I0647911

WINDFALL

TEMPE O'KUN · SLATE

Acknowledgements

Special thanks to: Megan for sunshine in the depths of drafts; Brandy and Jer for delving into strange furry lore; Carl, Eljot, Keiron, and Pedro for international investigations; Slip-Wolf and T-Kay for reports from north of the border; Ana, Apollo, Gouka, Kohaku, and Nic for dispatching the typos of madness.

Windfall

Copyright © 2015 by Tempe O'Kun

Cover and interior illustrations by Slate

Published by FurPlanet Productions
Dallas, TX
http://www.FurPlanet.com

ISBN 978-1-61450-253-1

Printed in the United States of America
First Edition Trade Paperback 2015

All rights reserved. No portion of this work may be reproduced in any form, in any medium, without the express permission of the author.

To Slate, for conspiring. To Sophie, for inspiring.

Table of Contents

CHAPTER I
On the Train

STRANGEVILLE (WED/9P)

S04E04 "Inside": After her grueling battle with the army of alien ghost dragons, Sandy finally returns home to Strangeville, but not everything is how she left it...

Max didn't really miss being a TV star. He did, however, miss Kylie, his co-star and co-conspirator.

In the six months since the show had ended, the husky had tried to fit in with the rest of the world. He'd moved back into his parents' house and his old, normal life. He'd caught up with the lives of his large, close family and the sights and smells of his childhood home, but it was weird not having Kylie around to fire off a wisecrack or save him from some awkward social situation. Really, it made sense: dogs excelled at missing friends.

Now, at long last, he sat aboard a passenger train as it rumbled down the long line of tracks between the Rocky Mountains and New England. When the trip started, he'd never been so happy to sit on so lumpy a seat— It'd be good to spend time with her again, even if it was only for a few weeks. As the countryside sped past, though, time had dilated to a crawl. He'd reached that anxious period of near-arrival found toward the end of every long trip. He stifled an impatient whine, breathed, and blinked to clear his mind. When his eyes opened, scenery still rolled past the window: trees, hills, rivers, power lines; all superimposed on his blocky canine face in the glass's reflection. He rested an elbow on his duffel and watched the rocky, wooded landscape roll by, knowing only a few hours lay between him and his best friend.

The train car rumbled, almost empty. Almost.

The mouse two seats ahead peeked at him over the back of her chair. She couldn't have been older than mid-teens, judging by her glittery bracelets and neon fur clips. She'd gotten on with her father about an hour ago and gradually started staring at him. The weight of her gaze pressed down on him, drooping his pointy ears and burying his nose further in the book he kept trying to read. Back on the show, he never dealt with fans in his day-to-day life, since filming ensured he never had a day-to-day life. Besides, he'd only been a second-string character, regardless of what the Internet insisted.

His phone buzzed, a blessed diversion. He dug the mobile from his pocket and swiped a paw pad across it.

Kylie Bevy: {The show jumped the shark when the director hired triplets to be in the background of every scene and wouldn't tell us why.}

Max grinned. Speak of the otter...

Max Saber: {What about the mirror universe panda with reverse-dyed fur?}

Kylie Bevy: {Hmm! I'd forgotten about her. XD How's the ride?}

He sighed, glancing up from his phone. The giggly mouse girl still stared at him.

Max Saber: {Train should be on time. Being stalked by suspected fan.}

Kylie Bevy: {Hunky huskies get stared at, especially when they're famous. Nobody stares in Montana?}

He looked up again. The mouse's whiskers bounced with the motion of the train; her gaze flicked away once he made eye contact.

Max Saber: {Well, we do, but we pretend not to.}

Kylie Bevy: {See ya soon, Maxie. ;) If you survive.}

The husky put his phone away and checked his watch. An heirloom with two time zones, his father had given it to him when he left for filming full-time. He kept it set half on Kylie time and half on family time.

The train rumbled on, tree shadows flickering against the windows. With every sweep of darkness, the fan crept a little nearer, appearing in the next closest seat.

Max closed the mystery novel. He'd already read it, but he'd been going over it again to pick it apart and figure out why he liked it. He relaxed his shoulders and smiled at the mouse, trying not to be huge and intimidating.

The scrawny young rodent seemed to encounter thinner and thinner air the closer she got. Her pink paws clutched a battered and very familiar DVD set.

He gave a disarming wag, his tail thumping the seat. "Hi?"

She bounced and swept away a nervous lock of hair. "Oh. My gosh. Are you Serge from *Strangeville*? Because if you're not, I'm sorry if I'm, like, coming off like a total weirdo."

Behind her, a taller, graying mouse had peeked around his chair to see where his daughter had gone. His eyes met Max's with a shrug of silent apology.

There'd been a time Max would've leapt from the train sooner than have this conversation, but Kylie had spent three years beating a semblance of social grace into him. "Um, yeah." He shrugged, rubbing the back of his neck. "But in real life, people usually call me Max."

"Ohmygosh! My friends are gonna be soooo jealous!" Her hyperventilation was prevented only by the air resistance of her braces. "This is soooo cool! Okay, okay, so like, what's it like being, like, a TV star?"

"I wasn't really the star—more like a supporting cast member."

She trembled with excitement, mobile phone charms clattering. "So what's it like?"

He contemplated the experience, then distilled it down: "You get up early, go to bed early, and spend most of your day working." It wasn't so different from farm life, really.

"Ugh!" Reality left a bitter taste in the mouse's mouth. "You make it sound totally like school."

"I guess so." He offered a smile.

She glanced down at the scuffed DVD box set, studying the cast list in search of a conversation topic. "Is your name really Max Saber?"

"Yep." A polite nod. "It was a birthday present."

"Like, really really?" She donned the look of a reporter gunning for a scoop. "It's not, like, some kinda stage name?"

The husky glanced at the middle-aged mouse opposite her original seat. They traded shrugs across the aisle. "Saber is an old husky name. The casting director wanted to add a second X to Max, but everyone else said that was too cheesy."

"Yeah, you wanna keep things, like…genuine or whatever." A pause. Wheels turned in her mind. "I didn't like it when they tried to ship you with that fortune-teller bat lady."

Max couldn't suppress a wry smile as the conversation took a familiar turn. He shrugged. "Yeah, I don't think anybody liked that."

"Why didn't you get together with Cassie at the end?" A cheery scoff bounced her whiskers. "Everybody knows you should."

His ears drooped, suspecting where this line of dialog led. "Um, that was really more the writers' call."

"Oh…" The mouse seemed to run off the edge of the conversation, then scrambled back onto it. "Soooo, are you guys dating in real life?"

Max squirmed. The inevitable question; the writers had always flirted with the idea of them flirting. "We weren't really dating in the show…"

"Yeah, but you know what I mean!" The mouse cornered him, blocking all escape from the seat or conversation. "Where are you headed? I mean, if it's okay that I ask that. I don't wanna, like, train-stalk you."

"I'm going to see Kylie, actually." He retreated against his carry-on luggage as he realized what he'd said: those words would keep her glued to the spot until one of them got off the train. Still, he thought, no way out but forward. "Cassie from the show."

Sure enough, a quiver traveled up the mouse's entire body, from tail to ears. "Oh my gosh! Did you finally propose?"

"What?" His ears shot up again, flushed hot. This wasn't the first time a conversation had taken this route. The fandom seemed determined to conflate him with his character, and Serge and Cassie had been the target of a lot of speculation over the seasons. "We aren't dating in real—"

"Does she actually live out here?" The rodent looked around, as if Kylie would spring out from the luggage racks. Then she focused like an awkward laser back on him. "It's totally awesome you two're together like that!"

"We're just friends. And, I don't know, we were on the show together forever, so I figured I'd visit. I wasn't really doing anything back in Montana anyway." Max's family had gotten used to his presence around the house after so much time in Hollywood, and it had taken some work to get them to endorse a two-week trip to the Eastern Seaboard. In the end, his mother's parting hug had been less "have fun, honey" and more "come home soon."

"Ya-huh!" She jabbed an unsteady glitter marker in his direction. "Would you mind signing my Season One, please please please?"

"Okay." He took the box. "I'll sign on the disc I actually appeared on, how's that?"

She nodded, whiskers whipped with enthusiasm. "Sure!"

Sitting up straight, he autographed the DVD with her squeaky felt-tip marker. It was his first signing in some time. At home, surrounded by people who'd known him from diapers, he'd felt foolish playing the Hollywood big shot. "Why do you have this on a train?"

Her pink paws lifted at how obvious the answer was. "In case I need to watch it on the way!"

"Ah, okay." Max gave a slow nod. "Aren't you kinda young for *Strangeville?*"

"Nah, my parents know I'd just watch it on the Internet anyway."

"Can't argue there." He handed the box set back.

A quiet hiss of deceleration. A train station rolled into view out the windows.

Her dad rose from his seat and gathered their bags.

"Ohmygosh! This is my stop!" She fumbled out her phone and held him and her father hostage with it. "Can I take a picture with you?"

He took a deep breath and tried to seem cool and friendly. "Sure." With a good-natured shrug, he stood, careful not to bump his head on the overhead rack.

Shoving the phone into her dad's hands, she scrambled over and hugged Max with disturbing strength.

The canine gave his best smile. The last thing he wanted was to seem all jaded and bitter.

A screech of brakes brought the train to a gradual halt. The mouse grinned back, colorful braces shining. "It was super awesome meeting you! Say hi to Cassie for me! Thanks so much!"

He chuckled. "Kylie, you mean. And sure."

The mice disembarked. A few more people loaded onto the train, but none seemed very interested in Max—save for the mouse girl who waved so hard she seemed in danger of spraining her wrist. As the train pulled away, the husky waved goodbye to the mice on the platform, then sunk into his seat. His thoughts lingered on Kylie. Before long they'd be together again, without any of the rigors of filming, getting into weird little adventures and feeling special for more than their moderate fame and his considerable tallness. He liked that idea. At least the weirdness with her was weirdness he enjoyed.

CHAPTER 2
Watching the Clock

STRANGEVILLE (MON/8ᴘ)

S01E01 "Pilot": Following the deaths of their globetrotting parents, otter sisters Sandy and Cassie must pick up the pieces as they begin to suspect that they were orphaned by supernatural forces...

Kylie Bevy sprawled, webbed paws spread across cool countertop. Her supple lutrine body flattened further as unending minutes pressed down on her. Strong afternoon sunlight poured in through the windows of the downtown antique store to fill it with sleepy, old-timey warmth. The afternoon might have tempted another twenty-year-old part-time employee to nap, but Kylie was too wired.

"Staring at the clock won't get his train here any faster, you know."

With a sigh, Kylie pried her chin off the countertop and flicked auburn bangs out of the way of the glare she aimed at the scrawny orange tabby who shared her shift. Technically Shane was supposed to be training her, but the job was simple and business slow, so he'd been passing the time with old music magazines. The feline adjusted his outdated jeans and leaned against a shelf of knickknacks. He lowered the unironic article on the evils of rock 'n roll and arched an eyebrow from beneath the hood of his overlarge sweatshirt. "Why don't you go into the back room and sort some silverware? I promise I'll call you when it's quitting time so we can head out."

Kylie gave a noise of frustration and glanced back at the clock, which had been stuck at 4:42 for at least twenty minutes. It had been slowing down since noon, and she worried it'd start going backwards if she didn't keep an eye on it. "I wouldn't be able to get anything done in fifteen minutes anyway. All I'd do is wind up having to put it all back right away, and then we'd be late leaving, and then we'd take too long to get there and no one would be there to meet Max when his train arrived!"

Shane pushed his glasses up the bridge of his nose and gave her a wry look. "His train isn't due 'til almost six, and it's only a twenty minute drive to the station, and then we'd have nothing to do but stare at the clocks. At least here you're getting paid for it."

"I don't wanna risk being late!" With a chitter, the otter bounced up from the countertop. "He'd have camped out there overnight if it were the other way around, just to be sure."

"Why's he even taking the train? It's a long way to Montana." The tabby's tail gave a teasing swish. "Big-time TV star can't afford a plane ticket?"

She waved a dismissive paw. "You'd think so, but tagalong kids aren't super high on the cast payroll." Being on the show had given them both a tidy nest egg, but they were hardly rich. "Besides, he likes scenery."

"You seem pretty hung up on this guy. Is this, like, a cross-country booty call or something?"

With a blush, Kylie studied the scratches on the countertop as her tail curled around the stool. "No, we never hooked up or anything, no matter what the fan sites say. He's just...Max. He's my best friend." It was most of the truth. "We were the only teenage regulars and spent a lot of time together." She shrugged. "It's been almost six months since we saw each other, right after the show ended."

"You act like you were never apart." He lowered the magazine to eye her with slitted pupils. "Didn't this show have breaks in shooting?"

"We shot a lot of episodes per season and we were in basically all of them to some degree. And it wasn't worth shipping Max home if they might need him for a pickup scene a week later, so even when we weren't on set, we were hanging out. Eventually, he just moved in with us." She crossed her arms and leaned back against a wall, tail curling around her knees. "It's been weird not talking to him every day."

Shane flipped a few more pages and paused to examine an advertisement proudly touting a thirty-year-old computer. "No calls? No texting?"

She heaved a sigh, shoulders slumping. "We text all the time, but it's not the same, y'know? And the Internet on his ranch is too crappy for video chat. Besides, his sisters tease him if he talks to me for more than twenty minutes at a time." The idea he'd soon be around, with that easy wag to his tail and ready smile, lifted her spirits. Max made no secret of enjoying her company, which meant she didn't have to do anything special to keep him entertained. She almost succeeded in suppressing a bounce of excitement. "It's going to be really good to see him again."

The tabby cat peered over the magazine at her. Triangular ears rose under the thick fabric of his sweatshirt hood.

The otter beamed, hands in her lap, giving him her most endearing smile. Her little round ears pinned against her head. She couldn't pull off the sad puppy face as well as Max, but he had taught her what he could. "Really, really good."

He heaved a long-suffering sigh and turned back to the clock. "Fine. It's only ten minutes to closing anyway. Lock up and I'll go get my wheels." He tossed her the keys on his way out the door.

Kylie snatched them mid-air, wriggled in happiness, and scampered over to hug him. "Thanks, boss!" In a blur of excitement she closed the till, locked the back door, turned off all the lights and flipped over the sign that lied about how sorry she was they were closed. She padded outside to wait for Shane. The little town sat quaint and proper, spreading down the hillside to the sea.

On the way out the door, however, she almost tripped over an exquisitely-groomed cocker spaniel lounging on a lawn chair. Cindy Madison, taking a break from pretending to work at her family's tourist trap next door. Her honey-brown fur gleamed in the afternoon sun as she lay at an angle calculated to make everyone driving past look at her boobs.

On another day she might have asked the canine to move, but with places to be, Kylie decided to let sunbathing dogs lie and squirmed past the chair. In passing, though, her anxious tail bumped Cindy's foot.

"Hey, watch it!" The dog stirred, crossing her ankles. "My new fur conditioner's gotta set and I don't need you wiping it all off."

Kylie heard her co-worker's old van fire up in the parking lot, around the back of the building. Resigned to spending the next minute in Cindy's presence, the otter sighed. "Hey Cindy. Good to see you too."

The canine remained in her pose. "Shutting down the junk shop early?"

Resentment bubbled up through the otter. "I figure you're working hard enough for the both of us."

The cocker spaniel arched a disdainful eyebrow at her, scarcely tilting her head. "Ugh. Unlike some people, my public still appreciates me.

Besides, there's only one way in, so anyone who wants something'll have to walk past me anyhow…" Her head shook just enough to toss her ears. "It's called business sense, duh."

"Glad you've got it all figured out." Glancing at her phone again, Kylie saw time had remained frozen.

"Whatever." She turned up her own, slightly newer phone, blasting terrier yip-hop from the tinny speakers. "At least our store gets a customer once in a while."

The otter simmered, trying to think of a scathing comeback. As much as she hated to admit it, Cindy and her assets were probably better than a billboard for business. Then the otter remembered why she was waiting and suddenly stopped caring about the other girl. Shane pulled around from the parking lot in a faded minivan. Without another word to Cindy, she hopped in and they rumbled off toward the highway.

The cat smirked. "Enjoy your little chat with Cindy?"

Kylie buckled up and crossed her arms over her less-impressive breasts. "As much as anyone ever does."

"I learned in the third grade: just stay out of her way. I don't know why my sister puts up with her." Shane adjusted the sun visor as they took the first ramp out of town. "So, no offense, but your show's a little repetitive."

"Watching Season One, huh?" She elbowed the cat. "About time."

"Lots of stock mythological creatures." Orange paws gripped the steering wheel as he watched the road with mild disinterest. "And, if everybody knows your character gets psychic visions, why don't they ever listen to her?"

"They don't really start to believe her until Season Two. They get into a little subplot later where my older sister thinks aliens gave me hallucinations. Give it a chance." Her limber body wriggled to get more comfortable on the angular seat. "The series finds its groove."

Shane pushed back his hood for added peripheral vision, then smirked. "When Max shows up?"

Soft joy washed through her. She giggled. "Everything gets better when Max shows up."

"Apparently." He rolled his eyes, whiskers quirking in a smile. "This guy'd better be amazing with how much you're talking him up."

Almost half an hour passed before a small city rose up around them. They exited near the transit hub. After a brief parking adventure, they headed into the train station. Signs for buses, trains, and a convenience store greeted them, while passersby milled around ignoring them. They found the right platform and the otter felt a minor burst of anxiety well up from her guts.

She bit it back and made small talk. "I wonder what replaced us anyway? I never really found out."

Shane didn't look up from his phone. "Frisky Blues."

Still leaning against the platform railing, she turned to look at him. "Do I want to know?"

"Probably not." He shrugged and looked up the tracks. "It's a police drama with mostly foxes, and no one can go ten seconds without having sex, or talking about sex, or making terrible sex jokes. The whole thing sets vulpine social progress back about fifty years."

"Huh, I wonder what my mom thinks of that..." She double-checked the schedule. "Max should be here any minute." She straightened her hair, then her vest, then verified none of Cindy's beauty products had smeared onto her tail. "Do I look okay?"

The feline groaned. "Sheesh, Ky, he's seen you before." For the tenth time, he checked out the antique railway maps enshrined on the walls. "You'd have to look pretty nasty for him to get right back on the train."

She stuck her tongue out at him. "Seriously, Shane."

"You're fine." He looked her up and down. "Nothing has pooped in your hair. This time."

"That wasn't funny!" She punched him in the shoulder. "Pigeons are gross!" Resting her paws on the safety railing, she bounced with anticipation as she looked up the tracks. "I think I see it!"

The train rumbled into the station, brakes squealing to a gentle stop. The doors opened, unleashing a small flood of travelers. A pack of wolf cubs with tired parents in tow exited the train first. A herd of giraffes in pinstripe suits chattered out next, bound for the café. She scanned the crowd for pointy ears, but saw no signs of a husky. She scampered forward and peeked inside the train. Nothing. Where do you hide a two-meter canine anyway?

Maybe he'd gotten off at the stop before and missed the train? But why wouldn't he have called?

Someone touched her shoulder.

A voice echoed behind her, deep as the sea, gentle as a brook. "Umm, you're watching the wrong train car."

"Maxie!" She spun around and pounced on him.

The towering husky laughed, delight shining in his blue eyes. His white-furred arms wrapped under hers and lifted her off the floor, high enough for her to see his swishing tail over his shoulder. Something important fell back into place in her heart. His words rumbled against her through a layer of fluff: "Hi, rudderbutt."

The otter squeezed him back, face buried against Max's broad chest and sighed into the solid bulk of his body. She could feel him inhaling, reacquainting himself with her scent, like the hug had been the point of the entire trip. She pulled back to examine him, arms still around his waist. Her gaze danced across his lips and she stomped on the wild urge to touch them. Instead, she looked up into his ocean blue eyes. "I missed you."

He patted her back, that same slow, warm smile she remembered stealing across his muzzle, making his eyes shine. "You too."

"You're looking good." She tried not to layer too much meaning into the phrase. "Your hair, I mean; you groomed your hair down. Not that the rest of you doesn't look good too."

He politely ignored her babbling and ran a paw over his ears. "Yeah, 'Serge' kept it a little longer. Kept getting in my eyes."

Released from the hug, she found herself touching his shirt. "I like it." She managed to peel her gaze away to look up and down the train. "Come on, let's grab your other bags and we'll get going."

The husky stooped to pick up the big, weathered canvas duffel he'd set down when he'd hugged her. "This is all I brought."

Kylie blinked. "Maxie, you're staying for, like, three weeks. You only brought one bag?"

Wide shoulders shrugged. "Bunch of clothes, grooming kit, a book or two, the old netbook they gave me on the show." That slow smile reappeared. His eyes found hers. "What else would I need?"

The otter slipped around his back to get a good look at the rest of him, then emerged under his opposite arm with a roll of her eyes. She grinned and swept a hand out behind her. "This is Shane—he's our ride."

"Hey." Max extended a paw with an acknowledging nod. "Thanks."

The feline stepped forward and shook his hand with a shrug. "Kylie's been bouncing off the walls all day. For the sake of our merchandise, I thought I'd better bring her down here."

"Yeah, I do have practice at keeping her out of trouble." The husky chuckled and glanced down at her. "If with only limited success."

"Hey!" She squeezed an arm around his waist. "You should thank me: without me around, you'd never have any fun."

He gripped her shoulder, still wagging. He didn't argue.

The otter breathed a happy sigh, pleased with the introduction; Max had trouble reading new people and Shane could come off as snide. Pleased, she bounced alongside them toward the parking lot.

Max wagged against the seat. Hard to believe he had three whole weeks with Kylie. He couldn't puzzle out the mood of her feline pal, but no one expected him to understand cats, not even cats.

The dappled light through the forest played across Kylie's delicate whiskers. She caught him staring and tilted her head toward the window. "I promise there's a town behind those trees."

The dog nodded, as if he'd been staring at the trees the whole time. Maybe he'd missed her more than he realized. He watched out the window as they crested a ridge and swung around the edge of Windfall. He sat up a little straighter. "Oh, wow, this is just like the show."

"Yeah, her mom basically copied the whole town." Shane swished his tail from the driver's seat. "I'd take you down Main Street, but we'd run into the credits."

Laura Bevy had been the executive producer and lead writer on *Strangeville*. Max had always admired how she could cultivate the chaos of running a television show while somehow keeping track of a teenaged otter daughter. Not that Kylie had been a been a bad kid, just precocious and stubborn—traits that had mellowed out around the time she was legally allowed to vote.

A parade of weathered wooden buildings drifted past. Various styles and eras, but most seemed several decades old. The town lay in a hill-strewn valley among a string of minor mountains, a gap where streams and settlement had collected. He hadn't spent much time on the East Coast,

but it felt like the backdrop for a romance novel about lighthouse keepers. Or maybe lobster fishermen.

They left Windfall behind. A winding, uphill road led on as they passed out of sight of all civilization. Gnarled forest limbs grasped from all sides. The road passed under a wrought iron archway; a rust-bled sign, dangling above missing gates, read "Bourn Manor." To either side, a crumbling stone wall extended into the woods.

Max turned to her. "Bourn?"

"We used to be the Bourns, but, y'know, stuff happened." She shrugged a little too fast. "Marriage mostly."

The husky's brow furrowed in thought, but he let the evasion slide. She'd tell him if it were important.

The minivan rolled up a long driveway, the mundane crunch of gravel counterpointed by the ornate mishmash of a house. The sprawling manor hunched, ancient and aged, against a backdrop of jagged pines.

The back half of the structure seemed to have engulfed a smaller house like some kind of architectural growth. Countless windows watched him from three long-forgotten stories. A walkway ensnared the nearby carriage house, between which struggled a twisty, weed-choked creek. Scabby paint whispered shades of gray. What little sunlight dripped through the trees threaded the ornate filigree of porch railings.

Max hopped out of the van and surveyed the property. "So. I see you've moved into a horror movie."

Slipping to his side, the otter wiggled a rueful shrug. "It's not as bad inside. We're reclaiming it, but it's slow going." She glanced to the open window of the minivan. "Thanks again, Shane."

"Sure." The tabby half-waved. "Talk to you guys later." The dented minivan chugged off, vanishing down the wooded hill toward town.

The canine squinted toward the roof. "What's the weather vane? I can't see from down here."

She crossed her arms. "It's a fish."

He grinned wryly. "Of course it is."

"Max!" The front door swung open. An older, stouter otter in a sea-weed-patterned blouse and beige slacks bobbed down the stairs and swept the dog down into an embrace. "Oh, it's so good to see you!"

Kylie rolled her eyes. "Sheesh Mom, let him get in the door first."

Wagging, he returned the hug, his arms on her shoulders. "Hi, Ms. Bevy."

"My wayward child returns." The middle-aged lutrine set a paw on either wide hip, looking up at him. "And I've told you to call me Laura."

A grin as he shrunk a little. "Yes you have, Ms. Bevy."

"Well, you're as proper as ever. And more handsome, if that's possible. Wouldn't you say, sweetheart?" The elder Bevy elbowed her daughter.

"Mo-om!" The younger otter squirmed back.

Her mother laughed. "I'd have picked you up myself, but somebody didn't want to wait for me to drive down and pick her up after work."

Kylie crossed her arms, tail slipping a little around the canine beside her. "In my defense, I thought he'd have more than one bag and we'd need the van."

Max shrugged, hefting the bag to his shoulder. Long-dead ancestors of the otters he knew had worn most of the paint from the boards of the porch. The overhang seemed faded, perhaps a bit warped, but sturdy. With another look up the looming house, he decided maybe he'd better see more than just the surface before deciding just how creepy it was.

"C'mon, lemme give you the tour." The younger otter took him by the arm, leading him up the porch. Its peeling paint crumbled under their feet.

The dog shrugged to Laura, who waved him along.

The front door creaked open, carved and heavy. Beyond lay a foyer, appointed with modern trappings against old wallpaper. The younger otter flourished a bow to the left. "Your room, Monsieur."

Max set down his bag in the entryway, amazed how far she could bend over. After six months out of their company, Max had forgotten just how much otters differed in construction from dogs. If he tried to bend like that, he'd end up in traction.

After a scant glance at the guest bedroom, she walked on, sweeping a paw to the next room. "Living room. Kitchen's back that way. Beyond lies wilderness."

He surveyed the landscape of sheet-draped furniture and dusty boxes. A stack of black-and-white photos revealed otters on their backs around a gramophone, knitting sweaters and mending fishing nets. "You weren't kidding about the place being full of old stuff."

"Junk is the preferred term." The lutrine rolled her eyes. "Legends tell of a garage somewhere back there; not sure I believe it."

Near the foot of the stairs, the husky slowed to examine a board of ancient keys. Each nail held at least one ring of them. Each ring held at least half a dozen keys, sorted by chronology and rustiness.

"The Keys of Mystery." Kylie jingled them with a wiggled of her fingers. "We found a drawer in the kitchen with like two hundred years of random keys in it. Whenever we find a door with a lock, it's like the world's most tedious game of Perfection. Let's head upstairs."

Following her, he set a hand on the railing. It wiggled under his weight.

She glanced back, creaking the old stairs. "Yeah, don't use that. Mom's got a contractor lined up to fix it."

His ears lifted in alarm.

She slumped with a small sigh. "No, there aren't any other safety hazards." She led him upstairs and into a tidied bedroom. The occasional box lay along the walls, still waiting to be unpacked. A light smattering of posters splashed color around the space—a tattered tribute to the pop sensation The Sugar Gliders sparkled beside the faded cartoon cast of *Majestica and the Defenders of Pegastar*. "None that I know about, anyway. The house is older than the telegraph or something ridiculous. Who knows what else is falling apart."

The canine's eyes flicked from the fresh phytoplankton-green paint to the new carpet to the wide bed. The room was a weird island of girly modernity in the spooky old house, like someone had spliced ten seconds of puppy cartoons into a horror movie. "Nice. It's very you."

"I like to think we have at least this much of the house settled." Her eyes lit up. "Case in point." She bellyflopped onto the bed. It sloshed back and forth. Her body rolled over every wave as she rolled to grin up at him.

A roll of his eyes did nothing to fade his smirk. "Waterbed."

"Waterbed!" She wriggled about on its surface. "You have no idea how nice it is not to sleep on a spring mattress."

With a shake of his head, he glanced out the window, noting a quaint greenhouse and pond. Kylie's mother seemed to be carrying some sort of flower pot in that direction. Further out, the forest closed in, scaling the ancient stone wall that ringed the estate. "So your mom…"

"Pounced on the master bedroom, which has a study and will soon have a hot tub." The otter sat up, rocking back and forth like a buoy on the waves. "It's all very impressive."

"And the rest of the upstairs?" He waved a digit around.

"More wilderness." She grabbed a pillow and propped herself up with it. "Peeked into the basement and attic—same deal. About two thirds of the house we've only been in to make sure there aren't any wild animals." Her tail swished over the sheets, stirring more ripples. "We'll explore while you're here. If you're into big rooms with spooky cloth-covered furniture, it's a really good time."

"This place is decked out like a costume drama." His paws rested on the window sill. "I keep expecting a butler to materialize."

She nodded, itching the soft, cream-colored fur of her neck. "Back in the day, between the family and the help, something like twenty people lived here."

Max glanced around and imagined his extended family stuffed into one building for more than a weekend. "Suddenly, even this house seems too small."

"Yeah, I don't think I could handle it either. The property has out-buildings; they mostly lived there." Her rounded muzzle flashed a smirk. "Mom and I just like you enough to let you stay in the house."

"Thanks, rudderbutt." Sitting beside her, his weight sloshed her up with a squawk. He watched her with amusement. Paws out spread, he managed to remain upright on the sloshing surface. "I'll try not to be in the way."

"No, please, be in the way." She gripped his arm. "It's been super boring. Mom hides out working on projects most days."

"Oh?" The canine's ears perked in an instant. "What's she working on?"

Kylie tipped a hand back and forth with fluid grace. "I don't think she knows yet. You know how it goes." She smirked up at him and thumped his chest. "Sorry to disappoint your inner fanboy."

She wasn't wrong. Getting to see Laura work from up close had been one of the coolest parts of the show and he'd been dying to know where she'd go now that *Strangeville* was finished. He changed the subject. "What about school? You looking at any colleges?"

She grimaced. "Not really. Still decompressing from the show. Moving across the country got complicated fast." She elbowed him. "You've got that covered, though."

He shrugged. Covered was a strong word. "Just some classes: this and that, seeing what sticks." A chuckle. "Liked the writing class I took, but the instructor seemed more interested in talking about his dream journals than teaching us how to tell a story. Kind of put me off."

"I always liked your stories. You should do what you enjoy." Her eyebrow lifted in his direction. "As long as it isn't acting."

"Hey!" He poked her flank in retaliation.

She flicked him with the tip of her tail. "Just saying, you're lucky Serge is basically you with a Russian accent and a penchant for dramatic lighting."

His legs crossed, adding a dapper tinge to his hulking demeanor. "I'll have you know I have an offer on the table even now."

The otter smirked. "That Ukrainian kibble commercial?"

"I could get you a part too." He settled an arm on her shoulders. "I'm told we have chemistry."

Her paw slipped around his back. "I might've heard that somewhere."

His tail swished against the blankets. "Seriously, though: without you, I would've just been a bit part. I don't know if I ever thanked you for that."

She patted his side. "Hey, it worked out pretty well for me too." A slight blush crept under her cheek ruffs. "I mean, I got way more screen time than I did as the tagalong kid."

"You weren't really a tagalong, since you brought skills no one else had."

"That's a generous assessment." She chuckled. "And then you showed up and we hunted monsters. We didn't have the best track record, but we did our damnedest."

"You were the audience surrogate too, especially in the early seasons. You'd ask the questions the viewer would be asking. Then the writers reached a point where you'd already have the relevant information, so they started handing the confused lines to me." He furrowed his brow. "And then they never stopped." He shook his head. "Serge was kind of dense."

"It made him cute." Her phone buzzed. She slid it from her pocket. "Mom says dinner's ready."

The husky raised an ear, with a glance to her mobile. "She texts you from downstairs?"

"Eh." She offered only a shrug and a smirk. "Big house." She stood, which caused the waterbed to become unstable and left Max in a slow tip backward. She giggled and lent him a paw.

Once he'd managed to scramble off the shifting surface, he followed her down the stairs. "Back home, we just bark at each other."

Max closed the door to the guest room, alone for the first time since he'd stepped off the train that afternoon. Without Kylie to hurry him along on a tour he could take time to get acquainted with his new lodgings. The room was dominated by a big, plush looking queen bed beneath a bay window. Pale, neutral wallpaper and dark carpet, kind of like a hotel room. An old, massive dresser stood guard in one corner, and it seemed even bigger once he'd tucked his few items of clothing into it. He pondered buying some new clothes after all, just to keep them company.

The bathroom encouraged him: small, but private and comfortable. The ancient plumbing only groaned a little when he went to wet his toothbrush, and while he brushed he couldn't help but notice how clean the counters were, how bright the steel of the faucets. Most the house he'd seen sat dusty and cluttered, only natural with just two people and such a big space to care for. Someone had gone to a lot of trouble to make his living space as comfortable as possible.

He returned to the bedroom and pondered his temporary home. He smiled, thinking back to his time staying with the Bevy's in Hollywood, pretending to be an actor. He wondered if all the time he spent feeling at home in temporary lodging had been what made his permanent bed in Montana feel so strange.

He shrugged out of his shirt and emptied his pockets onto the night-stand. First his pocketknife: a sleek, simple thing Kylie had given him on their second Yuletide together. Then a handful of loose change, the ruins that four days of dining carts and train stop convenience stores had made of the hundred dollars his father had slipped him. This he stuffed into his plain, thin wallet and set beside the alarm clock. Last was his keyring, used more for the little flashlight on the keychain than for the pair of battered steel keys to his family's house.

His eyes caught a flash of brass and he smiled. There, at the base of his bedside lamp, Kylie or her mom had left him a bright, freshly-cut house key. It was as warm a welcome as he could have hoped for. Sliding it in place with the others, he admired it on his keyring for a moment before it joined his wallet and knife in the pile.

The husky flung back the covers and climbed into bed. Even the thin blanket felt too heavy for the summer heat, so he let it drape over just his legs as he stared up at the ceiling. Seeing Kylie again had been really, really good. He'd almost forgotten how well they clicked, how in-sync they could be. The thought of spending a few weeks palling around with her made him smile in the darkness until the days of travel crept up on him and he fell asleep.

CHAPTER 3
SETTLING IN

STRANGEVILLE (MON/8P)

S01E20 "School Sucks": Cheryl the Vampire Cheerleader returns, this time with her sights set on Serge, the helpful neighbor husky. Cassie must protect him without revealing the truth of the supernatural world.

Kylie sprawled in bed, waging a war of silent protest with her old nemesis, the sunrise. Every time the light would creep across the sheets she'd whimper and retreat, curling in deeper to the blankets. She finally roused from hazy dreams to find the sun had climbed well above the horizon. A sigh of resignation sunk through the silence of the room. The lutrine rocked back and forth on the waterbed until it propelled her in a slow slither onto the floor. She staggered past various dusty rooms and downstairs, tail dragging. Coffee. Coffee needed to happen.

Staggering downstairs and into the kitchen, she slapped a bagel in the toaster and grabbed salmon and cream cheese from the fridge. As she set it down, she noticed it. There, before her, sat a salmon and cream cheese bagel, complete with dill and tomato. Just the way she liked it.

The lutrine stood there a moment, questioning her sanity. Mom would have corrupted any lox bagel with onion. One webbed finger poked it. Still warm; she hadn't sleepwalked down and made it herself. Then where—?

A polite cough arose behind her.

Max sat at the counter, ears tuned her way, a fork of scrambled eggs in his paw.

31

She struggled through a groggy blink.

He wagged, a small smile on his muzzle. "It's not gonna bite, rudderbutt."

She returned the smile, grabbing the plate and the empty mug beside it.

His deep blue gaze washed over her body.

Sitting across from him, Kylie chomped at her bagel. She swallowed a mouthful. "What?"

A pause, then he grabbed the coffee pot from its maker and poured her a cup. "I dunno. I haven't seen you in months and now I'm in your kitchen and you're eating breakfast in your underwear. It's like no time has passed."

A glance at the reflective side of the toaster revealed her wrinkled t-shirt and panties that had slipped a little too far down her hips for decency. "I look like I've been hit by a truck." She rubbed a paw over bleary eyes with a chuckle to cover the sudden wave of self-consciousness. Then she glowered at him. "You look like you've been up for hours."

"Farm kid. Up at dawn, regardless of time zone." The canine forked up the last of his eggs and ate them. He wagged, a small smile on his muzzle. She thought his eyes might have darted downward, but reality was slippery this early in the morning. "You look fine, though."

Before she could process that comment, he'd cleared his plate to the sink and started running the tap. As the otter fumbled for a way to tell him he looked good too, great even, her mother bustled past the kitchen.

The elder lutrine chittered a laugh and straightened her rumpled housecoat. "Max, honey? Are you...doing dishes? Sweet fishes, you've been here a day and you're already more useful than my other child."

Kylie grumbled over her bagel. "Hey!"

Ignoring her daughter, Laura Bevy leaned against the doorway, arms crossed over her sketch pad. "Would your parents be interested in trading?"

"Probably not." White paws buried in suds, he glanced over a shoulder. "They've already got more estrogen than they know what to do with."

Laura laughed. "We should count ourselves lucky you managed to escape the sister swarm to visit."

He nodded, spying a sly eye at his groggy friend. "Though the trade might be worth it to see Kylie try to do farm work."

"I don't have to sit here and take this abuse." The younger otter took another bite of her bagel and struggled to keep up a scowl as the perfect amount of cream cheese melted over her palette. She made sure to slurp her coffee extra loud, in retaliation.

Her mother cleaned her glasses on her worn-in t-shirt. "Been dating anyone?"

Kylie choked on her bagel.

Max placed a concerned paw on her back as she recovered. "Um, well, I wanted to be treated like regular old me when I got home, so I really just hung out with family and old friends." He slouched under the weight of shyness. "So no." He looked around for a place to divert the conversation and his glance fell on Kylie. "What about you, rudderbutt?"

"Me?" She looked up from licking the last of the bagel toppings from her finger webbing. Her hands flew to her lap, getting it all over her shirt. A thin laugh covered up the cream cheese catastrophe. "No way."

He nodded sagely. "Slim pickings?"

The otter struggled to maintain her dignity while scrambling for a napkin to wipe her whiskers. She puffed out her chest and dabbed regally. "High standards."

"Good." The husky wagged. "Someone'd have to be pretty stupid not to see how awesome you are."

"Thanks, Maxie. You too." Kylie felt the heat of a blush under her fur and brushed a lock of hair from her eyes. "If you'll excuse me, I seem to be slathered in cream cheese." She rose from the table and slunk upstairs before she could embarrass herself further. Cool bathroom tile slapped under her paws. Her clothes hit the floor. The steamy water of the shower helped wash away her indignity. A waterproof fur coat took a little extra time to clean, then fluff air back into. A short stopover to brush her teeth, hair, and whiskers, then back to her room.

As she crossed to her dresser the wall mirror caught her eye. The otter staring back at her looked cute and friendly, perfectly approachable. But she fell short of seductive.

She'd need to be more than cute and friendly if she was going to seduce Max.

In hindsight, she probably hadn't done herself any favors by rolling out of bed and staggering around the kitchen like a drunk, either. A plan of some sort would've helped too. Why hadn't she cobbled together some kind of plan for romancing him? Oh right: because reliable plans were Max's department. Kylie, by contrast, had just sort of assumed the right idea would come to her. Fat lot of good that had done her so far.

The lutrine looked her reflection up and down. She liked her body and couldn't think of anything she'd change, but a plunging neckline wouldn't do her any good. Nice hips, sure, but she'd put up with tight jeans on the show for years and hated the way they bunched up her fur. Her paws traced up her legs to her waist. She looked good naked: otter genetics had given her plenty of subtle curves, and a swimming habit kept them subtle. Not the kind of body that got you onto magazine covers, but enough to turn some heads in Hollywood. Plus, she'd always prided herself on what she considered a truly stellar vagina. Not that it'd do her any good in romancing him unless she decided to be a whole lot more forward.

She pouted at the mirror, but that only made her cuter. This whole business would've been easier if she were sexy instead of adorable. She'd heard she was cute from enough makeup artists and marketers that she believed it, but she was beginning to doubt that was going to be enough. She couldn't help noticing, as soon as she hit the age where she might be considered "sexy," whenever the studio provided promo shots to a magazine or TV talk show, the in-house graphic artists had always added a few inches of height and at least a cup size.

If only movies hadn't gotten her hopes up. The stereotype for otters was that they were either cute kids or sultry sexpots, and Kylie wasn't having a whole lot of luck with the transition. She longed for a scene where the childhood friend shows up in a slinky dress and everyone falls over her, but suspected she'd look like an idiot. She ran her paws down her long torso, smoothing the imaginary garment. Not many excuses to dress up in a supernatural tourist town.

Maybe she just had to rehearse. She slipped into a fresh t-shirt and panties, then posed a few different ways, wondering which would constitute sexy for a charming but obtuse husky.

She dipped her hips, trying to put a sexy sway in her tail. "Oh Max, you sure know how to butter a girl's bagel." The comment hung in the air, just long enough for her to really listen to it. "Ugh! What's that even mean?"

Gathering her composure, she tried again, leaning one arm against the mirror's edge. "Max, that little guest bed has such thin blankets. You might be more comfortable in my bed. You know, with me…" She shook her head.

Clearing her throat, she cupped her breasts, lifting them together. "Hey Max, do you think my boobs are small enough that I could get away with not wearing a bra? Well, maybe you need a closer look?" A pause, then a frustrated sigh deflated her.

She draped herself onto a chair and cast a gloomy look at the mirror. "Max, you're a total hunk and, like, the nicest guy ever. If you could just throw me on the bed and ravish me for a while, that would be really great."

With a sigh and a flick of her tail, she flopped back onto the chair and stared at the ceiling. She must, she decided, be the least smooth otter ever.

A knock rattled the door. "Kylie?"

Shock tumbled her off the chair with a squawk. Snatching up her panties, shirt, and jeans, she scrambled into them, struggling to support her weight on the thrice-damned waterbed. "One second!" Clothed, she fumbled to the door, opening it to see Max standing at a polite distance. They smiled at each other as Kylie struggled to calm her hammering heart.

The otter stepped back from the doorway and gestured for him to enter. "What's up?"

He followed a few steps, paws folded as he surveyed her room. "Your mother has volunteered you to show me the local sights."

Kylie could think of a few very local sights she'd like to show him, but instead grabbed her favorite vest from the chair. "She would."

A shrug rolled his massive shoulders. "I think your mom just doesn't want me to get lost."

"Yeah, you've always been her favorite." She stuck out her tongue. Her webbed fingers zipped up the vest, verifying her wallet was in its usual pocket. "Wanna start with the giant albino lobster or the house everyone says is haunted?"

"Haunted house sounds up our alley." He stood a little straighter. "Let's start there."

She swept her hands out. "Good choice! You're standing in it."

He perked his ears, but said nothing.

She grabbed her phone from the nightstand. "The tour's moving right along. Come on, you've only seen the livable parts."

His eyes caught on the various pieces of colored paper pinned to the wall behind her door, then peered around for a better look.

She stepped between him and the door. "Ready?"

The husky straightened at the obvious deflection, ears turning back to her as a question formed. Then he dropped it, gave her a wag of trust, and nodded.

With a paw on his chest, she turned him around and shepherded him down the hall, ignoring the flutter of paper as she closed the door after them. "Down the hall is Mom's room. Biggest habitable room when we moved in."

"Habitable?"

"Not covered in thirty years of dust and dead bugs. The otter soul can stand only so much cleaning." She padded down a fork in the hallway and opened a door. Beyond lay a columned walkway around a massive open space. A wooden floor below bore decades of dust. A scattering of half-packed boxes and cloth-covered furniture had been cast adrift in the cavernous chamber. Out the window, a massive swimming pool sprawled across the back yard. "My family used to have parties here."

Wide-eyed, he took in the entertaining room with a slack jaw. "For the whole town?"

She chuckled. "Pretty much." They rounded the corner to the tidy, dusty, and ancient bedchamber. Windows looked out on the back lot and stream. An ornate wooden door opened to a sprawling balcony. "This was the governess's room."

"Why's a nanny's quarters bigger than the master bedroom?" Max quirked an ear. He looked so out of place in his hoodie and jeans against the backdrop of the Queen Anne house. He touched a peeling strip of wallpaper to expose a spidery scrawl of charcoal.

Slipping between him and the wall, she set her paws on her hips and tried to act casual. "What would it take for you to be willing to raise a pack of otter kids?"

The husky looked around, as if imagining a flood of tiny Kylies barreling down the hall from the nursery at him, then nodded. "Touché."

Kylie eeled about the musty room before slipping past him and back out the door. "At one point they hired an Old English Sheepdog to herd them, who was apparently very good, but she quit after they dyed her fur while she was sleeping."

"How do you know all this stuff?"

She shrugged and tried to keep her smile from fading. "Oh, you know, family history."

Doubt flicked across his brow and Kylie had to suppress a pang of guilt. Keeping the truth from this poor dog, her closest friend, felt wrong. The moment passed quickly, though, and he bade her continue with a nod.

"C'mon." She took him by the wrist and tugged him down the hall. "Tour's this way."

He heeled, paws in his pockets. "What's next?"

"Next…" With a paw swept to either side, she gestured to the towering shelves all around. "…is the library."

The husky's muzzle tilted up as he surveyed the countless volumes. Even with about a third of the collection missing, the two-story library made for an impressive sight. "Wow."

"Comprised entirely of deep-sea fishing guides."

He shot her a questioning glance.

She stuck out her tongue. "Of course I'm lying, you dope."

He snorted with amusement.

They picked their way through stacks of old leather-bound books. At least some were trashy romance novels, Kylie knew, as Mom's smutty reading habits had a long tradition in the family. "We're not sure where some of the books went. I figure some of the relations took their favorites when they moved out."

Max nodded and continued looking around. Padding to the far window, he looked down to see a sloping roof of glass. "Your mom's greenhouse?"

"Yeah, it's the old sun parlor." Kylie peered down at the lush plants, including at least one stout pineapple. "The gardening's good for her. Mom needs a hobby that isn't identical to work."

Down the stairs, and through more library. The husky wagged. "We really should check through all this."

"Lots of exploring left to do." She grabbed his paw and led on. "I didn't even show you the ballroom. Or the pool."

His ears rose. "Another pool?"

"The meeting pool, not the one out back. It's actually on the other side of this wall." She rapped a knuckle on the fading wallpaper. "They sealed it off from the library because they didn't want the books molding."

They cut through a foyer, with a pair of cracked leather shoes standing guard at the door, probably her great uncle's; the second-to-last Bevy to live here. Kylie's mom had been the last. Then she left for twenty years.

Towers of fresh cardboard boxes signaled their return to civilization. They squeezed through the piles into the dining room, which led to what they'd been using as the front door. "This little section of the house we've reclaimed is actually the original part." She tugged Max down by the draw-strings of his sweatshirt and brushed stray cobwebs off his ears. "One of my ancestors worked as an architect for years. He designed the town hall."

"Cool." The husky straightened with a wag. "My ancestors mostly designed barns."

"We have one of those around, somewhere." She smirked up at him. "If you get homesick."

His stomach growled.

"How are you hungry again?" She squawked, poking his firm belly through the soft hoodie. "We ate like an hour ago!"

"You ate an hour ago. I ate at the crack of dawn like a normal person." He gave a polite shrug. Another rumble. "Besides, I'm not as efficient as you."

"We can head into town for lunch." The otter tilted her head in the direction of the family room. "Let's see if Mom's busy."

They passed Laura in the living room, pacing with phone in paw. "If we do novels, they can't just be watered-down episodes. I don't care who you have writing the forward. Wait, who? I thought he was dead. I don't care if the studio trusts him—I don't trust the studio. I made enough concessions to get it on the air in the first place." The elder otter gave them only a passing wave before grumbling back into the phone. "Why would I want pop stars reading the audiobook? Have you explained they can't auto-tune?"

Kylie suppressed a giggle, then waved to get her mother's attention and gestured to indicate they were stepping out. She snatched up her house keys from kitchen counter and led Max out the front door.

As they left the house, Max stopped, ears rotating toward a hammering above. He looked up, twisting his head toward a beaver waddling around the roof between plastic-wrapped stacks of shingles.

The otter touched his arm. "Contractor. I think his name's Joe. Mom's having the roof fixed."

Max raised a corner of his mouth at her. "The great reclamation continues."

"You have no idea." A roll of her eyes translated down her lithe form. "Nobody's actually lived here for close to thirty years, and some parts of the house have been empty even longer." She led him down the driveway, toward town.

The husky trotted after her. "You should consider getting a car. Your mom's not always around, and you can't just hoof it to town in the winter."

Kylie stopped, spun to face him, and squirmed a little bob of excitement. "Actually, I've got a car."

His ears popped up. "Since when?"

"Since we moved here and I claimed it. Mom said I could keep it if I paid to fix it." With a proud twitch of her whiskers, she led him over the creek that ran between the house and garage. Crunching across the gravel, she hauled the carriage house doors open, stirring calf-high swirls of dust. Inside, tarps shrouded the ghosts of forgotten hobbies. Here and there a fishing net or a mess kit peeked out, void of context. In the center of the clutter, a seafoam-green machine perched like a frog. It gleamed like one too. Its headlights watched with wet interest.

Max's head tilted at the vehicle. "What is it?"

Her dainty paws wrung with glee. "A car! An excellent car."

Head tilting further, he squinted at it. "...What else is it?"

The lutrine draped herself over the hood to run her paws over its shiny surface. "A boat."

His paws spread at the machine as he tried to grasp the concept. "Okay, so a pedal car crossed with a paddleboat—"

"It has a motor!" With a lash of her tail, the otter popped up. "It's an excellent car."

"You mom isn't just making you drive it because it's funny?"

She crossed her arms and cast him a narrow glance. "No."

He tipped a claw at her, his grin teasing. "And you're sure it's not a toy?"

"It's the ultimate car!" Her fists propped on her waist. "It drives on land and water. Amphicars are very popular with otters."

"I have to admire good marketing." He threw an arm around her shoulders. "It does float, right?"

"I assume so." She stroked her whiskers. "My aunt almost never parks her Schwimmwagen on dry land, and that's a similar design."

"You haven't tested it?" His gaze traced over the craft, finding a series of maritime registration numbers along the front fenders.

"I only just got it fixed!" A sigh escaped her muzzle. "It just sat here under a tarp for thirty years, so it needed a new battery and hoses and stuff."

"And tires." He prodded the fresh, firm rubber with the toe of his shoe. "You're sure it was worth the money?"

The lutrine crossed her arms. "Mom insisted it'd be a waste to buy a new car when I have this one sitting around."

"Your mother always did like to embarrass you." He rounded the aft of the car. Steering foils with floats to keep them level graced the hubcaps. Two full-size propellers hung under the rear bumper. A little banner with a kracken crest drooped from a miniature flag pole. "So this is the only car to actually need tail fins?"

"Not sure those do anything. They're not in the manual." She reached in the window and pulled a booklet from the passenger seat. "Comes with an anchor, though."

She snatched a harpoon gun from where it leaned against the wall, still loaded with a tarnished steel spear. "It even had this in the back seat."

The husky looked it over. "In case of sharks?"

"Of course. What else would you need a harpoon gun for?" She set the weapon back down on the dusty workbench. "And if you spill a drink, you're supposed to keep spilling until you activate the bilge pump."

Max nodded in approval. "That does reduce our odds of drowning a little."

She shoved the manual into his paws and drew the key from her pocket. "Hop in."

He offered a genial shrug and followed her order into the car.

The otter threaded her tail through the hole in the seat and popped the key into the ignition. After a few turns over and considerable willpower, the car fired up. She tugged it into gear and gripped the wheel as the machine puttered forward. A smile spread around her muzzle as they exited the carriage house. "Isn't it great?"

Folded up in the passenger's seat, Max poked his head out the window to watch as they crested the moaning bridge over the house-creek. "Great."

The little car grumbled downhill, rattling toward civilization. "The walk to town isn't bad, either, if you cut through the woods. It's how I get to work whenever it's nice out."

"But you can't drive this convertible in the winter either." The husky gave a coy nod. "Further evidence your mother only wants you to drive it to embarrass you."

She stuck her tongue out at him and steered toward town.

His best friend's fur shone in dappled sunlight. She looked better now than she ever had on set. Less harried. Nowhere to be but here.

Kylie caught his gaze. "Well, what'd ya think?"

The dog shrugged, enjoying the breeze through his whiskers, tinged with growth, gravel, and gasoline. "I wanted to smell the local scents. I guess I can't complain."

Forest rose around them, draped with moss and feathered with ferns. Sunlight pierced where it could, but shade hung from the canopy. The road twisted and turned just as much as the game trails they passed, though Kylie seemed to know her way well enough. "Some early settlers found the ground around here all ripped up after a big storm or something, and it had exposed a ton of silver veins." She pointed at a tunnel hunched in the hillside. "Set off a big rush." A bump in the road bounced them both. Kylie's muscular tail seemed to absorb the shock, while for Max the job fell to his shins against the dashboard. "By the time it ran out, they realized they could make more money selling the trees they'd cut down to mine."

He nodded and squirmed, trying to find an angle that didn't kink his tail or whack his knees on the dash at every bump. Out the windshield, what he at first assumed to be some kind of anvil hood ornament turned out to be a tie-off cleat for docking lines: the first reasonable part of the design he'd seen. His knee bumped the glove compartment open, spilling the contents of a tackle box, complete with pocket-size fishing pole. With a groan, he resolved to stow it all back when he wasn't folded into a fetal position.

The mustelid chattered on. "These days, the town's cashing in on 'supernatural' tourism. Basically, Internet weirdos have heard we've got a bunch of ghosts and goblins, so they drive up here to be separated from their disposable income." She couldn't suppress a smirk. "Having a TV show based on the town may have helped a little."

The canopy broke overhead, spilling them out onto a paved road at the edge of Windfall. She drove past an old lumber mill and into town, where the gas station and at least two knickknack stores had shelves of googly-eyed monsters staring in silence out the windows. They passed the nostalgia shop and she poked her head out the window to wave to her tabby coworker. Along Main Street, giant metal sculptures of space aliens directed motorists up to cute little eateries overlooking a rocky bay.

She pulled into the parking lot of a café with a giant albino lobster as the roof. The sign read Outlook Pointe. "Everyone in town calls this place 'Pinchy's.'"

The husky lifted an eyebrow. "That does fit better."

"Just come try it, smart guy." Bounding out of the car, she unfolded him from the tiny car and towed him inside, only to shove him into a booth. "I thought I'd miss the sushi in California. Then I discovered clam chowder. One taste of real New England clam chowder filled the sushi-shaped hole in my heart."

He smirked with a chuckled woof. "More like the sushi-shaped hole in your stomach."

"They're the same shape!" She opened a massive menu, unveiling a photo gallery of fish-based soups, fish-based salads, and fish-based desserts. "Mom used to take me here as a pup when we visited, but I always got the fish and chips. The place has looked exactly the same my entire life."

The husky looked up from the specials pamphlet, which asked if he'd found cod. Paintings of ships, lobster traps, and old rigging comprised the decor. Sure enough, from the faded menus to the worn tabletops to the knickknacks on the walls, everything looked like it had been there

for decades. The pair placed an order with a rhino waitress, whom Kylie greeted with a familiar nod.

A second rhino crashed through the doorway in a rush of panicked breathing. He turned to stare at Max, stammering: "Holy cow! Wow, okay. This is amazing."

The otter pinched the bridge of her nose and sighed over her coffee. "Hello Karl…"

He plodded over. "I mean, I hoped you'd be here, more than hoped: deduced. But to actually see you in person. Wow." Bouncing on massive feet, the rhino seemed to swoon on the edge of fainting.

"Hello…Karl?" Max extended his paw. "How'd you, um, calculate that? I'm Max, by the way."

"Oh, I know that, Mr. Saber." The rhino suppressed a squee, gripping hard enough to pop the husky's knuckles.

The canine winced. "Just Max, really."

Breathless explanation flooded the conversation. "You were spotted on a train on the only line that leads to Windfall." His wide fingers danced over the phone's touchscreen. "It seemed like a good guess that you'd be coming here, to the ancestral home of the Bevys. Oh my gosh, this is so cool!"

Kylie's finger webbing hid her face. "Max, meet Karl: our biggest fan."

"Only if you go by updates on the *Strangeville* wiki. Or by, you know, mass." He laughed, running a hand down his ample frame. "Is it weird if I ask you to autograph my horn?"

The otter gave him a look over her coffee. "Karl?"

"Right, sorry. You're real people who have lives. I'm just excited." His frantic little tail whipped the air. He stuffed his mobile into the pocket of his jeans.

Max lifted a finger off the Formica tabletop. "Hang on. I was…spotted?"

The rhino whipped out his phone again in one smooth motion, as if he'd been hoping for just that question. His thick fingers danced along the screen, pulling up an image of a very patient Max standing beside a teeny bopper mouse almost as excited as Karl. He grinned with pride. "It went

viral on the *Strangeville* forums last night. Everybody's been posting these great little snippets about you being a nice guy."

Kylie snickered and rolled her eyes at him. "Jeez, Max. That's the weakest smile I've ever seen. Was she standing on your tail?"

"I couldn't just brush her off; we were on the same train car." He sipped his ice water. "Besides, I remember being young and obsessive."

"Whatever, glory hound." She turned to the rhino. "How'd you even find us? Are you tracking my spirit energy now?"

"Just like that wolf in the Scent of Evil story arc! Ha! But no, my cousin Myrtle texted me." He waved to their approaching waitress, who gave a sheepish smile as she delivered their order.

The otter attempted a scowl, but it didn't survive the arrival of her steaming plate of chowder. Diving in, she scooped the creamy soup into her muzzle with abandon, spattering it on her well-groomed whiskers.

Karl, seeming to sense he'd get no further info for his wiki for the duration of the soup, started edging for the door. "Well, I'd better let you guys have lunch."

"Okay." Catching the scent of the cod special, Max tried not to drool as he shook the fan's hand. "Good meeting you."

"Oh man, you have no idea." A massive grin overtook his muzzle as he backed away. "You guys just go back to eating." He patted their table, making it rock a little. "I'm sure we'll bump into each other—eeee!—around town. Ohmygosh!" He trotted away.

Max watched him leave. "This town's more interesting than I thought."

Kylie deployed a napkin on her soup-coated whiskers. "Oh?"

With a smile, he picked up his cod burger. "I've never seen a rhino bounce."

She shot him a sidelong smile. "That doesn't bug you even a little?" She pointed a spoon at the door. "Him coming up to us like that?"

"I used to be a giant fanboy." He shrugged. "I still am. Getting a role just helped hide it. So I sympathize."

"You're a six-foot studmuffin." Her paws swept a gesture over him. "Not a lot of rhinos in television, outside of roles that require a character who chews a cigar."

Max leaned back against the lobster-red booth. "I like him." He chomped into his fish sandwich, then gave a thoughtful swallow. "He didn't even call me Serge."

With sunlight fading out the window and Mom upstairs in her study, Kylie wiggled from behind the entertainment center. She sat down on the sofa, stringing a display cable from the TV to her laptop. "I've been saving this for a special occasion: '*Revenginator Third: Hunt Future.*' Turkish film translated into Italian, now with bootleg subtitles by a non-native English speaker."

"Double translated?" Max emerged from the kitchen with one bowl of popcorn, another of popcorn shrimp. "I dunno; I like to at least pretend to know what the writer intended."

The otter bounced up in her seat at the scent of snacks. "Yeah, 'cause we're totally here for the plot."

The husky set both bowls on the coffee table. "Did we see the second one?" Wry smirk on his lips, his arms crossed over that wide chest. "Or the first? These movies kind of blur together."

"It doesn't matter." A webbed paw waved the notion away. "The original film, *Revenginator: Folly of Regret*, was a French film with a lot of shots of a guy smoking in the rain, telling us about a robot. *Revenginator 2* was an unrelated Italian film which stole the name for purely capitalistic reasons. This is an actual sequel to that film, but unauthorized, so it has none of the same cast, but it has an actor from the first film playing a different character. It's an ouroboros of bad cinematography."

The canine handed her the remote.

Her fingertip teased the play button as she looked his way. "Have I ever been wrong?"

He gave her a dubious look. "Yes."

She punched him in the shoulder. "You'll like it." With a wink, she hit play.

An opening shot of Paris stock footage flashed onto the screen, then cut to a high-octane gun battle down a street in some other city.

Ears perking, the husky aligned his muzzle on the screen. "Did he just take down a helicopter with his own severed leg?"

"I like how they're all bleeding carrot juice." She propped her webbed feet up on the coffee table, popping a shrimp into her mouth. "And they all become a slightly different breed when they have to do a stunt."

Max squinted through decades of VHS degradation. "The Manx they've got playing the cyborg turns into a calico whenever she does a backflip."

"Which would be okay, if she could walk instead of backflipping."

He nodded. "Design flaw."

The film flashed back to the protagonist's pre-revengining days.

"Ah, okay." Max talked over the layered dubbing. "The guy's wife gets killed, so he builds a killer robot that looks like her to avenge her. Makes perfect sense."

The otter tapped a claw on her lip, then pointed at the screen. "They keep calling her a cyborg, though. I think it's actually her."

"But we saw her funeral." His brow furrowed. "Did she punch her way out of the grave?"

A peal of laughter burst from the lutrine. "That would've saved this movie."

The last of the daylight left the sky outside and the breeze coming in through the window gained a bite of damp chill. As cars and buildings blew apart, the dog found his otter friend scooting closer and closer on the sofa to benefit from his warmth. She must have missed him a lot, since she slipped under his arm during the helicopter chase. He smiled; otters could be so touchy-feely. He'd missed her too.

Kylie groaned. "Aaaaand he's falling in love with Cyborg Wife."

The husky tapped a paw pad against his lips. "Legally, since death parted them, I think they have to remarry."

She writhed into a more comfy position on the sofa, curling up beside him. "Cyborg Ex-Wife sounds so wrong."

He gave a grave nod. "Even more dangerous, though."

"True." She giggled. "And stop staring at her boobs. She's technically dead."

"I'll stop when her nipples stop firing lasers." He watched said breasts lay waste to a platoon of allegedly deadly mercenaries. "Though she probably could've fired the lasers through her shirt instead of taking it off."

"And ruin a perfectly good tube-top?" The otter tugged at her shirt.

The canine's head tilted. "Does he have his leg back? He's limping around."

She popped another shrimp into her mouth. "He probably didn't have a full-size spare."

He laughed, which she must have felt, her cheek resting on his chest like that.

"If you ever get killed and I build a cyborg to avenge you, I'll be sure to make it look like you." She patted his knee.

"Laser cannons should to go somewhere other than my nipples." He examined his pectorals. "Doesn't seem practical."

Credits rolled, listing fifty Turkish names, the one original French actor, and an English-looking name as director.

With a charming smile, she propped her hands on his thigh and tilted her head toward the laptop. "Wanna watch another?"

He returned her smile, feeling, for the first time since the show ended, at home. "Sure."

A brilliant flash woke Kylie completely and Max not in the least. The younger otter found herself with her head propped on the canine's chest. With reluctance, she lifted her head to meet her mother's gaze. "What?"

Laura stood in the doorway with a mischievous grin and admired the photo on her camera display. "You two look pretty comfy."

"You'd better not post that for your friends." The younger otter grumbled, careful to let the sleeping dog lie. "The last thing I need is ten thousand middle-aged ladies telling me what a cutie-pie I am."

"You should have thought of that before you were so cute in your sleep, dear. Awww, look." The elder otter showed her daughter the picture. "The boy doesn't even drool. He's a keeper, honey."

She sighed and patted his side. "I'm aware."

They hadn't woken Max with their quiet conversation, nor were they very likely to. During production, the young husky had once been napping on set and slept through the filming of an intense firefight, complete with simulated grenades and gunfire and all the yelling of the cast and crew. He'd been upset with her afterward for letting him miss the action. In the living room, it took Kylie and her mother working together to haul him up onto his feet, and even then he was only half-conscious as they aimed him toward his room, gave the husky a gentle shove, and let momentum do the rest. He shuffled off to his bedroom and shut the door. A moment later, he hit the mattress with an audible thump.

By the time Kylie and Laura sat at the kitchen table, they could hear Max snoring.

"I've always thought he was a good kid." Laura set a steaming cup in front of Kylie and smiled over her own mug of chamomile. "I wouldn't have promised to keep an eye on him during the show if he wasn't. Let alone stay at my house while my daughter has a crush on him."

The younger Bevy propped her chin on her palm. "I know…"

"You and Max have had a good thing for a long time." A tinge of regret colored the edge of her voice. "You're still sure about changing it? You wouldn't be the first girl to mistake safety for romance."

"So I should just stop being attracted to him?" She crossed her arms. "It'd be a lot safer not to risk my friendship in the first place. I just don't know what to do."

"What do you think you should do?"

A sigh deflated her. "Tell him."

Laura looked up, webbed paws spread. "What happened to telling him before he got here?"

"I tried! I couldn't find a good time! 'Oh hey, by the way, while you're up here, I'd like to prove all the fan sites right and start making out' is a tough thing to work into a conversation with your best friend."

Her mother adjusted her glasses, looking as wise as possible. "I've found I regret more things I didn't say than the things I did."

The younger otter gripped her own whiskers in frustration. "I'm afraid of scaring him off forever, but I've only got—" Her eyes flicked to the calendar. "—nineteen days left!"

Laura rolled her eyes and reached out to grip Kylie's shoulder and plant her firmly in her chair. "First off: relax."

Kylie shrank a bit in her chair. "What if he says yes, but only for my sake?"

"Do you think he'd lie?" She took a sip of tea.

"No, I think he just likes to protect me." The younger otter sank in her chair. "I just need to find a way of finding out how he feels without risking our friendship."

"I'm sure Max feels the same way, honey, but I think you're forgetting who you're dealing with here. That boy would sooner step in front of a train than hurt you or make you uncomfortable." The elder otter traced a claw around the brim of her teacup. "I'm afraid you're going to have to make the first move."

"I know that. I mean, I'd always planned to, more or less. I just wanted to, I dunno, warm him up to the idea first." She shot her mother a mini-glare. "Don't say anything to him."

"I'll keep quiet and let you work your magic. Or at the very least, let you find some magic to work." The curvy otter winked. "So far, it seems like your master plan is to carry on your existing friendship, but with you wandering the house in your panties."

Kylie squirmed enough to make the chair creak. "That wasn't on purpose!"

"More's the pity. I thought you were onto something." The middle-aged lutrine smiled over her cup of tea. "A thoughtful gift is often helpful in this kind of situation."

The younger otter interwove webbed fingers around her teacup. "We could give him something from the show."

Laura examined a chip in her own cup. "Not exactly romantic, but it's certainly applicable."

The younger otter cast a glance out the dark window. "Not my fault I got bad flirting genes."

"I've got plenty of game; you're proof of that." Her mother stretched into a deep yawn. "Lucky for you, I don't think it'll take much."

Kylie muttered over her own cup of herbal tea. "I'll remember you said that when I've alienated my best friend forever."

"If it comes to that, being a wacky spinster has its upsides." The elder otter pushed up her glasses. "You'd be surprised how seriously people take you."

"The wackiness is what I'm worried about." She looked around the dark, sprawling house. "We have a family tradition of crazy. Bit of a turn-off for most people."

"Oh sweetie, try not to worry." Laura patted her daughter's paw. "Life's all about finding a way to channel the crazy."

"Like you did?"

A shrug rocked her back in the squeaky kitchen chair. "I suppose. Sometimes I wondered if it was this place that was the problem. People'd hole up in here for years and chase their demons round and round until nothing else mattered." Laura gave her daughter a wise look over her teacup. "I'd rather inflict my demons on a paying audience."

Kylie glanced to the door of the guest bedroom. "I'm scared of my audience changing the channel."

"You can't let the worry of something going bad keep you from having good things." She took another sip, then wiggled the tea from her whiskers. "I really don't think he's going to stop being your friend, no matter what happens. He's the loyal sort."

"You're probably right..." The younger otter gripped her teacup, letting the heat chase the chill from her finger webs. "What would you do if you were me?"

"Hmmm..." Her mother leaned back in her chair, pondering. She closed her eyes, setting a scene. "Invite him to a picnic." She tapped through the points of her plan on the table. "You show up in that new sundress of yours, with a nice bottle of wine."

"We're only 20."

"Then drive up to Canada to do it. Or pick something cheap out of the wine cellar. Do I have to think of everything?" She waved the concern away. "So you sit on a hilltop, slowly edging closer to him as you work through the wine. As the sun sets and he's just starting to notice what pretty eyes you have, the college marching band you hired comes out playing 'La Vie en Rose' and you gently take his muzzle in your paw and—"

"So I'm shipping a band across the border now?" Kylie tilted her head. "Won't they need passports? Am I renting a bus?"

"You know, lots of people pay good money for my advice. In fact, you can't have this one." She jotted down some hurried notes on her legal pad. "I smell a romcom brewing."

With a grumble, the younger otter slumped into her chair. "Glad one of us got something out of this chat."

CHAPTER 4
CAMPING

| STRANGEVILLE (SAT/4P)

S05E02 "Prickly Subject": The gang must track down Damon after it's revealed he took an important artifact with him when he left for LA. Serge is baffled by California culture.

Kylie bounced into the guest bedroom to find Max laying sideways on the bed, jeans clinging to that cute butt, accenting that fluffy tail. "So I was thinking..."

The husky looked up from his laptop and lifted his ears.

"We should go camping." How had she not thought of this before? What could be more romantic than sitting around a campfire? Maybe even snuggling up for warmth afterward? "I have a tent and sleeping bags and everything."

He wagged. "Sure. On the manor property?"

"Yeah, the back yard is nice and flat, once you stomp the grass down."

A grin spread up his muzzle. "It's not camping if you can see houses, rudderbutt."

"You wanna camp in the woods?" Her heartbeat capered forward down the road to hope. A little privacy might be nice. The otter hid her enthusiasm with a wiggle. "I mean, sure, that's cool."

"Cool." The canine sat up, reaching into his duffle bag. "Just let me pack. We're only staying out one night?"

Looking up from texting her mom the plan, she blinked. "You wanna leave tonight?" Her eyes flicked to the window. Sunlight traced long shadows across the driveway. "It'll be dark in a few hours."

"We'll be fine." He stuffed a toothbrush and flashlight into his back-pack. "Not like we're going that far."

She took issue with the husky's definition of "not that far."

Otters aren't built for hiking in the woods. They have short legs and heavy tails. Pine sap sticks to their fur where water would roll right off. Tiny, inedible shellfish buzzed about harrying her nose and ears—she'd never liked bugs that didn't stick to water. Roots and rocks tripped her whenever she looked up. Worst of all, she needed proper hiking boots; on the rough terrain, her sneakers kept pinching her toe webbing.

Max marched onward, tireless. Branches snapped unnoticed against his powerful frame. Tender blue eyes peered back over his shoulder at her, making sure she didn't fall behind.

The woods loomed, woven thick with hungry shadow. Just once, just at the edge of her hearing, a rustle or snap echoed through the woods. No matter how she looked around, nothing ever seemed out of place, save for an extra perk to Max's ears. Not wanting to ruin the mood, though, she didn't complain about the creepy forest or her sore feet. Still, though, her hackles refused to lay flat for ten more minutes. They pressed on.

After what felt like hours, they arrived at a clear hilltop.

He surveyed the area with a swish of his tail. "Perfect. Plenty of wood. Good drainage if it rains."

The lutrine collapsed like a warm jelly. "Ugh..."

With a sniff of concern, he crouched to put a paw on her back. He wasn't even panting. "You okay?"

"I'm fine." Her muscles ached. Had she really gotten this out of shape? Had she ever been in shape? The world seemed to think not.

The dog patted her on the shoulder, then pulled the tent from his pack. With a clatter of steel clinks and nylon whispers, he popped it up and staked it down before her eyes. "I'm going to find some firewood."

"I'll be here." Muzzle-down in the cool grass, she waved him away. "Unless a large bird of prey carries me off."

"Holler if that happens." He headed down the hill, toward a small wash of dead branches.

As Kylie watched him in the fading sun, she noticed more than a few antlers and bones tangled in the fallen wood. Was that normal? She'd have to ask, if and when her body started working again.

Songbirds warbled from the foliage. Crickets chirped down the slope. The sun sank, carving lines through the forest with tree trunk shadows.

The husky returned with a massive armload of dry branches, then padded back down the hill to return with rocks. Just as she wondered if he was showing off, he plunked them down in a ring a ways from the tent's entrance. He followed her gaze to a half-rotted pile of timber. With a gingerly pinch, he picked up a dirty skull. "Feral deer."

She knew that. The eyes were too far to the sides and the neck attached at the wrong angle, leaving little room for the brain. Still it looked enough like a sapient deer's skull to give her the creeps.

Walking up to the edge of the slope, he tossed it deep into the brush. It shattered on some unseen stone with a dry and hollow crackle. The sound echoed through the forest, distorted like a nasty rumor.

Even under the weight of weariness, Kylie found the energy to shudder.

One last trip down the hill, Max hauled up a wide, weather-bare log. With that in place, he knelt before the fire ring and started constructing some kind of tiny lean-to out of sticks and bark. With a woof of accomplishment, he pulled a matchbook from his backpack and lit the little structure. He knelt further to blow into the kindling.

Bent over like that, she got another great look at his butt, which was more than an exhausted otter could hope for.

Smoke rose from the wood, then the sputter of flame. That fluffy tail swayed near enough to stir air past her whiskers. At last, the canine stood and watched his crackling fire. "There we go."

"Mmmf..." With an agitated chitter, she tried to sit up, but found herself wedged under the weight of her backpack.

He unlashed the sleeping bag from her pack, then his, and tossed them into the tent. "I figured by the tent that you'd been camping before." A wide white paw lowered to help her up.

"I have been camping." The lutrine accepted his assistance and struggled to her feet. "In a back yard. In a city. Where 'camping' consists of being closer to the neighbor's duplex than your own."

With a chuckle, he sat down with her on the log. "I could've carried you if I'd known you were so wiped out." His elbow bumped her ribs, about the only thing on her that wasn't sore. "You're normally a tough little thing."

"Not tough enough." She slid out from her backpack and snatched the water bottle from it. She poured the last of the precious liquid into her muzzle. "I should've brought more water."

By the time she looked back to him, he'd already grabbed her another bottle. His backpack must have weighed more than she did. Crazy sled dog.

Heat glowed into the fur of her shins. Firelight fluttered along the surrounding grass and through the webs of her hands. "I never knew you were such a sporting dog."

He shrugged, brushing ash from his whiskers. "I'm a little rusty: usually don't have to blow on it like that."

The otter shook her head, remembering her little campouts as a pup. "Mom and I just use gasoline."

Thinking, he gave a slow nod. "Your mom's always been one for getting things done."

She leaned against him and looked out over the wooded landscape. "Maxie, this is super primitive." She wrung dirty paws together, a fine layer of grit between. "We're like, an hour's walk from the nearest shower."

A snicker snuck from his shapely muzzle. "Well, there's a pond a little ways over there. You could go for a swim if you're feeling sticky."

Kylie bit back a remark about precisely how sticky he made her. Still, it was too good an opening to let escape entirely: "Didn't think to bring my swimsuit. We'd have to go skinny dipping."

Silence. For a heartbeat, she wondered if she'd gone too far and tension wound in her belly. Had that departed too far from their normal old joking around?

But then he barked a laugh, a little louder than the stupid joke called for, a little higher than normal for the broad-chested dog. "Heh, y-yeah. Guess we should have planned ahead."

Grimacing, the lutrine unloaded her backpack: chocolate bars, graham crackers, and a jumbo bag of marshmallows. Using his pocketknife, she sharpened a suitable stick, jabbed a sugary cylinder onto it, and poked it into the cheery fire.

The marshmallow erupted into flames.

"Rotted fish guts!" The cursing lutrine waved the stick around, but only seemed to fan the flames. Her voice squeaked up another octave as she tried to extinguish the marshmallow. "Herring bones and fish guts!"

Paw to his mouth, Max woofed a laugh.

"Carp!" Her romantic evening burning away like a rogue marshmallow, she shook the stick harder.

The flaming blob sailed off, blazing, over her shoulder to splat against the tent.

With a yelp of shock, the husky jumped up and slapped a thick paw down on the flames to swat them out. Almost crying from laughter, his hot paw trailed back a black and white stretch of charred sugar.

The otter spat an indignant sputter. "I-it's not funny!"

"It's hilarious." Sitting back down beside her, he wiped a tear from his eye and got sugar on his chiseled muzzle in the process. "You almost burned down the tent!"

"Shut up!" She hissed with lutrine outrage, ears burning with a heat that had nothing to do with the fire. "I haven't done this in years."

Those big, gentle paws took her roasting stick, popped a fresh marshmallow on it, and leaned it on the ring of rocks. He spun it slowly, toasting the confection to a caramel brown. Three hundred and sixty degrees later, he pulled it from the fire and nodded with approval. He set a square of chocolate on a graham cracker on a napkin on a hot rock. Just as the chocolate began to reflect firelight, he squished the mallow onto it and placed another graham atop it. He handed the neat little confection to the otter.

Resentment still simmering, she took it in both hands. It looked really good. Against her spiteful judgement, she nibbled around the edge. The s'more dissolved with each bite into a crunchy, delicious ooze. In spite of the mood, she chittered with delight, tail swaying off the back of the log. "This is amazing, actually."

"Just takes a little patience." He began his roasting rotation anew. "And practice."

"It's not fair, Maxie." The lutrine munched away at her sticky snack. "You always seem to have a handle on life."

His muscular shoulders offered a shy shrug. "Whenever I go home from being a TV star, I'm just a beta who's good at heavy lifting. Gives a guy some perspective."

Her tail swayed to brush his. "Glad you could sneak away from the pack to come out here."

"You're my best friend." He bumped his knee to hers as he popped another mallow—a raw one, this time—into his muzzle. "Of course I did."

She smiled up at him. He still had a speck of goo sticking out from the corner of his muzzle where he couldn't see it, and it made him look so goddamn cute her bad mood took another hit. She, on the other hand, probably looked like the "before" picture in a public service announcement on basic grooming. Sticky traces of marshmallow fluff clung to her paws and whiskers, collecting a very non-seductive layer of dirt. She tried to wipe it away and only managed to smear it around and get it on her webs.

Silence reigned. They stared at the fire.

He fetched a bigger stick and poked a burning log to its side to get at the embers. Those gentle blue eyes stared into the shifting glow. "Really it's the big stuff I'm not doing so hot with. There are moments like this, where everything makes sense and I know we can deal with any little crisis that comes up. But then I try to think of what I'll be doing in five years and...I dunno."

She nodded, but said nothing. He was talking almost to himself and she didn't want to kill his momentum.

The fire popped and shifted and Max relocated his marshmallow to a safer bed of embers. "I mean, I probably don't have much of a choice. We've only got so many more years of guest spots and signing DVD cases before I'll have to get a real job. Maybe I should buy a car dealership. That's what washed-up TV stars do, right?" Pain hid behind the joke.

She reached out to give his hand a squeeze, favoring her clean fingers. "What about your writing? Haven't heard much about your projects lately."

"I haven't worked more than five minutes on any of them in months. Mom assumes I'm slacking if I'm on the computer. Gets me out working."

"That sucks." Though, from what she could feel through his hoodie, she couldn't argue with the results. If anything, he felt even more muscular than he'd been on set.

"She's practical. She has to be." Still watching the flames, he shook his muzzle. "She...doesn't understand yet; sees the writing, this trip, everything as just a way to cling to the past instead of focusing on a real job."

"She really thinks you're a slacker?" She brushed her bangs from her eyes. "'Cause I'd testify in your defense."

His paw patted her back. "No, she just thinks I'm crazy."

Kylie winced at the word. "Yeah, I don't think crazy fits you, Maxie. You have as good of a grip on reality as anybody I know."

Red sunset light painted white fur pink. "As a fanboy turned semi-pro actor turned amateur writer, I'm the wrong dog to talk to about reality." He pulled the steaming marshmallow from the campfire to cool. "But between me, you, and your mom, we've got the full spectrum of nuttiness."

"Heh, you're probably right." She fidgeted with a stick, breaking twigs off to throw in the fire. "I haven't figured out what I'm going to do next either."

"You could keep acting."

"I think I want to, in the long run. If the right role came along, sure, but I just spent five seasons on set. I should live in the real world for a while." She prodded the fire. "I have a bunch of relations in this part of the world I should get to know, but I haven't seen most of them since I was little. Hard to know where to start. Awkward to just cold-call them, ya know?"

"We'll have to trade phones." His gaze flicked to the rectangular bulge in his jeans pocket. "You can practice getting unsolicited phone calls from my family."

"And you can call my relations and play my public relations expert?" She gave a weak smile; her family could use some good PR, at least around town.

The big husky crossed his legs daintily and nibbled an imaginary pen. "So when can I pencil you in for an appearance with Kylie Bevy? Rare opportunity here!"

A laugh bubbled up from the otter. "Maybe you can act, after all."

Old memories and new stories rolled through the conversation. They used to have these heart-to-hearts all the time. Steady fire and warm laughter kept the darkness at bay. As night air cooled her fur, she scooted up against him and let him take some of her weight. He'd gotten her this tired, she reasoned, so he could prop her up. With sleepy nuzzles, her nose brushed against his shirt and under his chin. If she hadn't, over the years of their friendship, gotten him used to the constant physical contact otters enjoyed, getting this close might have gotten her further toward kissing him. As it stood, he just gave her a friendly hug.

Kylie woke to the unusual sensation of being crushed by a load of fuzzy bricks. With butterflyfish dancing in her stomach, she looked down to see Max sprawled out of his sleeping bag, halfway on top of her: muzzle on her shoulder, arm over her chest, shoulder kind of crushing her. Less of a loving embrace, more like he'd interpreted her as part of a mattress.

Steady breath stirred her hair. His scent, campfire smoke and pine, soothed and titillated her. She hadn't felt this close to him in months.

It made her heart flutter. Sure, the big lump of a dog wasn't at his most appealing right at the moment; feeling a slight dampness on her shoulder, Kylie wondered if he'd drooled on her or if it was moisture just from his breath. Maybe camping hadn't been as romantic as she'd hoped, but it hadn't been a complete pain...except perhaps about the rocks and sticks poking her back. She tried to imagine what it would be like to have him atop her in a more amorous context and savored the weight of him for almost a minute before she woke the big lug enough to roll him off her. Nothing like the threat of spinal injury to take the wind out of a daydream.

With a groan, he flopped off her, not really awake, their pelts clinging together with marshmallow residue. His jaws opened just enough to let his smooth, pink tongue loll out. His shirt had ridden up enough to expose his soft white stomach fur. Every second or so, his leg would twitch, just a little, like he was chasing something in his dream. All in all, she decided, he looked pretty cute for a big, goofy dog.

Not wanting to get caught staring at him like a creep, she slipped out of the tent to sit on a log. The barest ribbon of smoke rose from the doused campfire logs; even Max's methodical ways had failed to put it out completely. Tiny embers glinted here and there in the shadow of a branch-filtered sunrise. Forest birds sang the morning's praises as Kylie gnawed on a stale marshmallow.

CHAPTER 5
CRAZY WALL

STRANGEVILLE (TUE/8P)

S02E02 "Vision Correction": Cassie enlists her friend Serge's help as she tries to prove once and for all that her visions are genuine and not just her overactive imagination.

That afternoon, Max followed Laura through the cluttered attic. Sunlight swirled on dust between the stacks of boxes. It smelled like old cardboard and ancient wood. He ducked under the odd angles of the roof and tried not to step on any heirlooms. She opened a window to let in the morning breeze.

At her direction, he picked up an old dresser to be hauled downstairs. He grunted, arms straining around the bulk as he tried to maneuver it through the narrow attic door.

Laura hovered behind him, doing her best to peer over his shoulder, worried for the safety of house and houseguest alike. "Are you sure it's not too heavy, Max?"

He shrugged. "More awkward than heavy."

"When I grew up here, this old place was full of life." Laura looked out at the sheet-covered furniture. "By the time I left, it was empty." She set a paw on the husky's shoulder, steadying him. "Good to have warm bodies here again."

Max set down the dresser and hefted a few more boxes against a wall. He'd have been tired, but otters, being small, packed light boxes. "Are there cold bodies I should be worried about?"

"Mostly in the walls of your bedroom." She checked the contents of another box, then handed it to him with a laugh. "Actually, that's pretty good. Gotta get that in a script."

The dog woofed a laugh and followed her upstairs. In the attic, they grabbed a few more items, the sound of hammering and sliding shingles stifling all but the most curt communication.

"Thanks for the help." Laura set down an age-stained chair to shut the attic door, dampening the sound enough to resume conversation. "I'd planned on hiring movers for this stuff."

"It's not a problem." He shrugged. "Just earning my keep."

She rolled her eyes, motion traveling down her spine to her thick tail. "You're a guest, Max, and practically family; I'm not going to have you spend the whole visit hauling boxes. You wanna take a break?"

"Nah." Max navigated the living room, his arms locked around a water-warped dresser, muscles stretching shirtsleeves. He smiled and shrugged. "Got time on my paws until Kylie gets off work."

The middle-aged otter followed with the chair. The straw stuffing pulverized whenever she moved, curling fine dust into hot summer air. "With all the stuff in the attic, I'm surprised more of it wasn't ruined."

He nodded, then hefted the oak dresser, rotating it with care around a corner in the entryway.

She snuck past him to open the front door. "How'd that scriptwriting class go?"

"Fun." The husky guided the chest of drawers through the front doors, never straying from his steady pace. "Nice to be on the other side of the page. Not sure if scripts are my thing, though. Having action and dialogue be so separated feels unnatural. Had more fun figuring stories out than writing them down."

"That's how everybody feels." She opened the bay of her old hatchback. "You might remember from some of our *Strangeville* brainstorming."

With a grunt of agreement, he hefted the ancient wooden hulk in place. The car's suspension squawked its objection. He dusted the flakes of varnish off his shirt.

The curvy otter finagled the chair into the passenger's seat. "What else are you up to?"

"I don't really know." An earnest shrug. "I have this big cool accomplishment behind me and no idea where to go from here. I could go back to Montana, but I'm worried in twenty years I'll end up running a farm supply store or something."

A laugh rippled down her body. "A tragic fate."

His mobile rattled against the change in his pocket. He slipped the device out to find a photo of a grinning otter. "Text from Kylie."

"Better answer it." Laura dusted her paws and found her keys. "She's never been good at waiting."

He swiped a finger over the screen.

Kylie Bevy: {The show jumped the shark with the feral leprechauns.}

Max Saber: {Really? That's before the zombie bear with sharks for arms. Which we literally jumped.}

Kylie Bevy: {True! : o}

The husky stuck the phone back in his pocket.

Laura set her paws on her wide hips. "Tell you what: by the time you drop this off at the dump, she'll be off work. Why don't you pick her up?"

"Sure. She was grumpy about walking back from camping this morning." Max wagged as she handed him the keys. "A ride might cheer her up."

Smiling, Kylie stuck her phone back in her vest pocket. Having such ready access to Max made her wiggle with joy. She glanced around for something to distract her until he showed up.

Shane prowled through old vinyls, claws careful not to scratch the sleeves. "So, I thought you said this visit wasn't a booty call."

"It's not!" The otter unpacked a collection of ceramic knickknacks and a pantheon of dark god tea cozies.

The feline drew out an LP with a whisper of dust, reading the back with patient disinterest. "Only because he doesn't know it is."

"I'm working on that..." She stroked her finger-webbing, then occupied her nervous hands by pricing the bric-a-brac.

"Uh huh..." He swished his tail. "You could, you know, flirt with the guy. I've heard that can work."

"I don't think you realize what I'm up against here." She steepled her fingers, frowning in concentration. "Okay, story time. We had this one director on the show, skinny little squirrel named Ronaldo. He did maybe a third of the episodes in the early seasons. And he's got this daughter, about our age. Tall, big boobs, spoiled completely rotten. He used to bring her around for 'play dates' on set, like I wasn't, you know, working." She shuddered at the memory of long, awkward conversations spent trying to study lines while pretending to care about celebrity gossip.

Flipping another page, the cat scoffed. "And what, she tried to hit on this wonder dog of yours?"

"I'm getting to that. At first she shows up maybe once or twice a season—I assume whenever she couldn't weasel out of it. But then Max joins the show and, hot damn, suddenly we can't get rid of her. He'd been a permanent cast member for maybe six months when she first laid eyes on him, so I'd guess we were, what, sixteen?" She checked her math on her fingers, then barreled on. "Whatever. She starts piling on makeup and wearing low-cut shirts; he doesn't bat an eye. She shows up on days her dad's not even working, hinting at getting some 'private acting lessons,' like Max could act his way out of a paper bag."

Shane nodded. "And then you went into a jealous rage and threw her out a window by her hair."

"No." She sighed. The idea had appeal, in hindsight. "Max and I were still getting to know each other. He hadn't even moved in with Mom and me yet. Besides, it was pretty damn funny, like watching someone try to hit on a coffee table." A chuckle. "But the best it ever got is the time Max comes and finds me with this weird half-amused look on his face. Tells me he just found the director's daughter waiting for him in the costume trailer in nothing but her underwear. And he was still oblivious! He thought she was there to try on the outfits!"

"Not to rain on your parade, but this guy sounds kinda dense. Or gay." He considered. "Possibly both."

Kylie shot upright. "He's not dense! He's really smart. He's just, I don't know, humble. It honestly never occurred to him that this Hollywood bombshell would be throwing herself at some farm boy from Montana. As for the other thing…" She waved a dismissive paw. "Not a minute later she comes storming up, half-dressed and pissed. She jabs a finger to his chest and accuses him of making her look like an idiot. Tells him to take a good look because he'll never have a chance at her again and storms off. When he finally, finally figures out what she'd been after he blushes so hard I'm sure his head is gonna burst into flames. He looked like we was so embarrassed he wanted to burrow into the ground and die."

"That doesn't necessarily—"

"Besides, I've seen his porn collection." At Shane's look, she got defensive. "What? If he didn't want me to see it he shouldn't have left his laptop open."

"Uh huh." The cat drawled with divided attention, still paging through the old magazine. "Well, did the porn have otters in it? That would be a good sign."

"No. Three gigabytes and not a single otter. He was probably scared my mom or I would see it and get the wrong idea." She slumped. Finding otter porn on his computer would have been a perfect pretense for confronting the big husky. Okay, maybe not; this wasn't TV. But at least it would've given her some confidence. "So anyway, that's what I'm up against. If I'm too subtle, he won't notice. If I'm too forward, he'll get so embarrassed he'll totally shut down and I'll feel horrible."

"Well, if I see any skywriting that says 'dear Max, we should bang,' I'll know you've run out of ideas."

The lutrine grumbled, glaring out the window.

Silence sank over the room.

A smirk grew across the cat's face. "You know, you could start by reading him the fanfics where you two—"

"Hey!" Kylie abandoned the tea cozies and hopped onto a stool at the counter, tail swinging. "I didn't ask for your advice."

"They have to exist." His slitted gold eyes flicked up at her, over a faint smile. "I mean, come on: it's the Internet."

From outside, a cloying voice arose: "Oooh, you're new. I woulda remembered. Nothing's ever new here."

Kylie's small ears perked up, then drooped. "Ugh, sounds like Cindy's trying to attract some fresh prey to her venus fly trap."

"That's terrible." The cat snickered, half looking up. "It's probably some poor tourist who doesn't know any better."

Cindy yipped a flirty laugh. "You got plans tonight, big guy?"

The otter tilted her head in thought. "Yeah, most tourists wouldn't be Cindy's type. She likes big brawny canines like—"

A deep canine tenor: "Actually, I'm just here to—"

Horror dawned across Kylie's face. "Oh carp." She leaned back on the stool to spy out the window.

Max stood on the sidewalk, finger pointed with the polite desire to leave.

Clad in a string bikini, the spaniel tossed her hair in just the right way to make it flash golden in the summer sun. "Did you just move here? I love getting to know new people."

Kylie flailed off the stool, knocking it over. One foot stuck in the dowels, she dragged it across the store with frantic hops. With an incredible clamor, she managed to scramble out the open doorway.

Cindy stood with her back to the otter's shop, trapping the giant husky on the sidewalk.

Max's eyes met Kylie's and telegraphed his need to be rescued from this very forward new person.

The otter smiled, brushing a lock of hair from her eyes, shook the stool from her foot, and shrugged.

The cocker spaniel donned a sneer. "Oh look, everyone's favorite celebrity has-been."

Excusing himself with a shrug, he skirted the cocker spaniel's lawn chair. He wagged to her side and smiled down at her.

The lutrine's grip closed on his elbow. "Hey Maxie."

The other dog peered over the lenses of her expensive sunglasses. "Oh." Her gaze swept over the two of them, then blasted a quick glare where Kylie held Max's arm. "You two know each other?"

"Cindy, Max is my co-star from *Strangeville*." Kylie pulled him a little closer. "He's big and charming and not interested in you."

"Whatever, tuna-breath. He knows he's interested in this." The sunbathing spaniel crossed her arms and leaned back, spreading her legs a little. "Especially compared to you." Looking at Max, she flicked a dismissive tilt of her head at Kylie. "And considering your family's…tendencies."

Kylie stiffened.

Max bounced a confused look between them.

Cindy's eyes lit up, pouncing on a weakness. She turned to Max, her voice a purr of innocent curiosity. "Did no one tell you? She and her family are this stupid town's favorite boogeymen."

The otter stood horrified and silent, desperate for a means of shutting the bitch up without proving how crazy she was.

The cocker spaniel sneered, first at Kylie then at the town in general. "All the old farts go on and on about the whackjob otters up in their mansion. Then like, twenty years ago one of them goes extra batshit, burns down someone's house and takes off into the woods. They say on a full moon you can still hear him rambling about the monsters in his head." She ended on an ominous note, waggling her fingers, expression mocking.

"You—" The lutrine sputtered with fury. "You don't know what you're talking about!"

"Oh have you not told him?" The spaniel lay back on her sun chair. "I suppose, if I came from a family of lunatics and arsonists, I wouldn't want to tell people either."

Max lifted his eyebrows at her. A quick glance with Kylie, then he waved. "Nice meeting you."

"See you later, stud!" Cindy waved, sliding her shades up. "Look me up if you don't wanna get stabbed in your sleep."

Kylie dragged him inside, shutting the door. A deep grumble rose from the pit of her stomach. Max wasn't supposed to find out like this. Now he'd think she was a time-bomb of mental illness, which she might possibly be, but Cindy dumping all the crazy on him all at once certainly didn't help her sanity.

The dog raised his ears at her, eyes kind. His heavy paw rested on her shoulder, light with concern.

She patted it. "Shane, I think I'm gonna take off."

Feet propped on a table as he flipped through an old Platinum Retriever comic book, the cat shrugged. "Sure. You might wanna leave through the other door."

The otter padded off to the back room to grab her bag. Standing at the other side of the doorway, she took a few deep breaths. Here she was, letting that petty little jerk get to her, while Max acted like an adult. He always seemed to be in such control of his emotions. Not for the first time, she wished she found it so easy. If nothing else, it wouldn't give Cindy such ready ammunition.

In the other room, she could hear the dog and cat chatting. She peered from around the corner, past rows of shelves, where she just happened to be able to hear them.

Tilting his muzzle back out to the street, Max lifted an ear. "What's her deal?"

Shane sighed. "She was really popular in high school. Got halfway through a semester or two into college, decided it was too hard, then came running back to a social structure that didn't exist anymore. Then Kylie showed up and people liked how she treated them like they existed even when they weren't within earshot."

The husky's brow furrowed. "And now they're, what? Deadly rivals? She's gotta be a year or two younger than Kylie."

71

The cat waggled his paw around in ambivalence. "Cindy's been pacing around town since September, trying to wrap her head around the fact that no one cares she was prom queen anymore. Then she takes one look at—What'd you call her? Rudderbutt?—and decides this is a good chance to prove she's still top dog. I guess it's some kind of canine thing?"

Max only shrugged.

The cat continued: "Anyway, Kylie tries to ignore her, but that spaniel's got a way with biting comments. I guess she can't help getting mad."

Conversation lulling, the two had just enough time to blink at each other before the stockroom door squeaked fully open.

The otter emerged and dragged her best friend and the remains of her best-laid plans to the back door, grumbling: "Stupid lousy Cindy Madison with her big mouth and her flowing locks and her mind-control bikini..."

They took the long way around the block to Laura's hatchback, well out of cocker spaniel range. The silence on the drive home got louder and louder. Anger burned a blush on her cheeks. She knew she shouldn't get this upset, but she really wanted to reconnect with Max and blurting out that the town thought her family was crazy wasn't a great start. Moisture started welling up in her eyes, blurring her view of the road ahead. She bit her lip.

"So that's Cindy. Wish she'd introduced herself first." Max reached one hand from the steering wheel and put it back on her shoulder. "She seems...intense."

Kylie looked his way, brushing the hair from her teary eyes.

He patted her shoulder. "That's Montanan for asshole."

The lutrine couldn't help but laugh; a curt, sputtering laugh that did nothing to unwind the tightness in her chest. "Ugh! Max, she drives me crazy. She even thinks I'm lying about being older than her."

Ears cocked, he looked away. "Well, she does have a few inches on you, in several directions."

She punched him in one massive shoulder. "Shut up, Maxie."

Still driving, the husky didn't react except to smile a little. But, before long, he looked thoughtful again, still watching the road. "So...arsonists?"

The otter deflated a little. "I'll explain when we get to the house, Maxie. I promise." She wrung the edge of her vest. "I just… I was waiting for the right time to tell you, okay?" She ducked her head so she couldn't see his expression.

Minutes later, they pulled up to the house and parked. With a heavy sigh to break the silence, she led him inside, then upstairs, then into her room and shut the door. The big dog followed close behind her, hovering, worried. She paused at a folio tacked to her wall. "Alright, before I show you this: context."

Max sat on her waterbed, patient tail curled around him as the surface sloshed.

"O-okay." A chill gripped her hands and feet, distress squeezing her heart. She took a deep breath to fight the stammers. Best to give him all the info before he could jump to conclusions. "Mom thought it might be nice if I had some kind of connection to the new house, since I'd never lived here, so she gave me the old family journals that inspired *Strangeville*. Turns out…"

She trailed off, one final hesitation. It was too late, though. Max would never let it go now that he was worried about her. She bit the bullet: "It turns out my family has a history of going nuts…for the past few hundred years. And they keep journals recording just how crazy they get." She opened the folio, unfolding it further and further, taking care not to knock anything loose. As she went, she affixed the paper with tacks into the plaster. By the time she'd finished, it extended around the corner and halfway to the window.

The wall stood plastered with notes, old photos, and string.

His gaze skimmed the connections, taking it all in. "And this is…"

She sighed, hugging herself. "That's the Crazy Wall."

Those ocean-blue eyes swept back to her. "And this is tracking…?"

"Everything. Anything. I don't even know yet. Ugh!" She gave him a weary smirk. "Does not wanting to talk about the Crazy Wall make me crazy?"

He patted the bed next to him. "I don't think talking would be a bad idea."

"I've been trying to trace some family history." She sat. "This is a timeline of the Bevys here in Windfall, color coded. Red is 'local eccentric' crazy. Blue is institutionalized crazy. Yellow is missing, presumed crazy."

His muzzle dipped in a slow nod. "I'm sensing a pattern."

Still in shock, her breath came out a quiet sigh. "They all start with 'I've found these journals—going to read them for a lark' and end with 'the Universe is out to get me—run for your life.' That's why the house's been empty this long. Crazy has a way of making people want to leave." Tears welled up in her eyes, keeping her from looking at him.

If she'd been looking at him, she might've seen him coming. Instead, two strong arms wrapped around her and crushed her against that massive chest in a powerhouse hug.

"Aw c'mon, Maxie." She pawed at his chest, the last of her self-control slipping. "I-I'm okay."

He didn't budge, which was wonderful and terrible. In fact, he squeezed her tighter. He rumbled in her ear, a sound of wordless love and support, and the dam broke. She didn't cry, exactly, but a few tears snuck out as she breathed long, ragged breaths against his shirt. Her chest heaved as they stood there in her room, letting months of slowly-building dread out in one long go. He hadn't run, the hug said. He wasn't going to run.

He loosened the hug just enough to rest his chin on top of her head. "You're kind of an idiot, you know that? Why didn't you just tell me something was bugging you this badly?"

"Because it's weird, Maxie! I mean, whatever's going on's obviously genetic and that means it might get me too and then I'll go nuts and you'd never want to—" She was cut off by a renewed hug, and he held it until she'd calmed enough to put her thoughts into better order. "I was so happy to be seeing you again, Maxie. I didn't want to ruin it with the news I was probably gonna go insane at some point."

"Your mom's not insane, at least by the standards of television producers." Satisfied, he let up on the hug, but stayed close. "I think you're jumping to conclusions."

"It's all in the journals. Maybe you should read them." With a sniffle, she ran webbed fingers through tousled hair. "You don't have the crazy gene."

His wide paw rested on her shoulder.

She touched it and smiled. "Mom always said I came from a family of eccentrics. Understatement of the century."

"And last century." His blue eyes felt serious and kind on her, before they shifted back to the timeline on the wall. "How far back does this go?"

"Seven or eight generations of Bevys lived here. In our excavations of the house so far, I've found four generations of journals, including the guy who built the house and my great uncle." She drew a box of mismatched diaries from under the bed. "Same song, stuck on repeat."

He inclined his head back downstairs. "Have you talked to your mom about this?"

"Oh, she knows about it. Using the journals to make a TV show was Mom's way of coping with a messed up family history." She wrapped her arms around herself. "For one, I try not to make her dwell on it. For another, pretty sure she thinks taking the old journals at face value is the first step down a road that ends in a padded cell. When she saw how into them I was getting, I had to convince her I was only looking for a genetic or environmental cause for frequent punching of the crazy card."

He took the top journal from the box, then sat down on the bed and opened it with care. He flipped through the hardcover, three-quarters blank and one-quarter gibberish. "Are they all in code?"

Kylie shook her head. "Just Leister's. Mom kept it thinking she'd crack it one day, but never had the time." She tapped a paw pad on a name on the inside cover. "Leister Bevy was my great uncle. Notice anything weird about that page?"

"Yeah, it says 'my favorite book.'" Ears up, the husky tilted his head at the book. "Why bother to write that?"

"Exactly. So I started thinking about it this winter: if I were encoding a journal for my descendants, I'd leave them the key."

A moment passed in silence. The dog studied her, looking through her into her ancestors. Then his eyes refocused. "This isn't his favorite book."

"Exactly!" She brightened as the two old friends shared a look of mutual intrigue.

He thumbed through another book and watched it descend into scrawls and gibberish. "So what is?"

"Some morbid philosophy text called *Notes on Life and Death*. I found it on his nightstand." She pointed down the hall. "Turns out that was the cipher—he used the first instance of each letter as a letter of the alphabet. The rest was just scanning the journal into the computer, retyping it letter for letter, and using the make-your-own-code feature on the Kibble Puffs website."

Max chuckled, breaking the tension at last. "Breakfast cereal saves the day. Good thing he didn't use cursive."

"I showed Mom, but she just said 'oh cool, I'll remember that for a spy thriller.'" Kylie pulled a stack of printer paper from the box and set it before him, dejected. "Doesn't make much more sense than the rest of them."

"Hm." He drew another journal from the stack and flipped through a few pages, then found a charcoal drawing of the house and drive, reading the text beside it. "What's a holt?"

"Otter term." Kylie tossed a weary gesture to the property. "This house, the hill, the woods: it's all the Bourn holt."

Those deep blue eyes scanned the inside cover page. "Wait." A thick paw pad tapped the yellowed paper. "This one's maiden name wasn't Bevy or Bourn. She married into the family."

"And promptly went crazy." She slumped, elbows on her knees, head down, hands on the back of her neck. "So someone else with the crazy gene married into my family."

Max touched her knee, waited for her to look up, then shook his head. "Genes aren't the whole story here. If you really believed that, you would have just gotten a blood test instead of going to all this trouble." He swept a finger at the Crazy Wall.

"I'm looking for a reason to hope that I won't go crazy." A frustrated groan clawed up her throat. "Or at least to find out what kind of crazy I'm prone to."

His heavy paw patted her thigh. "Pretty sure we'll find that first one, rudderbutt."

She brightened at the 'we' in that sentence. "Sorry, Maxie. I was trying to find a way to tell you without freaking you out."

"Is this why you've been acting like you've got storm clouds tailing you?" He lowered the jumble of paper, eyes full of concern. "This must have been bugging you for months. Why didn't you say anything?"

"Because—" She gestured uselessly at the Crazy Wall, at the months of worry and uncertainty it represented. "Because it's weird! I'm weird! The whole reason we even met is because my mother turned a history of mental illness into a TV show!" This wasn't the reaction he was supposed to have. In all her anxious predictions, this conversation had ended with him buying an emergency train ticket back to Montana. One way. She picked at the edge of her bedspread and focused on her toes as they kneaded in the carpet. "You liked the show a lot when you thought it wasn't real, but I thought I'd better work up to it being based on the true story of my crazy ancestors."

She didn't see his arm until it wrapped around her shoulders. He pulled her into a hug and she dared to breathe again. "You were scared and you needed someone to talk to. I'm glad you can talk to me."

Kylie didn't trust herself to speak, so she just pressed herself against the solid warmth of his chest and let a long, rattling sigh escape her. She wrapped her arms around him and buried her muzzle in his shirt, feeling saner than she had in months.

CHAPTER 6
The Past

STRANGEVILLE (TUE/8p)

S02E01 "Property Values": With the Fathomless Gateway in the basement temporarily shut, Sandy must decide to continue the fight or sell the house while she still can.

The next morning saw Kylie hunched over the kitchen table, nursing a cup of coffee like it held the answers to her problems. She hadn't slept much, still riled up from the talk the day before. Max had been understanding last night, but he might still have second thoughts about staying in a house with a couple of mentally-unstable otters. Not likely, but some guys didn't like surprises. She chased the thought from her bleary mind.

Caffeine was better than sleep anyway: easier to summon on command. She'd only made one mug, since the husky was somehow always perfectly chipper without it. Then she realized his absence from the kitchen, where he'd normally be wolfing down a bowl or three of cereal. She padded over to his room and knocked. The door swung open.

Sitting up in the small bed, a dressed and showered Max pored over old records on his laptop. He looked up. His tail thumped the mattress. "Hi."

"Hey." She leaned against the doorframe, wrapping her paws around the warm cup. She tried not to think about warming up against Max's fluffy frame instead. "What're you doing?"

"Checking the journals against census data and public records for the house." He tapped a claw on the screen. "None of your ancestors living outside of Bourn Manor show indications of being crazier than average, and only about one in a generation went crazy here."

"Great: I'm an only child." Still, a fine mist of relief dispersed through her mind. She took a sip of coffee, letting the heat flood her muzzle. "Granted, not all craziness shows up in census data."

The husky's ears lifted with concern. "No, but it's an interesting pattern."

She set aside her worries of imminent madness, slipping into the room. She figured Max might have the right idea. Better to look for answers than sit around worrying herself sick. "Okay, so what could be in an old house that would make people go crazy?" She counted off on webbed fingers. "Hallucinogenic fungus, isolation, lead pipes, chemical imbalance, ancient curse…"

"Well, if it's anything like the curse from Season Two, we should learn about the cure after the first commercial break. This place does run on a well, though—could have lithium in the water or something." He jerked a thumb at a map on his laptop screen. "You know, from those silver mines you mentioned."

Kylie glanced at him. "Been poking around the Internet, have ya?"

He shrugged, blushing. "I didn't get much sleep last night." Clearing his throat, he sat up straighter. "Anyway, I called the hardware store—they sell well-water test kits. We can run down there whenever."

"You're cute when you're smart, Maxie." Slipping out her phone, she pulled up some satellite imaging of the property. "I don't think there are any mines uphill of us."

"Wouldn't have to be uphill if it's a deep enough well." Another shrug, this time while closing his laptop. "Anyway, we could look around the house too. Lots of rooms full of old furniture and boxes. Maybe there's weird mold or something."

The otter's gaze narrowed. "This sounds suspiciously like cleaning."

Max smirked. "I may have been talking to your mom before you got up."

Her sleek arms crossed while her tail swayed in amusement. "You don't need to kiss up."

He sat up a little straighter on the mattress and patted her shoulder. "Nothing says I can't help you both."

"Okay, but first: breakfast." She padded over to the cupboard, retrieved a box, and shook it at him. "Your day's cereal ration."

"Mmmm, Baco-Puffs." The husky licked his lips.

Hours passed. After a quick trip to the store, they set about their investigations. The otter looked through the glass of water holding a test strip, watching Max through the distortion. "All the bands are turning blue or green."

A vaguely husky-shaped blob studied the box. "Those are the nonpoisonous colors."

She rose from the barstool, palms on the countertop. "Yay?"

The big dog turned the box over to examine the other side. He didn't look terribly satisfied either. "Partial yay. We don't have an answer, but we're not being poisoned." He pitched it into the garbage with a wry smile. "Good thing, too. If I picked up heavy metal poisoning, I'd have a hard time convincing my family to let me visit again."

Next came the excitement of the mold test. As she had predicted, the collection process included a fair amount of cleaning. They tested the easy places first: Mom's study, the living room, the kitchen, and three bedrooms. Coming up with nothing in the first round of samples, they scoured the rest of the hulking edifice's vast and dusty drear for anything to scrape into disposable test tubes.

Upon returning to the living room, Max shook the last of the vials. "House's free of harmful mold, looks like. I put some aside to see if it grows, just to be safe." He placed a petri dish in the cabinet under the sink.

"And for what it's worth, I didn't really smell anything that seemed, you know, moldy."

Kylie sighed, draping backwards over the top of the sofa. "Great…"

He cocked an ear at her.

A roll of her eyes translated down her body. "No, I didn't want the house to have deadly molds. I just want a better answer."

Padding across the worn hardwood floor, he patted her stomach in a reassuring manner.

Kylie, head still resting on the cushion, smiled up at him, not shying away.

"It's probably just as well we tested for all this stuff." His wide shoulder shrugged at the room. "It's an old house."

The otter rolled off the sofa, then let her head tilt back with a forlorn breath and tipped forward at him. "Now what?"

He didn't budge as she leaned against him and thought for a moment. "You could stop eating strange mushrooms from the woods."

"I don't."

He stroked his chin. "You could start."

She swung her hips to swat his rump with her tail.

The husky just grinned and poked through the cupboards, as though he expected to find something more interesting than toaster pastries and cobwebs. "I have no idea what your family ate back then. Any old cookbooks lying around? A recipe for mercury casserole would explain a lot."

She brushed hair from her face and rested her cheek on a closed fist as she watched him bustle about the kitchen. His nose was working, she noticed, like he was trying to sniff out a clue. Adorable. "Sorry, we Bevys only document our descents into madness."

He spread his wide paws. "For all we know it was some kind of gill fungus on the local trout."

"We don't eat raw fish straight out of the river." Her fists propped on her hips.

His paw spread as if holding an idea. "Sushi."

"Trout sashimi?" She pressed her hands together under her chin in thought. "That's a good idea, but I don't think these ancestors knew about sushi. My family only discovered sushi in the 60s."

Max pondered, looking out the window as the beaver contractor unloaded more roofing supplies. "Has to be something…"

She looked up at him, then toyed with the hem of his shirt. "You're being really great about all this, Max. Most people would have just told me not to worry."

He smiled his winning smile, wrapped an arm around her shoulders, and pulled her tight against his chest. "This was bugging you, so we're gonna fix it. I'd hate to go back home and leave you all twisted up over this."

Kylie fought the impulse to nuzzle the tuft of soft fur poking from his collar. Her hand drifted halfway from his flank to his chest before she could stop herself, though he showed no sign of noticing. She hurried the conversation along with a clear of her throat. "So, um, now what?"

"Hmmm." The husky let her go and used the sofa as designed. He grabbed a journal from the coffee table and flipped through the pages one by one, careful with each yellowed leaf. "Skimmed these last night. Let me take another look; might find some leads…"

Kylie's phone buzzed. She swiped a web across it to wake it up.

Laura: {Honey, can you come up to the attic and help me?}

The younger otter patted Max on the shoulder. "Well, Mom has summoned me. Come save me if you find anything."

He nodded and smiled, looking up from the old diaries. The books, scaled to otter paws, looked so tiny in his.

She padded to the stairway, then paused, hand on the wall. "You know you don't have to do all this, Max."

"You'd do the same for me."

A twitch of amusement worked through her whiskers. "Make sure you give me a call when you think your family's going insane."

With a smirk, he settled back in the sofa and nosed into a book. "That ship has sailed."

Giggling, the lutrine bounced up the stairs. Two flights later, she poked her head into the musty attic. "Hey Mom. Did you need to talk about something?"

"Hmm? Not really." Her mother hefted a box onto an old desk, opening it with a puff of pulverized packing tape. "I just don't have time to accomplish much else before I head out, so I thought my darling daughter would help me clear out some of the attic for a few minutes."

Kylie rolled her eyes, but waddled over to a stack of suitcases and started exploring her family's untidy past. A dusty hour passed. She and her mother made a small dent in the attic's sea of clutter. They even found a cache of antique cannonballs, rusting in a far corner under a banner for some kind of crab festival.

Light streamed through the attic window, glimmering through the swirling motes as her mother continued sorting junk. The space stood packed to the rafters with cardboard boxes. She shifted one of them, which dislodged a billow of dust and a small baseball bat, which clattered to the floor. The younger lutrine sneezed and examined it. "Huh."

"Little league bat." Laura looked up, elbows-deep in an especially tall, rattly box. "It belonged to your grandfather." She poked her head inside, then came out wiggling spiderwebbed whiskers. "Couldn't bring myself to part with it."

"You mean it wasn't worth any money."

"Yeah, it's that too. It's got a weird stain on the end." She tsked her tongue at the club's business end. "Stick it in your great uncle's old room when you go down. Oooh, but try this first." The elder otter hefted a full-height garment bag. The bag appeared to be from an era when plastic was both coveted and dyed obscene hues.

Unzipping it, Kylie found a pleated and laced monstrosity in white. Nacre beads shone with iridescent splendor, heedless of forgotten years. "Whoa. I don't remember seeing this."

"I only show you heirlooms when I'm sure you won't destroy them." Seated, Laura peered up over her glasses. "It's your grandmother's wedding dress. In surprisingly good condition too; it's not even discolored. Why don't you try it on?"

Shedding her vest, she managed to nuzzle and hula her way into the garment, then got her mother's help in securing the various straps, hooks, and doodads. Before the dusty mirror, Kylie stood in her grandmother's wedding dress, which clung to her every curve. "Okay, so I'm the exact shape grandma used to be."

"Looks good on you. At least one of us might get some use out of the thing. For about an hour twenty years ago, I almost had use for it, but I was in the wrong end of the country at the time." Digging deep into a strong-box, Laura lifted and untied a roll of ancient canvas, revealing a polished seashell handle poking from each pocket. "Here we go…"

The younger otter perked up over her shoulder. "What're those?"

"Your great aunt's sushi knives, probably from her trip to Japan. We should start using these." She drew one, which sliced the heavy scabbard threading with a steel whisper. "Ooh, careful; they're sharp."

"They're only sharp on one side." She peered down the length of the blade. A little tarnished, but the straight edge gleamed like a katana.

"It's for right-handed people. Or left handers. A gal loses her grip on the particulars after forty years." The elder otter pulled another knife from the set. "This one's sharp on the other side—it's for shelling crab."

She took the implement and admired its form and balance. A glint of pearlescence gleamed and caught her eye. In another old box, she saw it: a perfectly-split nautilus. Wondering if one of her ancestors had eaten it, she shifted the knives to her other hand and picked up the shell.

Max walked in. His ears and eyebrows rose.

Only when she saw the husky's eyes widen did Kylie consider what she looked like, standing in a half-dark attic, wearing a musty old wedding dress and clutching an ancient seashell and a pair of wicked silver knives. "Uh, This isn't how it looks."

His eyebrows inched up.

Careful not to impale herself, she propped fists on her hips. "Okay, so it's a little bit how it looks."

An amused snort rose from her mother.

His eyes traced her up and down in that distant authorial way. Then he swished a little wag through the dusty air. "It looks nice, actually. Very classy."

"You don't know the half of it." Reaching into an old jewelry box, Kylie draped an intricate seed pearl torc around her neck. "Pretty swanky, huh?"

He looked it up and down. "That's more opulence than I'm used to seeing from any Bevy."

Kylie spun to a regal pose. "We were quite the affluent bunch once, darling, if you can believe it."

He woofed a little laugh. "I have a harder time believing your mom didn't sell it when she liquidated the assets."

The middle-aged mustelid shrugged. "Uncle Leister hung it up as a wind chime, so I didn't notice it." She hefted an old oak bucket, etched with intricate cameos. A few pearls rolled around the bottom. "Plus, we used to keep this by the table on oyster nights."

The younger lutrine let out a little whistle at the workmanship and wondered how much more information she'd have access to if her mother hadn't funded living in Hollywood with the house's contents. "Why didn't you just rent this place out?"

"That was Plan A: turns out no one wants to rent our old, creepy house." Her mother gave a dry chuckle. "Plan B collapsed too: the market couldn't support another haunted bed and breakfast."

Max smirked. "Too bad you don't have any fields—we could've put in some crop circles to give you an edge."

"No, no, Max, I said a haunted B&B. That crowd doesn't appreciate mixing genres." Laura's phone made an antiquated telephone ring. She set down a stack of old photos and frowned at the screen. "Sorry kids, I've gotta take this." She headed back down to her office.

After she watched her mother vanish down the stairs, the younger otter's arms sprung into the air. "We're free!" She waggled her body in celebration, then turned to let him see the row of buttons down her back, making sure her tail dragged along his ankles. She cast a little smile over her shoulder. "Help me out of this, would ya?"

Ears erect and pink, he swallowed and leaned in to undo the tiny clasps.

The fact that he seemed taken aback might be a good sign. Then again, as an otter and an actor, she might be placing too little value on the power of partial nudity. She cursed herself for not wearing more interesting undergarments. Then she forgave herself: Max's innocent little mind might overload at anything too scandalous. "How ya doin' back there, Maxie?"

"F-fine." His thick fingers fumbled. "Almost got it..."

As the last of the buttons sprung free, she slithered out of the garment. Heartbeat skipping, she hopped halfway into her shorts and shirt before remembering to be sultry. To compensate, she made sure to be extra sensual in zipping up her fishing vest. She stopped as soon as he looked, hoping it would draw attention to her cleavage.

Tucking the dress back into its garment bag, the blushing dog looked anywhere but at her. "Shouldn't we keep cleaning?"

"Max, Maxie, my dear dog." Trotting across the creaky boards, she pulled a shedding feather boa from a hat rack and tossed it over her shoulders. "We're just actors. Without her artistic direction, we won't do anything right."

The big canine nodded, then led her downstairs, past the serious business chatter of her mother. He plunked back down onto the sofa and flipped through an open journal on the coffee table. "I just had a section that might help us..."

She flowed onto the cushion beside him. "The one about sweet, bitter words in the tongue of darkness? Or the one with the writhing coils of inside-out serpents, lacking heads or tails?"

"Neither, actually. It's right at the end." He paged through the blank pages at the back of another journal, going too far and having to backtrack. "Ley lines, moon maps, ah! Here we go: 'I did it! I burned the bastard's house down. Need to get out of here before he sends his master after me. Leaving immediately. Have stashed supplies at shack. With luck, I'll be able to come back and reclaim this information for the benefit of all the world.'" He smiled. "Think that shack's still around?"

"Could be." Her gaze swept down page after page of ramblings. "Think there might be more clues there? If he was planning to come back there..."

He scooted closer to read over her shoulder. "It's certainly possible. Maybe even more journals."

Looking up from the entry, her whiskers brushed his. She shivered, then managed to climb back aboard her train of thought. "I read that back in the winter, so I didn't go out to see if it existed. I've only seen a couple of the outbuildings, but it's a big property."

His broad shoulders rolled a shrug. "I'm not sure the satellite maps'll show us much through the trees, but we can still do it the old-fashioned way."

"That works." The otter bounced to a more hopeful posture on the sofa. She looked out the window to a world aglow with afternoon light. Her muscles ached from investigating and helping her mother clean. "It's getting late. But we'll start looking tomorrow. Maybe walk the back acres." She patted his paw. "I'm gonna see what the dinner plan is."

Max nodded, watching her go. His gaze caught on her hips as she sauntered to the pantry, swaying with a sensual rhythm. Blinking, he made himself turn away. He'd found himself staring at her at lot lately. He'd missed her while they were apart, sure, but she seemed even prettier now than she'd been on the show. And had she always touched him so much? He shook his muzzle, clearing his thoughts. Maybe his sisters had a point in teasing him about crossing the country to see a girl. He must already be pretty desperate if he was imagining his best friend flirting with him. Furrowing his brow, he forced his attention to the map and started breaking the property into a grid so they wouldn't miss anything.

The husky got up and deposited the array of used water- and mold-testing supplies in the garbage. He contemplated the kitchen's trash can for a moment, then decided it was full. He tied up the bag and carried it out to the bins.

The canine stood staring at the garbage enclosure for a moment, nonplussed. It wasn't that the cans were small, or that there were only two of them; up till now it had just been Kylie and Laura in the house, and they wouldn't produce much waste. What made him grin was the haphazard, amateurish construction of it, slapped together from slabs of plywood and store-bought lattice with clusters of nails hammered in at odd angles. He pictured Laura, flummoxed by wild animals digging in the trash, taking matters into her own hands and grabbing whatever was at hand. With a wry shake of his head, he wondered if the handyman had seen this.

Something moved in the corner of his eye.

A dark shape raced from the bins.

He turned to the edge of the clearing, barely in time to see something, or several somethings, leap the stone wall, flash through the woods, and vanish in the inky black. A feral raccoon? Several maybe? Had to have been—too small to be people, and people couldn't move like that. He really needed to brush up on the local wildlife.

Staring into the night, he waited, watching, hand on the doorknob, but nothing else stirred in the windless night. He clicked the garbage bin shut, then headed inside and locked the door against the darkness. Just to be safe.

CHAPTER 7
Searching

STRANGEVILLE (TUE/8P)

S03E03 "Misplaced": Professor Egbert finally discovers where the Tribunal's enemies keep disappearing to—when he reads a cursed text message and wakes up in an abandoned subway station in New Jersey.

Late the next morning, they walked back to town, with the hope it could offer more information than the house had. Sunlight steamed away the morning dew; the wet sea air danced over Kylie's pelt. Shane had scheduled her for a half-day to cover him going to the dentist. Max, being a sweetheart, had offered to walk her into town and research at the library until she got off. They'd even stopped at the convenience store on the way, where she'd discovered anchovy potato chips. Not a bad morning, all things considered.

Until Cindy spotted them from another street over.

The two females spotted each other at the same time, across the single alley that separated Main Street from Windfall's residential district. Then Cindy vanished, only to reappear in their path a few blocks down, leaning against the wall of a building like she'd been there all day and trying to disguise her panting. "Hey, Max..." The honey-coated spaniel flashed her sweetest smile. Her expression soured on the otter. "And you."

"Oh hey, um, Cindy?" He gave her a polite, if distant sniff, then winced at her perfume. "How's it going?"

The spaniel peeled herself off the wall and sashayed toward them, tail swishing. "Just another day in this stupid town with its stupid people." She reached into the otter's open bag of chips, made eye contact with her, and popped one into her mouth.

Ignoring her, Kylie closed the bag.

The bitch smiled and tried not to cough at the fishy taste. Turning to Max, she brushed back her long, silky ears. "Need some non-crazy company?"

"Nah, I'm okay." Max shrugged and kept walking. "See you around."

The spaniel stood, pouting at the exchange, as they continued past.

Once they passed out of earshot, Kylie touched his arm. "I think she's wearing that perfume with the artificial heat scent in it." Even as a non-canine, it'd been a carpet bomb of musk. The cheerleader must have been carrying it around and blasted herself when she saw Max coming.

"I noticed." Max grumbled, walking a little funny. "That stuff's supposed to be for special occasions. She's going to have a lot of awkward conversations with other canids today."

Kylie stroked her chin. "Or more than a conversation."

The husky cocked his head. "You think she's on her way to seduce someone?"

The otter resisted the urge to facepalm. "Yes, Maxie. I suspect she may have been." She patted his shoulder. "She's dressed like a boy-seeking missile, off to blow some poor dude's clothes right off him."

"Huh." He adjusted his watch band. "How long has she been standing slightly taller than you and making sustained eye contact?"

"I dunno. Forever." The otter shrugged. "It's just a Cindy thing."

"And you always just stand there, shoulders straight, tail relaxed?"

She looked him up and down. Did it mean anything that he'd been paying attention? "I...guess?"

"No wonder she keeps challenging you." His bottle of root beer whispered open. "You haven't given her anything she knows how to react to."

"What do you mean?"

"It's a canine thing." He took a long drag on his soda, searching for the right phrasing. "Like, if you'd backed down, she would have known she was the boss of you. If you'd knocked her down a peg, she might have known not to mess with you. But just ignoring her?" He made a wavy, indecisive motion with his hand. "We don't really have an instinct for that."

"You canines and your body language and your hierarchies! How can anyone keep this stuff straight?"

He stepped over an encoded tile message embedded in the sidewalk. "I could get you a book—"

"I have the book! Mom got it for me when you came to live with us, but then you behaved like a completely reasonable person and none of it ever came up."

That got a wry chuckle. "Thank you. When I got on the show, I was a fanboy doing a guest appearance, so I knew I was at the bottom of the totem pole." He scratched at his jawline, pensive. "You and your mom never make rank matter, which I always found refreshing. Plus, most canines learn not to expect pack behavior from other species."

"Okay." She jerked a webbed thumb back at her adversary. "So why didn't Cindy?"

"Can't say. I just met her." He checked for traffic so he and Kylie could safely jaywalk. "Being a jerk isn't species-specific. She might just be one of those people who classifies everyone by whether or not she can push them around."

"So all I have to do is deck her and I can get on with my life?" Good news at last. Kylie slapped her fist into her open palm with an air of anticipation. "Good plan."

He shook his head, solemn. "Too late; you are now a walking chew toy. She's having too much fun being your nemesis to accept you as her superior. From her point of view, you've been getting everything she wants out of life without trying and this is her payback."

"Damn it." Mutters and grumbles tumbled from her muzzle.

"Rudderbutt, you know I think you're great, but you can be a little obtuse." He dug out his phone and skipped through the screens.

Kylie glared, incredulous, at the back of his head.

Oblivious, Max took out his phone signed into Howl, a canine social app that sent out anonymous messages in a limited radius. It was half social media, half bulletin board, and it kept local dogs with their social natures from cluttering the more structured services with their chatter or, worse, actually just howling to one another between rooftops. Max had never been much of a participant, but he liked to keep up on what passed for important news among dogs.

He let her peek and she watched the recent entries syphon in.

Howl: {Bacon half price at supermarket!}

Howl: {Someone lose this tennis ball? Kind of small; apparently much beloved.}

Howl: {Fidough's now has three kinds of sausage! Pizza time!}

Howl: {I have the best boyfriend! He bought me cologne AND ham!}

Howl: {New shipment of waterproof phone cases at Windfall Hunting Co.!}

Howl: {Hope these cases are sturdier than the last batch! Warrantee has a drool exception. D:}

Howl: {I got a Frisbee!}

Howl: {Frisbee!}

Howl: {New husky already attached to non-canid. Life is not fair.}

"Ha!" Max tapped a claw on the last message. "People think we're dating."

Kylie popped a chip into her mouth and crunched it. "Yeah, hilarious…"

"Hey, don't worry about it." He gave her a smarmy wink. "You and I know what's really going on, and that's what matters."

Kylie glowered at the sidewalk, waiting for him to throw an arm over her shoulder and exclaim what good platonic friends they were. At least she'd have plenty of time at work to figure out how to be seductive without resorting to chemical warfare. And hey, maybe Max would get lucky and find something to lend credence to his Kylie's-not-doomed-to-madness theory.

Max breathed deep, reassured by the musty tang of old paper. The Windfall Public Library stood silent around him, the only sounds the shuffle of carpeted strides and the rare rustle of pages. Down a hallway, the dog could see into the city courthouse. He liked small towns; they kept things simple; why have two buildings when you could have one? He carried an armful of surveyor records into the small study room and set the weighty volumes on a table.

The husky sat and started tracking down the holdings of the Bevy family since the town's founding. At first, he struggled to stay focused. The endless rows of property holders and property buyers were painfully dry. Eventually, though, he started to see the narrative inside the numbers: the waxing and waning of a powerful family. Together, these maps were like a book. He liked books. Movies and TV insisted on their own frantic pace, but books allowed him to stop and think if he needed to, or even cross-reference it with something else. Diving muzzle-first into the volumes, he soon discerned their system of organization and pored over the yellowed lot maps. Tedious hours passed, but the husky mushed on. Finding answers would make Kylie happy. He liked making her happy.

Various Bevy and Bourn holdings bloomed and vanished over the centuries, but Bourn Manor sat like a rock; only the outermost parcels ever changed hands. As far as the city was concerned, the house lay at the center of a vast undeveloped tract. No houses were listed as being built nearby. So much for the shack being the remains of another estate absorbed at some point. One by one, he sniffed out answers between the musty pages and tangy old plastic.

The door creaked open. Kylie slid inside, eyes widening on the stack of books and microfilm, which probably weighed as much as she did. "Sheesh, Maxie, leave some for everybody else."

Rolling his eyes, he pulled out the chair beside him.

She flowed into it, ample tail slipping out the hole in the back. "What'd ya find?"

He shrugged, not staring at her tail. He forced his eyes back to the books. "No surprises here."

"Oh, I wouldn't say that." She pulled a battered three-ring binder from her satchel and presented it to him.

"What's this?" The binder, thick with tagged and tattered pages, bore a nondescript black cover. The label: Sovereign Entertainment Studios - "Strangeville" Master Continuity Reference. Max's heart and stomach suddenly switched places. He stared, incredulous. "The series bible?" Max blinked at it, then at the otter. Sudden horror gripped him. "Does your mom know you took this?"

"Of course she knows!" The otter, unable to keep from beaming, bounced in her seat. "Open it, open it!"

He flipped the binder open. Inside the front cover, Laura's handwriting warned of bodily harm if this was altered, duplicated, or moved without permission. The bottom ring still had a length of chain where the older lutrine had bolted it to the writers' meeting table. He glanced a question at Kylie. His paws lifted away from the text.

The curvy otter groaned. "It's okay, Maxie." She bopped him in the shoulder. "She trusts you. Enough to let you borrow it anyway."

Thick canine fingers turned the page with care. "The studio let her keep it?"

Kylie quirked her mouth toward a grin. "She never asked."

"I assumed some staff writer hacksawed it off the chain and sold it online." In a show relying on plot twists, having a single physical copy limited spoilers getting out. It also meant every diehard fan on the planet coveted the binder. If Karl knew he was in the same county as this binder they would never get rid of him. "I always wanted a closer look at this. This is amazing. Thank you." He pulled her into a hug, resisting a sudden, crazy urge to kiss her.

She giggled.

He blushed. "Hey, so I liked the show before I got on it. I can like things."

"Yeah yeah, Maxie." She placed a paw on her breasts. "I know you auditioned for the show to get to me."

He shut his mouth with a smile.

Her hand and ears dropped. "What?"

He resisted speaking for a moment, then gushed. "Cassie was still the tagalong little sister in the first season. I actually found her kind of annoying."

She squawked: "Hey!"

"Her, not you! And I liked her more from the second onward." He squeezed her shoulders, then wagged down at the book. So many people he admired had put so much of their lives into this thing. "This is awesome. Very awesome."

"You're very welcome." She patted his arm, making no move to end the hug. Otters were friendly like that. It was kind of nice.

"I remember this!" He pointed at the page. "We totally jumped the shark when it turned out dragons were aliens and we didn't have the budget to show them, so they were also ghosts."

"Umm, pretty sure we jumped the shark with the cyber-demon living in a used modem." Her paw slipped along his back.

"I liked that episode. Terrible effects, but a solid story." He smiled down at her, then returned to paging through the book, careful not to tear the worn pages. "This could answer so many questions about the *Strangeville* mythos; like this part, where it explains how the fish people and the transparent-skull aliens hated each other before they got to Earth. I wish I'd had this for some interviews."

"Yeah, Mom wanted the surprise to inform our performance." She grimaced. "We'll have to do the DVD commentary someday. You can show off then."

"Wow…" He read on. "Unused story ideas." The back half of the binder contained sheet after sheet of scribbled-on looseleaf paper. "Including about a dozen scrapped sub-plots with you falling in love with guys who turn out to be monsters."

"Ugh. Those must be from the other writers." Her elbow bumped his ribs. "Mom barely even let our characters flirt on the show."

His tail thumped once against the chair.

Kylie glanced at it, but said nothing.

The husky slipped into reading, already getting lost in the text, his arm draped over her shoulders. "This is really great."

She smiled, relaxing against his fur. "Yeah, it is."

After an uphill trek back from the library, they emerged from the woods. Leaves fluttered on the sea wind to either side as they headed up the drive. A massive box sat on the porch, its scuffed cardboard out of place against the graying house and overgrown lawn. Taking up an entire shipping pallet, it was almost as tall as an otter.

Max tilted his head. "What is it?"

She nosed up to the shipping label, which bore Laura's signature. "Oooh, it's for me!" Her little caper of delight petered out. "Wait. ...I don't remember ordering anything."

Wagging, he had to admit his best friend was pretty cute when excited. "Maybe it's a spare Amphicar. We could play a deadly game of bumper cars on the lake. At least then I'd have a funny story to go along with the spinal contortions."

"Har har." Her sleek arms crossed. "Mailing info just lists some distribution company. Weird."

"Weird timing too." He sniffed at the box, but got only a muddle of shipping supplies. "This would be the point in the film when the main characters are warned off investigating."

"What, like someone leaves us a horse head in bed?" Her claws played over the sides of the container. "Do we know any horses?"

The canine pondered that for a moment.

"Too late! Opening it." Kylie's teeth snipped through the plastic tension straps. "It'll be like a present from myself!"

The cardboard sides of the pallet tumbled away to reveal pre-paid shipping boxes.

With a chitter of confusion, she clawed open the tape on one to find it stuffed with sleek black DVD sets. Each bore the *Strangeville* logo. Her mouth hung open as she pointed at the stack. "Okay, I would've remembered ordering these."

"Cool." Reaching into the open box, he drew out a copy. "I haven't seen the final season box art yet."

Arms crossed, she shot him a narrow glance. "Don't tell me you ordered them."

He woofed a chuckle. "Why would I order a pallet of DVDs to your house?"

"There's no note or anything." She traipsed around the pallet, looking for clues, but found only an inventory sheet. "What are we supposed to do with 3,000 Season Five box sets?"

Laura plodded up with a potted plant. "Sign them."

"I should've known." The younger otter sighed. "You could've told us."

"Yes, but seeing the look on your face paid me back a little for having to raise you." Her mother knelt by the creek that ran under the house's skyway, digging a hole for the plant. "We need to forward them to the distributor by Monday."

Kylie scowled at her mother's transformation back into an executive producer. "So we're all going to just sit in the living room and sign these forever?"

"Oh no, I signed my inserts for them over the past week." She made a little signing gesture with her trowel, which she accented with a smirk. "They're on the kitchen table."

A few hours later, the last of the special features chattered on the TV. Moving the boxes of DVDs inside had been an ordeal, though signing and inserting the 3,000 printouts for Laura was taking forever. The air conditioner droned to itself in one window, spilling cool air across the packaging-strewn floor.

"Ugh!" Her will draining, Kylie groaned and flopped sideways on the sofa. "My wrist is getting sore." She rotated her hand, dropping the pen. "What's your secret Maxie? Nightly practice?"

He rolled his eyes. "I've been signing every second one with my off hand. It's like a game: how close can I make them match."

"You're the biggest square, ya know that?" She shoved another paper into its case.

His nose tipped in the direction of an open case. "I'm not sure you should be writing 'Save me!' notes on the backs of those."

"It's meta." She wiggled her webbed fingers at him. "Our viewers will dig it."

The husky shrugged and kept her pile from spilling into the dwindling unsigned stack.

"So are you going to just keep one?" She waved the box set. "To complete your collection."

"Nah, I'm waiting for the Stranger Things edition." The dog waggled his eyebrows with obvious delight. "It has the deleted scenes."

She popped up on a wave of sass. "You already saw those in the daily reels! And acted in them. And we're going to have to see them again when we do commentary."

Nodding, he signed another copy left-handed. "Yeah, but I want the complete set."

"You're not supposed to fanboy over shows you starred in." Leaning in upside down, she scrawled her signature onto another insert.

"I'm only the star if you ignore literally the rest of the cast, including you." He tapped his name, tiny and near the bottom of the case. Being the end of the series, the DVD cover had a group shot of the entire cast. Serge was so far in the back that Max was pretty sure they'd just spliced in an old promotional shot. "Besides, it's a good show."

Her tail swayed to and fro against the back of the sofa. "Someday, I'm going to wake up and you'll have just become Serge."

Max slipped into his Russian accent like a well-worn glove. "We are inwestigating your missink uncle, Cassie."

"Don't use the voice on me!" She poked the ballpoint at him. "That was always so weird on the show. I'm only now getting used to not having to wonder what you're gonna sound like when you talk."

The husky snickered.

The TV babbled extra loud: "Here at Crystal Caverns, we want you to help celebrate our grand re-opening."

"Man, being an actor has ruined commercials for me." He jerked a thumb at the screen. "Look at this girl: I bet she didn't even get a rehearsal."

The lutrine perked to watch the screen. "I don't think that's stage fright... And I feel like I've seen her around town."

As the ad cut between different shots of winding, shimmering caverns, a bunny continued her slightly-petrified wooden narration: "Come walk along our brightly-lit and well-marked paths! Spelunker's Monthly called us the best-lit cave on the East Coast. Field trips welcome!"

"Huh." Still upside-down on the sofa, Kylie twitched her whiskers. "I would've done another take. That one had a weird vibe."

"Then it matches the rest of the town." Max met her gaze. "We could go check it out."

She crossed her arms under her breasts. "You only want to go because there's a pretty girl in the ad."

He held up the box set again and smirked. "The same reason you're front-and-center on the box art, even though you're billed third."

With a little pulse of joy at him calling her pretty, she eeled off the couch, turned off the TV, and signed a few more stacks of DVDs.

As the piles dwindled, the dog gave a deflating sigh.

"What?" She scooted a little closer.

"Nothing really." Those powerful shoulders shrugged. "This is the last time we're going to be doing this." He signed another paper with a wistful tone. "I've been noticing things like that ever since we got the news the show was cancelled. Last time I slept in your apartment, last time we shot a scene, last time I flew out from LA..."

Her paw landed on his shoulder. "You gonna be okay, Maxie?"

"It's no big deal." He flashed her a brave smile. "Gotta move on, right?"

"Not from everything." She bumped him with her elbow, then leaned against his bulk.

He hugged her close, resting that square muzzle between her ears.

She squirmed closer, enjoying his soft embrace. Max could be a little sensitive, but she liked that in a guy. He never sank so deep, though, that few words from her couldn't get his tail wagging again. She liked that too.

The forest loomed, aloof and ancient, as its undergrowth hid stones and scurrying creatures. Searching the property swallowed the next two days. Some parts of the woods prickled Max's hackles, though nothing ever came of it. He'd spent too much time in the city, filming the show. His father would scoff. He didn't even recognize some of the wild animal tracks, especially the ones with three big claws. Maybe some kind of large bird?

He and the otter walked on. Together, they tramped over moss-quilted earth and gnarled roots. Nothing to do but talk and joke around; it felt so right, so much like old times. Granted, he couldn't stop staring at her tail, what with her tendency to balance on logs, putting her butt at eye level.

Max tried to focus on his mental map of the property. She'd wanted to check out the property's link to the ocean, so they'd been walking along the low stone cliffs. Waves crashed over a rocky coastline. He hoped they wouldn't have to swim across the choppy waters to the tiny islands included in the Holt or, worse, drive her car there. After a ways, they found a shallow valley, which ended in a strip of purple-gray gravel beach.

An old structure hunched against the cliffside.

He lifted his ears at it.

"We're still on Bevy property." She swiped her fingertips over the satellite map on her mobile, zooming in. "That could be the shack my uncle talked about."

Max looked around, chose the least treacherous path, and plodded down it. Maybe if he led the way back up the hill later, he wouldn't be so tempted to stare at her tail. The pair picked their way down a narrow inlet to the sea. A dirt road once led down it, but wild plants had grappled it into submission.

Near the bottom, the otter perked up and trotted to the beach. She pointed to seaweed-ringed PVC pipe sticking up from the shallows. "Hey, an oyster bed."

He crossed his arms and smiled. "You're not gonna go oyster-crazy, are you? We don't have any way to get them home."

"Are you kidding? The oysters here are sharp. I need tools to take them on."

"Weapons, technically, then." The pebble beach crunched under his boots.

"I'm sure the manor has an armory somewhere." She hurried over to the sun-bleached building. About the size of a garage, it looked drafty, but stable. Max guessed it hadn't been maintained in about thirty years, which fit their timeline. The weather-beaten door wobbled as they opened it, holding on by a single hinge. A faded sign above the door read "Øysterholt" in ornate lettering.

"Huh." Kylie peeked around the dark space. "It's a boathouse."

His eyes traced the lumber track where a dinghy could fit. "With no boat?"

"I don't think this is what we're after." She shrugged, then poked at some pale fishing nets hung from a rafter. "Leister wouldn't have called this place a shack."

He nodded and followed her back up the slope. They'd found several outbuildings over the last few days, though nothing one could call a shack.

The structures, like this one, were weathered but clutching to the hill-sides, still furnished. Ancient tools, toys, newspapers, and even framed art haunted the buildings. Either they'd been abandoned in a hurry or Kylie's family never had the manpower to clean them out.

Adrift in his thoughts, Max's attention refocused on his friend's tail, which happened to be at eye level once again. The otter had managed to slip ahead of him and her supple body waggled up the slope. He averted his gaze to the sky, the rocks, the breaking waves, anything else. He couldn't afford to be such a horndog when his best friend needed him. He resolved to be more vigilant about not keeping watch on her rear. Behind them, the ocean surged and sank, eroding stalwart stone with every graceful splash.

The pair crossed back into the forest. Trees towered overhead, ancient and inscrutable; their shadows hung like black silk; their branches clutched at every turn. A few miles later, another inlet opened to the sea, spreading to choppy waves and spattered white spray. Brine wind swept through his whiskers. They wound their way down along the rocky shoreline. All along the tideline lay strips of pink-white dune. The dog crouched to examine the strange sand. Up the cliffside, a grassy road led into the woods.

Kylie spun a slow circle, tail curved after her. "Oh hey. I think this is Crab Beach."

"Crab Beach?" He combed fingers through the sharp, pale sand.

"Mom used to tell me how her family held parties at a beach where the crabs swarmed ashore every year. Guess it was this big annual shindig."

His ears perked. "Journals never mentioned this?"

"Not that I remember, but there's a lot of them." A shrug traveled down her limber spine. "Somebody probably kept annual tallies of crab hauls somewhere."

He rolled his eyes to keep them off the sway of her tail. "About the only kind of bookkeeping I could see you tolerating."

She nodded, paws rubbing together. "I'll take another look through the boring parts, see what I find. In the mean time, we should keep looking."

The third day, Max found himself dragged to a particular spot in the woods, instead of sticking to his search grid. Kylie had brought along a shovel and kept insisting their target was a surprise. He suspected "surprise" meant "manual labor." He wasn't disappointed.

Sunlight poured through openings in the canopy, flashing on Max's shovel blade as stabbed it into fresh earth and hit what felt like another rock. The canine panted in the summer heat. Even accustomed to farm work, his muscles ached. His clothes clung to his body, plastered with damp soil and clay. Brick-brown dirt stained his white fur. He huffed, tossing another shovelful of dirt out of the chest-deep hole he stood in. Who knew otters got so serious about burying things? "If there's a coffin at the bottom of this hole, I'm not going to be a happy dog."

"There won't be!" Kylie paced and peered into the hole, wearing floral-patterned gardening mitts. They belonged to her mother and had been designed for webbed fingers. She'd helped at first, but kept dumping the dirt on her own head instead of out of the pit. Otter geometry was not conducive to shoveling, so she'd taken up stone removal duty.

He lifted another scoop of dirt, this time filled with jagged flakes of old metal. Through his weary gaze, he examined the debris. "Huh."

"Ooh!" Her eyes lit up. "Let me get in there! If this is what I think it is, I don't want you to break it with the shovel."

"Fine, fine..." He climbed out of the hole, stuck the spade in the fill pile, and rested his weight on it. He did his best to puff and glare at her at the same time. "I hadn't expected my vacation to include grave robbing."

"It's not a grave—it's loot." Kylie hopped down into the excavation site. "Or a 'cache,' if you wanna be boring. One of the journals mentioned it."

The husky closed his eyes and tried to recover his breath, letting the cool earthy scent ease his irritation. His best friend, admittedly, had a habit of getting wound up about things. He reminded himself that he really liked her passion most of the time. Just not when it resulted in him working to exhaustion.

Inside the pit, the otter scrambled about, clutching a borrowed garden trowel. She poked and prodded with little chitters of otter interest. The tool clanked off something. She straightened with interest, cute little ears perking. "Hello, what have we here?"

He glanced to the cairn of stones they'd had to dislodge before they could start digging. "More rocks? A whole lockbox of rocks?"

The trowel prodded into a rusty shell that had once been some kind of steel. It flaked apart as she touched it, revealing smooth, shiny surfaces within. "Ho-ho! Look at this." She pulled a heavy glass bottle from the ruined box, wiped the dirt from it, then hefted it in triumph. "Still good!" Red liquid glistened in the sunlight, as did dozens of tiny silver fish suspended in it.

Max stared at the bottle.

The bottle won the staring contest.

He glanced to Kylie, happy she only had one set of eyes to look back with. "So otters not only bury their wine, they make it from minnows."

"Not wine: sauce." She cradled the ancient brown bottle, examining the play of light through the viscous substance. "And not minnows: anchovies. Caught, salted, fermented, and pressed like olives."

He squinted, suspicious. "Those look pretty whole."

"Oh, the whole ones are just garnishes." With infinite care, she set the bottle on the side of the meter-deep hole, then started poking around for more.

His arms crossed. "I've lived with you long enough that I thought I was cool with anything fish-related, but that's kind of gross."

"It was good enough for the Romans!" More dirt flew out of the pit.

He ignored the bottle's gaze. "So was lead plumbing."

"Hey, Serge got sucked through a time portal that one time." Kylie called from inside the hole. "You should know about this stuff."

Max crossed his sore arms. "I wasn't there for a history lesson; I was there to justify why my character suddenly knew how to fight monsters. Filming it only took like two days—they deliberately didn't show much of the training so I could spring in at the end and cut off the monster's head with a gladius."

"Another one!" She popped back up to brandish another bottle, this one green but with the same pale beeswax sealing it. "I thought Mom sold it all when she auctioned off everything in the wine cellar." She chittered and spun around, clutching the sauce to her chest. "This stuff is worth its weight in gold. And it's all mine."

"You're going to drink that goop?" A vision of the lutrine passed out and drooling tiny fish flashed into his mind. He wasn't sure how he would get her to the hospital with a car too small for him to drive.

"No!" Paws rubbing together, she cast a longing glance at the bottles. "Well, maybe, but it's a seasoning, not a drink."

"For?"

"Everything! Sushi, salad dressing, marinades…" She flashed an earnest smile.

Max ignored the surge of happiness in his chest and counted on his fingers for emphasis. "Marinating fresh fish in liquid fish with antique fish floating in it?"

"I know!" She performed a little happy otter dance. "Isn't it amazing?"

The husky chose not to comment and opted instead to sit with the mismatched bottles against a tree while the anchovies stared in judgement. Most seemed to have stayed right-side-up over the past century.

Kylie troweled about, but found no more bottles, only the bottom of the rusting strongbox.

Eye closed, Max leaned his head back against the tree trunk. "So we dug a giant hole in the woods to get you condiments?"

"And to verify the journals." She scrambled out of the hole and dusted herself off. "Most of the directions in them refer to game trails and bends in the creek and impressive trees. That stuff doesn't always last a hundred years, but a pile of rocks'll stay put."

His ears lifted. "A point of reference."

"Exactly." She padded across the soft earth and sat beside him. "Are you okay?"

A sigh groaned through him; he stretched his sore limbs. "You do realize all we verified is one landmark from one journal, and that you're all about this fish sauce."

"Hundred-year-old fish sauce!" She gripped his thigh. "It'll be like slurping history!"

For a moment, he just sat. Having her near, touching him, came as a blend of relaxation and thrill. He patted her hands. "In answer to your question, I'm tired."

"Sorry, Maxie." She stood and offered him a paw. "We should head back. Pick it up tomorrow."

He nodded and let her help pull him to his feet. His muscles complained with every movement. They started back through the woods. Another sunset sliced the trees to grasping shadows. He took stock of the day. No sign of the shack. For all he knew, it'd fallen down years ago. Though he couldn't complain about the company, he was beginning to wonder if there wasn't a better way to be spending his time. "I am happy you got your sauces, but…"

"Yeah, I didn't think they'd be buried so deep and I thought at least there'd be more of a clue down there. I'm sorry, Maxie. Turned out to be a pretty lame surprise, huh?" A squirm of remorse wove through her frame. "Feel like a movie? Tonight's viewing choices are Blast Radius and Brunch with Death." Still holding the bottles, she hopped down beside him from a rise in the game trail. "I'd be happy to give you a shoulder rub or whatever. Y'know, undo the damage."

He closed his eyes again, trying not to stare as her breasts reacted to the impact. Weren't bras supposed to limit that? What was he thinking, wondering about his best friend's bra? He must really be tired. "Isn't Blast Radius domestic?"

"Trust me, the dialog's so bad, you won't know the difference."

"Maybe." He glanced down at his clothes. "At the moment, I need to clean up or I'll end up devaluing your house."

She patted his leg with her ample tail and led him back toward their den of bad cinematography.

His ears twitched though, just able to detect, somewhere behind them, out of sight, a skittering echo between the trees.

Max took a very, very long shower. He felt more than a little irked. Kylie had always disapproved of his family expecting him to do their grunt work. She was usually the one encouraging him not let people boss him into doing their grunt work. And yet, he'd spent all day digging, doing manual labor just like his family would've had him doing. He didn't emerge until his fur gleamed white and his ears didn't feel like they had dirt in them.

Afterward he made use of the otters' pelt dryer so he wouldn't be running around damp all evening, rumbling in pleasure at the feeling of hot air under his fur. By the time he emerged, a little puffed-up but clean and dry, the sun was fully down and Kylie was nowhere to be found.

Laura had covered the dining room table in papers, her office desk being apparently too small to hold all the drafts, drabbles and research notes. One of her coffee pots sat at the center of the chaos, the scattered script a tribute to the caffeine gods. She hovered around the table and chewed a ballpoint pen.

He padded across the worn wood floor. "How's your next masterpiece coming?"

"Still a disasterpiece." The middle-aged otter peered up at him over her glasses. "Nice job on the fish sauce. I thought they'd all fallen prey to my shameless capitalism."

He glanced at the mismatched bottles on the counter, steeling himself for the flood of seafood to come. Not that he minded fish, exactly, but at this rate his fur would wind up oily as a Newfoundland's. "It'll make a good story someday."

"Everything does, if you're living right." She sipped from one of her prized mugs, the handle still looped with a plastic tie to keep cast and crew from absconding with it. "What about you? Any masterpieces in the works?"

"Stuck at the moment." He sat, the old chair creaking under his weight. "Had some video game ideas, but didn't have the expertise to do anything with them."

A nod bobbed Laura's whiskers. "What's your family think of your career path?"

He smiled. "I think they'd like me to have one."

"You know I'd give you feedback on anything." She examined a brace of notecards, then swapped their order in the timeline. "Those scripts you wrote weren't half bad."

His tail swished out the back of the chair.

She smiled. "I don't know if I ever thanked you for coming up here."

"I heard a house had space that needed taking up…" He sat up and puffed out his chest with a smirk. "…and figured I'd play to my strengths."

"Kylie won't admit it, but I think the big empty house was getting to her after all those years in little apartments." The otter gazed out the window, toward town. "I don't think the social scene in town has been everything she hoped for, either."

"Yeah, I...saw some of that." He spread his hands with a shrug. "Glad I could help."

"You always do." The otter tossed him a fond look, then glanced to the kettle. "Coffee?"

"Sure." After a day like this, he needed coffee.

She padded to the kitchen, again chewing the pen, and returned with a mug about a quarter full of milk. He usually drank it black, but the weapons-grade dark roast Laura preferred would keep him up for days if he didn't soften the blow, and she knew it. He grabbed the pot and topped off both cups.

She lifted hers in salute. "Consider this your first lesson in being a writer."

He wagged and sipped at his coffee. Lost in the aroma, he floated in a sea of smells until the rumble of a car up the driveway broke him from his revelry. The working half of the front door banged open, knocked by a proud otter tail. The dog turned to see Kylie trot in with three large butcher-paper parcels and a tiny propane grill.

The scent reached Max in an instant. Steak. Glorious, wonderful red meat. He surged to his feet to relieve Kylie of her burdens and scoop her into a hug.

"Hah!" She exclaimed. "I knew a nice porterhouse would make you forgive me. Ooh, extra fluffy." She nuzzled into the thick, dry-blown fur on his neck, cooing in a way that made his brain briefly fizzle.

He wagged harder.

"C'mon." She hefted the grill. "Let's see if I still know how to use this thing."

Fifteen minutes later, the trio sat on the patio, prodding at the steaks sizzling on the little grill. The sunset blazed against the wooded hills while Laura distributed plates, flatware, and cold cans of seaweed beer. As Kylie met his smile with one of her own, he couldn't imagine a better view.

Max distracted himself by fussing over the meat. He came from a long line of grillers, so he knew his way around a steak. The key was to sear the juices inside rather than drying them out. Even with only a selection of ancient and weird spices to work with, they smelled really amazing. By the time he dished them up, he was struggling not to drool.

The steak was divine.

It fell apart under the slightest pressure, releasing a rush of flavor across his tongue. Ancient instincts told him to wolf it down, but he made himself slow down and savor it. Still, he managed to finish before Laura and Kylie even got halfway done. Their progress slowed and slowed, until, in accordance with their established protocol, they let him help dispose of the leftovers. The otters might have said something snarky about his preference for red meat, but he was too busy preferring red meat to notice.

Afterward, Laura gathered the empty plates and waddled inside, amused.

Kylie patted her stomach and leaned back in the cool grass. They sat in a very comfortable silence for a few moments, until she finally regained the energy to start fidgeting again. "Couldn't help but notice you're using that boring, grown-up stiff-bristle brush you don't actually like again." With the back of her knuckles, she scrubbed a sheen of steak juice from her whiskers. "You do know your sisters aren't actually here to make fun of you, right?"

"I know." He shrugged. "I just thought I'd try out being a grown-up."

"Yeah, that's a waste of time." She rummaged into one of the larger pockets of her fishing vest. "Anyway, I got the kind you actually like. It's shaped like a ladybug. Sorry."

Cast in bright red silicone, it really did look like a ladybug. The flip side had a bunch of soft, conical bristles. It didn't even have a handle because it wasn't meant to reach anywhere; someone was supposed to use it on you.

She snatched the brush back, then tossed it from paw to paw. "You taking your shirt off or what?"

Max blushed under his fur. Adults were supposed to have their own grooming handled. It wasn't taboo or anything, just puppyish. She'd done it for him at least a dozen times before, and it had felt as natural as sharing breakfast. It wasn't a big deal. Really.

Brush at the ready, his best friend sidled up next to him, an expectant grin on her muzzle.

The husky took his shirt off, shrugging off the wave of awkwardness. He supposed Kylie was right; his sisters liked to tease him. They must have gotten to him more than he'd realized, if it was making him shy after all this time.

The rubbery bristles teased through his pelt, softly at first, then with massaging pressure. A pleased noise rumbled from deep inside him. "Mmmmm."

"Just like old times, huh?" She took her time coaxing the loose fluff from his shoulders.

He woofed a chuckle. "Your mom banishing us to the balcony so we wouldn't fill the apartment with fluff? Putting up with smoking neighbors? I think I like this better than old times."

She moved on to his back, hitting all the places he could never quite reach. Just like always, she hummed absently as she brushed him. She seemed to be doing a particularly thorough job, which was really considerate of her; she knew he wasn't as good at it alone.

Time slipped away from the husky as he was reduced to whimpers of entranced delight by tender tactile sensation. By the time she'd worked her way around to his front, the last of his shyness had drifted away like so much husky fluff. He couldn't think of a place he'd rather be. He leaned back, eyes closed in pleasure, giving the otter and her magic brush better access to his chest as he enjoyed the evening sun on his newly-thinned pelt.

The humming had stopped. Heat stirred his whiskers. He opened his eyes. Kylie looked up at him, her muzzle so close to his, as if she were thinking about kissing him.

He pulled back with a nervous laugh.

Tiny shy otter ears flicked down. Her fingers toyed with the brush as she looked anywhere but at him.

Great: now he'd embarrassed her. He really needed to get this swooning horniness under control. He didn't want to act like a creep toward his best friend. He cleared his throat and sat back in the grass, propped up on his palms. "Good job."

She plunked down next to him. At least she didn't seem offended. "Thanks."

Tufts of fluff drifted away on the breeze. Some tumbled into the swimming pools, mingling with the dust and dry leaves there. Others wove into the half-wild shrubs. A few sailed out into the clearing to tumble along before vanishing into the tree line.

CHAPTER 8
Steamy Dreams

STRANGEVILLE (WED/9P)

S04E12 "Chocolate Heart": An unknown person is causing havoc with a shipment of love-potion chocolates. Cassie, already coping with being in heat, unknowingly tries one.

Max closed the door of the guest room and let his weight rest against it. He ran his hands through his short head fur as breath burst out of him in a long, ragged sigh. He shuffled out of his shirt and pants and flopped into the little bed, determined to ignore the prominence in his briefs. Another few days like the last, he thought, and he was liable to die of a heart attack. Or maybe some kind of erection-related stroke.

A week into his visit, his attraction to Kylie had become impossible to ignore. Something had changed in the six months they had been apart. In the old days, her touch had been a comfort, a reassurance. It had kept him sane when the bustle of production had gotten to him. Now her touch was electric. Even brushing past her in the hall had become enough to send shivers down his spine. She might as well taze him for all the calming effect her touch had on him lately.

A hot blush lingered under his fur. Though the room was cool and the bed soft, sleep eluded the husky, teasing him almost as much as this indisputable erection, leaving him halfway out of his sheath and halfway out of his mind. He rolled over.

115

It had begun that first morning, when she'd stumbled into the kitchen half-comatose in panties and a t-shirt. He had very abruptly been aware of the way her creamy belly fur vanished into her panties and reappeared again on her inner thighs, of the way her hips rolled when she walked and how the motion traveled down her tail.

The moment had passed quickly, but it'd started some kind of ball rolling. He kept getting distracted by the fall of her hair, by the play of light on her fur. Whenever he got too close, he was blindsided by a sudden urge to bury his nose in the fur of her nape. He'd always known she was pretty, in an abstract sort of way. Everyone in Hollywood was beautiful. But it'd never struck him the way it did now, when she was relaxed and comfortable and they had nowhere to be but with each other.

With night falling, he'd found Kylie's mom tackling a mountain of laundry and asked if he could help. She'd told him he was a good kid and given him a stack of towels for the upstairs bathrooms. He'd headed upstairs, suspecting nothing. Just as he'd reached for Kylie's bedroom door, he heard the water turn on. Given that the bedroom door was partly open already, he figured her bathroom door must have been shut. He'd pushed it open and walked right in. "Hey, I'm just leaving some—"

Max and Kylie's bedrooms were on different floors in the same turret of the house. Consequently, they had a few things in common. One of those things was they each had their own bathroom. Another was an oddity in the layout that had the bedroom and bathroom doors lined up, so that in theory, if both doors were open, you could stand in the hallway and see straight into the shower.

Max knew this to be true, because that's exactly what had happened.

Clothes lay scattered across the floor, a colorful trail leading to the bathtub where Kylie stood with her back to him. Water beaded off her pelt, skittering along her curves like it was afraid to linger. She wore nothing but water and shampoo foam and it made his heart race with shocked arousal. That muscular tail swung from curvy hips, channeling suds from her back to the floor. Further upstream, her shoulders flexed, frozen in the act of rinsing shampoo from her silky auburn hair. Her scent had mixed with the soap, washing over him in a wave that seemed to grab him by the septum and tug.

The weird part was she hadn't seemed upset, not even when she'd snapped her head up to look at him over her shoulder. She's been surprised, certainly, but he could have sworn he'd seen the tiniest of smiles tugging at the corner of her mouth. She'd lowered one arm to cover the barely-visible curve of a breast and he'd realized he'd been staring. She'd been the one to break the silence. "Y-you can leave them right there, Maxie."

He put the towels down, backed away with a stammer, and raced a thundering heartbeat to his room. That smile, more than anything, was what was driving him crazy. Had it been real, or did his libido have him seeing things? If she had really been smiling, then a whole new, wonderful, terrifying realm of possibilities were opened. He tried to put the image out of his mind, but every time he closed his eyes she was there, smiling and naked, framed by billowing steam. Those hazel eyes invited him closer, her curves calling to his paws. He stifled a whine as his heart rate surged.

Night around him, days of building desire behind him, he traced a paw to his crotch. He slipped the waistband of his underwear down over his balls and let a finger trail across the swell of his sheath. No way he was going to get any sleep with a distraction this...urgent. He'd just have take care of it. Quietly.

Kylie scampered out of the bathroom, old floorboards creaking. Her thick tail flicked the bedroom door closed. Night air crept through the open window and clung to her damp fur. Giddy, she slipped out of her towel and tumbled into her waterbed, setting off waves. She usually slept in panties and a t-shirt, but with a cool evening breeze teasing her nipples and her mind and heart still racing, she had a feeling they would just get in the way.

Even through the fluttering glee of having him see her, she realized it wouldn't have killed her to have had something more suave to say. She'd

been leaving the bathroom door open during her showers for days, hoping he'd get a glimpse of her as he wandered by. And then, after all that waiting and foolish optimism, she'd choked when she'd finally snared him. She hadn't been expecting him to come bursting in with an armload of towels, and with no plan she'd just stood there gaping like a fish. She should've used her wiles on him. Why had no one ever taught her how to use her wiles?

Still, she'd gotten him to see her naked. And he hadn't instantly run off. That had to be a good sign, right? Part of her still couldn't believe it'd happened, that she'd arranged for it, hoped for it. Maybe it was a little stupid, but only if it didn't work.

With a self-indulgent smile she turned on her side and stretched out on the bed, feeling her sheets caressing her naked fur. Maybe she should've just bent over and lifted her tail. There probably wasn't any clearer invitation you could give a guy. She indulged in a shiver as she imagined broad, calloused paws taking hold of her hips and big canine teeth nipping playfully at her nape as his weight pressed her to the wall of the shower. But no, Max's politeness would've kicked in and he'd have run, apologizing, all the way back to Montana.

So she'd stammered something about towels instead of purring something sultry about him joining her. All of her plotting had failed to prepare her for the rush of tittering anxiety that had accompanied reenacting the shower cliché. The memory of his eyes roaming up her body made her wriggle. She had felt so exposed but still so very safe, because it was Max and she wanted him to look at her. It had been like jumping off the high dive: all the rush of falling with a soft landing at the end.

Webbed fingers edged under thin blankets and over the rich pelt between her legs. Moisture gathered on the delicate lips of her sex that had nothing to do with the shower.

Max's fingers closed gently around his fuzzy sheath. In a well-practiced motion, he worked it up and down along the firmer flesh within. His shaft responded with a swell and a dribble of precum. A slight whimper of pleasure escaped his muzzle.

He could go up there. Right now. Her bedroom was just upstairs, barely fifteen feet straight above him. She'd let him in. He imagined opening her door, her bedroom bathed in silver moonlight. She would be sprawled on top of the covers, naked and amazing, waiting for him. They could talk, or maybe they wouldn't even have to. Maybe she'd bounce over to him, full of nervous energy, and lead him by the paw toward the bed. Their eyes would meet, then their muzzles. She'd pull him close, craving his touch, so familiar and so new. He knew her scent like he knew his own. Even when she wasn't present, he could conjure its memory. How would it change when she was aching for him, wet and eager as she pressed against his chest?

The soft, but eager pinch of teeth on his lower lips would get him to open his mouth and their tongues would slide together. The husky wiggled his own tongue against the roof of his mouth, wondering how hers would feel.

Fingers along her inner walls, Kylie ran a free paw up her stomach to her breasts. She'd never kissed anybody, not for real, but she knew together they'd figure something out. Their tongues would writhe together as his hands ran through her hair, until they were forced to separate, gasping for air. His breath would breeze hot through her fur. He'd get that cute innocent happy look, all waggy and wide-eyed and grinning. She'd guide those big white paws in exploring her body, showing him all the places it felt good to touch. He'd tell her how long he'd waited, how much he'd wanted her all these years.

He liked her body. That much she'd seen in the way his eyes swept along her contours in the shower. Her big strong doggy would caress her sleek form, so caring, so gentle. He'd always been careful with her, careful of his strength and size. She'd climb up to straddle him, kissing him, feeling his stiff arousal against her crotch. She'd whisper in his ears how much she wanted him between her legs, between her folds. Then she'd drop a hand to his tented boxers and fish out his cock.

Would it be pink? Most of the husky hunks on the Internet had pink-ish-red ones. It'd have a knot too; she had to remember that. Would that fit inside her? The fanfics insisted it would fit just about anywhere she cared to put it. She'd push back the sheath and feel the smooth flesh throbbing in her paws. It'd feel so hot against her fingers. Once she'd taken a nice long look and couldn't wait any longer, she'd press him to her slick folds, letting him feel her juices.

Working faster against her clit, she imagined his cock in place of her fingers. Her back arched against the bed, sinking into ecstasy.

Max moaned, a steady drip of fluid soaking his knuckles. She knew that moan well; he made it whenever she brushed him. He'd grip her hips and pull her back on top of him. They'd scoot backward onto the bed. Somehow, he'd manage to remove his boxers in a sexy way, then lay back as she rubbed her juicy slit up the underside of his shaft. They'd pause with his tip at her entrance. She'd be really hot, really eager, and that naughty glint in her eyes would tell him just how much she wanted him. Her scent would sizzle with arousal, shooting desire down his every nerve.

Two delicate paws on his chest, she'd sink down, burying him in her slick folds. He'd watch his cock disappear into her pleasure-wriggled otter body, feel incredible heat and pressure surround him. He'd run his hands along her creamy tummy, cupping those perky breasts. Her body would start to bounce atop his, breasts bobbing, smile wide.

Kylie squirmed face-down in bed, humping her fingers deeper. Max would stroke her body as she rode him. She'd moan his name, gasping for him to play with her nipples. Her paw echoed what she pictured him doing to them. Her hips would rise and fall on his, tail and legs working to find just the right pace. He'd feel so warm, so filling, like nothing she'd ever experienced.

He'd never dated anybody, that much she knew, so he was probably just as inexperienced. He'd probably be a little uncertain, but with that fit, well-muscled body meeting hers, what could go wrong? She'd get him to knot her, though; that part seemed pretty straightforward. He'd work it into her, letting her take her time, stretching her to the absolute limit.

"Tie me, Maxie." She'd gasp. Then she'd grind onto him just right, at just the right time. There'd be a heartbeat of tension as her lips slid around the widest part of him, then he'd be completely within her, locked inside, claiming her. She'd be so tight and she'd love every inch of him as his knot swelled inside her.

The husky stroked faster. Wet fur and paw pads worked over his cock, his other hand rubbing his sheath behind the swelling knot.

Kylie ground her hand against the sheets, fingers soaked and sticky. Her hair fell in a tumble over her face, eyes screwed shut in pleasure. Her breath raced against the sheets; her heart thundered after.

He'd whimper, lost in pleasure, while he knotted her, but she'd lead his hand to her clit and show him how to finish her off and he would rub her just right to send her tumbling over the edge. They'd come together, climaxes fueling each other, hips jostling in frenzied passion.

Intimate muscles clenched, wringing together as if his cock were really in her. The otter squeaked in delight, burying her face in a pillow to muffle the sound.

Max bit back a growl. Hot, stiff flesh pulsed in his paws. His toes curled against the corner of the mattress, his knees spreading to give his paw room to work. He was so close.

His hips drove up, imagining her buried on his knot, tight and quivering and completely his. They'd be stuck, nowhere to go but deeper, nothing to do but come. His creamy canine fluids would flood her, rushing around his sensitive cock and into every inch of her passage. The image of her shuddering across his hips with moonlight kissing her hair and the curve of her breasts left him trembling.

Breathing hard, he shivered, eyes squeezed shut. His balls clenched and heavy spurts surged from his tip to spatter across his stomach. Into the night, to the ceiling that separated them, he whispered her name like some sacred word: "Kylie!"

Once they'd both climaxed, she'd lay across him, letting him wrap her up in his strong, gentle arms. Her legs would be around him, his around her tail. He'd keep her warm, buried in husky fluff, stuffed with husky cock. She'd fall asleep to the beat of his heart, safe and sated. Panting and hugging her pillow, the otter wiped her sticky digits on the bed sheets.

She heaved a breath, worn out by her own lusts, feeling sleep slipping into the corners of her mind. She tugged the covers half-heartedly up to her waist and sighed. It was a nice fantasy, but it wasn't real. Her bed felt as big and as empty as it ever had.

She turned on her side and settled in. A slender arm extended to where another person might have lain, the fur of her arm dark against the bedspread. She allowed herself a little smile. It wasn't real, but maybe it could be.

Max panted through gritted teeth, his chest heaving as the electricity of climax powered through him. Slowly, gradually, his muscles unwound and his vision refocused. His head flopped back as he stretched himself out on the little bed. His nostrils flared, searching for a scent that existed only in his imagination. The intensity of the experience floored the big canine. He had never fantasized about Kylie before. He hadn't known what he'd been missing. He wondered what else he'd been missing.

That thought was enough to bring him back to reality. He blinked in the darkness, prodding his sodden, sticky belly fur with a finger. With a grimace he pawed at the floor until he found his discarded shirt and set about mopping himself up. As he worked, he started to reflect on the situation, the glow of orgasm fading to be replaced by a twinge of guilt. Kylie had a lot to worry about without him adding another layer of complexity. She needed his help, and she deserved better than to have him distracted and horny because he'd happened to finally notice she was hot.

Belly fur drying, Max disposed of the evidence into the hamper and curled up in bed. Despite him knowing better, a hazy part of his brain suggested the only thing to improve his already pleasant afterglow would be a warm otter body next to him, curled in against his shoulder where he knew she'd fit. He allowed himself a wistful smile at the thought, then buried his nose against the pillow and fell asleep.

CHAPTER 9
Dog Day

STRANGEVILLE (SAT/4p)

S05E08 "Double Date": Tired of people assuming they're a couple, Serge and Cassie resolve to get dates to the winter formal, but there's something sinister about their chosen partners...

Max drifted to consciousness right around sunrise, as usual, but with slightly matted belly fur. He lay in bed for a while, soaking up the luxury of not having to get up and do anything. After a hazy period of time, his stomach grumbled a breakfast order. Stretching, he padded to the kitchen and reloaded the coffee machine. He poured cereal into a bowl, then found the vessel to be, like most things in the house, scaled for otters. After some quiet rummaging through the cupboards, he deemed the salad bowl too large, the colander too porous, and the skillet too shallow. The soup tureen was the first thing he found that looked capable of holding more than a few mouthfuls.

He sat at the table and munched his way through a quarter of a box of Kibble Puffs. His brain started to boot up. Shards of plot started to swirl in the silence of morning; he typed them out as notes and scraps on his phone between spoonfuls. After he finished, he placed the tureen in the sink and tromped back to his bathroom to grab a shower. As hot water raced down his fur, soaking him to the skin, he stood under the streaming water, lathered shampoo into his pelt, and appreciated the grandeur of having a bathroom for every bedroom. Good pressure, plenty of heat, and plenty of places to set soap: leave it to otters to design a good shower.

Several steamy minutes later, the husky emerged, toweled off, and pulled clothes on over his gleaming white fur. He retrieved his laptop and returned to the kitchen table. He tried to flesh out the fragments of literature, scattered though they were, and started trying to piece them together. Slow going, but no faster than most other times of day. Over the last week, he'd figured out writing in the morning wouldn't waste any Kylie time.

After a spell, the coffee aroma drew Ms. Bevy from her room upstairs. Clad in a rumpled dressing gown and sporting equally rumpled whiskers, she shuffled into the kitchen, grunted good morning, and poured a cup of the life-sustaining liquid. He knew better than to try interacting with her—she wasn't any more awake than her daughter in the morning, just more ambulatory. She tromped into the living room to catch up on whatever shards of Internet had accumulated on her tablet overnight.

Max puttered around on the computer until close to noon, at which point Kylie's shower came on upstairs.

He exchanged an amused glance with the older Bevy, who sat on the sofa, now more or less awake.

"Kylie's never been an early riser." She sipped her second cup of coffee. "More than once, I had to drive her to school in her favorite form of passive resistance against mornings: the blanket burrito."

"It's a wonder she survived filming." He thought back to some very early mornings as he loaded a bagel into the toaster for her.

"She's lucky I had to get up just as early." The lutrine kicked her slippered feet up on the coffee table. "And that I didn't listen when she told me to write her out of the day's scenes."

A few minutes later, the shower shut off. A damp Kylie thundered down the squeaky stairs, pulling on her vest.

Without a word, Max stood and handed her a bagel with cream cheese: suitable food for a walk.

She smiled a wag-worthy smile, then padded through the living room and bounced into her shoes. "Bye Mom!"

"Have a good day, dear." Her mother flicked through another email on her tablet, sipped her coffee, and found the cup empty.

Kylie eeled out the door. Down the driveway, the canine trotted after her. They crossed into the woods and followed a game trail under the canopy of rustling leaves. The lutrine bounced over logs and under branches with fluid ease, leaving Max to plow through them. A few more days and he'd have cleared a husky-shaped hole through the forest.

Even more impressive, though, she had the ability to munch on a bagel all the while without choking. "Should only be there a couple hours, so Shane can take a lunch." Her cute little ears wiggled as she swallowed another bite. "You ready for our little roadtrip?"

He gave a little woof of agreement as they emerged at the edge of town. The dog braced himself for yet another flirtation from the spaniel, but her chair sat vacant. He hugged Kylie goodbye and departed before Cindy could return from the powder room or wherever she'd gone.

Crunching back up the gravel driveway, Max trotted up the veranda and through the front door.

Glasses halfway down her muzzle, the middle-aged otter glanced up at him from the sofa. "And thus do you return."

He nodded. "In accordance with the prophecy, Miss Bevy."

She glanced down at the tablet. "You, Mister Saber, have gotten some offers."

His ears perked.

"Let's see." Her gaze skimmed the tablet as she flicked through emails. "A villain role—"

"Ooh." Settling on the recliner, he interleaved his fingers and leaned forward.

"—in a public service announcement about fleas. A flea suit may be involved."

"Please, no."

Her tail rolled in a wave atop the couch cushions. "And a chance to appear in a *Strangeville* fan movie—"

"That could be interesting."

She raised a webbed finger. "—filmed in a garage in Oregon."

He sighed, shoulders slumping. "Why do you even tell me these?"

"I'm your agent." She flashed a smirk, one he'd seen on his best friend a thousand times. "I'm obligated."

"Right." He crossed his arms. "Do you ever miss being my producer?"

"Sometimes. When I feel I'm sleeping too much and not stressed enough."

"It still feels like this is just another break, like we're due back on set any day."

"Everything's gotta end, kiddo." She shrugged, set down her tablet, and picked up her coffee. "Otherwise, we'd never have room to start something new."

He glanced at her askew. "Deep."

"Thanks." Dipping her creamy muzzle, she sipped at the steaming mug. "Saw it on this kitschy hand-painted sign in one of the souvenir shops."

"Ever have any regrets about how *Strangeville* played out?"

A shrug rolled her shoulders. "I tied up the big stuff, but the series ended with lots of untidy plot threads."

He nodded, not eager to dredge up painful memories. Even when she'd gotten her way on the show, it hadn't been easy to make. She had a vision and didn't like to compromise it, even for the constraints of reality.

Brushing hair back from her glasses, she took another sip of black coffee. "Life's untidy."

"Pearls of wisdom, from Laura Bevy herself." Wagging, he crossed his arms and sat back. "I should be honored."

"Don't assume I have it all together." The lutrine propped her chin on one palm, gazing upon her laptop. "I should be writing more, clearing these things out. Maybe I could do a screenplay for a certain badass porcupine co-star of yours."

"I saw a gif of him not too long ago emerging from an egg and scattering dead fish."

"See? I could help with that." She smirked. "Anybody can write meaning into meaningless surrealism."

As afternoon wind rustled the leaves of Bourn Holt, dappled sunlight danced over the stacks of dusty boxes in the massive ballroom. Max rolled an empty beer keg out into the hallway and under the gaze of portraits, which conspired around a disused fireplace. "Are you ever creeped out by the house?"

"Not really. I grew up here, so it's full of good memories for me." Laura glanced around, then over her shoulder. "And I plan to make more."

The dog nodded. As they passed the kitchen, his ears perked to pop music upstairs. Kylie must have gotten carried away picking out tunes for their drive up the coast.

"Plot exercise: why did I have half a dozen empty kegs in my ballroom?" She rolled the object in question through the living room and toward the front door.

The husky followed suit and examined his own keg. "Well, the obvious answer would be you used to throw wild parties here, but these aren't very dusty. I'd say you used to brew beer, but a brewery seems to be the only thing this house doesn't have. So I have to assume you're renting out storage space to local bars."

The middle-aged lutrine nodded, whiskers bobbing. "That does sound like me. But I have a seaweed-farming cousin up the coast on the border; he brews beer. Left these behind when they wouldn't fit in his truck for the return trip." She pointed to the label, which proclaimed the virtues of the "Thomas Creel Seaweed Farm & Brewery." It showed a smiling otter with seaweed in one paw and wheat in the other.

Glancing at her, Max cocked an eyebrow. "Seaweed beer?"

She crossed her arms over her breasts. "Your people eat frozen gravy on a stick on hot days."

The food part of Max's brain activated, and he found himself licking his chops. "Touché."

As Laura stopped to catch her breath, Max gripped a keg in either hand, hefted them, and set them in the hatchback with a soft grunt.

Laura gave a low whistle. "Sheesh, Max. If I were as strong as you..."

"You'd what?" His ears took a wry tilt. "Type harder?"

She chittered some sass at him and continued on her way.

After two more trips, he loaded the final kegs into the hatchback.

"He also brews a fine oyster stout." She noted his concerned expression. "Made with live oysters."

He dusted his hands and suppressed a shudder. "I'm sure it's delightful."

"Don't pander to me, young man." Grinning, she patted her paw on the metal rim of the canister. "Go get my foolish daughter. If you leave now, you can return these and get back in time for dinner."

Heading back into the house, Max trotted upstairs. Strands of bouncy music echoed down around him. He could've just texted her, but the thump of the beat upstairs suggested he wouldn't get much response. He crested the stairs and turned toward her room. Through a half-open door, motion teased his attention. He padded closer.

Inside, Kylie wriggled and wiggled, captivated by the song. Eyes closed, lip-syncing the caramel-corn lyrics, the otter bounced and grooved around the room. Her body shimmied to the beat of The Sugar Gliders, tail swaying. Summer sunlight glowed through her paw webs as they flashed around her body. She twirled and twisted, a melody given form.

Mesmerized, Max watched as her body moved in ways his never could. She moved with such freedom, born not just of dexterity but of utter confidence—as if no one had ever mocked her for dancing. He always had to be aware of himself, as much for social reasons as to keep from bowling someone over or hitting his head getting into cars. Grace wasn't expected of him, but his best friend swam through dance moves like water.

He might have watched forever, but she happened to open her eyes, see him, and freeze mid-bounce. "Max! Hi!" Jazz hands snapped to her sides, then fumbled to turn down her computer's speakers. "You saw that didn't you?"

Wagging, he shrugged. "Car's packed, if you're done wiggling around."

Max adjusted the passenger seat back all the way so his legs could stretch out. His ear tips brushed the upholstered ceiling as the hatchback puttered down the streets of Windfall on the way out of town. They stopped at an intersection. Out the window, a string of mumbled grunts rose from a hedgehog as he tended his row of immaculate topiaries.

Kylie gripped the wheel, waves of energy trailing down her tail in front of the back seats. He wagged through the gap in his own seat: after the recent stress, it felt good to see her having fun again.

They pulled into the supermarket parking lot and trotted inside. A weasel, surly and supple, argued with a manager about the establishment not carrying gold foil.

The manager nickered and pinched the bridge of her nose, rubbershod hooves squeaking on worn tile floor. "I'm sorry, sir: we only carry aluminum foil."

"Aluminum's not nearly conductive enough." With a furtive glance, the mustelid doffed his top hat to reveal a tattered lining of gold foil. "How am I supposed to block out the signals?"

Max opened his muzzle to explain that's not how transmissions worked, but felt lutrine paws grip his elbow.

His friend towed him along by the arm. "Don't encourage the crazy person, Maxie."

He allowed himself to be directed down an aisle and past a teenage buck eyeing a shelf of antler-growth cream. Soon Max found himself in the dog foods section, surrounded by familiar brands with scratch-and-sniff labels.

One hand still on his arm, the otter inspected a box of heart-shaped kibbles called Love Bites with a groan. "Dogs..."

"What?" He wagged and waved a cereal box. "It shows more restraint than Tennis Ball Crunchies."

"Oh, eww. I bet they taste like sneakers and feel like the inside of a sock."

"Mmm." He peered down the side of the box. "With natural nylon and rubber flavorings."

She jabbed a webbed finger his way. "You lie, sir."

"I do." He smirked as they walked on. "They're just corn puffs with green dye and white frosting."

Her smile bunched up. "I can't decide if I'm disappointed. Oooh!" She ducked off toward the snack section to scamper between the many options.

It'd felt so natural, Max had almost forgotten she'd held his arm. He wasn't sure what that meant. He grabbed some jerky and a root beer, then started looking for something his otter companion might enjoy. When she returned, his eyes narrowed with suspicion on her bag of barbecue potato chips.

Webbed paws clutched the snack away. "What?"

"They're not made of water chestnut pulp?" He folded his arms across his chest and did his best to look stern. "Not fried in fish oil or dusted with pulverized shrimp?"

"I don't think so..." For an instant, she studied the back of the bag, then poked him in the chest. "I can eat normal chips!"

He continued down the aisle, watching her from the corner of his eye. "I've seen no evidence of that."

She started to chitter up a retort as they turned a corner. "Whoa!" Her nose crinkled in distaste at the rows of specialty perfumes. "Ugh! This aisle smells like Cindy."

The husky nodded agreement. Even the most subtle of perfumes could get overwhelming when you put a thousand of them in the same aisle, all jiggered to different species. And not all of these were subtle. Musk hung heavy in his nose, weighing his every thought down to crotch level. He coughed at the faint burn kindling in the back of his throat, trying to wave the artificial heat-scent out of his delicate nostrils. "More like ten Cindys."

"Now there's a scary thought..." Tracked the odor to an empty perfume display labeled Estrüsse, Kylie squawked with shock and dismay. "Sweet fishes, she's stockpiling it. And it smells like half a bottle leaked onto the shelving."

Max only nodded, the scent buzzing through his brain to swell his sheath. He trotted back to the checkout as fast as discretion would allow. His companion bounced at his side, chattering on about how the town was just as weird as she'd promised. His glance kept trailing down the curve of her tail, without his permission. He decided, as he adjusted the crotch of his pants so he could walk a little easier, that he didn't like artificial pheromones.

A gangly greyhound cashier rang up their items with surprising speed and a shy retainer smile. "You two have a good night."

"Oh we always manage to." The otter looked up at him with a cute grin. "Right Maxie?"

He woofed a little laugh. "I guess we do, rudderbutt."

The greyhound's tail whipped up a wag as she bagged their items.

The husky nodded a polite goodbye, even as his ears burned. The cashier pup had gone starry-eyed, like she'd seen them as a cute couple. How would that even work? He'd have to lift her up to slow dance. She'd need a stepladder to kiss him. And with one partner twice the size of the other, sexual positions would get a bit limited. Doggy style might do. He glanced to the checkout counter and judged he could easily bend Kylie over it and ride her. Maybe clutching her tail for leverage as he sank in...

He shook his muzzle and tried to breathe out any residual heat perfume; that had to be the cause of his weird thoughts. Thinking about Kylie like this wasn't helping his unauthorized erection.

Climbing in the car, the canine busied himself by scrolling through the satellite map on his phone, trying to sit in such a way to hide an bulge in the folds of his jeans. "Okay, we have a full tank of gas, snacks, and directions. Anything else we need?"

Flashing him a smile, she switched the stereo to play from her phone. For the second time that day, the best of The Sugar Gliders sailed from speakers around Max. As his best friend wiggled and sang at the wheel, he felt his heartbeat speed as they took the ramp to the highway. With the seaside rolling by, though, and the way she drove, it was probably just because of the increased odds of a car crash.

A couple hours down the twisting roads, Max discovered the "Best of The Sugar Gliders" sounded uptempo and peppy and exactly like everything else Kylie's favorite band had ever recorded. At a fueling station, he also discovered maple candy was delicious. Upon switching seats, he discovered just how far pedals and a steering column can be adjusted.

At long last, they rumbled past a sign for the Thomas Creel Seaweed Farm & Brewery and up to a cluster of buildings around an inlet. A rocky shoreline curved to cradle a rippling sea.

A lone figure stood on the dock. The strapping and shirtless sea otter looked up from securing a small boat and padded toward them. Saltwater scattered from his shaggy blonde hair, pattering on the weathered boards or vanishing into the fabric of his wetsuit pants. "Can I help you?"

"We're returning your kegs!" She slapped a paw on the side of the hatchback, then bobbed brightly. "Kylie Bevy, and my handsome escort is Max, my former co-star."

"Sean Jib." He shook her hand. "Good to finally meet you. Your relations keep pointing you out whenever the show came on." The otter craned his neck up to meet his gaze, then clasped his hand, looked him over and apparently decided he needed to make a worse first impression. "Right, the Siberian sidekick. You looked taller on TV."

The canine chuckled, willing his ears to relax. "It's all about perspective."

"Uh-huh." His gaze left the dog after an instant, to make more time for checking out Kylie. Jib crossed sleek arms. "So what can I do for a couple of celebrities?"

Brushing back a lock of hair, the smaller otter fidgeted through her keys and opened the back hatch. "We're looking for my Uncle Thomas."

"The mad scientist is out, I'm afraid." His gaze flicked over her curves, then back to her eyes. "Some bar across the border called in for a restock. He'll be back in a few hours." He flashed a roguish grin. "Guess you're stuck with me."

Max leaned in to whisper: "So Thomas is...your mom's brother?"

Her fingers wiggled as she traced the family tree. "Mom's...cousin, I think." She stuffed the keys back into her pocket, then brushed potato chip crumbs from her vest. "Uncle's just simpler than saying 'second uncle' or something." A cute little shrug wiggled her form. "I should probably explain this stuff more now that we're not a continent away from my relations."

"Weird having Bevys back at the Holt." The male lutrine rounded the back of the car. "Boss brought me down there a couple times. Can't see anyone using it for anything but storage. That place gives me the creeps."

"Surprised they ever left." Max's ears perked. "It's an impressive place."

"Things got...messy." A flicker of wariness touched the older otter's face. "Way before my time, but I guess they used to head down for special occasions. Even that's stopped now."

Kylie wrangled one keg from the back seat to the grass. Jib grappled another with both arms. Max unloaded one in each hand, then went back for more.

The strapping lutrine farmhand tossed him a smirk. "You gonna be alright there, woofs? I'd hate for a big shot movie star to throw his back out on my watch."

The canine looped each paw through two handles, rose, and gave a casual shrug. He'd thrown around more than a little hay back with his family. This load felt about like a square bale in each paw. "I'll be okay." With barely a grunt of effort, he padded toward the barn.

Jib watched in shock as a dog twice his size carried four times as much without apparent effort.

His best friend bobbed around the group, paws in an anxious clasp whenever she wasn't rolling a keg along. "Maxie's a farm dog."

"Huh." Sass springing back to his whiskers, the handsome otter cast a look up and down him. "Wouldn't have guessed from that outfit."

A pang twinged through the husky's chest and straight up his hackles. This guy really rubbed his fur the wrong way.

With a deep breath, Max distracted himself with the surrounding scenery. Ahead, the pebbled estuary sprawled around them. Amazing how what he considered a short drive could lead to such different topography. Lacking the jagged shoreline of Bourn Holt, waves crashed here with barely a whisper. Even the brine smelled different, more alive here.

The dog then realized he'd kept silent the entire walk back to the barn. Lucky, no one expected the strong silent dog to say anything, so his little bout of reflection hadn't been remarked upon. Not that it would've mattered: Kylie appeared fascinated by the tubes and boilers of the barn's seaweed brewery, and Jib with her tail. With a roll of his eyes, Max set down the kegs.

Jib gave them a tour of the kelp beds, padding over the smooth stone beach and up the dock. "Nobody thought this was a good idea, but old Thomas made it work. Bred a whole line of seaweed just for brewing." He kept finding excuses to walk between Kylie and Max. The glib otter guided them through several cultivars of seaweed and expounded on the merits of each. "Depending on demand and weather conditions, we grow anything from dulse to sugar kelp to oarweed. We have heated tanks in the barn for the exotic stuff, but the real excitement is seeing the beds from underwater." He bumped Kylie with a conspiratorial elbow. "Wanna look?"

"Sure!" Without a moment's hesitation, she stripped down her underwear. Or possibly a two-piece swimsuit. Not that it made much difference, to otters. Years ago, he'd have been scandalized by her clothes flying off beside a random body of water, but he'd gotten used to it over the years. Birds flew, grass grew, otters swam.

The other otter doffed everything but his skimpy underwear too, though, which made the husky blush and flick his eyes away without thinking. Jib smirked and stretched into a glamor shot pose. "You joining us, woofs?"

Max shook his head. "Didn't bring swim trunks."

The farmhand tossed a smirk over his shoulder as he padded after Kylie. "Your loss."

At the end of the dock, she offered the canine a "won't be long" shake of her head, then looked out over the water.

Together, the lutrines flung themselves from the dock like fishing spears, vanishing with scant ripples. Their bodies wavered and darted under the surface. Here and there, they vanished and reappeared among the forest of kelp leaves and sandy hues.

Pelt soaking up the wet sea air, the husky watched from shore. He could swim, sure, but hardly did the verb justice compared to otters. He could jump too, but that didn't mean he could fly.

Ever the show-off, Jib surfaced only to burst from the water with acrobatic ease. He body surfed the occasional wave and ramped off them to jump buoys, laughing as the sea buffeted him about. His every flashy move cried for attention.

Kylie, though, traced and sliced the sea like a water nymph's dance off some ancient Greek vase, all joy and elegance. A streak of dark in the clear water, she wove between the heavy lines anchoring the seaweed to the pebbly bay floor. She breached the simmering surface with incredible speed. Her body spun with fluid grace and supple power. Evening gleamed around her body to scatter in sunset droplets.

At Laura's insistence, they'd entrusted Jib with a miserly bottle of fish sauce, which they directed be delivered to the still-absent Thomas. The farmhand weaseled a hug out of his fellow otter, sneaking a cheeky nuzzle in too. Kylie hadn't seemed offended so much as bemused by his antics. To settle the score, though, Max captured him in a farewell hug he'd be feeling for days.

In the car, they watched as Jib waved in the rear-view mirrors. As the hatchback rumbled off the property, Kylie rolled her eyes. "Man, that guy was checking out my ass the entire time."

"Oh good, you noticed." Max glanced at her, then back to the road. "You didn't signal for me to rescue you."

"Eh." She shrugged. "Weirdos have leered at me before."

"Not your type?" He bumped her arm and tried to force some joviality. "Pretty sure kelp wasn't the only thing he wanted your help raising."

She gave a nervous laugh, which was a little weird. They'd always joked about fans flirting with them before. "No, not really. Still, it's flattering to have a hunky guy notice me. I bet you got hit on all the time back home."

A tension released his chest, which was odd. Why should he care if she liked some guy or not? They were friends, not a couple or anything. He tried to chase a few late-night fantasies from his mind. "Huh. I didn't really notice any."

"Uh-huh." She didn't sound convinced.

He woofed a chuckle. "Had a couple guys from high school accuse me of thinking I was a big shot."

She crossed her arms over her seatbelt. "Jerks."

"I didn't know what to do about them feeling threatened and they didn't know what to do about me doing nothing, so we just stood there awkwardly until they gave up and left." He watched the sun set through the endless ranks of trees. "But no, I don't think anyone was really flirting."

"You're a good guy, Maxie." She stroked his shoulder down to the elbow. "Not to mention a hunk. I suspect you wouldn't have to look far for a girl who's interested in you."

The notion that Kylie might mean herself flashed through his brain. Probably just wishful thinking. She'd never shown interest in him before, so it was probably just him wanting to keep hold of her. He made a show of looking around. "You mean Cindy followed us?"

She punched his arm, snickering. "Don't joke about that sort of thing."

As highway miles rolled by, Max contemplated the painted lines glowing in his headlights. His best friend dozed against his arm. Her whiskers gleamed in the last dregs of sunlight. According to his phone, only an hour or so remained before the turnoff for Windfall. Should be back in time for a late supper.

In the quiet of the car, stray thoughts wandered his mind, most of which seemed to center on just how cute she looked like that, how much he wagged through the tail hole of the seat at the thought of her trust in him. Having her close felt natural, familiar. With so much of his life changing around him, the idea of a feisty little otter who could fall asleep next to him, as close to him as ever, made him wag all the harder.

CHAPTER 10
THE SHACK

STRANGEVILLE (TUE/9P)

S02E03 "The Nine Portals, Part 1": The Tribunal opens the Nine Portals, flooding the world with dangerous creatures. The gang must stem the tide before these monsters overwhelm them.

The sweet scent of live maples and the earthy tang of rotting leaves pervaded the old-growth woods. Sun crept through breaks in the canopy, setting columns of air aglow like light beneath the surface of a lake. After several more days of searching without a hint of the location, or even the continued existence, of her great uncle's shack, Kylie had begun to accumulate both aches and frustration.

She glanced to her companion. Max plodded along just as he had the first day. He'd always liked walks; he was built for them. Otters, meanwhile, were suited for traversing tranquil waters, not rocky terrain. The arches of her paws ached, the webbing on her toes was rubbing together unpleasantly, and her tail kept dragging through brambles and burr bushes.

"Ugh!" The lutrine leaned against a tree, propping her sneaker against it and massaging through the sole. "Why couldn't my family have built canals around the whole property while we were still rich?"

The canine shrugged, not the least bit winded or uncomfortable. "You live on a mountain. Seems impractical, even by otter standards."

Irritation twitched her whiskers. "And walking every inch of the property is practical?"

Max's ears twitched as he considered the question. "Yes, actually. If we walk in a grid and, you know, actually stick to it, we'll cover it all eventually."

A wavering groan rippled down her body. "I just dread walking back."

He crossed his thick arms. "I could carry you."

"No thanks, I'm not quite that pathetic." Wiggling her toes in the tennis shoes, she sighed. "Yet."

"Might be worthwhile to buy hiking boots." He turned his long white muzzle back toward Windfall. "I'm sure the hunting store in town would have something."

"Hiking boots?" Her fists propped on her hips. "What if I needed to swim?"

"You wouldn't." He smirked. "That's the whole problem."

They continued down a gully, under the precarious trees and shrubs that clutched its crumbling cliffside. Looking up the slope, Kylie stubbed her toe on a half-buried log and stumbled back, swearing. As Max held her steady, she cradled her aching foot with a grimace and wondered very loudly if all this stomping around was worth it. Whatever they might find, it could wait another day. Besides, as much as she appreciated Max helping her track down the crazy in her family, it wasn't doing much to clear up whether he wanted to date her or not. She only had two more weeks of him; maybe she should keep him at home a bit more, figure out how to bring the subject up. It wasn't fair to blow his entire vacation on a wild goose chase for her benefit, either. Even she could admit that was probably pretty selfish.

With a huff, she trudged on, contemplating that she might just be cursed. Then her eyes caught on pale slats of wood through the trees. Weariness forgotten, she dashed forward, wriggled through a gnarled, grasping cluster of trees, and stared.

The shack squatted against the wall of a crag, almost as gray as the rock around it. Roof half-collapsed, walls bowed, boards tilted like malformed teeth; time seemed eager to crush the tiny building. It seemed on the verge of victory.

Kylie hadn't been getting much sleep with the journals haunting her. Walking the property had eroded the last of her energy, or so she'd thought. Now she squeaked, bouncing and pointing.

Max nodded, then looked away when his gaze seemed to fall on her breasts. He'd seemed flustered like that all day, though it could just be her dreams from last night following her around. Nonetheless, he gave her an encouraging wag and they picked their way down the hillside.

Bounding up to the structure, she tried the door. It didn't budge. "What the heck? Is it locked?" She braced a foot against the frame, pulling on the knob.

"From the inside?" The dog's ears drooped.

Kylie winced, thinking of what it being locked from the inside might mean. Her curiosity burned unabated, even as dread crept up her spine.

Max studied the damp, rotting timber. "It's not locked. The wood's warped and it's stuck shut."

She breathed again. That meant they wouldn't find her great uncle's corpse in there. Probably. She gave the knob another yank. The sphere of rusted iron came off in her paw. She frowned at it. "Carp! What do we do now?"

Contemplative, the husky studied the ancient door, poked the yielding surface with one digit, then wound back and punched it with enough force to shake the entire building. His fist burst straight through the ancient, rotting wood. In one smooth motion, he gripped the crossbeam and ripped the whole door free, then dropped it to the stony turf.

Impressed, the otter gave a slow nod.

With a sheepish wring of his paws, he shrugged and shook the rotten splinters from his paw. "I always wanted to do that in real life."

She poked her head inside the structure. "What was it for, do you think?"

The decayed remains of a cot, an overturned trunk, and scattered shotgun shells with oxidized heads littered the floor. Max sniffed at the musty air, his breath swirling dust motes in the light that crept through drafty walls. "Hunting cabin, maybe?"

"Maybe..." They searched the cabin, but found nothing except a crumbling calendar and a few empty tuna cans. After ten minutes, Kylie plopped down to the floor with a groan. "Really? All that searching and it's empty?"

He crouched beside her, paw on her shoulder. "It's been here for decades. Someone else may have wandered by."

She propped her elbows on her crossed legs, fists under her chin. Her gaze fell to the floor, which lay powdered with orange lichen. The boards had warped and rotted as much as the rest of the cabin, spreading to reveal the ground beneath. She stared at the dirt, feeling at least as low. Then she saw it.

White.

Like bone.

A chill ran through her. "Maxie, I need you to rip up the floor."

His ears perked at her, his muzzle turning her way a heartbeat later. He set down a tatter of the cot fabric, which he'd been peeking under.

She pointed. "I think there's something under there."

Without a question, he wiggled his fingers through the gap and hauled the board up. Nails screamed, wood splintered, lichen pulverized. He worried the board back and forth until it came free, then tossed it on the ruined bed.

With shaking paws, Kylie lifted the pale circle from the earth. Light as old bone, smooth as ceramic, save for a tangle of semi-random lines. Etchings? Veins? It weighed as little as a sand dollar, but felt solid. Pinprick holes dotted the edge, for some purpose she couldn't guess at. It fit her two palms, dust and soil falling away, refusing to adhere. She lifted it for Max's inspection.

"I have no idea what that is." He sniffed it. "Must have been here a long time; only smells like the shack."

"Is it bone? Antler?"

He touched her hand, brushing it back from the disk. "Bone doesn't age that well, not in a place this damp."

"Pottery?"

"Could be." He squinted. "Looks like something from a gallery."

The otter watched the grooves dance in their infinite snarl. Trying to trace just one unfocused her vision. She squeezed her eyes shut and looked back at Max. "What'd we do now?"

The husky peeked into the floorboards, then gave the cabin a final glance-over. "Take it to your place and research?"

She nodded. Not that she imagined they'd be able to find out much— the disk looked like nothing Kylie had ever seen. She stuck it in one of the larger pockets of her vest.

They started to climb out of the rocky valley. Soil and scree shifted under their feet, boulders and branches lay scattered. Halfway up, she slipped and almost fell on her tail, but Max caught her by the arm. Big, strong paws handled her with delicate care. He flashed her a little smile, wagging as she found her footing.

"Thanks." Blushing under her fur, the lutrine tried to think of a way to bring up how much she appreciated that he was always there for her, how she wanted to be there for him, in a forever sort of way. She blushed harder. It sounded stupid in her head and it would probably sound stupider out loud, but she had to say something. She knew he'd listen while she fumbled through an explanation. "Maxie, I—"

Max shushed her softly, touched her elbow, and pointed out into the forest.

Fifty yards out, on the crest of a ridge, a feral deer posed with wild dignity, backlit against the evening canopy. Its ears rotated, listening to the forest as is glided through the dappled shadows to nibble on a low-hanging leaf. Light caught, glowing within its fur. It looked around suddenly, alert. Kylie supposed it had scented them.

Kylie crouched beside Max, fascinated. She was a cynical city girl at heart, and as much as she'd gotten used to the forest, nature still managed to strike her with its beauty now and then. To think, that elegant four-legged creature was related to every sentient deer she'd ever met.

Her eyes caught movement in the canopy. Something glossy and dark dropped from a tree, like a soundless, jagged nightmare. Iridescent black blades flashed through the deer. It tumbled into bloody shreds with a bisected gasp. The shreds twitched as predator and prey together hit the dense underbrush with an impact that shook the leaves.

Then the black thing, perched on too many legs and, moving in a way that was jerky and spastic and somehow fundamentally wrong, dove in and began to feed.

Cracks of bone and snaps of sinew echoed down the gully all around Kylie and Max. The otter jumped as she felt something grasp her arm. Max's hand. He drew her away. Her eyes remained locked on the black thing as it buried its front in gore, half obscured now by undergrowth. A few snaps of sinew later, it sat up, as if remembering its manners. Three front limbs plucked trembling strips of muscle from the kill, gorging them down a triangular maw. Blood rolled down the black carapace, trailing the plates to soak deep nooks. A trio of golden eyes shone with raw culinary contentment, mandibles clattering in obvious relish. Kylie's mind grappled with it from fifty meters away, unable to process what she was seeing.

The husky's arms closed around her middle. He shushed her squeak and dragged her to a rot-hollowed log, well out of sight of the creature, and hurried her into the narrow space.

Her thoughts bubbled into a frantic whisper: "Did you see that?"

Ears pinned back with terror, he crammed himself in beside her and whispered: "Yes!" He glanced around to ensure they weren't followed, then stopped, studying her expression. "Wait. Are you...happy?"

Her face did feel strained, as if by a paralyzed grin. "Do you know what this means? My family wasn't crazy!" She gripped his shoulders, then slackened, processing. Horror drained her of heat. "Oh my gosh, my family wasn't crazy. We're gonna die."

He put a finger to her lips, precluding further speculation.

They strained their ears, but couldn't tell savage eating from branches in the lovely light breeze. Now and again, Max reached his phone past the end of the log, watching the screen, checking if anything picked up on its camera. The recording icon flashed.

Kylie buried her face in his chest and concentrated on breathing. Quietly. Her heart thundered in her chest. The chill in her guts had spread to her fingertips and webbing. The log stunk of mold and rotten bits of wood kept falling in her eyes, which she barely dared to wipe away. More than once, she shifted, desperate to leave, to run, though this only resulted in Max holding her tighter. So she turned in on him instead, burrowing in against his chest, eyes screwed shut, as though he could protect her from that…thing. She opened her eyes to find the forest darker than she'd left it.

The husky climbed out, remaining crouched, ears scanning the woods. Sharp blue eyes scrutinized every bush and tree, but at long last he looked down to her and lifted his eyebrows.

The otter slipped out from under the log, her leg unresponsive and prickly from laying on it wrong. She stumbled.

His wide paws swept in to support her before she could collapse.

She glanced down at her leg, bending it to make sure it worked right. Cramped muscles ached as she tried to extend them.

Again, without a sound, he turned and drew her by the hand onto his back. Together, they picked their way down the shadowy hillside, away from the feeding site.

"Where're we going?" She breathed in his ear. "Home's back that way."

He shifted her higher on his back. "We're cutting down to the edge of the property, taking the road back."

She nodded into his shoulder. The long way, around Bourn Holt and down the highway. The way someone might at least hear them scream. She tried not to think about it, breathed in Max's scent, and told herself she felt reassured.

He carried her through the trees, jumping at shadows all the while, until they reached a narrow band of cleared dirt. Some kind of trail carved by ATVs or snowmobiles. By this point her leg was feeling better, but when she tried to slip off him his grip tightened on her knees, keeping her in place. With some distance and time behind them, Max must have felt it was safe to speak, albeit softly. "Well, that was exciting."

She squeezed his shoulders, curling closer as she croaked a hollow chuckle. "Yeah, no kidding."

He cleared his throat. "So...now that you know your family hasn't really been crazy all these years, I guess we're done with the investigations?" A strained, hopeful edge sharpened his voice.

The otter gave a weak laugh.

"Kylie!" The canine groaned, trudging on. "No. Absolutely not. I don't know what that was, but we need to stay away from it. This is real life; we aren't main characters."

"That...thing, or things like it, have been driving my family crazy for generations." The panic had subsided, mostly, replaced by gnawing dread and a deep, smouldering ember of outrage. "They wouldn't have obsessed like that if it weren't important."

He growled. She couldn't see his face, but his ear flicked her on the forehead as it pinned back. "We don't know what's going on, but we do know that part of it involves something that can rip a deer apart for lunch. What are we gonna do, lasso it?"

Her muzzle bumped his shoulder with a frown. Resting against his back, though, she couldn't help but feel protected. But who'd protect Max? Having him safe and across the country was one thing; she didn't know how she'd live with herself if something happened to him. She'd have to watch his back, she thought as she snuggled against it. Even now, as they fled from a monster, she felt safe.

So safe, in fact, that she fell asleep.

An hour later, aching from tension and exertion, Max trudged out from the woods to the roadside, hackles raised at every noise. Kylie had been quiet for the last ten minutes or so, but he could feel the steady rhythm of her breathing. He considered waking her, but then decided to let her rest.

If anything dropped from the trees, her being rested might help. He tried not to think about what would happen if it didn't.

An engine's hum echoed from behind him. The husky turned to see a battered pickup trundling up the highway, purring despite its obvious age. His gaze met the driver's and a sigh of relief left him as he recognized the beaver handyman Ms. Bevy had hired to fix up the manor.

The truck puttered to a stop. A beaver leaned out the window with a polite smile. "You kids need a lift?"

Max weighed the relative risks and then decided he could accept a ride from a beaver half his size. "Yes, sir."

"Hey, you're that pup who's staying with the Bevys." He leaned to see around Max's shoulder. "She alright?"

"Yeah." He helped the lutrine slide off his back. "We got a little lost and she's not used to walking this far."

The beaver gave an amiable nod and unlocked the passenger door. Gray tinged his temples and muzzle. Max guessed the handyman to be about forty, though he had trouble telling with non-canids.

Kylie looked around. "What the...?"

"It's okay." Whispering, he patted her back and guided her toward the vehicle. "Your mom's handyman's giving us a ride."

The otter murmured something and cast a worried look to the trees as she climbed in the truck.

Max followed. Remembering his manners, the canine offered a paw. "Really appreciate the ride. Joe, right?"

The handyman shook it around the bleary Kylie. "You got it."

"I've seen you around." Max positioned the otter between them, where she'd be safest. "You're the guy Ms. Bevy hired for the roof."

A chuckle warmed the cab of the truck. "And the porches, and the cellar door, and whatever else."

"Yeah, she can keep a guy busy." The dog nodded.

The handyman shone a buck-toothed smile. "Sounds like you know first hand."

Max shrugged. "I worked for her on the show for years."

"No kidding? Not a local then?"

"No, I'm from Montana." The husky rolled down the window a crack, summer air breezing past his ears, stirring a hundred scents past his nose. "Just visiting."

Joe nodded. "Weighs on a fella, being away from home."

Kylie, having stayed awake for as long as politeness required, curled up against Max and fell into a tense, twitchy doze. A length of silence and a stretch of road passed by. Max struggled for something to say, but recent worries pressed down hard on him, and anyway Joe didn't seem the gossipy type. In fact, it wasn't until they rounded the mountain and Windfall came into sight that their driver piped up.

"Bit strange to see someone living in the old Bourn place again." Joe cleared his throat and kept his eyes on the road rather than the otter draped over his other passenger. "That house of theirs is a local landmark. Been interested in it for quite a while. Thought it'd be nice to work on, so I made myself available."

The husky's ears perked. "Sounds like the Bevys have some sort of history around here."

"Folks around here love their spooky stories." The beaver offered a good-natured eye roll. "You hear stories about those otters putting too much stock in the local legends, but that's all from before you'd have seen my smiling face in these parts. I try to judge people on what I see."

"Seems like a good philosophy."

The beaver adjusted his old ball cap. "Take that Ms. Bevy. She's an artsy type and maybe a bit of a homebody, but folks around here like a little privacy." He adjusted his hold on the steering wheel, shifting gears with ease. "That's what's nice about a town like this: space to breathe."

"I can understand that." Max wagged, feeling tension drain away. He breathed a little deeper. After what he'd seen in the woods, the mundanity of small talk felt very reassuring, even if it was with someone he'd only seen before in passing. "Plenty of breathing room where I come from."

"Seems this new crop of Bevys isn't so much for the hubbub. Not so hung up on the way things used to be." He checked his mirror, then smoothed his well-trimmed whiskers. "And that's probably for the best. Gotta change to fit the times, go with the flow."

"Still learning that myself." The canine found his paw had slipped around Kylie's waist, even as his gaze stayed on the trees. The horror of monsters inhabiting the woods wrestled for mental real estate with daydreams of dating Kylie. The last few miles rolled by. With a final turn, they rumbled up the driveway of Bourn Manor. The dog climbed out and pulled a half-limp Kylie after him. With her on his back again, he waved to Joe. "Thanks again for the ride."

"Thanks for the conversation." The beaver tipped his hat. "One of the few things an old guy like me can do to amuse himself."

Max decided he liked this guy; at least he wore his opinions on his sleeve. He turned to carry his friend to the house. The pickup rumbled off. Every crunch of gravel reminded Max of the bone-snapping bites of the black thing. He shook his head and hurried on.

Upon reaching the front steps, he creaked through the door, then locked it behind him. Only then did he relax. The old house might be ancient and creepy, but the inhabited part brimmed with warm light and the smell of people he knew. He gave the lutrine on his back a gentle shake. "Kylie, we're here."

The otter oozed off him with a sleepy groan.

A plump figure in a fuzzy pink robe emerged from the living room. "There you are." Her gaze caught on her daughter slipping down from the piggyback ride. "Awwwww." She leaned against the stair rail, trashy romance novel in one paw, favorite mug in the other. "You two have fun out looking at shacks together?"

"Uh—" He looked to Kylie.

Her eyes told him to say nothing.

Shrugging, Max flashed a weak smile. "Just a leg cramp."

"Ah." She took a sip of tea, heading upstairs. "Make sure she gets to bed before she tips over."

He stood up straighter. "Yes, ma'am."

Up the stairs padded the middle-aged otter, while her daughter leaned against the door, arms crossed, waking up.

Max watched her with curious eyes, listening as Laura's bedroom door shut. "Shouldn't we tell the police or coast guard or something? Somebody with guns?"

"And say what?" She gave him a bleary look. "Our TV show was real? Everyone'll just say it was a publicity stunt."

"Ugh, you're right. The Season Five DVDs just came out." Max rubbed the scruff of his neck. "Does your family own any firearms or other weapons? Artillery? World War Two flamethrowers?"

"Aside from kitchen knives, I don't think so." She shivered. "But if these things were as dangerous to people as they are to deer, I think people would know about them." Her eyes darted to the window. "Something else is going on here. Something is keeping that thing from rampaging through town."

Ducking into the living room, he grabbed a throw blanket and draped it around her shoulders. "You think it's smart enough to avoid town."

"Lots of animals do." She glanced to the window. "Wild predators especially." A pensive moment gripped the air. She pulled the blanket tighter. "Max, this could actually be dangerous—that…thing cut a deer in half. I'm not gonna ask you to stick around just for the sake of my family's crazy."

The dog gave her a wry look. "Of course I'm sticking around."

"I don't think you understand." She cut the air between them with webbed paws. "You need to leave. It was wrong of me to drag you into this in the first place, but things have gotten dangerous now. You could get hurt if you stay."

He brushed her arm. "You could get hurt if I don't."

She looked up at him. Something bright and warm burst into being in her eyes and, before he could guess was it was, she had grabbed him by the front of his sweatshirt and pulled herself up to kiss him, with more passion than he'd thought possible. Her mouth felt softer than he'd even expected, and her nose warmed his. The blanket fell away. She wrapped her sleek arms around his neck and practically hung off him. As time slowed to a crawl around them, his hands hesitated against her ribs, then settled on her hips.

Finally, slowly, she drew her lips off his and let her eyes open again. A bounce to her posture lit the dim room.

Max stood, stock still, ears stiff, blinking down at her. His pulse raced over the chill in his veins, to the thrill in his heart. His mind raced to catch up. He was pretty sure he'd just spent a solid minute making out with his best friend. An unfamiliar taste teased his breath.

Kylie's beaming smile faltered as she searched his face. "Max?"

A moment passed. Max felt he ought to say something, but his brain had turned to cotton candy, his thought only able to circle endlessly on the fading tingle her lips had left on his. "You...just kissed me."

The otter nodded, eyes focused on his collarbone. "Umm. Yeah, I kinda did, didn't I?"

His ears flicked up, then down, then up again as he tried to get a handle on the situation. "Umm...why?"

She bit her lip, paws smoothing neurotically over the front of his shirt. "It just kinda happened. I mean, not that I haven't been thinking about it. I have. A lot. Since, like, before the show ended. And you're right here and you're being so, I dunno, heroic and I thought since you didn't seem to be getting any of my signals I should just go for it." She bounced on her heels, clutching fistfuls of his sweatshirt. She dared to raise her eyes to his. "You've been really, really amazing with all this weird junk and I don't think I can stand to go any further without you. I didn't mean to scare you or make you feel weird or anything, Maxie. If you want, we can just—"

Without really thinking about it, he reached up and clamped a paw around her little otter muzzle. He'd been instructed in the early days of their friendship to stop her when her mouth got a little ahead of her brain. "Kylie, calm down." His emotions were still a bit of a jumble, but he knew one thing for sure. "I'm not mad. I...liked it." The canine noticed, faintly, that his tail was wagging. He was having trouble looking away from her lips.

She blinked. "You did?"

He nodded, still dazed. His hands drew her hips toward him, holding her closer. "Can I...kiss you back?"

A shy, webbed paw traced his arm. "If you want t-oomph!"

His muzzle pressed hard against hers and her words vanished into a second kiss.

She melted against him, her body pressing close as his arms wrapped around to properly hold her. She was curvy and warm and had always felt so right against him. She wriggled in closer and he was abruptly aware of her breasts pressing against his chest. This time, the kiss broke to leave them both panting.

Max's tail wagged a mile a minute, dusting his hips.

Kylie giggled, what must have been weeks of tension escaping all at once. She bounced over to the sofa and collapsed onto the cushions. She tapped his usual spot beside her in invitation. Her eyes glimmered like stones in a stream bed. "I've been teasing you on purpose, y'know."

The husky stopped to cock his head at her, sinking into his customary spot. It was good to sit; the hike had made his legs rubbery even before she'd sucked his brainpower out through his tonsils. "You have?"

"Sure. You know, tighter pants, no bra." She licked her lips in a way that had Max's cheeks burning. "Leaving my bathroom door open."

Max tried to laugh off his embarrassment, pinching the bridge of his nose in his finger and thumb. "Thank goodness. I thought I was going nuts, or that I'd become some huge perv since the show ended."

She smirked at him. "Well, if you weren't at least a bit of a perv you probably wouldn't have noticed." Her face fell. She picked up a pillow and held it against her chest. "Maxie? This doesn't change...us, does it?"

He reached out and gently gripped her forearm, hauling her across the couch into a hug. "You're still my best friend, rudderbutt. Whatever else changes, that won't."

She squeaked and, with a nervous giggle, kissed him again.

Minutes drifted by in the dim room, the only light coming from the kitchen. Once in a while, one would remember the crashing reality of that evening, but it paled in comparison to this moment, which felt so much more real.

After a long spell of silence, the husky sighed. "We should get to bed."

She buried her face in his shoulder, making no move from the sofa.

He patted her arm. "Your mom said I should take you to bed."

Lithe arms tightened around him. "Mom can either find you sleeping with me here or in bed, but I don't wanna be alone tonight." Her voice, muffled in his shirt, held a note of weary imploring.

Max wasn't sure what Ms. Bevy would think about him sleeping cuddled up with her daughter, but it was probably better than what she'd think about him sleeping in Kylie's bed. Besides, with monsters stalking the woods outside, he couldn't abandon her. And it felt so right, so natural, to hold her. With a nod of surrender, he curled himself around her and dared to sleep.

CHAPTER 11
RESEARCH

STRANGEVILLE (MON/9P)

S01E12 "Slugfest": Cassie learns in a vision that her dentist is secretly a slug monster. She must convince the others before her upcoming check-up makes her a perfect target for being eaten and replaced by a slime-clone.

Kylie floated back to something resembling consciousness to the sound of chirping birds. She found herself on the sofa and muzzle-deep in Max's warm fluff. As she cuddled closer to him, something stiff poked her thigh. Assuming it a fold in his jeans, she reached down and felt more than denim. A blush flared under her fur, waking her fully. She didn't dare move her paw. She'd always figured morning erections were an urban legend perpetuated by horny fanfic writers. A wild notion of how to wake him up gripped her, tempting her to grip him. Mom had probably gone shopping and wouldn't be back for a while...how long did it take to give a handjob? Then reason caught up to her and drew her paw back up to her chest, willing herself to slow down. No need to rush. He wasn't going anywhere. The otter resolved not to go anywhere either, in particular not off the sofa and out of his embrace. Minutes passed as she lay there, feeling safe in a newly dangerous and unpredictable world.

With a deep breath, he shifted to nuzzle her ears.

"Hey." She squeezed his wide paw.

"Hey." His warm breath breezed through her hair.

"This is nice." Kylie buried her nose against his shirt.

He nodded. Those soft whiskers brushed hers.

"Can we just stay like this?"

His arm tightened around her shoulders. "Sure."

They sat silent as Kylie rested her cheek on his chest, listening to his heartbeat.

"Hey, just to, you know, verify…" He looked her in the eyes. "We totally saw a monster last night, right?"

Her arms squeezed a little tighter around him. "And then I kissed you and instead of running for the hills you kissed me back and we made out for a while?"

"Wow." The husky blew out a contemplative sigh. "Big day."

"Yeah…" With an unsteady smile, she nodded.

He breathed deep enough to lift her head. "Are we going tell your mom?"

Heat drained from her face as she blinked up at the dog. "Tell her about…us?" She cringed. Her mother had been super supportive up to this point, but she probably still had an "I told you so" stashed away for a special occasion.

Max rumbled a laugh at her expression. With only the barest hesitation, he leaned in and kissed her brow. "If you want to. I was talking about the flesh-eating monster killing deer on her property."

"Oh." Kylie flushed. "Oh, right. That."

The husky nodded, somber. "Why wouldn't you want your mom to know?

A sigh breezed from her chest as Kylie admitted the day had started. "Writing *Strangeville* was her way of denying any of this existed. She thinks our family was eccentric. I don't know how well she'd handle learning they were right."

The dog's stomach grumbled for attention, grinding the conversation to a halt. He offered a sheepish grin.

She perked, glad for the distraction. "Breakfast?"

His tail thumped the sofa. "Yes please."

They stumbled to the kitchen. Kylie piled various food components on the counter. "So…monster. We're calling it that, right?"

"I think that is the only biologically correct term for it." He nodded, spreading butter in a skillet. "Montana's really nice this time of year: wheat's growing in, weather's nice, hardly any flesh-eating monsters…"

"I dunno." A shrug trailed down her body. "Your family's always intimidated me."

He gave her a serious look, then raised a question with his eyebrows.

"We can't leave Mom." She wrung her paws and looked around. "This house is big for two people—I'm not going to make her live here alone. Especially not with something like that on the loose."

He crossed his arms, spatula in one paw.

"Fine!" She squawked, confounded. "I can't just walk away: I need to find out what's going on."

"Even if it's dangerous?"

"Not knowing anything is dangerous too." She gripped his arm, a tinge of desperation in her tone. "I need to figure out what's going on, Maxie."

Eggs landed in the skillet with a sizzle. "We need a plan."

The otter smiled. "Like what?" She set a frying pan on the burner next to his. Into her pan, she stirred her own ingredients: milk, onion, bay, thyme.

He shrugged. "Maybe we should stay inside for a while." His big white paws sprinkled seasoning on the eggs. "Like long enough to order a katana or two."

She raised an eyebrow and dropped kippers into the simmering mixture. "Katana?"

"Sure. You've watched just as many bad horror movies as I have." He loaded bread in the toaster. "Name one where someone gets killed while they have a katana."

Kylie's fists propped on her hips. "We've been safe outside all this time; just because we know about this thing now doesn't change that."

"True." He flipped the eggs as the toast popped up. "Wakizashi then?"

"Sheesh, Maxie, we're solving a mystery, not fighting demons."

"Don't think we can rule that out just yet." He buttered the toast with two elegant swipes. "Riot gear?"

The lutrine looked down at herself. "I don't think they make it my size."

The dog nodded. "Fully-charged cell phones?"

Watching the kippers cook, she laughed and grabbed a bottle of ancient fish sauce from the fridge. "That I think I can manage."

He scooped the eggs onto plates, placing hers on toast, since she was going to anyway. "And I'm walking you to work."

"Okay." She plated the kippers. "Anything else?"

His soft white paws settled on her shoulders and rotated her to face him. His ocean blue eyes met hers as he leaned down. The kiss came soft and sublime, strange and so familiar.

After their lips parted ways, she giggled. "Oh, right."

His nose bumped hers. "I've never had a girlfriend before and I'm not going to have her battling otherworldly horrors without me."

"You're sweet." She gave him a peck on the cheek as she carried break-fast to the table.

Max wagged and followed, a paw caressing her back. Amazing how easy him going from best friend to boyfriend had been. It'd seemed silly she'd worried so much about it. Now she only had to worry about alien monsters living in her backyard.

Hours passed and Kylie admitted she ought to go to work during one of them. Max joined her by the door without a word as she prepared to leave, ready to walk her to town. They kept to the main roads and watched every shadow for signs of predation. Tension only lifted off them as they entered Windfall proper. It looked oddly normal, though he now gave wary glances to the stuffed monsters leering from every shop window.

Ignoring a sultry look from a sunbathing Cindy, he followed as Kylie eeled into the consignment store.

"Okay, so the show totally jumped the shark when they had you date that girl who turned out to be a computer-generated banshee."

The husky padded in and gave this notion real thought. "What about the alternate timeline episode where we were played by the winners of the look-alike contest?"

"Oh right! I hear the director still has that Worst Episode trophy on his mantle." She perked as she noticed her co-worker. "Hey Shane."

The feline gave a bored wave from the counter.

"One second. Gotta put my bag in the back." She skipped off. At least she didn't seem worried about monsters at the moment. Maybe because work was too boring to be dangerous.

Alone with the cat and without anything obvious to say, Max clicked his claws together.

A cell phone buzzed on the countertop. Its owner made no move to answer.

With a nod at the mobile, the dog offered a genial smile. "You going to get that?"

"Eh." The cat shrugged. "People know not to call me about anything urgent."

Moments passed, but brought no obvious topics for small talk. The canine fidgeted. "So…still watching the show?"

"Yeah." The tabby sat up a little. "It's pretty good."

"How far are you?"

His slitted eyes flicked to the laptop beside the ignored phone. "Bad boy character's bubblegum girlfriend dumped him in the middle of a demon battle."

"Ah yes." The husky nodded. "He took that really hard."

"Totally."

Max flexed his paws, unsure what to talk about. "Say, we keep bumping into a rhino named Karl. Do you know him?"

The cat scoffed. "I seriously don't know what that guy did before your show…"

The canine nodded.

"Had to chase him off a few times when he found out Kylie was working here. I guess he's one of the people who thought the town got a lot more interesting once the show aired." Shane shook his head, whiskers swaying. "As opposed to the ones who were already believers and thought the show was making fun of them."

Max's ears rose. "What do you think?"

"It is what it is." The tabby examined a claw. "Kinda pointless to wish the show had never happened, or that it had gone on forever."

The husky took out his phone, intending to take notes, but wasn't sure what to jot down.

The cat managed a shrug.

Kylie returned and kissed the husky's cheek. "Talk to you later."

The dog's tail whipped up a small whirlwind. "Sure." He padded out the door, looking back at her and telling himself she'd be safe.

As soon as the door closed, Shane lifted an eyebrow. "You work fast."

"Didn't take as much convincing as I'd thought." The otter beamed after her co-star. "It's really great."

"Great." He batted his phone from the counter to his waiting palm, paw pads dancing over the screen in a flash. "I'll text Karl."

"What?" She squawked and straightened. "No!"

"Are you kidding?" He purred into a grin, then waved the phone to show he hadn't actually been typing. "I don't need more Karl in my life."

She shook her head, stooping to sort a box of dusty books. "Hey… have you ever noticed weird stuff around town?"

The feline crossed his arms with a shrug. "All the time."

"Meaning…?" The otter waited, crouched.

"We live in a tourist trap specializing in weird stuff. Some days I see five Martians before lunch." He lashed his tail and leered at the shelves. "A shop down the street gives out anti-mind control pendants to trick-or-treaters."

"I mean weirder than puffy alien stickers and keychain voodoo dolls." Her gaze never wavered from him. "Actual weirdness."

He brushed some dust from his paw. "I don't know what that's supposed to mean."

Kylie stood, keeping the social pressure up. "I think you do."

The cat sighed. "Tourists and locals pull weird pranks and schemes around here. It's the local industry. Sometimes, they even fool each other. Sometimes, you don't know where something comes from or how they did it." A spark of caution entered his slitted eyes. "If I were you, I'd be careful about sticking my neck out. Lot of people around here have a vested interest in the crazy. Nothing takes the fun out of the paranormal like someone asking a bunch of totally reasonable questions."

The otter processed that for a moment, then nodded...then realized that's just what she'd sent her boyfriend to do. He was her boyfriend now, right? She'd never had a boyfriend, so she wasn't sure how exactly when that became official. On TV, she'd have to fall into bed kissing him while the camera pans to a single long-stem rose or something; and then he'd awkwardly meet her parents.

Setting that tangle of emotions for the moment, she texted him.

Walking down the sidewalk, Max took a deep breath. He wasn't excited about trying to interrogate a bunch of strangers, but this was for Kylie, so he set his jaw and marched onward. At least he could hit up some book shops; the smell of books always soothed him. His phone buzzed.

Kylie Bevy: {Don't walk back without me.}

Max Saber: {Hadn't planned on it. Think you might need me?}

Kylie Bevy: {Or need to save you. ;)}

Heart still fluttering from Kylie's kiss goodbye, the husky smiled. He wagged down the sidewalk, looking up paranormal gift shops on his mobile, which seemed to infest the town map. The nearest: Windfall Wonders, was right next door to Kylie's shop. It was also, he remembered, where

Cindy worked. He glanced in the window, between light-up sea monsters, and found no trace of the cocker spaniel drama queen. The door set off a tinny, electronic burst of spooky organ music as he opened it and Max felt his expectations lower.

The small store was a bewildering mashup of New England and paranormal bric-a-brac. A shelf of sensational town histories occupied one wall, flanked by Elder God snow globes and carved wooden fishing boats crewed by tiny aliens. Max spied himself and Kylie on more than one cast poster for *Strangeville* tacked up behind the counter.

A middle-aged spaniel straightened and smiled, then handed a receipt to a pair of Pomeranians, who bounced with excitement at the counter. Taking their bags of merchandise, they bustled past him in matched UFO t-shirts, heading out to sniff out more treasures.

"Well, if it isn't our newest local celebrity!" He shook the husky's paw, generous ears swaying. "Charlie Madison. How ya doin'?"

"Pretty well." Max shook back and smiled. "You heard about me visiting? I didn't think that'd be news."

"Oh yeah!" His tan paws clapped on the countertop. "You're all over that Howler app. *Strangeville's* the best thing ever to happen to this town. Don't let anybody tell you otherwise." He punched Max in the shoulder with a wink. "The people who matter love the show."

"That's nice of you—"

"By which I mean customers. They can't get enough of this junk." A yippy laugh spiked through the shop. "You ever think about doing some merch signings here? Good for your career. Not to mention mine."

"Umm, I'm kinda still settling in." The monochromatic dog rubbed his own scruff.

"Of course, of course. We'll plan that later." The spaniel's tail swished. "The Bevys came up at last week's Chamber of Commerce meeting; some great promotional opportunities for *Strangeville* actors in this town." He jerked a thumb at a rack of *Strangeville* t-shirts. "You got a moment to sign some of these babies?"

"I guess? I mean, I was just wondering—"

A stack of shirts flopped onto the counter in front of Max, followed by a marker, followed by three complete DVD box sets, a first season poster, some keychains, and a Cassie bobble-head. The spaniel grinned. "Now, what can I do for you?"

The younger canine started autographing the garments with practiced efficiency. "I'm looking for information about Windfall. Any weird things that've happened over the years." He glanced at the aliens riding snowmobiles. "You know, actually happened."

"Hmm, now most people who come through that door want to be entertained. You're sure you're not more interested in a storyteller? I hear rumors about a *Strangeville* series revival, maybe a movie." His eyes gleamed, green as cash. "You know, the kind of projects that need a local expert..."

"That's all just rumors, as far as I know." He set his phone on the counter, its screen beaded with red markers. "How can there be so many gift shops in one town?"

His floppy ears drooped a millimeter. "Every diner and gas station with a knickknack shelf calls itself a gift shop in these parts." He waved dismissal at the mobile and plucked a laminated map off a stand by the cash register. "Lemme give you the heavy hitters."

The Open Chakra glistened with price-tagged healing crystals, sitar music and incense wafting thick on the air. Bead curtains and gauzy textiles hung from the ceiling. Max stood in the entryway, taking stock of the place. Light glinted through a spectrum of potion vials behind the counter. Shelves of statuettes traced the motions of a strange dance. Bins of colorful gems glimmered with plastic promise. Some kind of hematite tiara gleamed on a mannequin head, with a sign explaining how its magnetic magic helped mental focus. The shop felt odd—perhaps because he hadn't fought any dragons or trolls to reach it.

Behind him, the bell on the door tinkled. Max turned to see a family enter.

A middle-aged lioness prowled through the front door, a bouncing cub clinging to either paw. "Okay, kids, you can only pick out one healing crystal each. Mommy's going to take one for the headaches."

The siblings launched themselves away from her and touched all the merchandise.

The husky ducked under a hanging lamp, its dangling prisms clinking over his ears. A whiff of potpourri became a waft as he passed further into the store. Semi-precious stones at precious prices glimmered under a glass countertop.

On a clearing between the shelves, an Afghan hound in diaphanous robes sat crosslegged atop a tasseled cushion. Her ears twitched once, then she lifted her long nose to him. Her eyes remained closed. "We are each the Universe experiencing itself. How has fate handled you?"

Max weighed finding out monsters exist against Kylie kissing him. "Pretty well, I guess."

Ringed by candles, she rocked back and forth. "Tell me of your life, child. Are you overwhelmed? Underwhelmed? At the Open Chakra, we can help you meet your ideal levels of health and whelmedness."

"Really, I'm just looking for some information." His gaze fell on a bottle of Eastern Essences-brand goji berry anointment, its label featuring a serene, if pixelated, wolf.

A sigh stirred her long fur. "Oh, isn't that just the way of the world? Everyone's just looking for information. Better to seek fulfillment, don't you think?"

"Been working on that." His thoughts flicked to Kylie for a moment, then back to the task at hand. Anxious paws needed a place to be, so he stuck them in the pockets of his jeans. "I was wondering about how the town got associated with the supernatural in the first place."

"Leylines!" Her eyes sprung wide open, but skimmed right over him. Her paws spread toward the smokey rafters, then sank to the woven rug. "Conduits of power deep within the earth, you know. Tapping them requires properly resonant foci." She selected a rod of quartz from a velvet-lined shelf and cradled it in her paws.

The husky leaned, slouching a little, so as to appear less dominant if she ever looked at him. "I meant culturally."

She lifted an eyebrow. "You ask a lot of questions for a tourist."

"I'm careful what I buy." He touched a bin of discount chi stones. "And not a tourist, actually. I'm staying with the Bevys."

"Ah yes! So tragic!" Her paws clasped melodrama before her. "A proud family tree pruned by madness!"

"Yeah..." Max contemplated how to steer the conversation back to the specific weirdness he needed. "We're all broken up about the...pruning, but—"

"Ah!" The back of her hand swept to her forehead. "Step closer, young husky. I feel your aura..."

He padded closer and wondered how Kylie would feel about strange women feeling his aura.

Her pale paw shot toward him and quivered. "You've come a great distance, seeking your path in life."

Max shut his muzzle and waited to see if she'd reach a conclusion not obvious from his age and accent.

"I've..." Exertion dropped over her face like a theater curtain. "I've seen you before. In a past life, perhaps..."

After several seconds of silence, Max felt compelled to help. "A past life with television, perhaps?"

"Oh." Her long face fell, bliss giving way to belligerence. Her voice lost its musical lilt. "I thought you looked familiar." She stood in a sweep of gauzy robes and cast him a cold look. "Windfall was a perfectly respectable psychic energy nexus until your stupid TV show came along and made a mockery of us." With polite firmness, pointed to the door. "I'm afraid you must leave. Much of my merchandise is delicate and I don't want to risk it being corrupted by a Hollywood aura."

Max left without objection, dodging around the cubs while their mother scolded them for fencing with the rock-candy suckers.

Across the street, Windfall Hunting Co. presented itself as a legitimate outdoors supply, though the rack of Bermuda Triangle shorts raised a red flag or three. A jackal in an argyle smoking jacket guided him through the aisles of firearms and optics, past a mannequin in new khakis and an antique pith helmet. A book entitled *Monsters of the Windfall Woods* looked promising until Max found out it had been the result of a writing contest. The svelte proprietor somehow pegged Max as a deer hunter and warned the husky of the notorious lack of big game in the area, but assured him that turkey and water fowl were always a decent challenge. Max, who valued sleep too much to be getting up at four in the morning for any size of game, made his excuses and left after getting an earful about the time "that damn crystal-wearing hippy" lit a funeral pyre for the owner's hunting trophies.

He passed a liquor store called Primordial Booze, which prided itself on mysterious and ancient grains. One beer, Hops Circles, featured labels with an aerial photo of the crop circle the wheat was supposedly gathered from. A more exotic bottle, Karmic Cleanse, offered to purge him of toxins in unspecified, likely antiseptic, ways. In the central cooler, and looking tame by comparison, both the oyster and non-oyster beers of the Thomas Creel Brewery sat in their seaweed-green bottles, proudly labeled as "local product."

Further down Main Street, the Mystic Eye had a mutant pickled pig fetus on display just inside the door, complete with name tags for each of its heads. The proprietor was nowhere to be seen, but wet noises and the thrum of a small motor echoed from the back room. Max left without asking about any of the other livestock oddities that leered down from the shelves.

The shops only went downhill from there. Voice-changing monster masks, light-up ray guns, alien-shaped novelty candies: an endless parade of unhelpful trinkets. A trio of raccoons trundled a cart of squid-god-shaped cakes from Arkham Hors d'Oeuvres. He also passed what appeared to be a stag bar, The Hind Quarter, which he didn't feel the need to enter. The street outside wasn't much more informative: he passed a pair of armadillo twins conspiring in an unknown language and tourists waving strange detection equipment at every power line. At one point, a weasel in a hazmat suit skated past him, headphones pumping electronica.

Finding a game shop, three blocks from the end of Main Street, came as a pleasant surprise. Finding the rhinoceros fan from the diner working inside was also pleasant, if less of a surprise.

The rhino bounced around the shop, restocking games and tidying. A battered clipboard hung, dwarfed, from his massive hands.

Max stepped through the door, which rang a tiny bell. He stood still and let his shoulders relax a little, so as not to be intimidating. "Hey."

"One second, I'm just—" The heavyset male jerked his head up from putting a game on a high shelf and jabbed his horn through the bottom of the box. "Hey!"

The dog extended a paw to shake. "It was Karl, right?"

"Yes! Hi!" The young rhino tugged the box off his nose in a shower of game pieces. They plinked to the floor in a colorful spray. "Ummm… Don't mind those." He ducked behind the counter, shoulders bobbing as he picked them up.

"No problem." Deciding it would be rude to watch Karl collect all the plastic tokens, Max walked down the counter to inspect the wares, searching for a conversation starter. "Hey, is that the new *Mana Clash* set?" He picked up a booster pack.

"You play *Mana Clash*?" Karl's eyes went wide with glee as he dropped the tiny plastic cheese wedges into the box's new hole.

The dog shrugged. "I used to. Before the show. All my cards are in a shoebox back home."

"We have a pretty good pool of people who play in town." Rump in the air, Karl's tiny tail swished as he looked up with a smile. "I could lend you a deck if you want."

The husky gave a good-natured shrug. "Sure, but maybe later. I'm kind of on a mission right now: hoping to learn more about the town's history, but all the places I've checked out are creepy or touristy."

Karl taped over the impromptu opening with delicate care. The side of a game, titled *Gorgonzola*, proclaimed: 'Nonstop action! One look and she turns you to cheese!' He pondered the patch for a moment, then nodded. "A few places in town are more historical. Pinchy's has been here forever. Maybe the town hall or an antique store."

Max pondered, then settled on an angle the rhino might appreciate. "Yeah, I'm looking for something a little more in the theme of *Strangeville*." He flexed his sore paw. "But without merchandise they want me to sign."

"You could check out Curios & Quandaries." Karl spotted a stray plastic cheese and peeled back the tape to drop it in the box. "Mr. Tartle has some cool old stuff. Just don't touch anything without asking him. It can be hard to tell what's fragile." He grimaced.

"You're pretty good at directing people around town."

With a smile, the rhino shrugged. "I didn't get to be this influential in the fandom just sitting around. I've been researching the local origins of the *Strangeville* mythos and podcasting it."

The canine's ears rose. "Are you the guy who figured out Cassie had psychic powers three episodes before the big reveal?"

Tiny ears and massive fists twitching up, he brightened like a shooting star. "You listen to my podcast?"

"Mostly before the show. The studio kinda discouraged listening to that sort of thing while we were filming." He cast back through his memories. "Strange Times, right?"

Giddy with laughter, the rhino leaned back into his chair, which creaked but didn't buckle. "Wow, that's so awesome!"

"Well, I'm a fan too." The dog leaned against the counter. "Still making episodes?"

"Ever since the movie rumors tanked, it's pretty much just a fanfic roundup. Sometimes we trade theories with listeners, but even that's starting to slow down..." He wrung his hands.

The dog looked up from the map on his phone. "Fridays?"

"*Mana Clash*." The rhinoceros swallowed, finding something urgent to look at through the glass top of the counter. "If you want, I mean. No pressure."

"Sure." Max wagged. "I'm sure Kylie doesn't want me in her business all the time." He thought about just what kind of business they'd been up to lately and heat crept up his ears.

"Is it okay to take a picture?" The rhino waggled his phone. "To prove you came to the store?"

The dog woofed a laugh. "Okay, but only for you and the Internet." He paused for the snap of a photo, then stuck the map back in his pocket. "Anyway, I'd better check out your lead." He gave him a little nod. "Thanks for the help."

"Any time!" Karl squeaked with glee, tapping at his own phone before Max even got outside.

After endless tourist traps, Curios & Quandaries stood with silent dignity, a shining beacon of authenticity on the coast of a sea of mood rings and plastic alien masks. The old wood siding wore a coat of new paint, the second floor windows veiled by tan curtains. Even the "open" sign had been inked by hand. All in all, the shop came as a breath of fresh air, even with its smoky interior. What seemed at first to be a den of knickknacks hinted at something deeper the further he ambled into the store. A schnauzer smoking a pipe paged through a clothbound volume at the counter. His slate gray eyes rose to meet Max's. Something unnerved him about the other dog's look, like he'd been expecting a visitor.

The husky nosed around the store, with its rows of old books and shelves of curious objects. Strange stone faces, carved sigils, chunks of rock and metal in improbable colors. Max's attention caught one item in particular: a small piece of what looked like bone, carved and burnt. Upon closer inspection Max confirmed his suspicions. The bone bore the same tiny holes and unusual protrusions as the disk from the shack.

The smaller dog lifted the pipe from his teeth and closed the book he'd been reading. "Most people aren't interested in dusty old bones."

"Must be a dog thing." Max smiled, trying to be smooth, picturing this as a day on set. When the smaller dog didn't laugh, he hurried on, gesturing to the curios. "What's their story?"

"They were unearthed after a house fire." He glanced out the window. "Couldn't be identified as any known species, so they found their way to my shop."

"What do you sell, exactly?" His claw tip traced the edge of a shelf. "And who buys it? I don't see any price tags, just labels."

The schnauzer just smiled around his pipe stem. An old brass clock ticked above him.

Weariness and frustration catching up, Max took a deep breath. "Sorry, I've just been checking around town and getting nowhere."

"People in this town get asked a lot of crazy questions by tourists." The old dog took another drag on his pipe. "Slow down. Take matters as they come. I think you'll find it to your benefit."

With a blink, Max tried to parse meaning from that statement. "How?"

"For one, it will make you seem less like another tourist looking to confirm his pet theories."

The younger dog nodded. "I'd like to know more about Windfall itself. Kind of a...personal project. I heard it started around silver mines?"

A light of interest shone through the owner's graying muzzle. "Silver, lumber, legend: a strange town, with strange luck. I think I have a book that might get you started." With no more than a glance, he pulled a slim paperback from the shelf. He handed it over with a slight smile.

Max turned the book over in his paws: *Windfall: An Visual History.* A collection of old photographs comprised the cover. He flipped through it to find more photos, as well as timelines and painted portraits. "How much?"

"For you, twelve dollars."

Max pulled out his wallet and handed over the cash. "Thank you."

"You're welcome." The small dog pocketed the money in his vest. The clock behind him announced five o'clock with discordant chimes. "Afraid I was just closing up shop when you arrived. Stop by again, sometime."

Nodding, the canine allowed himself to be ushered out by a dog half his size. The lock clicked after him, then the lights, dropping shadow over the collection of promising artifacts. With afternoon sinking into evening, he looked down, pleased he had at least something to show for his day's work.

By the time Max got back to Kylie's nostalgia shop the otter was bustling about, shelving old records and locking the cases of vintage lighters as they prepared to lock up for the night. Shane was nowhere to be seen. The husky hunched over a table, reading the book among an array of hand-painted teacups.

The lutrine walked up behind him and set a paw on his shoulder. "Anything good?"

"A freak windstorm leveled the area, like a hurricane or a tornado or something." Max flipped to a map of the devastation. "It stripped trees out of the ground for miles, blew some out to sea. Some locals came up to investigate, found silver veins exposed at the surface, and plenty of downed trees for lumber. Town sprung up right then and there."

"Huh." She blinked, unsure what to do with that chunk of history. "Not sure what that tells us, but it's a good start."

He pocketed the book. It was an interesting start for a little town, but it would have been rude to continue reading with someone so pretty to talk to. "Have you noticed the locals being…cagey?"

The otter shrugged. "Not really, so long as the subject is my crazy family or my haunted house."

The dog nodded. "To be fair, I only talked to the people with something to sell."

She giggled, sprawling over him a bit. "And you thought they'd be founts of information?"

A sign deflated his chest a fraction of an inch. "I couldn't tell if they really believed something was going on or if they're just used to implying that to tourists."

Kylie watched Shane slink into the back room, carrying a box of decorative ceramics. "Yeah, they do that." She waited for the cat to disappear through the stockroom door. "Everybody swears something weird is happening, but they all insist it's their kind of weirdness."

The husky mulled the notion over. "What'd you think it means?"

She ran a paw over an old photograph of a silver mine. "I think it means we keep digging."

The two of them lounged on the steps of the sprawling back porch of Bourn Manor, wary eyes on the woods on the other side of the scruffy, neglected grounds. Walking Kylie home had lost the simple pleasure it'd had yesterday, now that spiky alien monsters seemed to dwell in every shadow. He noticed an unnatural stiffness to her posture, which left her only about as flexible as he'd be after mastering yoga. Putting an arm around her, he raised his ears. "You okay?"

"Sorry." She smiled and leaned into his warmth. "Just stressed out. I wish we could find out more about…what we saw, without confirming to the town I'm another in a long line of crazies."

He lifted her chin with a gentle paw and kissed her lips. "You're not crazy. If nothing else, we know that now."

That put a squirm back in her body. She hooked a leg over his lap, getting comfy. "Thanks, Maxie."

"And neither were your ancestors." His eyes swept the forest, just to be safe. "You just come from a long line of monster detectives."

The lutrine brightened. "See, that sounds so much better."

He patted her shoulder and thought for a moment. "Or it turns out that bone fragment was covered in mercury or something and we've both been hallucinating. But at least we can be crazy together."

The otter patted his denim-covered thigh. "Yes, at least we have that."

His tail drummed the porch railing. "I totally just kissed you."

"You did." A grin, then she hugged him tighter.

"It's weird how natural this is." The husky looked her in the eyes. "Kylie, what are we doing? Are we…dating?"

She shrugged. "I guess? Assuming paranormal research counts as a date."

"Is this the whole reason you suggested I come visit?" His head tilted in amusement.

She cleared her throat, scrupulously studying the floorboards. "Uh, possibly?"

His muzzle dipped and bumped his nose to hers. "Can I kiss you again?"

She grinned. "Definitely."

CHAPTER 12
EXPLORING

STRANGEVILLE (TUE/9P)

S02E05 "The Fast Lane": Serge puts his trust in Cassie and her friends when he needs their help to save his track team from a demonic scheme disguised as a new kind of steroid.

Nightmare clenched Kylie's jaw, leading her in feverish loops. Shouting, peppered with unpredictable whispers, shook the landscape of her dreams. The language was not her own, or any that she'd ever heard. Her mind's eye strained at flashes of living machines and spidery scrawls.

She thrashed awake. In a twisted sprawl of tangled sheets, she stared at the dark ceiling. Her whole face hurt. Her teeth, in particular, almost felt like they were buzzing, vibrating at some deep, unknown frequency. She groped her way to the bathroom, getting a glass of water in the dim starlight, letting the cool liquid clear her head a little. Her nerves still hummed with energy. Halfway across the room, she paused on the carpet. With unsteady paws, she padded over to the Crazy Wall, wondering how much of it was still valid. How many were right? How many were actually crazy? Which list was she going to join?

Eventually, her heartbeat calmed and her hands slowed their fidgeting. She'd had stress dreams before, but never this chaotic, this strained. Her stupid brain could've at least had nightmares about the alien monster she'd seen—that would've made sense. Sleep; she needed a good night's sleep to put this behind her. In the morning, she could approach this rationally.

Max would help with that. For a moment, she considered heading downstairs and demanding he comfort her, but the dog was probably fast asleep. She'd feel silly, making a big deal over a bad dream.

Crawling back into bed, the otter rolled up in a protective tube of blanket. Her muzzle buried in the pillow, she focused on taking deep breaths. Sleep returned slowly, as if waiting for her defenses to slacken again.

Days passed without them finding any sign of the monster they'd seen in the woods. Cheery summer sunbeams shone onto the carpet from the living room windows. Kylie oozed over the sofa, straightening her whiskers. A breeze curled in through the curtains, carrying the day's heat into the evening sky.

The door creaked open to admit Max bearing grocery sacks. "You won't believe who I ran into at the store."

"The monster?" She flashed him a look of faint hope, still laying upside down.

"Mr. Madison from the store next to yours. He's organizing some kind of *Strangeville* event, wants us to sign some merchandise."

"I don't believe it!" She tumbled off the sofa and sprung to her feet. "Cindy's dad? Tell me you said no."

The dog shrugged. "I threw him a bone. I figured it'd do us good to get out of the house for a few hours."

"I've been avoiding him since I moved here." Standing, the otter slithered in irritation. "And that's hard when you work next door to someone."

"You don't have to go." He set a large paw on her slim shoulder. He seemed a little sad about going alone. "But I did already text Karl."

A mutter of dismay escaped her muzzle. This is what she got for sending the canine out alone. "Karl's not really a problem. Cindy is."

"You're going to be living here for the foreseeable future." His ears rose. "Best to start smoothing raised hackles now."

Kylie crossed her arms. "I am not gonna hang out with Cindy in the heart of her lair."

Kylie sat at a card table, signing t-shirts in the heart of Cindy's lair. Max had used his sad puppy-dog eyes on her. Totally unfair. She smoothed her sundress and took some comfort in the fact that Cindy hated her being there just as much. Between that and being next to Max, she found it easy to put on a smile.

Meanwhile, the spaniel's sugar queen facade cracked to a scowl whenever she thought no one was looking. Her father had roped her into helping. She served snacks provided by the Windfall Chamber of Commerce, and dropped off by the handyman fixing Bourn Manor. Her dad even insisted she put on the store uniform, so she'd compromised on a shirt two sizes too small.

Max sat beside her, wagging all the while and discussing the finer points of *Strangeville* lore with fans. He'd been swarmed since the event started because he was new in town and doggedly eager to talk about the show. About a dozen fans had found their way to the store; the rest seemed to be normal locals wanting to get to know the new celebrities, or just people drawn in off the streets by the smell of brownies.

She leaned to whisper in the husky's ear. "I thought it would just be Karl."

He woofed a little laugh. "Would you rather it just be Karl?"

"Not complaining." She signed a poster.

The rhino stood in the knickknack aisle, directing wayward fans with a mobile phone and pure glee.

Kylie surveyed the crowd. All the fangirls, and some of the fanboys, wore tan vests of varying degrees of fidelity to the one she'd worn on *Strangeville* and afterward. "If we don't do something, fishing vests will become some sort of weird uniform in the fandom."

He elbowed her gently in the ribs. "Afraid that people will steal your signature look?"

"It's practical! I can keep all kinds of stuff in there. As opposed to this thing, which has no pockets at all and is just generally useless." She tried in vain to flatten out the wrinkles that two hours of sitting had put in the thin green fabric of her sundress. Max's focus shifted to follow her hand as it traced the curves of her belly and hips. Their eyes met and they both flushed and tried to hide a smile

The canine cleared his throat with a grin. "Anyway, I think you just had the easiest costume to duplicate; red leather biker jackets are expensive."

"It still only looks right on a porcupine to me."

Several of the fans lit up at the mention of the studio-mandated badass porcupine. A wolf brushed pink hair from her eyes. "Is Damon's actor gonna be here?"

"Nah, Max and I just happened to be in the area." The otter waved a paw. "Last I heard he got a role in some experimental indie film."

"A room with a view with a staircase and a pond type of movie." Max slouched to lean on the table, his voice a gentle rumble. "Very existential."

A murmur of approval rippled through the crowd.

Scribbling her name onto the back of an "always listen to Cassie" pin, the lutrine smirked. "Last time we invited him to a *Strangeville* event, he was in some desert, shooting dream sequences where he drags metallic cubes over sand dunes. And pretending he couldn't get phone reception."

The husky shrugged. "He seems to think the show hurt his reputation as a 'serious actor.'"

As the event wound down, Karl shook both their hands with frantic joy. "Thank you guys so much for being here. It's like having StrangeCon in my backyard." The rhino shook a cardboard box of game pieces. "And my friend's going to love that you signed his prototype *Strangeville* board game. See you later guys!"

Kylie leaned against the car and watched the crowd break up toward restaurants and parking lots. "I admit I got a little burned out on *Strangeville* after that last big publicity push." She smiled up at Max. "But this was fun. I mean, why'd we do the show if we didn't want people to enjoy it?"

He chuckled. "Karl changed your mind?"

"He's very...earnest."

Max watched the rhino bounce along at the head of the pack. "There's a little Karl in all of us."

Her lips quirked as the rhinoceros lead a few other stragglers in an *a cappella* rendition of the theme song. "Yeah, though there's nothing but Karl in Karl." She tilted her head at the bathroom. "Be right back."

He nodded, wagged, and started neatly packing away their pens and posters.

Smiling, the otter bounced toward the back of the store. The whole affair had been a lot less stressful than she'd remembered previous press events. Granted, there'd been no formal media and only the most informal of planning. She felt pretty good. Unfortunately, her path led past the the till, which brought her within range of a certain cocker spaniel.

Leaning on an elbow behind the cash register, Cindy yipped a snide laugh. "What a bunch of losers. And you're a loser for being their loser-queen."

"At least they care about something." The otter lashed her thick tail. "What do you even do in your spare time?"

"Oh, I have hobbies. Thinking of taking up a new one right now, actually." She peered down the counter at the hunky canine sorting pins and postcards into the promo box.

Kylie rolled her eyes and started coming up with a retort when her bladder reminded her why she'd gotten up. Pressing her knees together in defiance, she stood her ground. If things got ugly, maybe she could pee on something of Cindy's—that was a dog thing, right? She tossed a thin smile onto her muzzle. "Is it not being a bitch?"

"Being a bitch is an asset in this hobby." She leveled a superior glance at Kylie. "Everybody knows interspecies flings are a stud's last resort."

Rage boiled up in Kylie like a scalding hot spring. Her fists balled up as she suddenly longed for a choke chain.

Before the lutrine could squawk more than a sputter, Cindy's father appeared from between two aisles, clapped a paw on each of their their shoulders, and leaned between them. "Hey you guys! I bet the two of you have become great pals, what with all the time my angel-muffin spends outside the store gabbing with you." He yapped an oblivious chuckle.

For the first time ever, Kylie and Cindy felt the need to agree on something. Both grimaced and assured her dad: "Yeah, great...yeah."

"Great!" He patted both of them on the arm and drifted onward to drum up more business.

The otter, meanwhile, scampered off to the restroom before anything else uncomfortable could befall her.

As evening sunlight burned beyond the reach of branches, Laura stood on the porch chatting with the handyman beaver, complimenting him on how fast his roofing had progressed. Inside, at the kitchen table, Kylie hunched over her laptop as it played the video from Max's phone, frame by painstaking frame. Low resolution, wild camera movements, and the lack of any sign of the monster on film conspired to drain her of all enthusiasm. Slouching, she rubbed the strain from her eyes and popped the video back to the beginning to have another look.

Max set a heavy paw on her shoulder. "You're allowed take a break."

"I need to know more about..." She glanced out the window at her gabbing mother. "...you know."

"Nobody's been mauled by a monster this week." The husky stepped up behind her chair. "Or any previous week we know of."

She sighed, leaning against him. "Yeah, you're right. We need a night off." Her gaze flicked up to meet his. "You're on vacation. You should have nothing but nights off."

"I'm happy to help you, rudderbutt." He kissed her hair. "C'mon, let's go get set up."

Kylie grabbed her laptop and headed to the living room. She sprawled on the sofa, leaving just a slice of room for the husky beside her. "Did we watch *Ape X?*"

Max entered from the kitchen, carrying a clam juice and a root beer. "If it's the one where mountaineers dynamite a yeti, yes."

"Let's see…" She scrolled through her list of movies. "We could watch *Platypus Platoon* or *Please Stand By*…"

His eyes caught on the laptop screen. "Hang on. Why do you only have one episode of *Strangeville?*"

The otter sputtered a fluttered chitter, her webbed fingers grasping at justifications. "They take up a lot of room! I had to prioritize."

"And why did you prioritize this one?"

"It's good! I mean, not in the traditional sense…"

Max quirked an eyebrow at her and just waited for her babbling to lose steam. "Wait, is this the one where I wind up in a loincloth?"

"It's the time travel one, yeah…" Her ears and whiskers drooped with guilt.

Max snickered, opened his soda, and put his arm around her. "Good to know all that fanservice worked on someone."

That instant, Laura walked past the living room with a file box stuffed with script notes. She paused to look them over and gave her daughter a dorky thumbs-up.

Kylie waggled a paw at her mother, shooing her away as fast as otterly possible. She then draped herself over the husky's lap and pressed play.

The *Please Stand By* episode began and was terrible. Foam-rubber tree people waddled with menace on a tropical Hollywood backlot. They almost forgot to mock it, though; they were too caught up in the feel of each other. Their fingers interlaced, his fur tickling her webbing. She curled closer to him and rested her head on the armrest to watch his expression. Before long, the credits rolled and the stars had come out and neither of them wanted to leave the other's arms to go to bed. So they spooned and Kylie, to keep from wondering if all this would last, babbled.

"I used to be scared of this house as a kid when we visited." Her webbed paw squeezed his hand. "I like it much better now."

Max smiled, tail swishing against the back of the sofa.

"Mom moved out after my great uncle disappeared, before I was born." She sipped the last of her clam juice. "She came back when she was pregnant with me and started selling the old china, silverware, crystal, antiques, furniture…"

"That was before Hollywood?"

"Yeah, she used the money to get herself set up, pay for a sitter for me, stuff like that. She hit it big before she could clear most of the house out, though. That's why there's still so much junk."

"Your mom and I've been making progress on that." He patted her stomach.

"You've been really great, Maxie." She rolled over to face him. "I don't know what I'd have done if you weren't here."

The husky smirked. "My guess: call and demand I come out to help you."

She smiled. "And you'd have come, wouldn't you?"

"Of course I would." He stroked the gentle curve of her back, brushing his muzzle along hers.

"You're sweet." She lifted his chin, kissing his cheek. "This is so nice, Maxie. I'm glad we ended up like this."

"I'm sorry I kept you waiting." His paws caressed along her back in a way she decided was pretty spectacular.

"It wasn't so bad, really. I only figured it out myself right at the very end of the show. I saw everything winding down and everyone going their separate ways and realized you'd be leaving and it just sort of hit me, you know?" Her fingers played through his short haircut. "And I didn't say anything because I had no idea what was going to happen. I didn't know when I'd get to see you again, and I didn't want this weird thing hanging between us the whole time. It sucked, waiting so long to get you out here."

He shrugged those powerful shoulders. "You could have come out to visit me. Always room at the farm."

"Ugh, nooo." Her response was muffled by his shirt as she thumped her forehead against his chest. "Your mom would have made me do chores, and I'm allergic to the crack of dawn." She peeked up at him, one eye twinkling. "Though, it might be worth it, to watch you throwing bales of hay around with no shirt on."

"The important thing is: I'm here now." He leaned in, his nose ever so gently touching hers.

"Yeah, you are." She smiled up at him, caressing his cheek and drawing him into another slow kiss.

Losing himself in the kiss, Max slipped his paws beneath her arms and drew her close. Passion built to dizzying heights on their years of trust, their months of longing. She licked his lips, then inside his mouth, searching out that soft canine tongue. In the dark room, lit only by the television, they explored. Slender lutrine paws caressed his powerful frame while wide husky paws traced every contour of hers. He cupped her breasts, investigating their soft resilience.

She pressed his shoulder, rolling him to his back. He moaned as kisses rained down, her nimble form climbing atop him. Those sleek legs wrapped around his hips as small, needful noises escaped her throat.

Not for the first time in their make out sessions, Max felt an erection swelling in his pants. As usual, he shifted away so as not to hump against her.

"It's okay." Hands on his chest, she ground down against the tent in his pants. "I like it."

A blush burning his cheeks, he let her ride him. Soon, he found his hips bucking back.

Kylie lay atop him, wiggling her body, stimulating every inch she touched. The front of her jeans felt so hot Max could no longer attribute it to mere friction.

His shaky paws got lost in the sleek fur of her arms, her shoulders under her sleeves, her back under the t-shirt to trace the undersides of her breasts.

Otter eyes shone in the dim light. Her paw slipped to his crotch, gripping his erection.

Max whined, panting with need, the fabric of his pants stretched unbelievably tight. Their hips pressed together and stayed there. His cock swelled under her paw, stretching its fabric confines.

She rubbed up and down, sliding his sheath against the slick length through the denim, watching his every reaction. "Like that?"

"U-uh huh..." Heart racing, he lay back and enjoyed her attentions.

The otter giggled, nervous fingertips tracing his cock's outline. "...Can I see?"

Max's mind raced to catch up to the moment. His best friend wanted to see his dick. And most likely touch it. At last, he squeaked a very tiny "yes."

In the scant light of the television, she bit her lip. Those graceful paws fumbled at his zipper, pulling it down, down—

Floorboards creaked upstairs.

They froze.

A moment passed, chilling Max's blood. The last thing he wanted was Laura walking in on them. He might never be able to look her in the eyes if he got caught with his pants down on her living room sofa.

Kylie stared up, her cute little ears twitching at the ceiling. Her gaze drifted down to his chest, mischief rekindling in her expression. "Your room?"

She didn't quite meet his eyes as she asked this, and Max's heart quickened as he realized what she was really asking. He licked his lips, breathless. "Uh, yeah. Okay."

They hurried off the sofa, still a tangle of touches and kisses and Max trying to keep his unzipped pants from falling down. The best solution he found was keeping her pressed against him. Her strong, supple body fit to his with every step, leading him in a clumsy dance of passion. They bumped into furniture, rounding the corner to his room.

They paused one final time just outside Max's door. It had been left half-open, and the darkness inside suddenly seemed like the threshold to another world, a portal to someplace scary and amazing. He broke the kiss to catch his breath, retreating into the room, and she chased after him with a little mewl of need that made his blood boil. Allowing her to renew the kiss, Max shuddered, struggling to keep his head. Who was this incredible, sensual creature burying her fingers in his hair, sliding her body like sheer silk against his? What had happened to the impish otter girl who'd stood behind the cameras and pulled faces to make him flub his lines?

Sensing his hesitation, she broke the kiss, but only a little. She kept her fingers in his hair, kept his head down, kept their noses touching, breath mingling. An eager spark lit in her eyes, even if her voice trembled. "Come on, Maxie. Let's do this."

He grinned. There she stood, whiskers lit by soft moonlight, muzzle lit by a familiar smile. He let her recapture his lips, not bothering to suppress a whimper of need as she ground her pelvis against his tented boxers. When she gripped him by the shirt and pulled him into the darkened bedroom, resistance was the last thing on his mind.

He got a few steps in before belatedly turning around to lock the door. When he looked back at Kylie, she already had her vest unzipped and halfway off. It fluttered to the floor as she flowed out of her shirt. Max recognized the impatience of nerves in his soon-to-be lover. She was rushing to keep herself from chickening out. He watched, entranced, as her pants and panties fell away in a flurry of lutrine grace. Anxiety and desire tingled down his nerves. His hands didn't know what to do with themselves.

Walking closer, she smiled. Her modest breasts matched the immodest curve of her hips, her tail a sultry sway behind her. Her paw touched his chest, as it had so many times before, but never had his heart raced like this because of it. Moonlight touched her fur with silver elegance, wreathing her lustrous pelt with celestial illumination. The cream coloring under her chin flowed down over her breasts and between her legs. There, a pink hint of her slit teased through thin fur.

Max hesitated further, tail between his legs, eyes wide. Blood rushed like an icy river through his veins, an unusual sensation for the arctic dog. Confronted with the naked otter he loved, who loved him, he reached out and touched her bare shoulder.

She brushed her whiskers on the back of his hand, hazel eyes looking up at him over an eager grin. The sleek lines of her body flowed with every tiny movement, grace woven into her very being. Her tail swayed, lifted higher than usual. Closer and closer she drew, their attraction overpowering all other forces.

Cupping her cheek in a wide white paw, he studied her face, wanting to remember this moment. Her rich scent teased him, driving his length to swell further from its sheath. Deep inside him, catastrophe and wonder loomed, and he wanted to remember every instant of it. He leaned in, kissing her. Her lips brushed, warm and delicate, over his.

She moaned, breasts pressed just under his ribs. Paws wrapped around him, caressing his back, gripping the hem of his shirt and lifting it. She drew it over his head and off his arms. Webbed hands trailed the rich fluff of his chest. More kisses reassured him in the darkness.

A shiver translated through him, just enough to cause his pants to finally fall from his waist. He'd forgotten to button them and now watched with shy shock around the kiss as they deserted him. The front of his boxers tented out, bridging the space between them.

Kylie snickered, drawing back to smirk at his falling pants. Her paws helped them escape, then returned to do the same for his boxers. She knelt. Her round muzzle rubbed the bulged fabric, nuzzling up and down his tender length. Deft fingers curled over the waistband, tugging down. Further, further, cock stretching the garment into a pavilion, his sheath and balls on display in the dark.

His ears burned with self-consciousness, even as the rest of him shivered. He whimpered, paws wiggling and flexing, unsure where to be or what to do. Even just her tugging cloth against his tip felt amazing, the tension growing as fast as his erection.

At last, she pulled a little too far and his dick sprang up to bop her in the nose. A stunned gasp as she fell back, landing with a thump on her butt.

"Sorry!" He reached to help, tripped on his underwear, and almost fell on her.

"Eep!" She giggled, supporting his chest. Her other paw wiped at the spot of moisture he'd left on her nose. He could see her nostrils flared with a silent panting. "Stay quiet. Mom's upstairs."

He nodded and stepped out of his boxers, then helped her to her feet. Her belly fur brushed along the tip of his erection. He shuddered at the sensation.

Not letting go of his paw, she guided him to the bed. With lutrine ease, she slithered onto the mattress, drawing him clambering after. The bedsprings squeaked a protest under their combined weight. He wound up kneeling between her legs, erection jutting into the air. She gave it a long glance before drawing him down atop her, their kisses resuming.

He propped his arms around her, afraid to put his full weight on her lithe form, scared he'd hurt her. His cock bumped her thigh, sac tickled by fur. He took care not to rest a knee on her tail.

That thick tail bumped between his shins. Her tongue traced inside his mouth. A soft-webbed paw closed around his cock, stroked its length and girth. The quiet dark amplified her every soft intake of breath.

He tried to speak, but couldn't find words. Her fingers, her flesh, her fur: countless new textures brushed up his exposed skin. The muscular length of her tail rolled up in a wave under his balls. He panted, heart racing.

She took hold of his cock and guided him up between her thighs. Bathed in delicate starlight, her ears flicked back, muzzle in a nervous dip. Her webbing caressed his length, fingers exploring, taking stock of him. "Wow, Max, you're kinda huge."

His tip brushed her slit, warm and slick. The only sound he could manage began as a chuckle and collapsed into a moan. His shaft bucked once under her touch. "S-sorry?"

"Not complaining." A hint of nerves tinged her voice. Delicate moisture and heat greeted his tip as she rubbed it along her folds. Wet noises peppered the silence.

Max felt himself stiffen further, fluid dribbling from his tip. The first hint of his knot started to swell, stretching the sheath. Easing it back behind the bulge, his fingertips bumped hers, somehow embarrassing him even more. His voice softened further as she manipulated the stiff canine cock. "You're sure about—?"

"Really sure, Maxie." Pure affection warmed her tone, burying her anxiety. "I wouldn't want anybody but you."

His eyes misted; he closed them to keep from tearing up, then nuzzled her whiskers. "Neither would I."

Her tail swished against the bedcovers. She smiled. Her paw gripped the fluff of his hips, guiding him forward.

He pressed forward, glanced off. A trace of her fluids clung to his tip, chilling it in the hot night air.

With a kind chuckle, she reached down and lined him back up.

He pressed in again, the wet heat rising up his cock about an inch.

She squirmed, and not in a fun way. "Ow. Ow!"

With a whine of concern, he froze and bumped her muzzle with his. "You okay?"

"I'm just…" She reached down, spreading her folds a little wider. "Alright, try now."

Once again, he pressed forward, but the memory of pain had spooked them both and her passage bore down on his tip and kept him from entering further. The husky whimpered with concern and unsated need, arms quivering as they supported his weight above her. With effort, he pulled his attention from the incredible heat around his tip and opened his eyes. Kylie clung to his chest, eyes closed, her face a mask of anticipation and uncertainty. He brushed his fingers across her cheek, and her eyes shimmered as they opened to meet his. He leaned in and touched his nose to hers. "Do you trust me?"

The otter blinked and smiled, her arms releasing the fur of his chest to wrap around the back of his neck. "That's a stupid question."

He pressed his lips to hers, letting a fraction of his weight settle on her. He felt the tension unwind from her body, little by little.

She moaned the tiniest of moans into his muzzle, her thighs brushing across his pelvis, and he found he could press on at last.

He sank deeper and deeper, slow and unsteady, not wanting to hurt her. Slick, gentle pressure greeted him and clung tight to his every contour, like that's where he'd always belonged. Her scent, full-bodied and feminine, overwhelmed him, beckoning him to thrust all the way into her. He resisted, gritting his teeth at all the unfamiliar delights. His breath washed out in a shaking rush as he sank in all the way to his knot. He grunted with relief and anticipation, then studied her for reactions.

The lutrine wriggled, squeaking with joy. Her paw explored their connection, tracing her stretched lips and the base of his cock. She traced the swell of flesh to its supple sheath. "That's your knot?"

His muscled arms cradled her, though his weight still pressed her into the old mattress. "Yeah."

"Wow." Her fingers traced her stomach, feeling for his cock. She grinned up at him. "Maxie, you're inside me."

He nodded, returning the smile and adding a kiss.

The otter rocked back and forth under him, jostling his length within her. "You have no idea how long I've wanted this."

Max pulled back a bit, then sank back in. That incredible pressure still gripped his cock, massaging pleasure up its length. "I'm not...too big, am I?"

Kylie moaned into his fur. "No, no, it's okay, just gimme a minute." She wriggled a bit, as though trying to get him better situated. "How about you? I'm not, like, squishing you, am I?"

"No, this feels amazing." He thrust a little more. Unsure and unsteady, but liking the sounds she made, he ground and humped his way to something resembling a rhythm. All their years of reading each other couldn't keep him from slipping out a few times. More than a few, to be honest. A shared chuckle, though, and they had him back inside her, where he belonged. The husky grappled with the instinct to grab her and take her as hard as he could, but he could only go so fast and hard before the mattress or the headboard started to creak and thump, or her gasps got too loud.

She writhed around whenever his knot bumped her clit, the movement so wiggly it threatened to slide her free of him all over again. Undaunted and vivacious, she gripped him harder, angling her hips to meet him.

He thrusted, creaking the bedsprings and slowing if he caught a hint of a yelp in her moans, or whenever the headboard threatened to thump. He'd have to put some padding behind it. The dog watched his best friend shudder and gasp on his cock, feeling a new chapter in their lives open before him. His balls brushed back and forth along her thick tail.

She rubbed her fingertip in her juices, then toyed with her clit, pressing the tender nub against his shaft as it slid in and out of her. Tension rolled in waves up her frame as she rubbed faster and faster. Her breath ran to ragged panting. "Oh Maxie! Ah-ah!"

Max paused his motions, not wanting to hurt her, biting his lip as she clenched around him. He could feel her pulsing around his shaft, gripping with need. His hips bumped hers, never pulling out. His hand joined hers, rubbing her fingers a little harder on her clitoris.

Curling beneath him, her eyes closed as she moaned in orgasm. Bucking and shivering, her supple body rolled against his, pressing with desperation onto his erect shaft. "Mmmm!"

He held her, resting his cheek along hers, grinding his knot against her entrance.

Aftershocks shivered through her body, webbed paws gripping his back. She arched up. Her wet, swollen labia pressed his bulge as she engulfed his shaft once again. Her eyes closed, her breath evening out. "Ohmygosh, Maxie. Oh... Oh..."

Humping with gentle pressure, he stroked her hair and panted affection into her ear. The moment stretched on, basking him in the glory of his best friend panting with pleasure beneath him. That same voice that'd brightened long days of filming and chased off his homesickness.

"You got the knot in?" She looked quite pleased with herself. Her paw reached down that smooth stomach, feeling for a bulge where he would've tied her.

He shook his head. "Got too big to fit."

Fingertips reaching her stretched lips, she caressed the swollen base of his cock. "It gets…bigger?" Her voice held equal parts terror and delight.

Max's ears dropped with a shy smile.

She stroked his scruff. "Oh." A lopsided grin. "Did you, um…?" She wiggled under him.

"No, but it felt really nice." He shifted his hips. "Still does."

"Whoa, really?" Her whispers spiked in volume, then got quieter as if to compensate. "I thought guys couldn't help it once they were inside."

"Umm, well, my knot's not in…" He pressed forward to demonstrate, slick moisture squeezing out around his cock. That canine bulge pressed to her entrance, throbbing and eager in the quiet of the night. "Plus, I've never come with someone else around." Pulling a little ways out, he dipped his muzzle, shy.

"You could if you want to…" Her whiskers twitched, catching moonlight with her smile. "I mean, I want you to…"

He brushed a lock of hair from her face. "Okay." Drawing back, he slipped free, feeling her silky flesh caress his. Sitting up, his tip bobbed against her slick folds. His paw slipped down and hers followed. He stroked his bunched sheath against the base of his cock, rubbing paw pads against the back of his knot.

Slender otter paws joined in, caressing his cock, their webbing stimulating every inch of its surface.

He rubbed faster, thinking about where he was, who he was with, how much she cared about him. He climbed over her, stroking himself down into her. His tail dropped to meet hers. Soft growls of pleasure rumbled in his chest.

The lutrine gasped, hands massaging his slick shaft, feet tucked against his knees. "Ya close?"

"Mmhm!" He stroked faster. Breath caught in his throat. His balls tensed. Pulses of impending orgasm telegraphed up his length and through his body.

She rubbed faster, gripping here and there, still getting used to the feel of him in her paws. "Mmmmmm..."

Frantic with desire, he guided her paws behind his knot. The sensation of her soft, loving hands set him off. With a groan, he spurted along her forearm, then on her lower stomach, then her hip. He clenched his teeth, squeezed his eyes shut, and rubbed her fingertips harder on the back of his bulge, coaxing forth another few spurts. His mind reeled, swept up on the winds of bliss. As his orgasm faded to dribbles, he watched his pearly offering slip off her waterproof fur onto the bedspread.

Giggling, she arched an eyebrow at the pearly spatters across her belly. "Kinda missed your mark, huh Maxie?"

Still catching his breath, he could only answer with an awkward chuckle. "Yeah, sorry. That got a little..." He shuddered in aftershock. "...intense."

She slipped a hand down, the dark fur vivid against her paler belly in the low light. She curled soft fingers around his tip, pressing it against the sopping fur of her mons and earning a gasp and a fresh spurt against her wrist from him. "Don't apologize." A shaky paw brushed hair from her eyes. "It was kinda cool to watch."

His tail swished. "Here, let me help." Already committed mentally to washing the sheets, he used them to wipe up his sheath and her crotch, amazed how nothing stuck to her.

The otter shivered as the fabric stimulated her oversensitive flesh. The heat of her tender folds lingered on his paw pads. She bit her lip and savored his touch. Her paws stroked the fur of his back, drawing him close once more.

He cuddled her close, a sleepy haze drifting over his brain. His heart-beat slowed, his muscles relaxing, his cock withdrawing to its sheath. Maybe he'd been afraid to be attracted to her, for fear of risking their friend-ship. Here, laying together on an old, narrow bed, moonlight gleaming off her fur, that seemed more than a little silly. Their friendship remained, that connection now joined by a growing and greater need. As he snuggled closer, he knew he'd never let her go.

CHAPTER 13
Trending

STRANGEVILLE (MON/9p)

S01E03 "Egbert": Sandy is approached by an eccentric scholar of the supernatural, who claims he knew her parents and needs her help. But can he be trusted?

Sunrise bloomed outside, shining warmth between the trees, through the old windows, and onto Max's bedroom floor. Wakefulness settled on Kylie like morning dew. A deep breath led to a stretch, which led to noticing she lay in the arms of a handsome, slumbering husky. She abandoned the stretch and snuggled into the breadth of his chest, giddy all over again.

With his door shut, and hers closed upstairs, her mom might not have any clue about the impromptu sleepover. A very good thing, she figured. The last thing she wanted right now was an awkward talk from her mother. It was hard to decide if the older otter would censure them for rushing forward or poke fun and wish them luck. She couldn't decide which would be more uncomfortable.

Sex hadn't been like she expected. She and Max always read each other like a final draft script, but sex had felt clunky. Wonderful, sure, but not the perfect rush of super-sexy fantasies she'd expected. Wasn't sex with the guy of your dreams supposed to be mind-blowing? Also, she wished someone had warned her about being all sore the next day. Was that normal? Or because she'd chosen an enthusiastic and gigantic partner?

Max pulled her close, laying between her and the edge of the bed. They'd gotten close during filming, to the point of casual touching, but he'd kept even closer since seeing the monster. A tiny, irrational part of her worried they only got together because of what they'd seen. Dear, sweet Maxie; he might hang around her to protect her, but he wouldn't sleep with her just to make her feel safe. Would he?

She chased the concerns from her mind, rolling to face Max. "Good morning."

A soft smile rose to his muzzle. "Morning, rudderbutt."

"Mmmm." She wiggled against him. "So: confession..."

His ears tuned in on her, but he smirked. "Should I get tested?"

"What? No!" She swatted his arm. "You know we're the two only virgins in Hollywood."

A smirk as he pulled semen-stained sheets over their nude, entangled bodies. "Well, we were."

"Whatever! Let me talk." She blushed under her fur. "You know how there's fanfiction of...us?"

He suppressed a laugh against her forehead. "You read it?"

"I started as the show was ending." The otter chittered a nervous giggle. "Apparently, Cassie and Serge have wild sex whenever they're alone and off camera."

"Sounds like a plan to me." His paw caressed her flank, a moving bump under the covers. Those powerful arms wrapped around her, one leg finding its way over her thigh. "How'd we compare?"

Her head rested on his arm. Fanfiction might have overplayed how good the sex would feel, but the cuddling... Cuddling with Max, free to be as close to him as she wanted with nothing but fur between them, was everything she'd hoped for and more. Being buried muzzle-deep in his scent and warm fluff, that did blow her mind. "Pretty well." She patted his side. Sleep stole over her, dipping her into dreams more peaceful than she'd found since arriving in Windfall. Or possibly ever.

The otter awoke to the wild drumming of a tail against the mattress. Still under her lover's arm, she turned to see a very happy husky. "Hey Maxie."

A sleepy bump of noses followed. "Hey there, rudderbutt."

She nuzzled under his chin. "So, I had this awesome dream last night."

His arms tightened around her shoulders. "Yeah, me too."

"So...fun?"

"Mmm-hmm."

She smiled. Shy fingertips traced his arm. "Was that how you pictured your first time?"

"I think I pictured more candles and soft music..." He caressed her hip. "...but the important stuff was all there."

Her lips met his.

Stroking down her back, he kissed in return. "Plus, now I'm even more familiar with your rudderbutt." His paw groped her ample tail.

"Ee!" Her head nestled against the bare fluff of his chest. A shared, content silence wrapped around them, accented only by breathing. "I was scared things would change when we started dating."

His tail thumped the bed as he leaned in to kiss her on the brow. "You're still you, and I'm still me. I'm just allowed to notice what a nice butt you've got now."

She giggled, rolling closer against his chest. "You've got a nice butt too; nice and fluffy." Her hand slipped up and earned a whimper from him as she gently rolled his testicles along her fingers. "Wow, Maxie. Even your balls are soft."

He squirmed, panting against her ear. "Might want to hold off. Don't want to wake up your mom."

That stopped her cold. "Oh right. Forgot about Mom." She cast a wary eye at the door. Her eyes shot wide. "You need to go scout if Mom is out there so I can sneak back to my room."

His paw stroked up to her shoulder, his touch light and calming. "Do you really think we're going to be able to hide this from her forever?" He glanced over their entwined, blanket-covered bodies. "Her mom-sense probably went off the moment you lost your virginity."

Peeking under the covers, she blushed. "Oh yeah, w-we're naked, aren't we?" Her gaze flicked through the room. "Where are my clothes?"

"On the floor. And the chair. And the dresser."

The otter snaked out of bed, gathering garments. "Panties. Where are my panties?"

"Don't you remember?" He propped his paws behind his head and watched her naked form, quite interested. "You left them on my doorknob."

"Not even funny, Max." Fighting her way into her shirt, it somehow wound up inside out, forcing her to start over.

"Honestly, I think we can relax a little. Your mom probably saw this one coming." He watched her stumble into her clothes. "What's the worst she'll do?"

Her vest came next, pulled straight but unzipped. "Snap a picture, frame it, and engrave the frame 'I told you so.'"

"You're going to make me put on pants, aren't you?" He crawled out of bed and located his trousers, though his gaze barely strayed from her half-clothed form. True to his word, he seemed to be having a hard time taking his eyes off her hips.

With a quiet cry of victory, Kylie found her panties on the nightstand lamp. A few quick hops saw her into them, followed by her jeans.

The husky strutted over to the dresser and made a show of pulling on fresh boxers and pants, then drooped his ears at his own boldness. Still blushing, he buttoned her tail strap without being asked. And if his paws strayed a little while they were back there, she couldn't say she minded.

"Thanks." She spread her arms. "Respectable?"

Deep blue eyes flashed over her. "More than you usually look before coffee." His ears lifted. "Wait, where's your bra?"

"Upstairs in my dresser." She gave a knowing smirk. "I haven't worn one around the house since you got here. Not a great idea on a hike, by the way—learned that the first day."

A deep pink rushed to the insides of his erect ears.

With an exasperated groan, she puffed up her chest and wiggled for emphasis. "You seriously didn't notice?"

He gave a shy shake of his head, eyes locked on her breasts. "I noticed." He blushed even redder. "I just didn't know you wanted me to."

"Sheesh, Maxie." She leaned back, paws covering her face. "It's a miracle I ever seduced you." She turned to open the door for him.

A gentle husky paw closed around her wrist. He pulled her into a soft embrace, pressing her rumpled t-shirt to the bare fur of his chest. Then his muzzle lowered onto hers in a soft, slow kiss. His fingers trailed through her hair to cup her cheek. His eyes met hers, misty and sincere. "I'm really glad you did, Kylie."

The otter wiggled with joy against him. "Me too."

After another warm moment, she stepped aside and let him out the door. Padding through the entryway, he glanced up the stairs, ears perked for any noise, then poked his nose into the kitchen. He returned after a moment with a note.

Kids -
Gone to town to pick up replacement stair railing.
- LB

Kylie's sigh of relief stirred the paper. "Dodged a bullet there."

Max's eyes rolled, then his stomach gurgled.

She glanced his way. "Breakfast?"

Options bounced around his mind, evidenced by the set of his muzzle. "Waffles?"

"Sure!" She padded after him to the kitchen.

He smiled and started gathering ingredients: waffle mix, eggs, milk, oil.

The otter left him to whip them together and scampered into the dining room to rummage through boxes. Where had Mom put the small appliances? She searched, until, in the third box, it shone with promise.

With a triumphant squawk, she paraded into the room with a waffle iron, which she set on the counter and opened it to reveal fish-shaped spaces.

The husky groaned. "Of course. Where the heck did you find a fish-shaped novelty waffle iron?"

"It's not novelty! It's imported. Taiyaki are the waffles of the Orient." She dug through the various jars in the door of the fridge, letting her tail sway against his wrist.

His paws traced its contours. Rough paw pads sang over slick fur as he slipped a hand the wrong way against the fur and tugged the tail-clasp of her jeans.

A squeak bounced her upright, a jar of red bean paste clutched to her chest. "Hey!" A skip closed the distance, bringing her muzzle to his cheek. A kiss. Their eyes met in a sparkle of happiness. "You're lucky I like you, Maxie."

"No kidding." He wagged, then turned to measure batter into the iron, spreading it so it'd adhere to the surface when closed.

Kylie nestled in next to him and glopped bean paste into each tray, closing the iron with an expert flick of her webbed paws. She then pushed him back against the cabinets and kissed him again. Her tongue swirled around his, only stopping when a soft click announced the taiyaki had cooked.

After toasting a few more of the fish-shaped pastries, Kylie tossed them in a paper bag and headed to the door with a smile.

The husky followed, led by the smell. "Umm, where are we going?"

"That curio shop you told me about. I'd never even heard about it before yesterday." She swung the bag.

His muzzle tracked the bag, though his eyes stayed on her. "You think the owner knows something? What makes you think he'd tell us?"

"Because we'll show him the disk." The otter grabbed her satchel and backed out the doorway.

Closing the door after them, he leaned down to sniff at the pastries. "You don't think that'll make us look...?"

"Crazy? Max, I can either spend all my time telling people I'm sane, or hunt a monster and prove it." Heading past a stack of new shingles, she handed him another fish-shaped waffle.

The dog ate half the pastry in a series of happy chomps, then nodded.

They padded across the driveway. Cool shade welcomed them to the forest as they followed old game trails. The otter spun to survey her boyfriend. A lingering tension clung to his posture. His ears strained, perked upright and nose sniffing for any incoming monsters. She smiled his way, though, and took one of his big paws in hers. Like he'd said, nobody had ever seen monsters this close to town. His eyes met hers. A smile grew on his muzzle.

The ground sloped down to Windfall, easing each stride. Her gait bounced even more, though, mulling over the events and sensations of last night. A little sore now perhaps, but he'd filled her so well. Her muscles clenched just thinking about it. And the doggy had more to give; they hadn't even worked his knot in. Maybe if she took a nice hot shower first, she'd be stretchier? Maybe he could join her? Possibilities swirled into daydreams, ceasing only when she realized they'd stopped.

Max, ears cocked and amused, fish-pastry in paw, watched her watch him.

The otter wiped the obscene smile from her muzzle, then shrugged with a blush.

Silent but smiling, he wiped crumbs on his jeans and drew her close. A soft nuzzle grew into a kiss, then bloomed into several more. The soft sound of wind on leaves swept around them, the landscape alive and brimming with wonder. She lived in a world with monsters now, but she'd found something else with Max, something that made moments like this utterly safe.

The kisses tapered off, leaving them standing in each other's embrace. Max tilted his head onward, tail swishing in the breeze. They continued through the woods. As they finished the last of the pastries, their steps fell on sun-hot sidewalks instead of mossy earth. They ambled through town, past locals with places to be and tourists looking for the same. Even after months in town, the degree to which weekends enlivened it amazed her. The streets flooded with tourists and locals, eager to lose money in the gaudy shops. A few people whispered and pointed, but no one stopped them for autographs, which she took as a blessing. Slipping through the last of the bustle, they reached the curio shop, only to find a closed sign.

Kylie groaned. "Seriously?"

Max's thick paw settled on her shoulder. He drew a rumpled list from his pocket and consulted it. "Plenty of other places to check out." He pulled out his phone and opened the map. "Shrubs of Mystery maybe?"

"That's an actual landscaping business, Max. Mom buys plants there." She brushed a lock of hair from her muzzle, trying to look flirtatious. "Anything else you're in the mood for?"

"Hmm." The canine peered down the street toward the center of town, pointy ears erect and scanning. "I guess we could find something to do around town until it's open."

She nuzzled his throat and watched his ears perk, felt his heartbeat accelerate. "Or we could find something to do back at the house."

In the quiet shade of the storefront, he kissed her. A quick touch of lips as their hands found each other's hips, followed by a lingering smile at one another. He wagged.

She wiggled as a glow of joy spread through her body. Nothing could ruin this moment. Nothing.

Behind them, someone's phone played a fake camera shutter sound.

They spun to see a massive rhino holding a minuscule phone, bouncing on his toes and making a sound like a teakettle.

The otter swept both hands to the sides. "Karl, are you kidding me?"

Grinning, he gave them a bouncy shrug. "No one online would've believed me—it's every shipper's dream. You guys have even more chemistry than on the show!"

Max blushed, frozen.

She advanced on the rhino. "Gimme the phone, Karl."

The fan cradled his mobile against his chest, looking sad. He glanced back and forth between them, hoping at least one would cave.

Repelled by guilt, she pinched the bridge of her muzzle. "Max, tell him he's gotta delete that pic."

Still pink in the ears, the husky shrugged.

"Max!" The otter eeled between him and the rhino, unsure what to do. "You're supposed to be on my side."

The husky offered half a smirk. "He'll just take another one, or someone else will. Unless we're going to stop kissing in public." Pondering the notion for a moment, his expression soured a little. "I vote no on that, by the way."

Meanwhile, Karl typed with astonishing speed on his phone. "You guys don't have to worry about anything. I'll make sure it gets good spin. Have you always been dating, or is this a new thing?"

"It's uh, new." Max cleared his throat under the weight of Kylie's glare. He turned to the hapless fan. "Though, uh, we should probably wait until we tell her mom until we have a press release or something."

"Oh." The rhino froze. "Oops."

The dog's ears rose. "Oops?"

"I kinda already posted it." The massive fan squirmed. "It sounded like you were cool with it."

Kylie groaned. "This is so going to bite us in the tail…"

With a deep breath, the dog patted her shoulder. "I'm sure it'll be okay."

She head-butted his chest once in slow motion. "Aren't you supposed to be the shy one?"

"I am, but I'm trying to be realistic: you're my canon ship now." He gave her shoulders a tender squeeze. "Besides, who's really going to see—?"

Across the street, the civilian garb of a cheerleader caught her eye. "Oh carp!" She grabbed him by the elbow and dragged him behind a stand of fresh vegetables.

Max heeled, but lifted his eyebrows.

"Ugh. Cindy." The otter hissed. "Just act natural."

"The only acting I know." He studied a rutabaga, then glanced around. "Where'd Karl go?"

The otter scoured the street, but found no sign of their massive fan. "Stupid rhino ninjas."

The stand's deer proprietor froze in surprise at her grumbling, but that was nothing new. Deer were always freezing about something. She had trouble looking the poor guy in the eye after what they'd seen in the woods. Instead, she watched Cindy from the corner of her eye.

"Never known you to have a blood feud." He presented her with an eggplant. "How'd that even start?"

"I got a lot of attention when I got to town, which meant less for Cindy. Since she gains nourishment by having people stare at her cleavage, she attacked me as a rival for her food source."

"You let her get to you, huh?"

"I'm used to dealing with adults. I mean, look." She nodded across the street where Cindy stood with a friend. "Even her friend can't stand her."

"Oh?" Max leaned out into the open to stare, without a hint of subtlety.

"Don't stare. She can sense it." She poked him with the eggplant and hauled him back into cover. "See how her friend slouches whenever Cindy's not looking. She clearly wants to be somewhere else. Clara or something is her name; I've seen her before."

As they watched, Cindy yapped all the way to a shiny red sedan, hopped inside, and made a cursory attempt to invite her friend along before driving off. The brown and white rabbit sighed, hefted her plastic shopping bags and headed across the street.

"Doesn't even want a ride." The otter squeezed an avocado, then nodded with approval and pulled out her wallet. "Can't say I blame her."

Max nodded, still watching the bunny.

She glanced over some other veggies. "Hey, do you like cucumber in sushi? Max?" She turned to the husky.

But the dog had gone, dashing down the street toward the bunny.

The lagomorph flinched, drawing her bags against her in shock, as the muscled canine charged over.

Max stooped to pick up an aerosol can. "Excuse me, miss." He offered the glinting canister. "Dropped this."

She took it with a harried smile, brushing a floppy ear from her cheek. "Thanks." She glanced from the hunky husky to Kylie, considered them a moment, then bounced off.

He strutted back, wagging.

The otter leaned against the stag's display stand. "Great job, Sir Ocelot. She's totally not going to bring this up to Cindy and draw her evil eye once again upon us."

"Did you see what she was carrying?" He smiled. "Pepper spray. Pole-cat-brand pepper spray."

"Lots of girls carry pepper spray."

"A can you could put on a keychain, maybe. Not one you could use to douse a fire."

"Maybe she's going to use it on Cindy." The otter scoffed. "She'd make my Yuletide card list."

"Why would she need wildlife-grade pepper spray? Does she work outside?"

Accepting her change, she took her bag of vegetables. "Nah, just in one of the tourist shops."

"Not a lot of wild predators around here." His eyes glimmered, assuring her of his supposed cunning. "Nothing for them to eat. According to the guy who owns the outdoors shop, the big game in Windfall has always been scarce. It's a real drain on the hunting industry."

"How could you possibly—?"

"This could be a lead."

Kylie crossed her arms. "This could be a pain in the tail."

His grinning muzzle dipped to bump hers. "If we're nice to her, she might convince Cindy you don't want attention and that she can have it all to herself."

Arching backward, she released a groan. "It wouldn't work: Cindy's more of an attention black hole. An insatiable vortex that consumes all in its path." She patted his arm. "But it's cute that Hollywood hasn't corrupted your innocence."

One wide paw settled on her hip. "I think people are pretty decent."

The otter lifted a digit. "A week ago, you thought that monsters weren't real. Shows what you know."

"Good that we know now." He squeezed her a little closer. "I like learning new things."

"Yeah." She leaned into him, his closeness lifting her heart. "Me too."

A bell tolled, chiming out the hour. A few people on the street noticed, but most continued on without a glance at the town hall's bell tower. Max stared, though, with that singular confusion dogs got when trying to focus.

A moment passed. The bells stopped. She looked up at him. "What?"

His gaze narrowed on the bell tower. "The book our shopkeeper friend sold me had photos from an exhibit in town hall."

Kylie's arms crossed. "You wanna check it out, don't you?"

"Last I heard, we were hunting the monster." He glanced down at her, amused. "Unless you have a better idea."

"Just one…" She bit her lip, slipping him a coy look. "…over and over…"

The husky's ears stiffened with interest. A soft whine escaped his muzzle.

"…but Mom's probably back at the house by now." Reason caught up with her libido. Sighing, she swung the bag of vegetables against her knees. "So we might as well look at old homestead photos."

His paw closed around hers, gentle and strong. Hand in hand, they headed for the center of town.

Pamphlets stirred as they opened the door, pinned to the cork board like a still-twitching insect collection. Cool shade and old tile welcomed Max and Kylie to the quiet interior of the town hall. A single sleepy clerk oversaw the lack of activity from a scuffed counter. At the heart of the room stood a massive landscape painting of the area at the town's founding: rustic shacks, heaps of downed trees, and minecarts brimming with silver.

Between a rack of maps and a table of coupon flyers, glass enclosed a timeline from the town's founding to the last time someone cared to update it, which seemed about half as recent. At the ancient end stood a pillar of bone, a meter tall and charred up one side. A selection of photographic plates and informational cards hovered around it.

"The Windfall Cataclysm." The canine tapped the glass with a claw, just in front of a painting of leveled trees. "The storm that flattened this forest enough for people to settle it."

She padded to the burnt pillar. "And they celebrated with postmodern art?"

He studied the placard. "This bone totem was found near the center of the area leveled by the storm. Archeologists believe it to be a tribute to the spirits of fertility and good harvest."

"Archeologists!" The otter rolled her eyes. "They're gonna find your laptop in a few centuries and think it's a fertility idol."

The dog nodded and glanced her way. "They wouldn't be wrong."

"Max!" Her webbed paw batted his elbow.

He crouched for a closer look at the totem's base. "Yours has fanfiction of us."

"Okay…fair point." She rummaged in her satchel, found the bone disk, and held it up against the glass. "The carvings look the same."

He nodded. "Meaning the most abstract totems ever."

"Maybe they eroded?" Slipping the disk back into her bag, she put a hand on his shoulder. "Who knows how long these things had been out in the rain before people found them."

The dog looked up. "Bone weathers more like wood than stone; it cracks and splinters, but this…" He pointed through the glass. "…looks smooth, almost like one solid piece. But if it were petrified wood, it wouldn't have burned like this."

Kylie took a picture with her phone. "Could be a hoax."

He stood. "Yeah, but why hide part of the hoax in a shack?"

"I'd hide pieces all over." She shrugged. "So more people would find them."

"Hmm." Studying the display for another moment, he flipped through the pamphlets for any references to the pillar, then surrendered with a shrug. "The only mentions of the totem use it as shorthand for mysterious relics in town. They use it as clip art on anything supposedly supernatural."

"So they think they understand it, but they don't, but they use it to symbolize what they don't understand? That's pretty meta. Maybe it's art after all." She opened the door to a gray sky. The air smelled of thrown dust and rejoicing greenery. Wind stirred bits of litter down the sidewalk. "Looks like rain out there."

The husky's blue eyes traced the street, watching as vendors pulled displays indoors. "Yeah, we'd better get back. Curio shop can wait."

They ducked out the door and jogged north, droplets of rain scattering around them. The otter tossed back a catch-me grin, then zipped off with her tail raised and swaying.

Entranced for a moment, the canine shook off distraction and water to give chase. Block after block, he gained on her. After a few minutes, they reached the edge of town, clothes close and heavy with rain. She paused a bare instant, watching the droplets dance down the branches, and he grabbed her tail. A squeak, then she dodged into the woods, jumping logs and mud puddles. Caught in brush and harried by branches, he fell behind. The otter hopped onto a stump to gloat, only to see him burst through the impediments with a playful growl.

Far behind, dark clouds rolled in from the sea. Curtains of rain followed and stirred the forest into a tangle of sound: spatters against trunks, taps on rotten logs, and splats into mossy ground. Lightning flashed above, thunder snarling at their backs. Together, laughing, racing, they jogged to the old game trail and scampered uphill toward home. Steep slopes and slippery soil tripped them here and there, but never enough that a quick hand from the other couldn't haul them back to their feet. Rain scattered off her face and neck to soak the neck of her shirt.

Halfway home, her breath kept cutting short and each step came harder. She gasped, then writhed as large paws snatched her from the ground.

Without breaking stride, he scooped her up and carried her against his chest. His loping strides bounded them up the hill. The smooth ripple of muscles through his body against hers brought back a flash of last night.

"Hey!" She squawked a laugh, squirmed a lot, and gripped him close. "Put me down, you lunatic!"

"You're lucky I don't use you as an umbrella." Breathing hard, he lifted her a little higher in jest. Now that he'd caught her, he loped into an easy jog.

She tucked her whiskered muzzle under his chin. "I'm nobody's umbrella!"

A laugh rumbled through his chest to her. "Then why are you waterproof?"

Dripping wet and laughing, he carried her up the driveway and set her on the porch. They stood in each other's arms and caught up to their breath, then caught up on kisses. Their muzzles met in a mix of passion and summer rain. Lightning crackled above, wind sweeping the woods, but nothing could break them from making out against the screen door. A wild urge rose in Kylie: she imagined him making love to her as the storm thundered like their hearts, the wind howling with her lover as he came inside her, leaving her as wet inside as she was out. Someday, she promised herself. For now, she groped his back and tail, then opened the door so they could tumble inside. They could just slip into his room without her mom hearing from upstairs; it would be the perfect plan.

At least until her mom leaned in from the living room and yelled: "Hey kids, you're trending!"

Kylie blinked, torn from her building frenzy. "Trending?" Then she groaned as her mind flashed back to the meeting with Karl and his stupid smartphone. "Dang it, Max." She bopped his shoulder and hurried inside.

The dog doffed his soaked hoodie as he followed, then stood dripping on the entryway tile, looking amazing in a tight t-shirt. "How bad is it?"

Pushing up her glasses, the elder otter glanced down at her laptop and scrolled through social media posts. "Very good, at least for the DVD sales. Outside the fandom, I don't think you're famous enough for it to appear on any but the most desperate TV gossip shows."

"Just the kind my mother watches…" Worry crept onto his muzzle as he felt for his phone. "I'm going to hear about this."

"She almost found out about it before I did." The middle-aged lutrine smirked. "I'm impressed. You two went from living in denial to making out on the streets and I never even knew. Well, I mean, I knew, but it's a better story if I didn't."

Kylie froze from wringing herself dry. "Mom!"

"Hey, the Internet found out you were dating before your mother." She poked a webbed finger at the couple. "I'm allowed to tease."

The younger otter scrambled for a change in topic. "Uh…you get your stair railing?"

Laura glanced out at the car, out in the driveway getting a thorough rinsing. "I was waiting for Max and his muscles to be home to unload it. It can wait till the weather clears."

"I'm as wet as I can get." He finished checking his phone for messages and set it on the table. "I don't mind."

"Fine, go." The elder otter rolled her eyes. "I might as well exploit your fondness for my daughter. Just don't hurt yourself."

"Sure thing, Ms. Bevy." He stretched his arms, shaking off a little of the rainwater.

"Laura." She wiggled her whiskers in annoyance. "Seriously."

He smiled as he padded back out into the rain. Wind clattered the door shut after him.

"That boy has terminal politeness." She shook her head at the retreating husky, then turned to her daughter. "Sounds like you had an eventful trip to town."

Kylie shot a glare in the direction of town, hoping it would hit Karl. "What's the best way to kill a rhino?"

"Wait for her to die of old age." The elder otter tapped away at her keyboard. "They're three hundred pounds of armor plating, sweetie." She didn't look up. "Glad things are going well with Max. Guess your scheme worked."

Her daughter bit her lip. "Yeah, I was over-thinking it. Thanks for being cool." She gestured to the house, then shook water off her tail. "Compared to how you could be, I mean."

A wry look lifted her mother's eyebrow. "Sweetie, if I were going to object, I probably would've done it in the three months you were planning this visit. You know I think Max is a sweetheart; the boy lived with us for three years." She drained the last third of her tea in a single gulp. "Besides, you're both adults; I figure I ought to at least try to be one."

Max wrestled a massive box through the door, then set it down with a thud that rattled Laura's teacup.

The slender lutrine jumped at the noise. "Holy mackerel. What's that even made outta?"

"Wrought iron. Very classy." Laura smiled at the husky. "Thank you, Max dear."

"Sure thing, Ms. B—"

"But!" She jabbed a digit his way.

He straightened, ears perked. "But?"

"You're only allowed to date my daughter if you start calling me Laura."

Max chuckled, ears drooping in playful defeat. His tail swished, scattering raindrops on the floorboards. "Yes, M—Laura."

CHAPTER 14
The Cave

STRANGEVILLE (SAT/4P)

S05E05 "Crystal Clear": After aquiring cursed costume jewelry, the gang investigates a local new-age shop whose wares are slowly draining the life force from buyers.

Late morning light filled the house, banishing the shadows that conspired in the countless nooks and corners. Even a lingering tension from a half-forgotten nightmare steadily evaporated in the morning sunshine. Kylie bounced downstairs and crossed the entryway to Max's room. As she touched his door and it drifted open, she heard him talking on the other side. Even before she could make out the words, the tone of his voice stopped her at the threshold.

He cradled a phone to his drooped ear and paced around the bed. His large white paw almost covered the mobile, but he held it with care. "No, I don't think she wants to move down there. Because her mom is up here and they just finished moving in. Yeah, I know you're out there. And that you're my mother."

She stood in his doorway and made no move to hide. Wouldn't want him to think she was eavesdropping. Besides, she could hear everything better this way.

The husky didn't seem to notice. He mostly played with his watch, phone pinned between his shoulder and cheek. "I really don't know if that means I'm staying up here. We haven't talked about it. We'll talk about it. Nothing's off the table."

Tension gripped her guts. She'd tried not to think about it, but he'd only ever planned to visit for a few weeks. The memory of the long, lonely months apart burned at her. Could they really go back to just talking online? When would she even get to see him again? She'd just gotten Max; could she even handle being in a long-distance relationship?

"Yeah, love you too. Bye." He stuck his phone back in his pocket and turned, then lifted his ears as he noticed her. His expression brightened a little. "Hey."

"Hey." She leaned against the doorframe. "I think this is the part where I pretend I didn't hear any of that and we let the tension build up 'til we have a big fight."

He grimaced. "We've both seen way too much TV."

She nodded at the phone sticking out of his pocket. "Was that your mom?"

He nodded, pocketing the little plastic brick and looking unhappy.

A deep breath as she put on a brave front. Max's mom was hard to describe, though the word "matriarch" always sprung to mind. Max's descriptions of his family farm conjured images of an ant hill, with dedicated workers serving under a domineering queen. The strongest memory Kylie had of the woman was of her towering in their little Hollywood apartment, saying goodbye to her only son for the first time and clearly resisting the impulse to stuff Max back into the truck and speed back to Montana. The otter tried for a diplomatic tone. "That sounded a little tense."

He closed his eyes and groaned. "My parents never really understood why I wanted to do the show. Dad, at least, thought it was a great opportunity. Mom took it personally."

She swished her tail in consideration, then lifted a spread paw. "So why'd they let you?"

The husky blinked and considered for a moment. "I guess because I really liked it. And you and I hit it off. And…I don't know, it just all came together. Besides, nobody knew I'd be on the show for three years."

"Or that it'd be on the air that long." Her arms crossed. "And now you're supposed to pick up where you left off? Start slinging hay bales or whatever? Do they need another pair of hands that badly?"

"No, it's a dog thing." He swirled his fingers at the complexity in an effort to distill it. "Mom's the alpha, and she wants me back because I'm part of her pack."

The otter perked. "So are we a pack now?"

He pondered that for a moment, then nodded. "Sure. Though your mom doesn't exactly flaunt being the alpha."

Kylie snickered, but the noise faded fast in the quiet bedroom. Anxious paws carried her forward. "They don't like that you left again?"

"They don't like that I've been gone for years and don't show much interest in sticking around." He sat on the bed, hands spread on the bedcovers. "Leaving the pack's not taboo or anything; they just miss me."

"So you're not going back?" She winced, scared of possible answers. "Right away, I mean?"

"They miss me, but I'd miss you more." He touched her arm. "And they don't need my help fighting monsters."

She hugged him and nuzzled into his neck fur, then pulled back to study his expression. With her standing and him sitting, their gazes were almost level. "She's not going to come here and carry you away by the scruff, is she?"

A single wag stirred the sheets. He patted her flank. "We shouldn't give her the idea, but I'm probably in the clear for now. I'll stay as long as you need me."

She tried not to think too hard about that sentence. She needed him in more ways than she could count. Instead, she changed the subject to something she hoped he'd find a little more pleasant. "I have the day off again." Her webbed fingers caressed his cheek fluff. "Anything you wanna do?"

His pointy ears dipped, tinged with pink inside. Those broad shoulders gave a shy shrug.

With a chitter of excitement, the otter scampered to shut the door. In an instant, she flowed back onto his lap, her shorts-clad legs spread around his. Her muzzle ran along his, drawing him into kisses. Swift and sweet, each kiss led into the next, chasing her heartbeats faster and faster.

Wide paws caressed her back, smoothing her vest. His tail swished over the blankets. Warm breath stirred her whiskers. He pulled her close, closer.

She toyed with his ears, their fur running like silk under paw pads and webbing. Her thick tail slid up and down his legs and ruffled his jeans. She scooted forward, so the base of it rocked against his crotch, savoring the growing warmth there. A juicy thrill tingled between her folds. Just a few layers of fabric between him and her, between him being inside her, pumping her full of thick canine cock. "We can be a little wilder this time." Her nose brushed his. "Mom's out working in the greenhouse."

The husky bucked and squirmed under her. The bulge of his crotch pressed between her legs as they rocked together. With great care, he kissed along her jawline and down her smooth neck.

A tide of desire rising, she gripped the back of his shirt, lifted it, and caressed under it. His chest fur fluffed through her hands. Seeing him without a shirt on the show had been titillating, even before she had a crush on him, but touching him sent her mind racing. Memories of their night together flash-flooded her mind, leaving her gasping at his every caress. Eager now, her hands dove to the front of his pants, where they groped and squeezed, and started to undo his fly.

He whimpered with delight, but set his paws on hers. "We took things kind of fast, you know, before." Those deep blue eyes looked up at her with doggish devotion. Their whiskers touched as he licked her chin. "Maybe we should start from the beginning; take things a step at a time."

With a grin, she kissed his nose. "Okay, Maxie." She traced a fingertip where his hip met his thigh. "What's our first step?"

"Well, you could take your clothes off." He put on a cocky grin, even as his ears found a deeper shade of pink. "I'd like a better look."

She flashed him a smirk and a sassy sway of her hips and tail. "Didn't get a good enough look in the shower?"

A nervous chuckle accompanied a shy dip of his muzzle. "Not even close."

Heart soaring, heartbeat fluttering, Kylie slid off his lap. She shrugged out of her vest and drew the t-shirt over her head. The garments fell to the carpet in a pool of soft fabric. Next, unsteady webbed paws unzipped her shorts, unbuttoned the tail strap, and let them slide to her ankles. Biting her lip, she tugged her panties down with nervous mirth. Twisting her arms back, she fumbled through the clasps of her bra and tossed it aside. With a little smile, she belatedly tried for a striptease, but found no sexy way to kick off her shorts and panties. Nude now, only the familiar assurance in his eyes kept her from feeling exposed.

Max sat bolt upright and watched with rapt anticipation. His toes curled against the carpet as if he were fighting the urge to pounce her. That white-tipped tail drummed a rhythm of excitement on the mattress. "You look amazing."

Blushing, the lutrine rolled her eyes and swayed her tail. "C'mon, Maxie." Her paws tried to wring the nerves from the moment. "I wanna see you too."

"In a minute." His big snowy paws settled on her hips, pulled her into a kiss, and guided her to the bed. With soft blue bedroom eyes, he flashed her a smile. "I want to try something."

With a happy squeak, she put her hands over his. "Oh?"

He sat on the edge of the bed and drew her forward until she stood between his knees, then into a kiss. Her pelt pressed against the soft cotton of his jeans, a delicious jolt of friction. His lips lifted from hers, the warm rush of his breath the only warning before they descended again, this time on her nipples. Her startled intake of breath only pressed her closer to him, and the electric rasp of his tongue across her sensitive flesh made her grip his shoulders to steady herself. He gave a happy little rumble, and the thought that he liked the taste of her kindled a fire that started in her belly and settled deep between her thighs.

He licked with deliberate patience, teasing her stiffening nipples in turn with lips and tongue. Those big, warm paws slipped down off her hips to cup the curve of her ass and knead, pulling the otter closer and making her shiver all over again. By the time he turned, easing her beside him onto the bed, she was panting through clenched teeth, her fingers buried in his short, thick hair.

Regaining some degree of her senses, she wriggled onto the bed and swam up the sheets to the pillow. Giddy, she grabbed a pawful of blankets and drew it to her face with a coy smile.

His fingertips outlined her every curve. They started at her shoulders and spread over her breasts before brushing her flanks and along her arms. Tracing next down the length of her tail, then up from her toes to her calves to her thighs, he smiled at the way her short fur flipped back down as he let it go.

Wiggles of anticipation danced down her body. Tickles and titillation interwove across her nervous system. She loved the feel of this powerful canine treating her so tenderly.

He nuzzled her breasts, lapping again at her nipples. His blunt claws scritched through her pelt. Those thick paws explored along the sweep of her hips, then down to grip the curve of her rump and startle a squeak of surprise out of her. With a growled chuckle, the large canine leaned in, holding her by the hips. His wide tongue lapped at her stomach to stir her creamy fur.

Giggles bubbled up from around the same place. She felt herself relax a little. Same old Max, just with the simmering heat of longing layered over his familiar warmth.

He knelt between her legs and spread her thighs with infinite care. His nostrils flared as they took in her scent. That wet black nose hovered over her slit. His fingers edged closer and closer. His eyes met hers. He waited, ears cocked, wagging. The gentlest touch traced her outer folds.

She grinned up at him and spread her legs further. Her heartbeat thundered ahead with her thoughts. Her best friend was caressing the light fur of her crotch, exploring her. Her toes and tail curled in anticipation.

His fingertip sank into her. He watched her expression, husky ears tuned to her. "Is this okay?"

"Mmmhmm." A contented sigh breezed through her body as she rocked her hips, inviting him further.

His finger slid into her folds, exploring all the while. The rougher texture of his paw pad traced around the inside of her passage. While careful with his claws, he didn't seem to notice the ticklish effect his fur had on her. In, then out. And again. A little faster now, the friction stirring heat deep within her. He worked a second digit inside.

Her hips pivoted to help him touch everywhere. She thought back to all the times she'd used her toy and that warm night she'd had him inside her. Still hard to believe. Hard to believe that such a sweet, darling dog wanted her in all the ways she wanted him.

He crawled up the bed to lay beside her. One arm supported her neck while the other massaged back down her flank, leaving a slight trail of her own fluids. A breath later, his paw played again over her tender slit, caressing and spreading its supple pink lips. His fingers, soaked with her moisture, stroked in and out of her. The now-slick fur teased her every surface. His knuckles bumped her stiff clitoris, which sent bursts of pleasure up her body. She squirmed with desire.

His voice, barely a whisper, teased at the fur of her ear. "You're so warm, Kylie. Do you like this?"

A squeak of desire escaped her throat and she nodded frantically, willing him onward. This close to climax, she'd always speed up, push herself over the edge. Max, though, continued slowly exploring her. The tension built and built, wiggling her hips and tightening her grip on the sheets. He studied her reactions, ears tuned to her every moan, and caressed those textured paw pads along every inch of her vaginal walls. Wet, gentle noises filled the room, punctuated by his panted breath and the swish of a wagging tail. With those long, thick fingers, he could reach so much deeper inside her than her finger webs would allow. Her hips bucked up against his hand with trembling urgency.

She whimpered and writhed.

Her heart raced.

Her teeth grit.

Her breath and patience ran short. She moaned and reached down to rub her clit with frantic abandon. "Oh! Mmmm!"

Max growled in approval, licked her neck, and at last fingered her faster.

Her gasps came splashed with chitters of joy. Thighs clenched around his hand, her body rolled across the bed on waves of bliss. When the last great wave of delight had crashed over her, she flopped to the mattress, bounced once or twice on the springs, then lay dazed, her boyfriend's room hazy through the blur of pleasure.

The husky licked her cheek as amusement rumbled deep in his chest. "You totally made that squeaky noise when you came."

She rolled back and forth in his arms, so sensitive that the blanket against her nipples was electric. "Shut up! It felt good!"

He patted her flank. "You're adorable, rudderbutt." His muscled arms held her close.

Wiggling back against him, she lost herself in his warm fluff. Her tail found its way between his legs as she held his hands. Her entire body hummed with afterglow. She drifted in and out of dozing, cuddling with her husky pillow. Moments passed. Beat by beat, her heart finished racing. Afterglow faded from her supple body. She leaned in and kissed him. "My turn."

With a smile, Max rolled over and sat on the edge of the bed. Those gentle eyes held the patience of an old friend and the eagerness of a new lover.

His girlfriend slithered through the last of her post-orgasmic haze and off the bed, whereupon she attacked his pants. They proved impervious to her efforts, even after she'd unzipped his fly and unclasped the tail strap. After a few squawks of frustration from her, he lifted his rear off the blankets. She then grabbed at his boxers before they could mount the same kind of resistance.

Naked, he sat, tail wagging in avid anticipation. His cock poked a little ways out of its sheath, a triangle of red against his pure white stomach.

The lutrine knelt between his thighs, nuzzling his sheath, fondling his balls. "They're really warm." Her wide nose brushed into his fluff. "I should've guessed, huh?"

The canine whimpered.

Seeing his crotch for the first time in good lighting, she blinked at the emerging tip of his cock, easing back his sheath to reveal more of the crimson flesh. "Huh. Not the color I was expecting."

Max gripped the comforter, trying to hold onto some shred of composure as soft, as webbed fingers cupped his balls. "You've...you've thought about the color?"

Kylie bit her lower lip, her smile mischievous as she coaxed more of him into the open. "I've thought about a lot of things, Maxie. The color. The texture." A dainty finger explored across his tip as her voice dropped to a simmering whisper. "The taste..."

She figured choking on her partner might spoil the mood and decided against trying to take his full length in her muzzle the first time. Instead, she settled for working the tip and using her hands on the rest. Remembering how he'd stroked himself their first night together, she caressed his shaft, running webbed paws all over his length. His sheath felt so soft compared to the shaft or the swelling knot. Her hands gave it little strokes in time with her taking him deep in her muzzle, which resulted in some very satisfying noises from the canine. Pulling off for a breath, she gripped his knot to maneuver him. Her hand squeezed just a little too hard behind that swell of husky flesh…

A gasp.

He shuddered, his balls twitched, then a pulse of tension rushed up the underside of his cock. A shot of thick canine semen surged against her lips to drip down her chin. The dog bit back a wild howl, reining it back to a desperate moan.

By the second blast, she managed to get her lips back around his tip. A heavy, salty surge of flavor flooded her mouth. That shaft of naked flesh pulsed again, and this time she wiggled her tongue against the head of his member.

An ecstatic whine emanated from the dog. His eyes squeezed shut. His body trembled.

The remains of his first blast of semen oozed from her chin down over her hands. Softer pulses followed, tinged with salt, woven rich with musk. He leaned over her and gasped. His panted breath stirred her hair, hot with a hint of toothpaste. Even after he stopped spurting, she held him in her muzzle, enjoying the sounds she drew from him with every suckle.

When at last she pulled off, she worked the fluids around in her mouth with approval and ran her paws up the whites of his thighs. A thin strand of saliva and semen connected his cock tip to her lips. Chin propped against the base of his dick, she looked up at him and licked her lips. "Good?"

"Very." He panted for breath. His chest rose and fell as his erection started to fade.

Curious otter paws drifted back to his crotch. She watched as his knot shrank, after a minute or so getting small enough to slip back into his sheath. After seeing how he reacted to her paws, she squeezed down on where it would be buried inside her. She'd been a little intimidated, but, having seen it up close, she found herself more eager than ever. "I thought knots stayed hard for like half an hour?"

"Depends on where you put them." Shaky paws cupped her face and wiped a drip of cum from her chin. "You have no idea how good that felt."

The otter eeled up onto the bed to snuggle at his side. "I may've picked up on your subtle signals."

He smiled and breathed and held her close.

Kylie gave a soft, happy sigh and nuzzled into the plush fur on Max's throat. Her hand played along her belly, her whole body still tingly and satisfied. "I'm starting to really like this bed."

He rested his chin between her ears. "It does have a good track record."

They lay back on the sheets, letting time drift by. Their scents hung thick in the air. She hoped the room would air out before her mom came home. On a whim, she reached up and coaxed the window open, just to be safe. She curled back up against Max, feeling one of his massive arms wrap around her shoulder, and let sleep creep up on her. She had barely closed her eyes when her stomach grumbled. With no small effort, she summoned the will to move once again and rolled to face him. "Wanna get some lunch in town?" She wiped the last traces of his semen from her paws to the sheets. "After we clean up, of course."

He blinked, but squeezed her shoulders. "Uh, sure?"

Noon banished shadows and gleamed off the previous day's rain. Restaurants had started to fill with lunch guests, including the patio of Pinchy's, where several cubs sported paper lobster hats. Otter instincts roused at the scent of chowder, Kylie still refrained from scampering to the front of the line to demand the creamy delight du jour. They waited in line and bought two containers of soup, which they ate as they walked.

At the window of Windfall Hunting Co., Max stopped to look inside. "I've been thinking: if we're going to cross paths with this thing, we should probably have some kind of plan." His gaze met hers. "And by plan, I mean implements of destruction."

Kylie cocked an eyebrow. "You're a big strong farm type. Can't you just punch it?" The lutrine made two tiny fists and socked the air in front of her.

He lowered her fists. "Kylie, how many horror movies have we seen?"

"I dunno." She looked up to tally them in her mind, then gave up. "A lot."

The dog nodded. "And in how many of them has punching the monster worked?"

"Hmm. Valid point." She turned to survey the displayed sporting goods. Her ears twitched in consideration. "What would work?"

"I dunno." A shrug rolled his thick shoulders. "Claymores?"

The otter cocked an eyebrow. "The swords or the land mines?"

He blinked, a bit nervous. "Which do we have?"

Her paws spread against the cool window glass. "Neither, probably."

"Pity." The husky crossed his arms. "We could strap claymores to claymores for double the destruction. It'd be straight out of *Revenginator*."

With a smirk, she nodded at the window. "Or we could buy a gun."

He gave her a wry look. "I know how to pose with a gun, not shoot one."

She bumped his hip with hers. "What kind of farm dog are you?"

His deep blue eyes rolled. "The kind who spent his formative years doing shoulder-rolls around a Hollywood backlot instead of learning to hunt."

"Hmmm." Cupping her paws against the glass, her glance zipped further into the store. "Think monsters are vulnerable to pepper spray?"

"I guess? I mean, acid in the eyes is probably a bad day for anybody. Still, we should play it safe and buy the biggest can they sell." He paused.

"Wait." A second ticked by, thoughts forming behind the husky's furrowed brow. "Didn't that bunny friend…?"

"Yeah." Realization sprang through her. "You don't think…"

The dog spread his paws. "We could ask her. Do you know where she works?"

"Remember the touristy cave TV ad? That's where I'd seen her." The otter snapped her fingers, then grimaced. "Do we really need to hang out with Cindy's pal? We could just wait for dark and sneak into the caves."

"Yes, because we're cool with hunting monsters but not with paying admission." He flicked through his phone's map. "Crystal Caverns?"

"Yeah…" The otter gave a resigned sigh and a nod. "That's the place."

The Crystal Caverns had far more than just cave tours. The giant, enthusiastically-colored sign out front said so. Walking at Max's side, Kylie passed troughs where a group of pups pawed through pebbles, yipping with joy to their parents when they found a chunk of dyed quartz. Before them, an old badger ignored everyone and lectured on strata at a geological pace.

The otter smirked. Max still showed some of that puppy enthusiasm now and again, extra amusing coming from someone twice her size. She liked a little cuteness in her hunky television stars.

The main building, composed of hewn rocks, sat half-buried in a hillside. The pair ducked inside, entering a gift shop stocked with suncatchers, stone wind chimes, and plastic miner's helmets with LED lanterns. At the front desk sat the brown and cream bunny from earlier, now clad in a prismatic polo shirt emblazoned with the shop's logo. She bounced upright. "Hi there!"

"Hello again." Max gave a polite nod.

Kylie followed with the requisite smile.

A look of brief horror crossed the rabbit's face as she recognized them. She froze except for her twitchy pink nose.

The otter waved her worries away with a webbed paw. "This isn't about Cindy. Or me."

Brushing her floppy ears from her face, she relaxed a little. "So why are you here?"

"We just had a couple questions." Max sat on the stool next to the counter full of rock-candy. "If that's okay."

"It's okay, really." The bunny adjusted her whiskers, looking mostly at him. "Thanks for your help back in town."

"Sure. Actually, that's one thing we came to ask about." He leaned on the countertop. "Is there some reason you need a can of wildlife pepper spray?"

Nerves swept the bunny once more. She gripped the counter. Her emerald eyes bounced from the window to the cave entrance and back to them. "Yes? Maybe? I don't know?"

The lutrine groaned. "You should tell us so we can leave before Cindy finds out we're here and drops the drama-bomb you're so scared of."

"Oh, that's not the problem." The bunny wrung her paws. "Cindy and I aren't joined at the hip, and I don't think she's very funny anymore." She fiddled with a novelty pen display. "We hung out in high school, and when she moved back I just sort of got pulled in. Sorry, am I babbling?"

"It's okay. My name's Max and you already know Kylie. She babbles, too." Ignoring his friend's sputter, the husky extended a hand. "What exactly is the problem?"

"Sarah Warren." Her soft, fluffy paw shook his. "And, well…" A nervous simper. "This is gonna sound crazy."

The otter leaned against the gift shop door. "Try me."

A deep breath, then the bunny continued. "I've wanted to tell somebody about this, but everyone seems to think I'm just trying to drum up business for Haunted Cave Tuesday. People are supposed to stay on the walking paths, but I've been exploring since I started here. Something is totally living in the caves. I've heard…noises."

"Don't your caves have speakers in them to make creepy noises?" The lutrine lifted an eyebrow.

The bunny shook her head. "The speakers are rigged up to hidden doorbells in the passage so I can trigger them on the tour. And they all play bargain basement sound effects off an old CD. This is different."

Kylie crossed her arms.

Max nodded. "So do you have some kind of evidence?"

"There's a passage, deep in the caves. Just a little chimney connecting our tunnels to the old mines below. Something keeps leaving animal carcasses in it." She paused, as though expecting them to stop her. When they only stared expectantly, she continued in a rush. "They're always gone within a few days, sometimes within hours. Nobody has seen any kind of predator in the woods for decades; you can ask the local hunters. But every few years, they all get together and scour the woods for whatever keeps killing the wild deer and turkeys. Never turns up anything."

The husky gave a slow nod. "You think it's living in your cave?"

"Or unliving?" The lutrine wiggled her fingers, then regretted saying anything. She had an unfortunate habit of snarking at people whom she suspected might dislike her. The last thing she wanted was to confirm the bunny's fears of being mocked.

"Oh." Sarah pulled out her phone. "I took some pictures. See?" Offering the screen to them, she cycled through images of bloody trails along the cave floor, along with more distant shots of carcasses and one closeup of a rough rocky ledge crisscrossed by long, deep furrows. "I don't know of anyone or anything with claws that big."

The dog waggled his mobile. "Could I get those pics?"

"Sure." The bunny swiped her paw across the screen, entering his phone number.

While they exchanged info, Kylie looked around. Among the crystal-growing kits, she found a placard telling the legend of a prospector who hid his silver cache in the caves, then one day vanished without a trace. "You must be the only place in town not banking on a monster myth."

"That's not the sort of story that gets people into caves." She tittered a nervous laugh.

Kylie twitched her whiskers, but softened her tone. "But you're willing to tell us."

The lapine pocketed her phone. "Look, I'd like to know what kind of giant predator might be living in my workplace. If you two are willing to help, then, yeah, I'll tell you what I know." She led them to the back of the shop, then opened a door into a cave. She grabbed flashlights off a shelf on the other side and brandished them at Max and Kylie. "And if this is some kind of trick and you're here to make fun of me, I'll totally abandon you down there."

Max and Kylie stood staring for a moment, at this apparent portal to another world. Stone flowed down the walls, ringed like inside-out trees. Occasional drips of water pattered the floor. A row of lights ran bolted to the ceiling, the only sign of civilization's existence. They exchanged a glance of shared hesitation.

"C'mon." The rabbit gestured for them to follow. "I've led this tour before, y'know."

The pair padded after her, entering the cavern. Crystals glimmered, glued to the walls, scattering light from the lanterns overhead. The cave expanded in asymmetrical ways, natural furrows in the stone sweeping up and away, leaving plenty of places a deer-slaying monster could drop down from.

Max leaned down to the otter's ear. "See, this is a place we could use claymore claymores."

"Please stay with the group and don't wander off the lighted path or we'll have to use the buddy system." Sarah led them without hesitation down the twists and turns, deeper and deeper, past waterlogged diagrams of the planet's layers. "The town's earliest records don't make much mention of these caves, but somebody must have known, considering at least one mine hit them."

Max perked his ears, then twitched as they scraped water off the low ceiling. He crouch-walked under the low ceiling. "At least one?"

"Even I'm still exploring this complex. There's something weird about these caves." Her soft chuckle got lost in the convoluted space. "I love tunnels as much as the next bunny, but I keep getting lost in these. That just doesn't happen..." Her heavy ears swiveled up. "We offer full spelunking packages, but you'd have to go back and sign a waiver."

Kylie twitched a drop of water off her nose. "No waivers for the monster lair?"

The husky stopped, let the otter pass, then put a paw on her shoulder to stay connected through the twisting passage. He looked ahead to Sarah. "Just the place you took the photos is fine."

She nodded and took them further down, at last reaching a wall with a crack.

Surrounded by the echoing sound of dripping water, the three stood staring into the gap.

Max looked around in confusion.

Kylie watched their guide.

The bunny tossed back her ears, exhaled, then wriggled into the gap. A tight squeeze, but she vanished into the black. From nowhere, her anxious voice called. "You coming?"

Max whimpered. "Is there another way around?"

Sarah chuckled. "No, but it's right here."

The otter shrugged. Max was clearly struggling to clamp down on his worry, and she wasn't about to make it worse for him by showing nervousness. She dove into the crack; a tight fit, but manageable for a scrawny otter. She emerged on the other side to find the rabbit leaning against a wall looking down a break in the floor, varying in diameter, but large enough to shimmy down.

The bunny pointed her flashlight down the chasm. "The floor's too level in there. You can tell it's a mine. You can even see some railway ties from where they were using carts."

The lutrine peeked over the edge and saw a stone surface maybe ten meters down. Dark streaks marred the rock. "And that's where you saw the remains?"

"Yeah." The rabbit's gaze never left the hole.

Kylie backed away from the edge, slipping on a wet patch and landing on her tail. In a frantic scramble back, she clutched the wall, heart racing. "Ow." She clambered back to her feet and dusted the water off her pelt.

Max whined, his nose poking into the gap behind them.

"I'm fine, ya big baby. Not my fault you can't fit." The lutrine cupped a paw over his muzzle and pushed him back. "Coming up here was your idea. I just wanted to have lunch."

The bunny twitched a nervous foot at the ledge. "Aren't you going down?"

"Fuck no. I'm even smaller than you." Her arms crossed. "I'm thinking we jackhammer this gap until burly, monster-fighting types can get through."

"Kylie." The dog's voice reverberated through the gap. "You know I've only fought monsters made of foam rubber, right?"

"The owners won't let you jackhammer the cave walls. For a number of reasons." She edged past Kylie and squeezed back through the gap. "But I felt a breeze when I was down there, so it has to connect somewhere. I'm guessing one of the old mine entrances is still exposed."

Grumbling and contorting, the otter managed to slither back into the main chamber.

Once she emerged, Max padded a little closer.

She patted his chest. "You can stop freaking out."

"I wasn't freaking out." He straightened with transparent bravado. "I was totally fine with you going into the death hole without me."

Kylie turned to their guide. "You know a lot about this stuff."

The bunny smiled with pride. "Yeah. My family dug a lot of the mines, back in the day. We've been in charge of them the whole time." She gestured vaguely at the string of Yuletide lights leading back toward the entrance. "In, you know, one way or another."

He gave her a makes-sense shrug. "We could check sat maps; look for other entrances."

"No need. I already have them on here." Sarah waggled her smart-phone. "For emergencies and stuff. They're probably all overgrown, but..." The lapine's fingertips danced across her phone as she sent another file.

The canine glanced down as his mobile lit up. No signal this deep in the earth, but wireless transfers worked fine.

"Those are the ones I know about, but I haven't been in most of them. Like I said, I'm still working on these caves. Also, the tunnels punch through into mine tunnels in a few places, and I've got no maps for those. You might go through half the town underground before you find where this thing is getting in." Sarah flipped her ears over her shoulders and guided them back up the winding path to the shop.

Kylie stepped back into the sunlight and kitsch of the gift shop. "Can you take us down there?"

Max's ears popped up.

The rabbit froze for an instant, assessing the idea. "I go on lunch break in like twenty minutes." She bit her lower lip, looking back into the caverns. "If you guys want to wait until then, I guess I could." She made them sign a waiver, then ushered them outside and got on her phone.

The pair stepped outside and sat on a stone bench looking over the sifting troughs and fool's gold panning station. The old badger grumbled her way through an explanation of various types of granite. Birds chirped, likewise unaware of any monster roaming below the surface.

The husky looked at her askance.

Kylie gave a defiant squirm. "What?"

He sat back. "So we're going in the cave."

She flipped her paws forward. "We have to. We need to find out what the creature is."

"We're going into an enclosed space to seek out a large carnivore."

"And bringing one of my own." She patted his knee. "I'm sure you can deal with whatever it is."

"We're not on TV, rudderbutt."

"Fine, we'll take a look around, then scoot if anything seems sketchy."

The dog crossed his arms and set his lips.

Eventually, the badger gave up on teaching the pups anything and muttered her way into the store. Seconds later, the brown-and-white bunny exited in tight-laced running shoes. She bounced in place, settling into them. Her long, supple ears flopped in time.

Kylie clucked her tongue. "Just have to outrun us, huh?"

She dangled a lop ear. "I don't get it."

A webbed digit pointed at the athletic shoes. "Because the monster will stop once it catches us."

Sarah rolled her eyes. "No signal down in the mines. If something happens, I need to get out of there fast if I'm going to get help."

"Right." Unconvinced, the otter glanced around. "So, where's the entrance?"

"This way…" Her fuzzy paw gestured for them to follow her.

The trio trudged into the leafy woods surrounding the Crystal Caverns. They filed down a ridge, then deeper into the brush. After scrambling up and down a few hills, they reached the weather-beaten, root-strangled beams of a mine entrance. A deep, earthy smell wafted from the tunnel.

Without a whisker of hesitation, the rabbit led them inside. A heavy click turned on her flashlight. Her dandelion-yellow shoes gleamed in the dank dark. "People claim they see ghosts down here. I can see why."

Max fished out his pen flashlight, comically small in his massive paws. "You don't seem worried about crawling around through unstable old tunnels."

"Being a rabbit certainly helps. And when I'm down here, I can almost feel the presence of everyone who dug them." She touched a rough rock wall. "Knowing that somebody dug out every inch of these tunnels, it makes me feel connected to everyone who dug them, you know? It's…peaceful."

Kylie looked down at her sneakers squishing in the mud, then up at the almost-as-muddy ceiling. "Helps you ignore the half-mile of rock above your head."

"Oh." Her tail fluffed. "We're not that far down."

"Don't mind her." Max held the otter back, calling ahead to their guide. "She'd feel safer if the tunnels were flooded."

"I would!" The otter squawked. "It'd slow down falling rocks!"

"Having well-dug warrens fall on you is about as likely as a house falling on you." Still walking, she glanced back at them. "It's all about proper maintenance."

Max straightened, then had to duck under a low rafter. "Have these been maintained?"

"Oh heavens no. Not in years." She chuckled at the absurdity and brushed an ambitious root aside. "They're just the old family mines."

With a suspicious glance at the walls, the otter performed a grouchy little dance that failed to shake the mud from her shoes.

Sarah hopped deftly from rock to rock, avoiding the mud. "How'd you get onto this stuff, anyway?" Her emerald eyes flashed back in the dim light. "Did my brother put you up to this?"

She stomped to a stop. "Your brother?"

"He works with you."

Kylie ticked down the list of coworkers. It was a short list. Only one person on it: a cat. "Shane?" She tried to think of a way of asking if one of them was adopted or from a previous marriage or something, but couldn't think of a way to not sound nosy.

"Yeah." Stopping at last, Sarah's flashlight beam angled up a steep chimney of stone. "Look familiar?"

"Is that where we looked down?" She turned to the bunny. "And you wanted me to shimmy down that?"

"The trick is to brace your hands and feet against the sides." She spread her stance wide to demonstrate. "I've gotten up and down lots of shafts like that."

Trails traced the stones here: dry, dark, and ruddy. Kylie knelt to examine them. What she thought at first were tool marks looked more like three-clawed scratches gouging the rock. She snapped a few quick photos with her phone, the flash startling in the deep darkness.

A faint noise echoed down from some unseen tunnel, distorted beyond deciphering.

"Guys, I really don't like hanging around here." She held very still. "We should go back."

Max looked up from pondering some kind of lumpy white mushroom.

"We just got here!" The lutrine chittered with irritation. "We should at least take a look around."

Her floppy bunny ears lifted a centimeter, the only movement on her whole body. "No, I'm getting a weird feeling. We should probably get out before something happens."

The otter met her boyfriend's eyes, but they darted back down the entrance. He swept the tiny flashlight down the various side-tunnels, his free paw on his pocketknife. With a quiet huff, she trudged back through the muck back to the path that'd led them here.

With the darkness closing in, the three of them retraced their steps at a much quicker pace. Once outside, the sun shined through a canopy of cheery leaves. Crickets chirped. Songbirds tweeted.

They tramped back toward the Crystal Caverns in silence. At about the edge of the parking lot, she stopped, as though it had just occurred to her how insane this all had been. She turned to point a finger at Kylie. "None of this gets back to Cindy."

"And give her more gossip to smear my family with?" The lutrine crossed her arms. "No, thanks."

She led them back into the gift shop, then paused, watching. "You're not as nuts as Cindy said."

"These last few months have been kinda stressful." Max offered a farm dog smile and shrugged in Kylie's direction. "Normally, she's even saner."

The bunny simpered and straightened her polo. "Just try to stay out of this thing's way, whatever it is. And Cindy's, if you can."

"We'll try. And we'll let ya know if we find anything." The otter extended a paw.

Sarah took it. "Thanks." Her ears flopped to the sides a bit and she looked relieved. "Hey, thanks for coming by, too. I had no one I could talk to about this stuff and I felt like I was going crazy."

Kylie ignored Max's pointed elbow to her ribs. They said their good-byes and headed outside.

Max studied his phone. "Think she suspects it's something more than some wild animal?"

The otter's feet squished through the damp earth. "No, not unless she's trying to send us to our deaths."

"About that..." His eyes met hers, mouth a fixed line of worry. "We lucked out this time, but we still have no plan for dealing with this thing."

"You have a point." She patted his shoulder. "But we need proof. You know, we'll capture it or something."

His eyebrows rose.

"Or just take some pics." She shrugged, heart pattering at the thought of jumping the giant black switchblade-monster. "Whatever we do, we'll be careful."

The big dog grumbled, but said nothing else. Walking at her side, he flicked over to a map on his phone and zoomed in, then held it out for her. "The city of Windfall only lists the mines they used for utility tunnels. Guess the old silver miners weren't very good about keeping records."

She groaned. "Back to walking through the monster-infested forest."

He studied her for a second, then threw an arm over her shoulders.

The otter nestled against him. Her stomach gurgled. "Wanna try lunch again? That soup's wearing off."

He wagged. "Sure it is. You just want more chowder."

"It's good!" She watched his tail, amused. "That bunny totally stared at your butt."

Max twisted, trying to stare at his own rear end. "You always say that. Why would anyone want to stare at my butt?"

"Big guy, the simple fact is you have a butt worth staring at." She slipped an arm around to swat his rump. "And I've got four years of video evidence to prove it."

After food, they headed back to Curios & Quandaries, which by this point had deigned to open. The door's tiny bell jingled as they entered. They grimaced their way through clouds of pipe smoke and past shelves packed to the ceiling with weird little knickknacks and oddities.

The schnauzer shopkeep sat up at his station, perusing a document in his white-gloved paws. "Welcome, madam, and welcome back, sir. Your previous purchase suited you, I hope?"

"Yes, sir." Max set his shoulders back, every inch the statuesque husky. "Actually, we're hoping you could give us some more information."

"Antiques, antiquities, and *objets de curiosité*: all flow through here with equal ease and each carries a story." He rolled the parchment up with swift care, then guided it into a varnished wooden tube, which he capped with a plug carved to resemble a rose. The scroll vanished under the till. "Just what sort of information are you looking for?"

The otter stepped forward to rest interleaved fingers on the counter. "I'm researching my family's history."

One digit pressed his spectacles up his muzzle. "And who are you?"

She tried to keep her expression neutral. "Kylie Bevy."

A slim eyebrow rose. "Bevy? Now that is interesting." He tapped tobacco into his pipe, then lit it. "Tartle's the name. Looking for more ideas for your TV show?"

"The show's over. Mom's moved on to other projects." She resisted the urge to snark at the tiny dog. "I'm just trying to get a handle on my family history."

"A loaded topic." He rose and puffed into an aisle of his shop. "But I may just have something for you..."

They followed. The shelves held an array of small wonders. A delicate golden chain coiled up an iron spike. A glass sphere of water and fungus teased at motion within. A perfectly articulated gauntlet shone in a display case, carved from a single bough of petrified wood. An ornate cuckoo clock clicked and ticked on the wall as a parade of wooden velociraptors circled its base on a precise mechanical hunt.

Near the back, the mustached canine stopped and stooped, releasing smoke from his mouth like air from a dropping airship. He drew a volume from a row of mismatched leather-bound books, then held it out to Kylie. "This might be of interest."

She took and opened the hardback. In a swirl of dust, its yellowed pages blossomed open to scratchy handwriting, all in code. She turned to the inside cover and found a very familiar name. "Leister Bevy...that's my mom's uncle! How'd you find this?"

"Your family's holt has a reputation." The old dog stuck his thumbs in his waistcoat pockets. "The town knows better than to throw away something related to it."

Kylie clutched the book to her chest and bounced. "I don't know how to thank you."

The schnauzer watched with amusement, stroking his ample whiskers with the stem of his pipe. "Money would be the traditional means."

Max gave the journal a wary look. "Didn't someone steal that from her family's property?"

The schnauzer waggled his mustache in offense. "If I'd been overly concerned about rightful owners, it never would've made it back to you." He sat back on the stool, tail wagging under the hem of his vest. "Consider it a finder's fee."

Wallets and hearts lighter, they left the curio shop. Max sniffed, snorted, and finally sneezed, trying to clear the pipe smoke from his nostrils. It'd smelled like the guy had been puffing away in there for hours. He glanced up at the curtained second story, wondering if the owner lived above his shop.

Walking at his side, Kylie flipped through the encoded text, then froze, blood chilled. She held the book open. "Look familiar?"

The husky peered down, then froze too. On the page, in nervous fountain pen, crouched a black figure on jackknife legs. The same jagged form they'd seen plummet out of a tree and onto a wild deer. The reality of their chase rushed back into the husky's mind. "Yep."

"We need to translate this." Her paw traced the yellow-edged page, over the old ink.

He rested a paw on her shoulder. "Think it's the same code as before?"

"I know one way to find out." She glanced up, in the direction of the public library.

Once inside the old brick building, they hurried to a scanner and spread the important looking pair of pages inside it. Kylie retyped the scans, transferred the cipher from her phone, and ran the whole mess through the Kibble Puffs website. The ancient computer churned through the decryption.

Her webbed paws danced over the keyboard. "It's a little surreal, all this."

The dog blinked back to the moment, having been trying to think of a way to download the Kibble Puffs decoder for safekeeping. "Yeah?"

"We're basically acting out the plot of a *Strangeville* episode."

"This never would've made it past the censors."

Kylie noticed a flash on the screen and hopped with glee. "It worked!"

"Sort of." The husky squinted at the screen. Words and sentences looked complete at first, but some contained nothing but a jumble of letters and numbers. He turned the monitor for Kylie to scrutinize.

The otter frowned. "Yeah, Great Uncle Leister had really bad handwriting. I had to do a lot of guessing."

A distant librarian shushed them from a passing book cart, then vanished back into the stacks.

The lutrine leaned over Max for a better look, her voice low. "Okay, so it's not a perfect translation. We can clean it up later." She ran a claw tip along a line of somewhat jumbled, but decrypted text. "'Ley lines'... something...'not just lines of power around the Earth. We're not that important.'"

Max pointed to another line. "'Vanguard of an invasion.'" He blinked. "Ominous."

They skimmed the next few entries and ran a few lines through the same process.

"'The monster has an accomplice in Windfall. He's encouraging the rumors of my madness.'" A shock translated through her body. "Accomplice. Someone's working with that thing? That means—"

"—it's intelligent." The husky stroked his chin. "Explains why he coded the journals; he didn't want the accomplice reading them. Or the monster."

Kylie sat in a free chair and flipped through the book, past several illustrations of alien creatures. "Or monsters." She pointed to one that looked like the unholy offspring of a parrot and a tick, then scrolled to that part of the translation. "He calls these 'skitters.' I think it says they live in the old mines."

"I remember these. They're called skitters in the show too." Max tapped a claw tip on the screen. "We did that episode where the house got infested with them."

"Ah yes, I always forget things that were green-screened in." Her gaze flicked to him, then back to reading. "My great-uncle must've told Mom about them at some point." She smoothed her whiskers and leaned forward at the computer. "His other journal mentions them too; says they drift in on ethereal winds, whatever that means."

"Assuming they also exist."

"Well, yeah. I guess my uncle could've been crazy and correct at the same time." A few more pages, same process. Kylie then added the step of flopping back in the chair in disgust. "Ugh! This'll take forever to fix! All the words are coming out wrong. And then it turns to pure scribbles—I can't even tell if it's the same code!"

The dog nodded. "At least we have something."

"I know." She spun around in the desk chair. "I just want a button I can press to solve this problem."

"Somebody probably would've done this already if it were that easy." He finished scanning the journal.

Kylie's phone buzzed and she pulled it from her pocket. "Hey Maxie, do you like fish tacos?"

A beat, and then he woofed a laugh, earning another dirty glance from the reference librarian.

"Oh grow up." She spun in the chair and swatted him with her tail. "Mom made us supper."

Mirthful, he uploaded the scans and offered her his paw.

She took it and stood, and walked with him out of the library. "You're lucky I like you."

He responded with a snicker and wag. "I know."

Kylie awoke, heart racing, chest tight. Lingering tendrils of nightmare scrabbled at the edge of her mind. Every move revealed sore muscles. She forced her jaw to unclench and rubbed her tongue over sore teeth. Night's deep shadows clutched every corner of the room, animating every pool of darkness with the fear.

The dream itself escaped her. What little she could grasp of it consisted of tangled phrases, quivering movements, and stars sliding slick across an inky sky. She burrowed under the imagined safety of the covers, but couldn't escape her worry. The dreams kept getting worse. Some rational part of her brain claimed it was just a few nightmares: not indicative of actually going crazy.

Her gaze traveled around the room. A familiar space, now that she'd spent the last few months colonizing it. She glanced to the posters on her wall—then paused. No matter how she squinted at the letters, she couldn't force them into words. Biting her lower lip, she stared at the blank ceiling. Clearly, the language part of her brain was still asleep. That made sense, right?

She closed her eyes super tight, breathed in and out a few times, then dared a look back up at the posters. *Majestica & the Defenders of Pegastar*: eight-year-old Kylie's favorite thing in the world. At least she could read again. Had it just been her imagination? Was her imagination going crazy? No, that was a crazy thought…like something a crazy person would think.

241

After holding out for a heroic several minutes, she scrambled out of bed and peered out the bedroom door. No obvious intruders to be seen, so she chanced a dash to safety. Padding into the hallway, she creaked down the stairs and the shaky railing. She avoided looking out any windows in case a killer was posing outside them, or in case she didn't recognize her refection. That had to be an irrational fear, but so was the fear of losing the ability to read.

The cold doorknob rattled at her touch, the door groaned open. The big fluffy form of a husky lay atop the bed. A look of complete canine contentment hung undignified from his muzzle.

She leaned in the door. "Maxie?"

He grunted.

Of course he wouldn't wake up. "Max!"

He grumbled, grunted, and looked up at her. "Huh?"

She trotted in and shut the door behind her, so nothing could attack her from behind. "Is it okay if I sleep here?"

The dog answered only with a mumble, but scooted back. One paw lifted the sheet.

Scampering to the bed, she hopped in and curled up against him. At this point in a movie, the character would usually need a fortifying shot of whiskey. Did they even have whiskey? Would artisan seaweed beer do the trick?

Powerful arms enveloped her.

She rubbed her paws together, safe, but still unsure. Part of her wanted to make him talk more, just to make sure she could still understand him. But how would she explain that? Just checking that I can still understand speech. You know, no big deal.

His thick muzzle pressed to her ear, affection carried on gentle breath. "Night, rudderbutt."

CHAPTER 15
SKITTERS

STRANGEVILLE (TUE/9P)

S02E18 "The Inopportunists": Sandy runs afoul of a group of fame-hungry paranormal investigators who risk unleashing an ancient demon in their search for evidence.

Max stirred from sleep to find an otter tucked in beside him. Her breath rose and fell in her chest against him. His paw eased down her sleek curves. She nuzzled deeper into his fluff.

He lay a gentle kiss on the bridge of her muzzle. "Hey."

Opening her eyes just a little, she smiled up at him. "Hey."

"So, not that I'm complaining…" He patted the base of her ample tail. "…but why are you sleeping with me?"

"Lots of reasons, um." She squirmed, tapping her little claws together. "I mean, because I like you. And I've liked you for a really long time. And I like who I am when I'm with you. And you're built like a marble statue covered in shag carpet, and—"

He rested a paw on her breastbone, putting an end to her evasions. He resisted the urge to slip his hand lower. "No, I mean literally. You just sort of popped in here last night."

"Oh." She sunk down, drawing the covers up to her nose. "I had a bad dream."

"Oh?"

She nodded. "But I slept fine cuddled up with you."

"You don't have to wait until you have a nightmare." He drew her close, nose to nose. "You can sleep with me anytime. As long as your mom won't be upset."

"I don't think that's going to be a big deal."

"You think she approves of me?" His tail thumped once under the sheets.

"She wouldn't have taken you under her wing if she didn't approve." She wiggled her whiskers at the walls. "Or let you in the guest bedroom."

He considered this for a moment, then nodded. "I just don't want to make her uncomfortable."

"Like Mom's never had a boyfriend or girlfriend."

"It's a loyalty thing." He shrugged. "She wrote my favorite TV show, then let me act on it, then let me date her amazing daughter."

"Hey!" She punched lightly him in the fluff. "I'm the one who 'let' you do that."

"You know what I mean, though."

"I do." Her wide lutrine nose brushed his. "I should probably head to the shower before my mom notices I'm in here. Wouldn't want to scandalize her."

"Especially when we haven't even done anything scandalous." He groped her tail.

She squeaked and play-bit his shoulder, then bounced out of bed. "Plenty of time for that once she leaves."

Birds chirped and sun shone through the first-floor windows. The dog wagged into the kitchen and distracted Laura by helping make breakfast. After greeting Kylie coming down the stairs as if for the first time that morning, he'd watched as the two otters descended upon the lemon-salsa salmon, sliced melon, and toast.

After a second helping, Max licked his chops. Not all dogs liked fish, but Laura sure knew how to prepare it; grilled salmon in particular.

He made himself useful, disposing of the napkins and wrapping up the leftovers.

"You kids sure you don't want to come with me to ChimeraCon?" Plates clattered as Laura cleared the table. "You still have time to pack."

"Thanks to *Strangeville*, I've been to enough sci-fi cons for a few decades." Kylie slid past Max's front with a swaying otter gait that drew his gaze like gravity. "Besides, we've got more exploring to do, right Maxie?"

Max stared, the last piece of toast forgotten in his teeth.

The younger lutrine smirked at the reaction, then eeled out the door to load her mother's bags in the car.

Laura, stack of dishes in her paws, cocked a wry eyebrow.

He continued munching on toast and hoped his ears weren't as pink as they felt as he bagged up the garbage and moved to haul it outside.

A throat being cleared caught his attention. "Max, dear?"

He perked his ears to the middle-aged otter.

Resting the dishes in the sink, she flashed a gentle smile. "Story exercise: frazzled single mother is leaving her daughter with a handsome single guy in a big empty house. And even though this kid is solid and pretty much part of the family, she still feels the need to take him aside and have a conversation. How does it go?"

The husky blinked. Laura was leaning over the counter, cradling the dregs of a cup of coffee with a smile of perfect serenity, and he was suddenly reminded of the time in fourth grade when he sat across the table from his parents, trying to justify a bad report card. His girlfriend's mother arched an eyebrow in expectation and he realized she actually expected an answer. He cleared his throat and thought for a moment, then straightened and met her gaze. "Um, how 'bout: 'Kiddo, you know you're welcome as long as you like. I trust you and I know how happy my daughter is that you've started dating. That said, if you ever hurt her, so help me you'll be naked, shaved, and on the train back to Montana so fast your head will spin.'"

The older otter smirked, an expression of mischief so like her daughter's it unnerved him. "Ooh, good threat. I like the added touch of humiliation."

She drained the last drops of coffee and eyed the bottom of the mug like there might be some she'd missed. "Feels like it needs a prop, though."

Max considered, then smirked in return. "She gives him a cup of cocoa before she starts talking, to lull him into a false sense of security. When she's done she leaves and he sniffs it like he's afraid it has saltpeter in it."

That got a laugh as Laura rose from the countertop and plopped the dirty mug into the dishwasher for Kylie run later. She patted Max on the shoulder as she made her way to the door. "There might be hope for you yet, kid."

Max couldn't help but smile at the praise from his sort-of mentor. Still, the conversation had shaken him a bit. "Um..." He began in a tentative squeak, and felt his ears flatten as Laura turned in the doorway to face him. "I'm not sure what the poor guy might say after that, to reassure her."

This time there was no irony in Laura's smile. She looked amused, and a little proud. "He wouldn't need to say anything, Max." She hefted her suitcase, waiting in the front hall. "I'm heading out. You two have a nice weekend."

He nodded and smiled, ears and tail drooped in deference. He waited until the door had closed behind her to slump back in his chair. That had been an...interesting conversation. Still lost in thought, he polished off his hot chocolate, collected the overfull garbage and made his way to the door.

Outside, the air was hot and still. He had stopped halfway to the garbage cans to listen to a cicada in the distance when Kylie ambushed him with a grope and a giggle. "I can't believe she's leaving us alone in the house." The lutrine gripped his arm and followed him along.

The dog smiled. "She trusts us."

"Poor old fool." She shook her head at the family hatchback as it puttered away down the long driveway. She hopped up on tiptoes to kiss his cheek, pulling at his arm. "C'mon, let's go celebrate that trust by making out on the living room sofa."

Max lifted his ears and tried to organize a tangle of feelings into words. Failing, he deposited the trash bag, then snapped the bin's lock in place.

Her little clamshell ears quirked, head tilted his way. "You're locking them?"

A nod dipped his muzzle. "Yeah. I think something was getting in there."

"Like what?"

"Actually, it was weird." His brow furrowed as he glanced into the forest. "Might be my memory playing tricks on me, but it didn't seem like any animal I've ever seen."

"Was it Karl?" Kylie groaned. "Did he finally cross the line from 'faintly amusing' to 'time for a restraining order?'"

He let the bad joke slide and shook his head. "Smaller than Karl."

The lutrine twitched her whiskers. "Well, that narrows it down."

He shrugged. "Smaller than a breadbox."

"A breadbox? What is this, the 50s?"

"Fine, the size of a footstool. Really fast too." Max scratched the fluff under his chin. "I assumed it was a feral raccoon, but—"

A branch snapped in the woods.

On instinct, they both snapped their attention toward the tree line. Max finished, subdued, "But knowing what we know now..."

Kylie inclined her head to the house. She cracked the door open with her heel and eeled backward through it.

He followed her inside and clicked the lock behind him. Between glances outside, his eyes caught hers and he raised his ears.

The otter crossed her arms. "Skitters?"

Max's eyes widened. "Hey, there's an idea. I guess I didn't recognize them without the half-assed CG."

Her tail swayed, eyes gleaming. "Have you seen one lately?"

"No. I guess they can't get in the bins."

She flowed around him to peer out the window, then cast a smirk back. "What if we invited them back?"

The rest of the day consisted of heading to town and purchasing monster-catching gear and snacks. Kylie arrived home drained from just running around. Weariness clung to her eyes as she stretched toward the entryway ceiling. "I think I need a nap."

"Okay." The husky plunked down on the sofa and grabbed his laptop from the magazine stand. "I'll poke at some writing."

She trudged upstairs and flopped face-first into bed. Limp as a jellyfish, her motion came entirely from the resulting waves on the waterbed. Sleep. Nightmares and the fear of them had robbed her of it for the last several days. She should be safe sleeping now. Who ever had a nightmare on a sunny afternoon?

Unconsciousness cloaked her mind, unbidden but welcome.

The otter drifted into soothing emptiness. Tendrils of stress gripped her mind. Stars, always stars, slid against the oily backdrop of the night sky. No matter what space her dreams entered, it always folded in on itself and turned inside out. Familiar faces muttered and yelled in unknown languages.

Her sore eyes opened on a cheery afternoon. She worked her stiff jaw, feeling like it'd been gnawing on clamshells.

The journal they'd gotten from Tartle lay open to an especially inscrutable page. The script degenerated as it went, denser and smaller and stranger, breaking from the lines of the paper to spiral and intertwine. The last pages of the journal, where Leister would have realized he was running out of room, ran almost black with ink.

A scrape of text caught her eye: "using a hidden entrance."

She snatched up the journal. The scrawls and scribbles all made sense. She tried not to notice that none of the English did. Instead, she bounded downstairs, clutching the journal to her chest. "Max! Max!"

The big husky jumped to his feet, tiny netbook bouncing to the sofa cushions. His ears pinned back, hackles up, ready for a fight.

She waved the journal in his face. "I can read it now!"

His massive shoulders relaxed a little, though his muzzle stayed aligned on her.

Having used her fingertip as a bookmark, she popped the book open and started reading again. "'The monster dwells underground.'" She paused, paw on her hip. "That could mean all sorts of things, with all these mines around…"

He nodded at the text. "Keep going."

"Right!" In a giddy haze, she babbled onward. "'It's using a hidden entrance. I grabbed the disk and bolted down a tunnel. To my surprise, walls spring open before me, aiding my escape. I must keep track of the disk, hide it here. Whispers are getting loud.'" She turned the page, but found eldritch scrawl too dense to read. "Seriously? It's too messy to read!"

His ears popped straight up. "Which word was disk?"

She flipped a page back and jabbed a claw at the page, onto a scrawl that looked like a drunken spider's path through a drop of ink. "This one."

His eyebrows rose. "Incredible."

Nerves caught up with her. Maybe she'd deluded herself into thinking she'd finally decoded the journal. "Or crazy."

"Probably not…" He traced down the line she'd just read. "That same word appears here."

"So?" Worry whispered from the back of her mind, as a familiar, awful lump settled in the pit of her stomach. She had thought, after seeing the monster in the woods, she wouldn't have to worry anymore, that her family had been vindicated. Even the ramblings in all the old journals hadn't been enough to douse her relief. But now that was slipping away. She was doomed after all. She should have known better than hoping—

Heavy white paws thumped on her shoulders as Max stooped to look her in the eyes, concern and admonishment written across his face. "Hey, stop that."

Kylie blinked. "What?"

"You're freaking out. I can see your wheels spinning from here. You're not going crazy." He picked up the journal and bopped her on the nose with it. "Last time I checked, losing your mind didn't teach you new languages. Something else is going on here."

"Oh." Her gaze fell to the battered leather book. Her brow furrowed. "Yeah, you're right. That's weird."

He grabbed his computer. "Can you read it again, so I can record it?"

"Ummm…" She nosed closer, then back up from the text, frustrated by the impenetrable jumble. "Apparently not?"

Max grunted, not looking up from his typing.

"Ugh!" The English words clicked back into clarity with an unpleasant lurch. She pinched the bridge of her nose to chase off the vertigo. "It's gone. And we barely got anything. Assuming you're right and I'm not just losing it."

He raised a digit. "We got that the creature is living underground."

"Somewhere…" She flung her hands out to either side. "But how'd I suddenly start reading code? And why'd I snap out of it?"

"Not sure." Max took the book from her and paged through it. "Maybe it'll happen again."

She scratched sheepishly at her arm. "It happened last night, too. Or at least, I stopped reading normal words for a few seconds."

He stroked his whiskers with a slow nod. "Okay, so it happens when you sleep." He raised an eyebrow at her. "Is that why you've been sneaking in with me?"

"'Sleep' would be a generous way of describing what I've been getting the last couple nights." She rubbed her tired eyes. Her lithe body slipped onto the sofa beside him. Her blunt muzzle nuzzled into his chest. "In my own bed, at least. Looks like you're the cure."

Concern tinged his voice. He curled and arm around her. "To the insomnia?"

"Insomnia, insanity, whichever." She leaned her head against his shoulder. "You help."

His ears dipped in concern. "You still look really tired. Want me to let you sleep for a bit?"

She was way ahead of him. Lulled by the steady rhythm of his heartbeat and his free paw on the keyboard, she faded into a snooze. For the first time in days, dreams allowed her peace.

Starting at dusk, they had a stake out watching the trash bins they'd left open in the yard. They read and re-read the journal entries on the skitters, but those held limited info. Laura called after nightfall. And if she noticed how tired they sounded over the phone, Kylie especially, she didn't say. Max suspected she thought he'd been keeping her daughter up doing something scandalous. He wished she were right. Spending their investigation time in the bedroom instead of the backyard would have been just as productive, and a lot more rewarding. But taking a photo of these critters was important to Kylie, so it was more important than his libido. If only she didn't smell so amazing, or insist on nuzzling along his neck as they watched the trash cans. How was he supposed to be vigilant if she kept turning him on so much?

About an hour after they'd started talking about giving up, Kylie sighed and wriggled a little closer against his warmth. "So...how's your family?"

Max had been on the verge of cracking and hauling her off to the nearest horizontal surface, research be damned. The question did more to douse his enthusiasm than a bucket of ice water to the crotch. Dreading the topic, he shrugged and waggled his phone, which he'd been keeping at the ready in case one of the skitters showed up. "Oh, they're okay."

"No, seriously."

Despite the dark, his fingertips found his wristwatch, fiddling with the double time zone controls. "They want me home. Every time I finagle another few days here, Mom gets more worried it'll be permanent."

A spark of what might have been hope in her eyes.

He pretended not to notice.

"Missing you is easy." She kissed his cheek. "And really tough."

He settled an arm over her shoulder, still leaning over the back of the sofa.

She nuzzled up against his shoulder, her paws tracing his broad back. "It's really none of my business, but you are an adult."

"Barely. And not in her eyes." He shuffled to get more comfortable, pressing a little closer to her. He laid a forlorn chin on the window sill. "You never seem to have these problems with your mom."

"Probably because all we ever had is each other." A shrug telegraphed down her supple spine. "Only child, single parent; I guess we're just lucky we don't get too worked up about most things." A giggle bubble through her. "Should I send a thank-you card for letting me borrow you?"

He woofed a quiet laugh into the throw blanket, never taking his eyes from the open window. "Nah, it's just idle howling. So long as I come home—" His ears shot up.

Movement rattle against the plastic bin.

A flat-bodied creature squiggled up the contours of the trash can, segmented body wriggling side to side. It hesitated on the lip of the open trash can, sniffing, or looking, it was hard to tell. Then it was over the edge and diving in with abandon. A beak munched on food scraps while at least half a dozen beady black eyes kept a quivering watch. A row of nasty-looking quills flittered along its back. Half a dozen jointed legs creaked as they sifted through the refuse. Alien as it was, it looked nothing like the monster they'd seen while searching the property.

Holding their breath, the would-be researchers brought their phones to bear and snapped a few rapid shots apiece, the flashes blinding in the nighttime gloom.

The creature hissed and scrabbled in panic on the smooth plastic. It leapt from the bin and rippled to nothing in midair.

"What the halibut?" Kylie scampered to the front door and poked her head out. "Did it get away?"

Close behind, the dog flipped through the photos he'd taken. "No, it... disappeared."

She brought her head back inside to glare at him. "The heck does that mean?"

He gestured helplessly at his phone. "It sort of...wavered, and then it was just gone. Like a crossfade." He held the final image up for her to see.

She scowled at it. "Do you have some weird settings on? Those pictures look fake."

He turned it back around and inspected it, nodding as he considered. Apart from being see-through, the creature cast a shadow that didn't match the direction of the light from the camera flash. The effect left it strangely illuminated, as though light hit it from every direction at once. The monster looked more like a bad overlay than part of the real world. "And not very good fakes, either. The CG on the show was more convincing."

Closing the door, she flicked through her own images. "Ugh! Mine are bad too. People really would think we're just trying to drum up attention for the show."

Paw on her shoulder, he padded back to the living room. "And that we can't be bothered to do it properly…"

She flopped back down onto the sofa. "The journal said something about them being 'not properly anchored' and 'capture not possible.' Guess this is what it meant."

"It wasn't a total waste." Max shrugged. "We have a second data point now. If the skitters are real, it means your great-uncle's journals are at least partly reliable."

"Oh that's reassuring." She flailed her arms in exasperation and wriggled against the cushions. "I really need every memory vampire and gorgon and hungry vapor from *Strangeville* showing up in my life."

"They're not built like the thing we ran into in the woods. They're too flat, too clumsy. Way too many legs."

"So we've got two kinds of monsters?" Her gaze cast out the window as she chittered with dismay. "How many more are we gonna find?"

"I don't know…" He sat next to her, careful not to land too hard on the sofa springs. "The other question is why no one else has evidence of them. Even we got some bad photos."

"Maybe they have! We could check online." She tapped some search teams into her phone, then winced at the stupidity of the results.

Max peeked groggily at his watch. "I don't want to dive to that particular depth of the Internet right now."

"What about the monsters?" She pointed out the window at the disturbed trash bin.

He patted her shoulder. "Assuming we're not tripping from a gas leak or something, they'll still exist in the morning." The dog leaned back into a massive yawn, stretching to spread his fingers and toes. "We should go to bed."

She grumbled, but didn't resist as he stood and pulled her to her feet. They padded back to the dark entryway.

Just as he turned toward his room, she gripped him by the tail.

The big husky looked back at her with quiet curiosity.

Uncomfortable with the shadows around her, she squirmed. The silky warmth of his fluff brushed her finger webbing. "We just watched weird aliens eating our trash from the living room. You're not leaving me alone."

In her grasp, the fluffy tail swayed gently. With a soft smile, he towed her upstairs and into her bedroom.

She closed and locked the door behind them. Shedding their outer clothes, they crawled onto the bed together, pulling the blankets up for safety. His muscled frame sank a ways into the waterbed, propping her higher than she was used to. Very carefully, he held her close. His breathing settled into a steady rhythm. Time evaporated in the warm dark under the blankets, impossible to measure except against his calm, powerful heartbeats. It was pretty cool having him around, having a friend and, now, a lover she could rely on even when the world broke its own rules.

Her fingers played over his thick hands as her paws and tail entwined with his. Under his arm, the otter watched the "Thanks, Maxie. For everything."

The dog snored.

She squawked with outrage. How could he sleep after seeing monsters? It was completely unfair, her barely getting any sleep and the big oaf can conk out anytime, anywhere. She wrung her paws and fretted. Could the skitters get in the house? Had they always been? She muttered and grumbled, unhappy but unwilling to leave the safety of his arms to check. Would he wake up if they came in the room? Would she?

A faint whine rose from Max's broad chest. His paws twitched, pantomiming a run.

Oh great, now he was going to keep her awake. Wasn't sleeping with someone supposed to be romantic and peaceful? What was he even dreaming about? He didn't seem to be enjoying it. Normally, he slept like a log—

She flailed out from his embrace and bounded up, stiff as a board. Her palms bounced on his shoulder. "Max! Wake up!"

"Mmf?" His sky-blue eyes struggled to focus on her. "Huh?"

"What were you dreaming about?" She bit her lip.

He blinked in the pale starlight, then shrugged. "I don't know; something about stars, except I was in the sky with them."

"You just had a nightmare!" Her body wiggled up into a bounce, sending shockwaves across the waterbed. "That's great!"

Ears up, he tilted his head at her. "I guess?"

"The nightmare, you fluffy fool." She gave him a gentle shove. "The one I've been having."

He bounced a little on bed, patiently perplexed. "Okay?"

"It's gotta be something in this room." She looked around. "Maybe the water in my new waterbed is psychically radioactive or something." Her paw prodded the rubbery surface.

He gave a wide yawn, blinking thoughtfully. "Hey, where are you keeping that disk?"

"Of course!" She yanked open her nightstand drawer and seized the bone disk. "That has to be it! I bet it's trying to take over our brains, like it did Leister."

He propped himself up on an elbow. "Well, it's not very good at it if it only works when you're asleep next to it."

Kylie contemplated the disk in her paws for a moment. It looked pretty flimsy; she could probably crush it with her teeth if she needed to, but the world probably wouldn't take an otter-gnawed artifact seriously. She decided to hold it only with her claws. "What'd we do with it?"

"I don't know." He sat up on the edge of the bed. "Sleep in my room for now?"

"Good start." She stuffed it into one of the journals and shoved it back into the drawer. "Well, tonight's been a bullet train into and out of Crazy Town."

He lead her out of the bedroom. "I keep telling you: you're probably not crazy."

"You keep saying 'probably' and you'll drive me crazy." Reaching back, she pulled the door shut as much to stop her mom saying anything as to block alien dream transmissions. "C'mon, aspiring writer: you should know this is the point in the story when you tell me I'm not insane."

He took her hand. "You're not insane."

She squeezed his in return. "Thank you."

His big white paws creaked down the old stairs. He stayed closed to her. "We need to know what we're doing with here."

The otter slipped into his bedroom, repeating her locking ritual from upstairs. "That would be nice."

"Other people must've seen some of this weird stuff." He settled onto his second bed of the evening, this one all creaky with springs. "We could talk to Karl; he's snooped around town for the show's inspirations."

She shook her round little muzzle. "No, we want someone who won't blab that we asked them. Don't want it getting back to the big monster's accomplice." She paused. "Somebody who's lived here long enough to know the lore, but who hasn't bought into it." Some of the slump left her shoulders and her faint smile lit up the dark. "I know just the person to ask."

CHAPTER 16
CHAMBERS

STRANGEVILLE (TUE/9P)

S04E06 "Inside and Inside": While cleaning his grandmother's attic, Cassie and Serge are abducted by a possessed Russian nesting doll that wants to emtomb them.

The next morning, Kylie puttered her Amphicar into the store parking lot and hopped out. With a quick look around to check for Cindy, she eeled in the back door and past the shelves of items yet to be sorted, tagged, and eventually destroyed by customers' offspring.

As she emerged from the back room, her feline coworker looked up from his phone at the till. He pulled his headphones off and slung them around his neck. "Weren't you doing the tourist thing with your new bunk buddy? What're you doing in here?"

"Didn't take us long to see the stuff worth seeing." She wove through the shelves toward the storefront, pretending to examine the merchandise as she tried to think of a way to steer the conversation where it needed to go. In the end, she figured she might as well begin one awkward conversation with another. "The cave tour was kinda cool, though. I didn't know you had a sister..." She let the unasked question hang.

The cat slunk back on the stool, as his tail flicked back and forth with vague amusement. "Yes, my sister is a bunny, like my dad. Sarah was in vitro, before you ask. Egg donor. And I was sired by an old friend of Dad's."

"I didn't want to pry." She shrugged up to the countertop. "You must get tired of answering that question."

"Eh." The tabby shrugged, gesturing through his phone's file tree. "Just one more way she complicates my life." He reached to show her a photo of himself, Sarah, a male bunny, and a female cat. They stood in front of the local high school, with the rabbit in a graduation gown. "Senior year, some new kid saw we were close and asked if I was getting some tail. I explained to him that we'd come out of the same uterus."

The lutrine laughed. "Bet he wasn't expecting that."

He flicked through the rest of his mom's social media gallery: on vacation at some sunny beach, as babies covered in cake, dressed up as cacti for a grade school play.

Her ears flicked up at a picture of him with a longboard. "You skateboard?"

"Used to. We live at the lowest point in town." He shrugged. "I gave up because it felt like those spiraling coin-funnels at the mall, always leading back to my house." With a roll of his eyes, the cat withdrew to the music section and started alphabetizing. "So were the Crystal Caverns as enchanting as the advertising says?"

She hesitated for a moment. "No, but we got her to take us down into the mines."

"Seriously?" He hissed, straightening. It was the closest to angry she'd ever seen him "I told her not to keep poking around in those mines. Dad's as gung-ho about caves as anyone, and even he's told us all our lives to stay out of those." His thin arms crossed. "Don't encourage her. Bad enough she still lets Cindy drag her around."

Kylie's clawed grip on the countertop tightened. "What if she has a good reason to worry about those mines?"

"Everybody does." He ticked through the albums with his claws. "They're all at least a hundred years old and no one looks after them anymore."

"That's not quite what I meant." She cornered her feline coworker at the vinyl shelves. "Shane, sit down for a second."

He blinked at her, confused by the change in the conversation. With a playful lash of his tail, he sprawled into a reading chair. "Is this an intervention? I swear, the catnip wasn't mine."

"What? No. Focus." She took a deep breath. "This may sound…crazy, but monsters live in the forest. Max and I saw one."

"Duh."

She blinked. "What?"

"Yeah, you might've noticed nobody really goes in the forest." His slitted green eyes rolled. "Except for the tourists."

"We saw this little skittering thing—" She stammered to a halt as her brain tried to backpedal and rejoin the conversation. "Wait, what?"

"Lots of legs, lots of eyes, about the size of a breadbox?" He made little creeping gestures with his fingers. "Yeah, they're around."

Her webbed paws tried to strangle him from a distance. "You've known what they are this whole time?"

"I sometimes go to the Chamber of Commerce meetings for the free snacks." He shrugged. "They talk about what they should leak to the paranormal crowd to encourage tourism."

The otter sputtered. "Are these things dangerous?"

"Nah." He brushed back a stray lock of hair. "They're like, I dunno, seagulls. Show up, grab some scraps, then they're gone again."

She sat down on a squeaky barstool. "And nobody's ever captured one?"

He shrugged. "If it were possible, I'm sure someone would've managed it by now."

"We tried to take some pictures, but…" On her phone, she flipped through the disappointing images for him.

The cat smirked, sharp teeth glinting like slices of moonlight. "Yeah, they're not photogenic."

"Where can I find them? They look like of like bugs, so we thought underground, but we didn't seen any in the old mines."

"I wouldn't go there." He crossed his arms, the stripes on them not quite lining up.

"Why?"

"The mines are dangerous." The feline shrugged, sorting dusty records. "More than abandoned mines should be."

"What's that supposed to mean?"

"Back when they had actual silver, the workers got weird injuries, said they saw strange things down there. But the silver kept coming in, so nobody cared. Now, about once a generation, somebody wanders in and comes out…different. Hasn't happened with my generation yet and I figure it shouldn't be anybody I like, including me. Or even my little sister."

"Comes out different?"

He groaned. "Yeah, they can't stop talking about the shadows of other realities and stuff."

"Shane!" The otter tumbled from her barstool behind the counter. "Why didn't you tell me about this before?"

"Like I said, didn't want that to happen to someone I liked. Pretty clear I can't keep you out of this. I'd like at least to keep you safe." He shrugged and fiddled with his headphone cord. "Besides, you wanted people to think you weren't crazy, and dealing with this stuff has a tendency to make people go crazy. I thought you wanted to avoid that. Also, the new Tactical Love album came out." One orange finger tapped his headphones. "You should borrow it."

She clawed up the counter and back to her feet. "Why haven't you told the cops? The media? Anybody?"

"Tourist trap town claims it has monsters? But for real this time?" He rolled his eyes, leaning back against a bin of vinyls. "Everybody who claims that sort of stuff gets labeled as crazy." His eyebrow arced at her. "No offense."

Reeling from the revelation, she stammered for questions. "How'd you find out about them?"

Another shrug. "It's all just rumor. Even at the Chamber meetings people pretend they're just kidding whenever they talk about this stuff, even though we all know better. You wanted facts."

"And you never followed up on any of this?"

The cat groaned. "I work in this store because I'm one of the few people in this town who isn't obsessed with supernatural junk." A deep sigh weighed down his shoulders. "Please, don't tell Karl about this."

Her ears popped up. "Why?"

"If he found out the show was real, he'd never shut up."

"But these things are real!" Kylie bounced around, twisted between anger and fluster. "We saw one kill a wild deer!"

He cocked an eyebrow. "What are you talking about?" He tapped at the frozen, oddly-lit homage of the skitter on her phone. "These things couldn't kill a wild rabbit."

"It was bigger, like a person. And it wasn't built like the skitters: more like a big predator." She arched her body forward in imitation. "It had a black armor shell and legs growing out of its back."

Surprised silence spelled over the feline for a moment. "Well…nothing like that's ever come to town." His arms crossed over his narrow chest. "But can you see why I've been keeping you from this stuff?"

"Ugh!" The otter leaned back like a bent sapling and groaned. "Can you tell me anything useful about the mines?"

"Dunno." He rubbed his scruff with an anxious growl. "The town's built on them, for one. The sewer and water lines run through them. Power lines too."

"Power lines?"

"Oh yeah, years ago, they ran the entire power grid through old mines running under the town. Guess they thought it'd be cheaper than digging new tunnels."

"That doesn't seem weird to you?"

"Actually, it sort of made sense." He watched her with ears cocked. "That way, they shored up the sketchy parts. If anything is living down there, it's probably been sealed off."

"What if it wasn't?"

The feline shrugged.

Her whiskers straightened at a realization. "Wait, if you know about all this stuff, how have you not gone nuts?"

His tail swished as he fixed a label. "That's the difference between knowing about something and being obsessed with it: you have to care about something for it to make you crazy."

"So indifference is, what, your special gift?"

He lifted a half-hearted fist. "Apathy power: activate or whatever." Amusement faded from his muzzle. "You're going to check out the mines, aren't you?"

A bounce traveled up the otter and emerged as words: "Of course!"

His green eyes grew serious for a moment. "That's exactly why I didn't tell you about this."

"Which is why I'm not yelling at you."

"Don't get killed." A faint smile and a tail flick. "With my luck, the owner'll hire one of your fans. They actually are crazy."

"Fine." She pulled her keys from her pocket and headed for the exit. "But, in return, you have to give me whatever info about the town I ask for."

"Anytime." The tabby shrugged. "You're the first person who didn't get bored with this job after three weeks and leave. I'd prefer you not die."

She paused in the doorway. "Aww, you care."

"Yeah, it's exhausting." He indulged in a long, languid stretch. "I can see why I don't do it much."

Max watched his girlfriend bounce in the front door clutching a large shoebox. Well, large for an otter.

She plunked down at the kitchen table, then popped open the box and crammed her feet into a pair of new hiking boots.

His eyebrows lifted. "Finally learned your lesson?"

"We're serious about this now." Her webbed fingers fumbled at the laces.

The dog knelt down to help her into the boots. "We haven't been until now?"

Her heavy tail traced the floorboards behind her chair. "Shane fessed up about the monsters around town."

"Okay." He cinched the last row of laces and tied it in place. "What's this tell us that we didn't know?"

She crossed her arms and groused. "That he's a jerk for not telling me sooner."

"Anything else?" Leaning onto the table, the husky steepled his fingers. From the pot at the center of the table, he poured her a mug.

The otter raised the steaming cup in both paws, taking a sip. "The town runs its power lines and sewer through the mines."

"Tell me we're not going in the sewer." Max examined the pristine white fur of his paws. "I'm not as washable as you."

She stirred her tea, then added more sugar. "It stands to reason there'd be access somewhere."

"This is sounding like a sewer plan." His voice rung resigned.

Her eyes met his. "The creature could totally be down there."

"So sewer plan with a chance of monsters." His ears sank and his massive frame slouched. "When have those episodes gone well for us?"

"It's our best lead." The otter stroked her whiskers and tried to keep her nerves in check. At least she had a hunky husky for backup. "We've gotta go down there and try to get some evidence, monster or no monster."

Max heaved a canine sigh, then grabbed a small aerosol can from his pocket and tossed it to her.

She caught the slim canister, then examined it. Pepper spray. She gave him a grim smile.

The husky met her eyes with a confident nod.

Before noon, they stood at the first mine entrance in a little gully near the Crystal Caverns. The flashlight beam traveled twenty feet before darkness ate it. Rotting beams creaked under the weight of the world above, eager to collapse. The canine fought back a slight whimper, not eager to charge into an unstable mine.

Kylie held the large flashlight in her slender paws. "This plan seemed logical until just this second."

"And now we're charging down an abandoned mine to find a dangerous monster." Max took the spool of twine from his backpack and tied one end to a tree near the entrance. From what he'd read in the Windfall guidebooks, silver mines weren't built for ease of navigation. His gaze met her hazel eyes.

She nodded.

Side by side, they entered the mine.

Half an hour later, they tramped out, slathered with mud.

"Okay, that was gross." The otter unlaced her now-sullied boots and dumped out clods of muck. "From now on let's stay above the water table."

"I thought you liked water." The husky wrung out his tail.

"That wasn't water. I'm made of more water than this stuff." She scraped a pawful of muck off her back and splatted it on the rock-strewn grass.

The next candidate had a cave-in a few meters from the entrance.

As they clomped along in hiking boots toward their next site, Max could see signs of frustration building in the otter in the arch of her shoulders, the set of her jaw. They picked their way around rocks in a narrow gulch. A stream hurried past them, vanishing down a pebbled slope. At the entrance, he tied the twine off again, then glanced her way.

Brushing drying flakes of mud from her pelt, she washed her paws in the stream and steeled herself with a deep breath. Before Max's eyes, the frustration rolled off her like so much rainwater. "Okay, let's try this again." She marched into the mine ahead of him, flashlight ready.

The dog couldn't help smiling. Pound for pound, she was tougher than anybody he'd ever met. He followed.

A stone wall blocked their progress. The otter squawked with frustration. "Another cave-in?"

"It's like they just stopped digging." Max touched the solid granite surface. "This might be a test mine that didn't pan out."

"I don't think so." She pointed her flashlight around, down, and up, then paused. "What's that?"

At first, the dog saw nothing. Then he crouched. Tucked behind a rise in the ceiling clung a small white object, about the size of his thumb. The material looked familiar. He sniffed at it, but smelled only earth. "Mushroom?"

"Not like any I've ever seen." She curled a finger, gesturing him closer. "Gimme a boost."

He bent and let her step in his hands, then lifted her to touch the object.

"Hey cool!" She bounced down, playing with his ears in excitement. "It's got the same kind of etchings as the disk. You remembered it, right?"

The canine dug through his backpack, drew out the white bone disk in a zippered sandwich bag, then handed it to her.

She held the disk up, studying it through the clear plastic. "We're onto something here."

His ears rose. "What're you going to do with it?"

"I don't know." She waved it at the ceiling. "Hit the mushroom thing with it?"

"It's not a clam." He tilted his head at the protrusion. "At least, I don't think it's a clam."

"I'm not gonna break it." Her damp paws slipped over the bag as she tried to open it, but she managed to get the disk free. Faint lights flickered around its periphery, through the pinprick holes. A strange buzz hurt her teeth.

The wall shook.

Max grabbed the otter and shielded her with his body, ready to dash back toward the entrance.

"Wait!" Kylie gripped his arm.

He waited for the mine to crush them, but the only sound came from his spool of twine rolling on the uneven floor and a dry rattle like dry bones over rock.

Before them, in the trembling beam of her flashlight, the stone changed color and texture and dilated open like a sphincter in the earth. A sizable space lay beyond, filled with organic shapes and glinting lights. The entrance stood bone-white and solid once more.

The otter stepped from his embrace and into the newfound chamber. Its size seemed impossible to judge; if the beam of their flashlight could be trusted, it had to be at least a hundred feet across. A snarl of walkways and columns twisted in all directions, meeting and diverging, obscuring the vast blackness with their bony tangles. The floor lay concave, bulging out in all directions to support the chamber. Strange items and vessels perched on shelves and fused with walls or the floor. A steep ramp led to a central spire, which stood in the exact center of the space. All these structures had been sculpted, or perhaps grown, from that same white bone.

They trod with care down the incline to the cavern floor. Along one wall, they found a trio of egg-like sacs, translucent and yellow, braced by bone structures and fed by quivering veins. Inside, lumpy shapes pulsed, suspended in hazy gel. Max snapped a few pictures of them, then the space as a whole.

Kylie's gaze traveled the ovoid chamber. "What is this place?"

Max's booted paws tracked mud onto the lumpy floor. A sucking sound spooked him; he lifted his paws to find the grime slurping away into the floor. He surrendered a nervous chuckle. "Paranormal tourist attraction?"

She tapped the butt of her flashlight on the bone, which gave a solid reverberation. "It's better than anything we had on the show."

Max looked at a bundle of wires vining down from the ceiling, which fed into a hungry maw of bone. Some dangled, hair-thin and drifting on his breath, others chugged, pumping fluids unseen. "Laboratory? Shop? Rumpus room?"

"More like a creature." Her paw traced the sloping walls, the texture of which danced under her fingers just like the bone disk. The disk glinted here and there out those pinprick holes.

"Everything does look…grown. If it's alive, it's not going to be happy we crawled in." He made a sweep with his phone and recorded the surroundings. "Or maybe it will be, which is probably worse."

As his eyes adjusted to the dark, glimmers of light burned around him. At the chamber's center stood the spire: conical and a meter tall. Faint lights pulsed along it in strange patterns.

The otter climbed up the ramp and touched it. Gentle at first, then harder as she noticed its give, like a loose tooth. Twitching golden nerves writhed where it joined the floor. "This looks just like the one in town hall. Just not burned." She turned to him, eyes glittering in the eerie light. "Maxie, I think we hit the jackpot here."

The husky, taking video with his phone, gestured for her to stop. "Don't touch it."

She beckoned him closer. "Your knife."

He pulled it free and handed it to her, taking flashlight and disk in return.

With a flick of her paws, she snapped the blade out and started sawing the ropy nerves that held the spire in place.

"You're totally touching it." With a whine of worry, he sidled closer to her. "I think we should leave."

"We're going to need proof." She sawed at the connections, which hissed and bled ooze. "More proof than a frantic mobile phone video or fake-looking pictures."

The husky pondered this notion, happy for something concrete to distract him from the surreal space. The flashlight's beam flared over levers and divots, worn smooth with use. He made sure to get footage of the claw-marks in the bone console. A spinning bone orrery held spheres of pale gold, though blackness blotted his vision if he looked too close. Nearby, a small trough held tiny, familiar disks; miniature copies of the device-organ in his hand, but at various stages of development. His claws tapped over them, finding one loose. He handed it to Kylie. "Looks like we found the source of your uncle's disk. Looks like its growing more."

She studied it for a moment, then resumed cutting. Steam rose from the twitching nerves. The knife burned her paw, forcing her to drop it more than once. After half a minute of steady work, she sliced the last connection and raised the blade in triumph. "That should do it."

"Kylie? We should probably go…" He pocketed the blade and edged toward the door, though he stayed within arm's reach of the otter. "I don't want to leave too much of our scent around here."

The lutrine yanked the pillar free of its socket with a discordant symphony of wet snaps. "Got it!" She hefted the thing in her arms, staggering with the weight of it down the ramp. The severed nerves writhed like tendrils, still bleeding their yellow goo.

A rumble shook the room. The walls shifted, flexed, and rippled. The bones clattering returned, all around them now, echoing in the swallowing space. Structures collapsed upon themselves and each other. The room drew smaller, pillars fitting together like a set of fangs.

Kylie watched, transfixed, in awe. Then she grabbed his paw. "We've gotta get out of here."

He nodded and hurried backward, up toward the entrance, then spared a single glance back.

Half the chamber had folded away. In the distant wall, another wall spread open. With four legs on the floor and two on the ceiling, a being issued forth into the writhing space. Its black body contorted over collapsing chunks of bone-wall as its claws worked levers with frantic abandon. Three golden eyes gleamed his way, then a mouth at their center unleashed a shriek of otherworldly fury.

Max and Kylie ran.

The cavern collapsed behind them, crunching atop the black being and its panicked motions. Walls folded in without hesitation on their master, fusing floor and ceiling as the pair ducked out the entrance. Behind them, the stone clenched shut, sealing the mysterious chamber, and its occupant, in merciless granite. Down the tunnel, supports flashed bone-white, then flowed like putty, collapsing the earth above. Rock and dirt tumbled off his back. His tail hid between his knees. With the entrance a meter away, Max grabbed Kylie by the vest and hauled her out of the sealing mine and into the safety of daylight. They spilled onto the rocky ground, the dog yanking his foot back as the entrance closed around it. A gout of bone-white powder roared after them. Cold blood rushed through him even as his throat burned from the dust.

They panted and coughed at the shore of the stream, well clear of the collapsing tunnel. They glanced back to see it crumble into the hillside. Scree tumbled in a sheet and plunked into the water at their feet. They panted, covered in dust, and exchanged a glance.

The dog looked her over. "You okay?"

She nodded. Shaken but standing, Kylie still hugged the conical alien device to her chest, its amber connections now limp as severed intestines. Patterns of translucence still pulsed with light.

The otter beamed.

He wagged and put the disk in his backpack. They'd just defeated an alien monster and walked away with proof. Not a bad day. But the way Kylie took his paw, and the gratitude and trust in her eyes as she pulled him toward home, felt like the greatest victory of all.

Together, they tramped out of the creek bed and tried to shake the dust from their pelts. The forest around them loomed quiet, as if in reverence for the mayhem they'd just caused. Not a single bird or insect called.

Kylie bubbled and bounced up the incline. "Soooo…" A happy chitter interrupted her as she hefted the glowing bone column. "…we have proof now. We can show this to everybody and the whole world will know my family was never crazy. Also, we'll have discovered aliens."

"Yeah." Max nodded, dust shaking from his fur with every step through the woods. "Not sure who we could show it to."

"Oh right. We're famous." The otter slumped a little. "Dang."

"Plus: we crushed the monster, but what if it still had an accomplice?" He met her eyes. "Might come after us for killing their buddy if we start bragging about it."

270

"Right." She trudged up the hillside. "So we look into that, then figure out a way to tell the world."

He lifted a digit. "Or there could be more than one monster."

The otter looked alarmed for an instant, then shook her head. "The journals always say it's unique."

The husky mulled over a moment of moral quandary. "Was it okay to kill that thing?"

"That really dangerous monster that's been making my family go nuts for generations? That was charging right at us?" She sputtered and pointed back toward the mine. "Yes, I think that was justified."

"Might've been the last of its kind." He shrugged. "I've just never made a species extinct before."

"If it had accomplices, they'll have no idea we did it." Her deft paws checked that the flashlight still worked, then stuck it through a loop on her vest. "Gives us the advantage."

"What'll we do when we find them?" The dog cocked an ear, then brushed some dirt from his scruff. "Can't collapse a mine on them."

"I dunno; get a restraining order?" Her hand found his. "We'll figure it out. Besides, it might have been coercing them. They might thank us."

He nodded, then gripped her paw.

The otter's smile lit the woods. "We totally have proof, though."

He wagged. "Yep."

"Thank you." She stretched up and kissed his cheek.

"For stumbling into danger with you?"

"For staying." Her shoulders rolled in a shrug. "You didn't have to."

The dog stopped, placed his hands on her hips, and kissed her. "Yeah, I did."

The lutrine wriggled with glee, still holding the dripping alien spire.

He tried to ignore the last time he'd seen her wiggle that much against him. At least until they got back to the house. He slung an arm around her. "C'mon, rudderbutt. We'd better go wash up and stash the evidence somewhere safe." His head tilted, eyes shifting her way. "We're telling your mom, right?"

"She never saw the journals as anything but a way to make something useful outta our family's mental illness." She quirked an eyebrow. "Might take some convincing." Her paws patted the light-pulsing bone device. "Too bad she's at that sci-fi con or we could start that awkward conversation now."

He glanced to the spire. "In the meantime, it'll make a charming den lamp."

She laughed, a beautiful noise that ran down his soul like a creek over stones.

The canine found himself staring at her. From somewhere deep in his chest, a smile rose to his muzzle.

The light in her eyes caught his.

Happy to be alive, happy to be together, they tromped further into the forest. Though other monsters could be hiding behind every tree, Max contented himself in the fact that he at least wasn't in this alone.

CHAPTER 17
Loose Ends

STRANGEVILLE (WED/9p)

S04E20 "The Calm after the Storm": With the member of the Tribunal imprisoned for tax evasion, Sandy and her friends rush to unravel the last of their plans and come to terms with their victory.

Pulses of sickly yellow light emanated from the guest bedroom closet. The alien pillar twitched a nerve ending now and then, but remained otherwise inert. The nerves on the bottom had stopped leaking, too, and the jagged edge she'd left cutting it free had long since healed. The pale glow grasped out at the otter and husky sitting across the room.

Seated on his bed, Kylie looked up from the journals on her phone. "Ya think that thing's radioactive?"

Max thought for a moment, then got up and shut the closet door.

A look of incredulity colored her sleek features.

"We did carry it all the way from the mine and we're not dead." Beside her on the mattress, he picked up one of the old journals. "Maybe we can buy a Geiger counter in town."

"Windfall would be the town..." She flicked to another page on her mobile. "I put the scans on your phone. You don't have to read those physical copies."

He looked the book over and shrugged. A soft wag breezed over the sheets. "As long as we're not in town, the accomplice won't see."

"So..." She blew a lock of hair from her face. "The monster's dead."

The canine scratched his whiskers and looked up at her. "The big one is dead. We still know very little about the skitters."

She waved the thought away. "We should show that pillar to the police or maybe some reporters. Authorities of some sort."

"We can start with your mother when she gets back on Tuesday." He flipped open the journal. "This does concern her."

The lutrine sighed. "Can't we do something less awkward? Like hold an international press conference?"

A shadow of worry flickered over his mind. He set a paw on her knee. "If we do, the monster's buddy may come knocking."

"What about that weird schnauzer with the curio shop?" Her webbed toes flexed against the carpet. "He knew a lot about my family, and he's the only one in town to really get involved. Think he might be the one?"

"He sold you the journal." The husky waggled the slim volume. "Don't know why the monster's accomplice would help us find it." He shrugged. "Would've been much easier to help the creature find us."

The otter swept the journal from her phone's display. "I'm texting Shane; maybe he knows something about the place Leister burned down." Her webbed fingers tapped over the glass surface. "We should dig the lair back up too and look for clues."

The dog smirked and turned a page. "I forgot my tractor at home."

Her phone buzzed. "Shane says he used to walk by the burnt-out house on the way to school. People claimed it was haunted until the new owner tore it down."

"Hmm." Thoughts worked through the gears of Max's mind. His head tilted as he stared into space. Unfortunately, that space held Kylie's rump, so his thoughts kept going astray.

The otter noticed him staring, oozed around so her gaze met his, and lay with her creamy stomach exposed from under her t-shirt. "Something on your mind?"

The canine blushed and blinked back to attention. "Ask him about your curio shop friend."

Silence swept the room, then another message buzzed in. Her hazel eyes skimmed the text. "He also says that schnauzer's lived above his store since before the fire."

Max plunked a search into his laptop's keyboard. "The guy in the house was a recluse. Porcupine."

She rolled her eyes. "So much for the schnauzer."

Gaze back on the screen, the husky winced. "Police never found his body after the fire."

"Holy mackerel!" Kylie's whiskers quirked in horror. "My great-uncle killed the guy?"

"Maybe." He squinted at the screen. "Only reference is this newspaper article from twenty-five years ago. The guy was rumored to have inherited the haul from a mine. Sold chunks of silver now and then to keep afloat."

"Almost like he had a monster mining for him."

"Yeah…" The dog's ears dropped as he performed the mental math. "Even if he survived the fire, the journals references go back fifty years before, with him mentioned as an adult. If he was only our age then, he would've been at least in his seventies when the house burned down and almost a hundred now."

A confident nod dipped her round little muzzle, then smacked her fist into a webbed paw. "We can probably take him in a fight."

He smirked at her spirit. "On the other hand, a hundred year old wouldn't be much help as an accomplice."

She quirked an eyebrow. "You think the monster posted a job offer for a replacement?"

"The porcupine could've." The canine's claws tapped on another of the journals. "Leister's journal never mentioned an accomplice to the accomplice."

Her fingers steepled and tapped her lips in thought. "I wonder how the porcupine got the job in the first place."

His brow furrowed. "Maybe there's something we missed."

"Yeah." She returned to her scanned copies. "I guess it can't hurt to know as much as possible before we break this story to the world."

A cloudburst tapped against the windows. Outside, thick billows floated in a blue sky, drizzling over the canopy of trees. The forest colors deepened, half-lit.

Max read on. Another diary speculated that no storm could level a mountainside like that Windfall had been; it speculated someone had been mining already and that their powder house had gone up. Notes in a different hand countered that this scenario would take far more explosives than any miner would keep on hand. The husky cleared his throat. "Hey rudderbutt..." He patted her rump. "...if you ever make footnotes in these, please initial them."

The lutrine chittered a chuckle. "I use sticky notes."

"Right." He glanced to the colorful bits of paper poking from some of the journals. "Still, it would help if we could sort out whose handwriting is whose."

"Ugh." She tossed her phone onto a pillow. "I'm learning my family being right doesn't mean they weren't also crazy. This one goes on for like eight pages about how the Universe is big and he is small."

The dog cocked an ear, then rubbed a paw around her midriff. "Maybe your ancestors weren't as used to being the smallest as you are."

She wriggled up into his hand, her fur silk under his paw pads. "Shut up, Maxie." Her webbed finger poked his flank. "I've seen Cosmos. This isn't news to me."

"This journal was written in what?" He checked the top of the page. "1925? Yeah, the bigness of the Universe was news then."

She threw an arm over her eyes. "Bleh."

He sniffed at her. "Break?"

The last of her will escaped in a small sigh. "Yeah..."

He smirked. "Know what we haven't done in the week we've been dating?" His paw slid up her torso, drifting under her shirt.

The lutrine caressed his thigh and flashed a coy smile up at him. "What?"

"Dated."

Realization blinked across her face. "Huh... I guess you're right."

A smirk quirked his muzzle. "Unless monster-hunting counts as a date."

The otter couldn't suppress a smile of her own. "In my family, it might…"

He stood and offered his hand. "I'll treat you to the best Windfall has to offer."

She took it with a roll of her eyes. "It's called Pinchy's and we go there all the time."

His ears lifted. "Is that a no?"

"Of course not! I love Pinchy's." She curled around him to get to the door, every inch of her supple body sliding around his. "C'mon, you can buy me a clam platter."

Together they padded down the game trails to town, mindful of the rain-damp earth. Every wet branch slipped its damp leaves over Kylie in a refreshing caress. Behind her, Max's pelt soaked up every drop of water in a three-foot radius and he kept having to stop to brush the worst of it off. She waited for him, considering not for the first time how ill-suited a husky was to this environment. Now that they'd accidentally avenged her family, would Max succumb to pack pressure and go farm corn or whatever?

On cue, he patted a waterlogged paw on her shoulder, which chased off her doubts for the moment.

She touched his hand, then brought it down to be held. Because of their difference in height, she had to get the right angle in their hand-holding or feel like she was being led into a fancy ball. "I kind of feel stupid now for waiting and worrying, knowing you would've dated me whenever."

He thought for a moment. "You know how you can have a favorite song for years without really thinking about the lyrics?"

"Yeah?"

"Then they just sort of click in your mind and you like it in a whole new way?" He squeezed her paw with a shine in those sky blue eyes. "That's how I feel about you."

A wiggle of glee translated up her body. Unable to think of a response sweet enough, she dragged him down for a quick smooch. The swish of his tail scattered rain from leaves and told her he understood.

At Pinchy's, she drowned her trouble further in a sea of fish, then sat watching the sun set over the ocean in a slow, autumn shimmer. Eventually, Max convinced her to take him for a walk. He paid the bill and they started for the door. A few booths down, the beaver handyman picked his way through the spicy tuna, grimacing when he got a hot bite.

"It's funny living in a town this small." She took the dog's hand as they stepped out into the rain-shined street. "Shane says he's lived in the same neighborhood as our contractor since he was a kid."

A giddy rhino trotted up to them through a cluster of tourists, excusing himself as he bumped their souvenir bags. "Hi guys!" His shirt depicted anime versions of the cast.

Kylie groaned. "Karl, your torso does weird things to my face." Her paws set on her hips. "We talked about this."

"This is a new shirt. The rule shouldn't apply. Besides, this isn't you! It's Kasi-san, right? No? No? Okay." He rubbed his gut, self-conscious. "Hey, would you guys wanna be on my *Strangeville* fan podcast? We're talking about what forms a revival of the series could take and—"

"Hey..." Max cocked an ear. "Record this."

The rhino fumbled his phone to record mode.

With a smirk, the husky put on a thin Russian accent. "Previously, on Strange Times..."

Karl tittered in glee, then stopped recording. "Don't worry, I can edit out my laughter and stuff. This'll be great."

Max crossed his arms with a smirk. "But seriously, we haven't heard anything about the series being revived."

"Is there anything new about merchandising you can tell me?"

A drip of water fell on her ear, which she twitched off. "Karl, anything I tell you'd just end up on the Internet again."

"Well, yes." His tiny tail swished, smacking the building next to them. "That's how the world advances."

The otter groaned.

The rhino's massive hands wrung. "Aw come on, I bet you guys have all sorts of inside info. We talk about this stuff all the time on my podcast."

She grumbled. "Karl."

"I say mine, but it's actually a collaboration—"

She glared. "Karl?"

The rhino tapped his massive fingers together and babbled on. "We've interviewed a special effects guy, but nobody who'd—"

Max got a sly smirk. "Season Three was a dream."

"Really?!" A gasp shook the rhino. He stood in stunned silence for a moment, ears flicking as thoughts rushed through his brain. "Oh my gosh, that makes total sense!"

"Not really. Just a personal theory." The canine woofed a chuckle. "But calm down; I'll be on your podcast."

"Seriously?" Karl bounced, shaking the pavement a little.

"Seriously?" Kylie's whiskers and shoulders drooped.

"Sure." The canine spread his hands. "Why not?"

The rhino pulled out his phone again and began tapping with frantic delight.

Her gaze locked on him. "What're you doing?"

"Telling the Internet I landed you as a guest." The rhino's dark eyes remained fixed on the tiny screen. "This is gonna be awesome!"

"Ugh." Kylie took her boyfriend by the arm and led him away. They walked on, leaving Karl to the fan forums.

The young rhino seemed not to notice.

Max just grinned.

The otter scowled. "Season Three was a dream, huh?"

The canine nodded. "Total conjecture, but it fits the lore."

She raised an eyebrow at him.

An amused shrug rolled his wide shoulders. "What? I like the show."

"I've been avoiding that podcast for months." Orbiting in a supple circle, she chittered at him. "Now you're encouraging him!"

"I like him." Max wagged.

With a squawk, she bounced in protest. "You like anyone who's not scared by your hugeness."

"That's possible. I like you…" He scooped her up in a hug and kept walking, letting her legs and tail dangle over the sidewalk. His muzzle brushed her ear. "…and I seem to remember you enjoying my hugeness."

Her whiskers sprung out in scandal. She oozed over his hands and rolled like a wave back to her feet. "That's different! The rhino's completely nuts."

"So?"

"Okay, so that didn't stop you from liking me." Her arms crossed over her breasts. "But my point stands."

"Let the guy be excited." He rubbed her shoulders. "*Strangeville* to him is like fish to you."

"What, nourishing, but leaves you wanting more?"

"Exactly."

"That's not a fair comparison." The otter waddled on with emphatic gestures. "I'm supposed to like fish—I'm an otter!"

"And he's a fan. Just let him do his thing."

The lutrine grumbled as they headed down the street.

Standing in the living room, Max took a deep breath, steeled his resolve, and gave his ears a resolute perk. Then he drew the phone from his pocket and dialed. Two rings, then a click as she picked up. He cleared his throat.

"Hey little bro." His sister answered. "How's life in otter space?"

"Hey Aggie." His middle sister usually stood up for him, but she still took him by the scruff now and then. And her tone of voice certainly pointed in that direction. "Doing fine."

She practically panted with anticipation. "Let me guess: you're not coming home because you're dating that otter girl you like so much."

He sighed. "Pretty much, yeah."

"Who made the first move?"

A moment of hesitation crawled by, but brought no good way to evade the question. "She did."

"Ha!" She woofed with triumph. "Called it."

"Are you betting on my happiness?"

"Would you rather I bet against it?"

Pinching the bridge of his nose, he groaned. "Just put Mom on the line."

She chuckled. "Good luck, runt."

He rolled his eyes; he'd been taller than Agatha since he was a fifth grader. Hearing her call for his mom, he braced himself. It would've been one thing if he'd gone to college on the East Coast, but this was just to shack up with a girl. Well, and to hunt monsters, but he couldn't tell her that part.

The phone clattered as it was handed off. "Hello?"

He forced himself to smile. "Hey Mom."

"Well, if it isn't Traveling Max." The whistle of the pressure gauge signaled canning in progress. "Been missing you around here."

He smiled a little. "Miss you guys too."

Another moment crept past. In the background, canning lids popped with a metallic ping as they cooled. "I take it you're calling to say you're still not coming back."

"Not right away." He paced the carpet, phone cradled against his ear.

"Thought you were just going to visit. Go scent-smelling and all that." She adjusted something with a grunt. "Now, you're staying there."

"Yeah, the plan changed." He rubbed the nape of his neck. "You know I want to spend time with the family. But Kylie and I, we just started dating and I don't want to move back across the country so soon. Is that Aggie in the background? Tell her to shut up, I can hear her snickering."

His mother paused just long enough to have stared down the laughter. "You're an adult now, so I won't lecture you, but you barely settled in before you took off again." She paused, probably adjusting some aspect of the canning process. "The pack's not the same without you. Thought I'd get some time around my son after all these years."

"I came home between seasons." He looked out the window. When he'd signed on to *Strangeville*, they'd admitted the show represented a once in a lifetime opportunity. Living half a continent away to date an old cast member, though, would be a much harder sell. As he listened, he grabbed the brush from his room and gave himself a once-over; grooming always calmed him.

"I was young too, you know: I've made impulsive choices in my day."

The phone buzzed on his cheek. He looked, still listening.

Kylie Bevy: {You should come up here when you're done...}

His tail swayed.

Pertinent arguments from his mom echoed through the mobile. "You're sure you're not just trying to cling to the glory days? What about college? You just bailing on that too?"

A sigh from deep in his chest evaporated his desire to talk. "I'm not giving up on college. Lots of people take a break. Better than burning out and getting bad grades." His free hand gestured into empty space. "It's not like I've disappeared into the back alleys of Amsterdam; I'm in New England with people you know. And unlike on the show, I'm not sleeping on their fold-out or in some cramped spare room. I'm moving up in the world." The husky chuckled, but decided not to mention he hadn't exactly been sleeping alone.

"I'm just saying we miss you." She sealed another can. A shade of vulnerability reached her voice. "I miss you."

His paws carried him on an endless and automatic tour of the living room. "I know you miss me. I miss you too. And I'll be home before too long; I promise."

"Don't think I won't hold you to that." A slight growl entered her tone. "This plan of yours changes every time I talk to you."

He traced a paw along the top of the sofa. "Alright. Bye, Mom."

She gave a soft sigh. "Bye, pup."

Hanging up, he padded upstairs, wagging that he'd bought himself some time. Mom would cool down and, in the meantime, he'd have more adventures with Kylie…of various sorts. On the way, he double-checked she wasn't still on the line.

The otter checked everything was in place. Lights down, candles lit, soft music playing: perfect. A nervous giggle escaped her throat as she sat back on the bed. Her legs crossed and uncrossed as she wondered which looked more enticing. Her tail flowed over the covers, a cream-and-cocoa curve she hoped would lead his gaze to her rump.

A creak on the stairs and he turned the corner into her room, still pondering his phone.

In her sultry voice, she leaned back on her hands, lifting her breasts. "Hey Maxie."

"Hey, rudderb—" He paused and looked up, his ears going further and further erect. "You're naked."

"Almost." She writhed on the sheets, toying with the hem of his favorite old t-shirt.

The insides of his ears turned an adorable shade of pink.

Her hips rocked back and forth on the sloshing waterbed as she wiggled in anticipation.

Max drifted close, attracted. He eased onto the bed, so big but so careful. One paw curled over her hip as the other lifted her chin to a kiss. Tension clung to his muscles, though it eased as her paws roamed his back.

Her tongue slipped over his lips, then lapped at his own. The warmth of his mouth and the fur of his arms chased away the cold of the world.

His fingers traced her thigh, then brushed the thin pelt over her slit. A cautious fingertip spread her, then explored just a little way inside her. He slipped in, one knuckle at a time. Breaking the kiss, he nosed under the t-shirt and began a tender licking tour of her nipples. Two fingers now sunk into her passage, stroking in and out along her growing moisture.

She bit her lip at the delicate pleasure rolling through her body, hips rocking. Tail curling and uncurling on the covers, she arched under his powerful form.

Heartbeats later, his lips began trailing down her body. Wide, caring paws spread her legs. His muzzle hovered over her naked crotch, eyes tracing her folds.

The otter's thick tail curled up a bit, trying in vain to cover her. Her knees slipped a little closer together as her gaze fell from eye contact under the weight of the moment. "You don't have to…"

A swish of his tail stirred the silence. "I know." His claws combed her dense pelt to relax her. A playful gleam sparked in his eyes, even as a blush lingered in his ears. "I get to." His sturdy white muzzle sank between her thighs.

Kylie allowed herself a shiver of anticipation, head tilting back, eyes drifting shut as his soft breathing washed across her most tender places…

Cold shot through her.

"Eek!" She wriggled, knees squeezed on his ears. "Your nose!"

"Thorry." The husky looked up from between her thighs, peering over her bare breasts. "I, uh, don't actually know what I'm doing here."

"Like I do?" She smirked, anxious. Anxious paws gripped the hem of the t-shirt. "Even I can't bend that far."

He sank back down and licked with redoubled enthusiasm. As her legs relaxed, his tongue caressed her folds with eager interest.

The otter lay back, head rocking from side to side, hips wiggling with abandon against his now-warm nose.

Again and again, he licked along her slit, then pressed further. He delved deep, that long silky tongue curling up inside her. Every little wave of motion teased pleasure from her flesh.

284

Her muscles clenched at the pleasure. Her breath caught. Tense teeth dragged along a trembling lower lip. When she could stand no more, she reached down to guide his lapping muzzle up to her clit.

That silken tongue traced over her sensitive bud. Breath traced tender flesh. Raw pleasure raced up her nerves.

Awash with pleasure, her body rolled upon the waves of orgasm. Her slippery walls clenched down as his soft tongue rubbed ever faster on her nub, drawing out the climax as long as possible. Knowing her best friend enjoyed lapping up her juices compounded the exhilaration as her body tensed, arced, and at last flopped to the sheets.

In a dreamy haze, she drew him up her body, slinking higher on the waterbed. Their kisses raced, one into another, just like their heartbeats. His paw slid under the old t-shirt to caress her breasts. She arched back, enjoying the feel of his rough paw pads on her nipples, then helped him pull the shirt over her head. Her own paws responded in kind: first relieving him of his shirt and hoodie, then his pants and boxers. At last, they lay together, naked, panting, and lost in each other's fur.

Strong paws traced her body, one drifting down to line him up with her entrance. Wet heat greeted her folds as his tip brushed them.

"Wait."

He froze, concern in his arctic eyes. His weight shifted off of her and onto his elbows.

Her paw touched his chest, rolling him to one side. "I wanna have you on the bottom this time."

The dog let her move him, waterbed sloshing beneath them. Kylie couldn't help but lick her lips as her eyes travelled down his long torso, with its vivid black and white markings. As his tender blue eyes beckoned her, His paws waiting for her next move, raised and bent at his chest. His sheath was plump and heavy, crimson tip peeking out into the open air, begging for attention. Between his knees, his trapped tail tried to wag. He was hers for the taking, and she loved it.

She crawled over the waiting dog. With a brush of whiskers, her lips met his. The kisses shifted to nuzzles and whispered breaths, then back to

kisses. Their tongues traced together with velvet friction. His breath traced hot against her cheeks.

Grinding up at her, he moaned into her open mouth. As she sat up, she could feel his tail swishing under hers. Those powerful hands stroked her pelt, exploring, caressing. Ears flat, he looked up at her with a whine of adoration.

Her paw wrapped around his sheath; her finger webbing brushed his exposed tip. She stroked him back and forth a few times and watched him writhe in pleasure against her water mattress, ripples traveling under the sheets. Hot precum dribbled against her webbing, which she examined for a moment. A lot like her own moisture, though this smelled muskier, more canine, and very male. Sweeping a leg over his hip, she wiggled down against his crotch and guided him into wet, welcoming folds. Slow and steady at first, she sank onto him. Having him inside her felt amazing, even more so with the slick combination of his saliva and her juices. "Oh yeah.

Mmm..." A chitter of delight escaped her muzzle. "You feel really good in me."

He spread her wider until her labia met his sheath and eased it down. Only the slightest bulge hinted at the knot to come, yet she felt so filled, so loved. Those big white paws gripped her thighs, grinding her down against his hips with adoring whimpers. "Kylie! Mmmm! Oh..."

Testing the waters, the otter rocked her hips a few times, adoring the feel of his hot length inside her. A smile spread over her muzzle as she heard his whines of delight get louder. She chittered with glee and bounced atop him in earnest. "Yeah... Mmm, fill me up, Maxie."

The dog gasped and gripped the bedcovers. His canine bulge swelled, slipping in and out of her sensitive folds. It stretched her, teased her, filled her with eager need. It got tougher and tougher each time to press him back inside.

With her rudder for leverage, she thrust hard against him, biting her lip as his knot battered her entrance. She tried not to smack his balls with the thick base of her tail—he'd always been so careful with her, like he was afraid he'd break her. Despite being half his size and not a canine, she craved his knot. The idea of him being so close, being so deep, as intimate as two beings ever could be, added tender ferocity to her thrusts. His friendship, his love, his heart, his knot: she wanted every bit of Max. "Harder! Give in to me! Yeah, right there!"

Hind paws braced on the foot of the bed, the husky humped up at her. His teeth set in restraint, careful not to hurt her. Those paws gripped her hips, strong as her desire. Always so protective. His touch drifted down, massaging his soft-furred sheath against the back of his firm bulge.

The waterbed threw off their motions; she'd have to get used to having someone else involved in her antics under the covers. Palms on his chest, she slammed down and pressed hard. She thought loose thoughts, relaxing her muscles against the tension of delight. His knot edged inside her with great effort, little by little. Just when she thought she couldn't take any more, that they'd have to try again another day, it popped into her. She gasped and felt his bulge settle inside her. Her folds closed behind it, sore from stretching. His bulge throbbed larger inside her, expanding to fill her. With a shudder, she soaked in the unexpected sensation of him swelling to fit her just right, like they were meant to fit. A shared moan passed between them, accompanied by a pulse of fresh fluids.

He bucked under her, eyes closed, muzzle frozen in a silent howl of passion. A second throb raced up his shaft, this time joined by a flush of heat inside her. Another hot bloom followed the first, then another: hot, thick husky passion.

A blush simmered under her fur. He'd knotted her. Now he shot load after load of his seed into her waiting and tender passage. She felt it well up around his cock, trapped inside by the tie they shared. The idea, and the incredible reality of it, sent her fingers in frantic circles over her clitoris. Pleasure built upon itself to dizzying highs, then cast her off the edge into a world of roaring sensation and wet heat. A cry of orgasm shook the dim room; only a moment later did she recognize it as her own. Unabated, her hips ground down on his, his sheath bunched up against her hot and tingling labia, his shaft buried so deep inside her.

Heartbeats racing, they panted together for an endless moment. His paws fell to the bed, the surface of which rolled in waves that echoed their enthusiasm. He looked up at her with pure canine devotion, tongue lolling out the side of his thick muzzle.

Still straddling her lover, still bound by that exotic bulb of flesh, she felt his hips grind up at hers. Kylie took full advantage; she wrapped her arms behind his neck and showered his face in kisses, stroking her fingers through the soft, thick fur behind his ears, reveling in every little happy sound she drew from him. She brushed her nose along his cheek and the side of his muzzle, kissing his smile. She flashed him a giddy grin. "My Maxie."

His warm gaze shone her way, eyes lidded with post-coital drowsiness and deep satisfaction. Strong paws caressed her ribs. He angled his muzzle up a fraction and brushed his lips against hers. When the kiss faded, his voice rose in a gentle murmur. "Who else's would I be?"

She flushed with pleasure and pride, then nuzzled further into his fur with a delighted squeak. Not bad for an otter who couldn't find her wiles with both paws. In all her life, for all that they'd uncovered, she'd never felt safer.

CHAPTER 18
THE GATEWAY

STRANGEVILLE (TUE/9p)

S02E23 "Hitch in Time, Part 1": Serge is sent back in time, where he struggles to learn to fight in Roman boot camp without doing anything to change the future as the others scramble to rescue him.

Wrapped in each other's arms, the lovers cuddled in sleepy satisfaction. Long after the knot had gone down and slipped free, Kylie kept her face buried in his chest fur. Together they breathed and drifted between wakeful snuggles and dozing. She shivered whenever he shifted to make himself comfortable or lifted her chin for a long, lingering kiss, which teased his soft fur across her hypersensitive flesh. The slow, sensual cuddle kept the embers of passion lit through the dreamy haze. Kylie knew it would only be a matter of time before the tension became too much and they made love again, and for once she was happy to wait and let it happen, to savor the simple pleasure of being in bed with her best friend and lover.

Downstairs, glass shattered.

Max's ears shot up.

She clutched him, then scrambled out of bed and into a t-shirt, vest, and shorts.

The dog, meanwhile, jumped into his blue jeans, then opened the door and peered down the staircase.

Footsteps. Clanks. The thump of closing cabinets.

Heart racing, Kylie flipped on the lights. She spied through the stair railing and saw a beaver poking through the contents of their living room. A very specific beaver, in fact: the town handyman. "Joe?"

He looked up and walked nearer the stairs, meeting her gaze with oily ease. A shattered dish lay at his feet. His gait consisted of pained jerks and hyperextensions. "Hi, kids."

"It's the middle of the night! What're you doing here?" Kylie brushed loose locks of hair from her face. "If—if this is about the remodeling, Mom's gone."

"Just looking for something of mine. I doubt she could help me find it." Joe smiled a little wider. His eyes never left hers. "But you will."

Max stepped off the stairs and stood at his full height. Two meters of solid canine, corded with muscle and prickled with hackles, towered over the beaver. His eyes narrowed at the rodent.

With a jittery look around, the otter padded down to the landing. "How'd you get in?"

Wearing an inoffensive grin, Joe jingled the ring of keys on his belt.

With the hope of letting Max get the drop on him, Kylie slunk past a shattered lamp and around the beaver's back. He looked pretty rough. His clothes were ripped, but free of blood. Her eyes met his, trying to draw his attention but stay out of reach. "You okay?"

"Oh, had a little accident…" With a genial smile, he stroked the missing straps of his overalls. "…but I'll be just fine." He chuckled, which spread a gash on his flank. The wound exposed, not wet gore, but obsidian plates within.

Blackness crept in the edges of the lutrine's vision.

He hunched, a strange bulge writhing under his shirt. A claw burst forth and pinned her to the wall.

Max dove at the plump beaver. Ivory fangs shone around a snarl.

The rodent's arms folded out into claws. One flicked out and flung the dog across room.

With a crash, the canine knocked the easy chair over. Breath yelped from his lungs. Wheezing, he got his feet under him, paw clutching his side. Ears flush to his skull, he circled the grinning handyman.

The beaver stretched to tower over Max, potbelly vanishing as he unfolded new limbs from inside his arms. His head tilted, eyes glinting amber. His chin lifted. A third eye winked and glittered under his jaw. "Give back my equipment or she dies."

Head ducked, shoulders forward, a deep growl echoed from the husky. "What?"

"I thought you Bevys had finally gone and changed. I thought you'd leave me be." His tone oozed warmth and cheer, like giving directions to a lost tourist. "Either you go fetch my things or I kill you both and search the house." His grip tightened. His head pivoted backward to the husky. "I've waited too long. I'm leaving this rock tonight."

"Don't do it, Max." Kylie struggled against the wall and tried to pry loose the talons around her neck and shoulder. "It'll kill us as soon as we give it back."

The dog stood and squirmed against her command.

"It's *wearing* Joe!" The lutrine struggled in vain against the obsidian claw. "You really think it'll just leave us alone?"

"Oh, I'm the same old Joe, miss." He looked straight up, or at least his muzzle did. With all his shifting and jostling, he resembled less a beaver and more a beaver-shaped leather bag, stretched taut over something rigid and writhing within. One jagged claw doffed his ball cap so the bottom eye watched Max while his top two locked on Kylie. "Don't make killing you the most efficient way for me to fix this."

She put on her best scared-idiot-girl expression. It didn't require much acting.

That polite smile remained, frozen on the Joe-creature's face. Its head tilted down, just a little, toward her. Two of his eyes stayed cheery, the new one under his chin an ember of rage: all three stayed locked on hers. His upper lip rose to reveal a third, sniffing nostril. "Smells like you kids were having a little fun. I'd hate to ruin the evening with a gristly murder, but I'm afraid I'm just plum out of patience."

"Don't hurt her." The canine's voice rumbled like leashed thunder. "I'll give you back what we took. The spire and the disk, both."

"Max no!" The grip tightened around her chest. "Ghk!"

Guttural shadows crept into Joe's voice, but his tone remained clear and polite. "I'd suggest you hurry…"

Max spread his paws. "Just don't hurt her." Backing up, he padded into his room. His stormy eyes never left Joe until he rounded the doorway. A clatter, then he returned with the disk and pulsing bone pillar under one arm. He crouched beside the stair railing box and held the items out.

The Joe-thing beckoned with a talon, his false hand dangling like a loose sleeve. "Give them to me."

"Let her go." The canine didn't flinch. His blue eyes flashed to her.

The otter spotted hackles pricked down her boyfriend's back, his stiff posture, his bristled tail. She gave the tiniest nod. Then, with all her strength and a mighty squawk, kicked off the wall.

Joe staggered, knocked off-balance by the force. His torso bent at a fantastic angle, tail slapping into the floor to steady himself in a way that should have been impossible.

In a smooth arc, Max drew an iron rod from the box, leapt, and swung it into the side of the creature's head. The bludgeon struck with a crackling thud, scattering yellow nerve endings and shards of black shell.

His face paralyzed in a well-mannered smile, Joe shrieked and rounded on Max. He raised his claws to rip the dog apart.

With a frantic twist, Kylie seized a digit holding her and chomped, teeth piercing a rubber exterior into something like lobster shell.

The yowl spiked. Claws at her throat bore down with crushing force. Talons exploded from the beaver's flat tail and streaked toward her.

A second swing of the iron rod crushed the creature to the floor. Teeth gleaming against a snarl, Max pummeled the beast. The black spindle fell again and again, smashing flesh and breaking carapace. Fine drops of yolky gore scattered from the bludgeon with every blow.

The lutrine tumbled to the floor, then fumbled to draw a slim aerosol can from her vest pocket. Cold and heavy against her palm, a flick of her thumb popped off its safety cap. She scrambled to her feet as blows fell on the thrashing creature.

The polite face roared at his attacker, three pincers reaching out from its torn mouth. Joe reared up and knocked the husky on his tail. It pounced onto him.

Flat on his back, Max jammed his makeshift weapon into the beast's three mandibles.

With a shriek, the creature pranced back and scaled the china cabinet backwards with unnatural ease. Six claws gleamed in the kitchen light. He arched back to swing a scythe-claw through the husky.

The otter aimed the spray can and thumbed the trigger.

A torrent of red fluid struck Joe's eyes and writhing mouthparts.

A keening screech scoured her mind. Joe recoiled and wiped desperate limbs against his face. Red liquid welled in every gap in his shredded mask, clinging to the flesh beneath. The mask's mouth worked wordlessly as the creature snarled.

Kylie stepped over Max and hit the trigger again and again; shot after shot of pepper spray blasted the creature's face. It beaded against his carapace, flowing down his head like crimson tears.

Flailing, the Joe-creature staggered back, bracing against a wall. His three eyes fell upon her, a swollen trinity of hate.

Cold fury flooding her veins, she raised the canister for another shot.

Disguise in ruins, face a swollen mess, the creature scrambled away on six limbs in a haphazard, spastic retreat. His tail claw gripped the disk and pillar. His front limbs yanked open the door, and he vanished into the inky night.

Still coughing from the pepper spray, Max stood beside her, one paw on her shoulder, iron spindle still in the other. Yellow ichor dripped from it, traced with red.

In a numb panic, she gripped his bare fur. Adrenaline pulsed cold through her veins as they hurried back from the choking cloud of aerosolized pepper oil. A crimson trace curled from his palm, spreading into his pristine fur. She grabbed his arm, paws clumsy with shock. "You're bleeding!"

He set the rod down on the tile, then flexed his paw. A bloody scrape glinted on his palm pad to stain his white paw fur. "I'll be fine. You?"

"I think so." She rubbed her shoulder and breasts, aching from the crush of the Joe-beast's hand. Shaky, she rose and headed for the stairs. "Be right back."

With a look around and without a word, he padded after her anyway.

Upstairs, she grabbed bandages from the bathroom, then a baseball bat from her great uncle's room. She placed the latter in Max's good paw while she wrapped the former around his bloodied one. "So you don't destroy your paw." She crept down the stairs with him at her heel.

Max hefted the bat, child-sized to start with and about the proportion of a billy club for the huge dog. He shot her a questioning glance. "We're going after this thing?"

"The evidence my family's not crazy? The monster that broke into my house and tried to kill us? The reason my family's been going crazy for generations? Yeah, we're going after that. This could be my only chance to stop it." She shook the pepper spray canister. "Sounds like it's got more shots, but we'd better play it safe." Stuffing it in her pocket, she bounded over to the kitchen and began rooting around for dangerous utensils. "Maybe get the old harpoon gun."

The canine patted her shoulder.

She popped up like a nervous buoy, floating on a sea of adrenaline.

"We don't know if or how the harpoon gun works." His blue eyes flicked to the ladle in her paw. "And we need a plan."

"The plan is to stop him from doing whatever crazy bullshit he has in mind for those things you gave him. Or to take his picture, at the very least." Kylie jabbed at the darkness with the scoop. "He has to be going back to his lair."

His ears rose. "So there's more to it than what we destroyed?"

Her paws gripped the ladle. "Or he dug it out again."

Max cast a determined glance at the forest.

Kylie snatched a pair of sushi knives and stuck them, scabbards first, into her jeans pockets. Not that she knew what to do with them, but it was better than nothing. She'd have carried more of them, but her vest pockets weren't big enough.

As she turned, Max stood in the somewhat-destroyed entryway. Yellow ichor shone along the ancient hardwood. Plates lay smashed, chairs flung about the room. With a conflicted and quiet whine, he worried a small object between his paws.

"What's that?" She pointed at it.

With great hesitation, he revealed the item with a wet jingle. "An unidentified set of house keys."

"These have to be Joe's keys! Oh, nasty." She took the slimy key ring with ginger claws and rinsed it in the kitchen sink.

He tilted his head to the scene of the battle. "Maybe I shouldn't have picked them up."

The otter squalked. "Are you kidding? Now we know he can't skip town—he's gotta be going back to his lair." She bounced from foot to foot. "We can totally catch up to him!"

His bandaged paw closed around the handle of the baseball bat. "That's just what I was afraid of."

Stars hung cold in an inky sky. Lutrine and canine stood before the entrance to the mine, which lay buried under a ton of stone.

Max sniffed, bat in hand. "Hmm. Unless he can phase through rocks and leave no scent, I'm thinking there's another entrance."

Glum, she sat down on some moss and swept the woods with her flashlight. "Yeah, but where?"

Max's eyeshine glinted in the white, wide-beam light. "Also important: how do we find or open that entrance without the disk?"

"Oh." Her paw slipped into a vest pocket and drew out something resembling a sand dollar. "I stole the smaller one you found in the lab."

Pointy husky ears rose. "And you assumed Joe couldn't sense it or something."

She shrugged. "If he could sense them, why'd he bother taking a hostage?" Her paw rubbed the bruises forming along her breasts.

Max gave a slow nod, then gestured with the bat at the bridge overhead. "The caves ran under Windfall."

Her fingers traced the etched bone disk, then she looked up. "So the entrance might be in town."

"Makes sense." He tapped his claws on the length of the bat. "Hmm. If our monster is its own accomplice, then who was living in the house your uncle burned down?"

"The monster in accomplice form! Joe!" Kylie bounced to her feet. "Come on."

"Okay." He followed over the mossy ground. "Where's Joe live?"

Kylie froze, then sputtered. "No idea." She smiled. "But I know how we can find out…"

The night hung close around them, broken only by the occasional car rumbling down the block. The buildings in this part of Windfall held a sense of age, but constant upkeep. Shane's family's yard stood fenced and groomed. A lawnmower stood in one corner, not put away.

Phone still glowing from the text, Kylie bounced in place on the steps. If Shane fell back asleep instead of coming down, she'd drag him out by the tail and beat Joe into submission with him.

Max stood behind her, the slim bat buried in his pocket. His heavy paw rested on the pommel as those stormy blue eyes watched the street. The angle he stood at more or less concealed the bludgeon.

Shane stumbled to the door, rubbing his eyes, phone still in hand. "What's this about?"

She poked a digit at the tabby. "You said Joe lives around here. Where?"

"Three houses down." He blinked, pointed, and stretched. "What possible home maintenance emergency are you having at four AM? Toilet detonation?"

The otter took a deep breath. "He's actually an immortal alien monster who's been battling my family for generations."

"Huh." The cat yawned back into the house. "Well, goodnight." He closed the door.

Upstairs, a light clicked on in an upstairs window. A floppy-eared shadow materialized into Sarah, who studied them with the same steady concern she'd expressed guiding them in the Crystal Caverns. Arms crossed, she watched the pair standing in her yard.

Kylie shrugged up at her.

The bunny only quirked an ear, like she wanted an explanation later. Then she turned and vanished deeper into the house, probably to catch Shane on his way upstairs.

Husky and otter stood in the street for a moment, then the dog slung his backpack over his shoulder. They hustled up the block, past the Amphicar, to the house Shane had pointed to.

Slinking up the sidewalk, her nervous paws pulled the pepper spray from her vest and toyed with it. "How'd you know this would work on aliens?"

"I didn't." Max tapped a claw at the ingredients list. "But I got you the brand with tarantula venom, to hedge my bets."

With a look of worry, she held the can a little further away. "Harsh."

"I just had to trust you wouldn't blast yourself with it." He smirked and slung an arm over her shoulders, drawing her close. "Or me."

She felt a little safer and a little more trusted. Most boyfriends didn't entrust their girlfriend with chemical weapons.

One story tall and in good repair, the house languished a color-starved pallor. A familiar work van stood outside; Max's paw traced over the hood to find the engine cold. They moved with care down the walkway, wary of the lawn gnome. Joe seemed too practical to have a lawn gnome.

Creeping up the front steps, the husky turned to her. "We're sure this is his house, right?"

"I don't know!" Kylie's whisper came out more frantic than she'd realized. "Shane said it was!"

He nodded, braced himself to bash the door down, but froze when she waggled the keychain at him. She flipped through the keys, at last finding the right one. The lock resisted. It dawned on her they could have the wrong house, not matter what a groggy feline said. Then the key turned, not with worn surrender of heavy use, but with the slick grind of having sat untouched for years. The door swung open at her barest touch, oiled to silence. A scarce whisper of breeze came as the only indication sound still existed in the world.

The husky offered her only a shrug.

They proceeded inside.

Inside, the house seemed just as normal. A bit too normal, like a set designed for a passing shot. Darkness draped over every surface, puddled in every corner. They tiptoed in, but found not a single squeaky floorboard. A clock, a television, a living room set: old perhaps but in excellent condition.

Flashlight beam cutting through the gloom, Kylie's eyes fell upon a picture frame. A heartbeat of panic followed. Joe wouldn't have family photos—this had to be the wrong house. She froze, transfixed by the strangers in the frame, wondering whose home they'd just invaded. She recognized none of the people and they seemed to be all from different species. One of them held up a sign with pricing and photo size info. Only then did the otter breathe again. "That lazy bastard; he never took out the display photos that came with the frame."

Max tapped a digit against his lips for silence and led onward. They slunk downstairs, finding a stark and empty basement. Bare studs lined the walls around a pristine concrete floor. If the upstairs had been an underdressed set, this room sat naked. The canine padded into center of the room. "Smells like Joe's been here. And it smells like the mine." He looked around, but found only a few three-clawed scratch marks in the walls. "Don't see any door that could lead there, though."

"Oh." The lutrine pulled the small disk from her pocket. Tiny lights flickered along its periphery. Her teeth buzzed.

The concrete floor rippled and split open under him. He dropped with a flail, a yelp, and a thud.

The otter raced to the edge of the concrete maw. The edges had become bone-white. "Ohmygosh, are you okay?"

Dazed, the dog shook his head. He waved her concern away. Yellow light flickered off his silver wristwatch. "I'm in one piece."

"Stay there." Tension still gripped her. They'd fought off Joe together, but if he found them separated... She shuddered, then tried climbing down, but found the walls of the passage too steep. She hurriedly scoured the room for something to climb down with. That ladder on Joe's van would do, but the night had gotten a lot scarier with Max down a hole. After a tense second, she grabbed a sturdy chair from upstairs and lowered it down the hole. Using it as a platform, she hopped down the bare bone wall. The dog steadied her shoulder as she landed on the lumpy white floor. Around her, the space hung empty, as if this tunnel gulped shut when not in use.

They pressed on. Down, down, diving into darkness and thrumming organic contrivances. Pale spires and pillars grew in the dark like toothy fungi. The machinery moaned a discordant drone. A journal entry surfaced in her mind, one about a noise that sank into your bones and couldn't be shaken, and how her great-uncle had begun hearing it in every distant echo.

Max took her paw.

Shoving the memory aside, she gripped his uninjured hand and headed further into darkness. Slowly, slowly, a light grew around corners. Down the cave's throat, they found a chamber tangled with grown equipment.

Yellow light swallowed all other colors. They ducked through the pulsing glow into the cavern, climbing over smooth, white spikes.

She recognized it as the cavern they'd collapsed, only...crumpled. Now a fraction of the size it had been, pillars of fresh, clean bone strained under the weight of the roof. The ceiling hung barely high enough to stand in some places. Scree and jagged rocks lay in piles around the floor.

In a pit at the room's center, an archway of bone perverted the reality within it, twisting it into impossible shapes. Beside it, an obsidian form hunched, manipulating knobs and arteries with swift claws. Joe straightened from his console, obsidian and six-limbed. He sighed. "You kids'll be the death of me."

Movement at her feet made her jump. The remains of his beaver disguise pooled on the floor like a discarded robe, mouthing his words.

"You're the one who broke into our house and tried to kill us!"

Joe didn't respond, only fine-tuning a few prickly knobs.

Keeping Max in sight, Kylie lit a cluster of glass spheres with her flashlight. Each held strange shapes writhing within, set on a countertop that pulsed with clotted ichor. Above it, on a diagonal strut, hung the rack of small bone disks they'd stolen from last time. Beside it, a row of brittle, bleeding alien machines sputtered and chugged, held together with duct tape. With her free paw, she drew one of the sushi knives and prodded a tube. The blade nicked a small hole in the membrane. Clear liquid glopped out, setting an acrid tang to the air.

The whole chamber rumbled. Bone struts clattered together like cannibal wind chimes. Dust curled in thin curtains from the ceiling.

A throaty buzz rattled inside Joe's control console. His back arm adjusted a lever. "Are you trying to kill us all, missy?"

The leak slowed to a drip.

The otter lowered her knife, watching the flashlight beam catch on the scabbed-over cracks in his carapace. Why had she stopped? She shouldn't be listening to him, he was a hideous space monster. Her mind flashed to the disk, to Leister's journals, to voices clawing at her dreams. Had the nightmares implanted a suggestion in her brain? Some kind of crazy safety protocol, to make her hesitate?

Except a quick glance to Max found him likewise appraising the situation—and he was the sanest person she knew. So instead of getting stabby right this instant, she straightened to stare the monster down. "It's over, Joe. You've got nowhere left to go."

"Just one place, actually." He lifted a claw to the shimmering snarl within the archway. "The ley lines have converged and my portal is opening. If you just let me go home, we can all walk away from this happy campers."

The old photograph of the Windfall Cataclysm fluttered to her mind. Cold panic raced through her. "You're lying."

"Oh, I'm not." The handyman tweaked a tiny dial with long talons. "And you shouldn't risk that I am."

"Whatever!" Kylie stood and brandished her flashlight. "It's a machine—just turn it off."

"Afraid I can't do that, miss." The angular, obsidian form hunched, tweaking finger-bone levers. "And if you knew enough to find me, you know it's too late to stop me. You should leave; this lab's going with me. The last thing I need's a Bevy following me home."

The otter's eyes flicked to her canine companion. "He's bluffing."

Max lifted an eyebrow at her.

She lashed her thick tail. "He's probably bluffing." Her flashlight beam cut the darkness, catching on the twisted and torn beaver disguise. "Are there more of you? Is this an invasion?"

"Afraid it's just the opposite: I'm never coming back." Joe's arm cracked a few joints longer to reach a dial. Yellow ichor shone on his sleeve. "Who in their right mind would invade this backwater world?"

Kylie swallowed fear and revulsion. "Again, we're just supposed to believe you?"

Max found the larger disk they'd stolen the first time and lifted it from its cartilage socket. The machinery hummed and pulsed, unabated.

"A bit late for that, kids." Bending his head the wrong direction, looking straight at the husky through a jumble of bone apparatuses, Joe chuckled.

"Hundreds of years of calculations I could have done in five minutes on any civilized world."

The husky furrowed his brow.

A soft click of shadowy mandibles echoed from Joe's mouth. "You'll get pulled through if you stay here. Trust me, being trapped on an alien world gets old, and with your lifespans I wouldn't like your chances of getting home."

The dog's expression darkened. He slipped the disk into his pocket and gripped his bat. "How do we know we won't end up with another Windfall Cataclysm?"

"Ah yes. That was a mistake, ya see." The creature watched them from his bone platform, his many limbs working levers and bladders. "Got impatient after I finally found a suitable spot for the portal. Didn't double-check my work. Wrecked what little equipment I had and cost myself another two centuries trying to replace it. Never expected the locals to build a town in a mysterious crater. It's a wonder life survived on this planet."

Max shrugged at his girlfriend. "That does make a certain amount of sense."

The lutrine spun to face her companion, arms spread. "You're agreeing with the giant murder-monster?"

"Now hang on there, missy, I've only been eating the wildlife." The creature's voice, polite as always, blended with the strange hum of energy. "Two hundred years of blending in, and I haven't killed anybody yet. If not for your family, nobody would even know I wasn't a beaver."

A sputter of disdain rose from deep in the otter. "I'm supposed to believe my great uncle just ran off?"

That frozen smile taunted her. "I always expected him to come back, possibly with friends. Some folks wouldn't take kindly to my presence here." He turned back to the dog and repeated: "She's going to be pulled through if you stay here."

Max raised the bat.

"Buddy, we're beyond that." A joint popped in the chitin of his neck. Without breaking eye contact, he continued working the gnarled controls.

"The ley lines have converged. The array is already active. Even if you took me down, you only have a few minutes until it reaches critical mass. So unless you know how to shut this all down properly, you could blow the whole valley off the map." One limb lifted to clack long claws in some arcane gesture. "Again."

The husky padded closer, down an aisle of strange apparatuses. "How do we know we can believe you?"

"I guess you don't." The three-sided face craned backwards to eye the pair. Within the depths of his gaze, alien emotions roiled.

"You tried to kill us!" The otter's ears pinned back. "And now we're just supposed to let you go?"

"I just want to leave." That trio of golden eyes tightened on Kylie. On the floor, the beaver suit gave a half-hearted flop of disgust. "Scaring you struck me as the sure-fire way to get my equipment back."

Max growled, but paused his advance on the alien. A careful toe pushed the discarded costume off a ledge, but it caught on a spire of bone, contorting even further.

The alien's genial voice became endearing. Dangling and boneless, the beaver face twitched to a sweet smile. "Say now, what would you have done?"

"What is your equipment anyway?" Kylie popped up from behind a spindle of webbed bone. "We might as well know."

"The spur is a power supply. It's some fine work, if I do say so myself, considering the lack of proper tools on this planet." The creature jabbed a claw at the pillar, which glowed bright on a sloped platform. "The disk stores calculations I need to travel home. Like one of your floppy disks, or whatever you kids have these days, but ten-thousand times more powerful."

The husky stepped back, shuffling through the tangled web of struts toward Kylie. "How do we know you won't come back for revenge?"

"And risk getting stuck here again? So I can get beaten to death by minor cable TV stars?" Claws lashed out from his tail-leg, seized a ledge, and catapulted him to a higher platform. He prowled forward on three legs. "No offense."

Watching him carefully, the big husky offered a slight shrug. "Eh."

The otter raised her phone and snapped a picture.

A jet-black claw flashed toward Kylie. Before the otter could even jump back, it sliced with metallic ring and sent half her phone clattering away. He clacked his mandibles at her. "Not that I'm above a little petty vengeance, mind you."

She squeaked in shock, then chattered angrily. "My phone!"

At her reaction, the three-meter long creature wriggled with what could have been delight. "Maybe I've been a little hard on you kids, though you have caused me every kind of headache." He tapped a vicious claw against the side of his skull, and the dangling, lifeless beaver face gave her a ghastly wink. "Getting that disk back saved me decades of calculations. So here's some free advice: pick your fights a little more carefully. There's a lot of nasty critters out there, and you'll find there are things besides your boyfriend that might like the taste of otter."

Outraged beyond words, Kylie shoved the broken halves of her mobile into a vest pocket.

"Well, I'd better get a move on." With shining talons, he clacked across the uneven floor. His obsidian carapace stretched, towering over the equipment and the couple. His polite tone never wavered. "Remember to leave once I do. Don't want you kids tagging along, and I doubt you're interested in being crushed in a cave-in." He swept a talon at the controls.

The portal flashed, leaving a purple afterimage in the otter's eyes. A sudden decompression popped her ears. A wave of distortion rippled from the archway. Wind whipped through the chamber, flinging loose objects into the portal. She dodged through the tangle of white surfaces to Max's side.

Alien bones and lightweight power tools tumbled around them, bouncing into the twist in reality. Each stretched and spiraled into the strange abyss. One by one, they vanished, swallowed by an unending throat of shimmering energy.

Eyes on them, Joe stepped back into the gateway. His battered carapace shone in the yellow light. He tumbled backward and spiraled in on himself as the twist gulped him down. His upper body stretched and bent in unthinkable ways, as the portal stretched him like taffy to fit into more dimensions.

Another pulse of decompression yanked the breath from the otter's lungs. Wind whipped down the throat of the cave, shoving at her back. With a squeak, she tripped forward, then stopped short. A glance back revealed Max gripping the back of her vest with one paw and a heavy column with the other. With floor under her feet again, the lutrine tried to watch the crumpling gateway, even as it strained her vision. Tears pooled in the corners of her eyes as the shadow that'd haunted her family for generations slipped forever away.

Joe plummeted into the eerie depths of the portal.

As if pleased with the taste, the twist in reality grew wider, the pillar of bone glowing with blinding glyphs and veins, brighter and brighter. The spire stretched sideways, the white floor under it rippling to pump it along. The snarl in space devoured the shining sliver of technology. Its subtle patterns smeared across misshapen new dimensions. Its light spilled over countless landscapes of alien geometry.

Kylie watched in wonder.

Max picked her up and ran.

Wide-eyed, She stared over his shoulder at the room's disintegration. Around them, the chamber snagged in jagged angles. Instead of melding in upon itself, it jolted and spiked around them, impaling consoles and flinging equipment. As the cave-in reached the archway, it snapped the bone frame in after it, shredding the room into the twist. Joe's discarded flesh-costume flopped and fluttered into the breach.

The husky loped back up the passage's throat as the floor receded under his paws. Up, up, up the ramp he sprinted.

All around the cavern, collapsing walls tumbled into the twist. Only concrete, dirt, and a hole in the floor above remained.

The otter gripped her boyfriend close, heart racing against his. With a running start, he dashed up the steep and lumpy incline to the basement.

The last of the shattered bone fell away into the portal. Rough stones and clods of dirt tumbled after, followed by hunks of concrete and a floor lamp. Max spotted the staircase and sprinted toward it. Kylie wondered where they could go if the portal kept going and swallowed up the world after them.

Just before it passed out of sight, she caught a final glimpse of the portal. Sated, the twist undid itself with a fizzle and a pop.

They paused at the foot of the stairs. He set the otter down. The cave, dark now, stood in silence. She groped for her flashlight, a blade of illumination in the inky gloom. She swept its beam along the rocky walls. "Is that it?"

Broken boards fell from the ceiling. The house groaned. A crack whipped up the foundation like lightning.

"We'd better go." He hurried her from the concrete basement floor.

They dashed upstairs, finding every light in the neighborhood on. She placed a paw on the husky's chest. "We'd better take the back door."

The house creaked again. Somewhere, wood splintered like a gunshot. Decoy photographs fell from the walls.

Together they hurried out of the monster's lair, through the handyman's backyard, and into the welcome embrace of night. Kylie's body buzzed from danger and elation. Only Max's hand on her shoulder kept her grounded. On the streets, small groups wandered and gossiped, speculating on everything from gas mains to earthquakes.

An Afghan hound in a silk dressing gown swooned down the road. "I can feel it! An incredible psychic convergence!"

"Oh calm down, Martha." An elder rabbit fluffed his poof of a tail at her theatrics, arms crossed in a stance that seemed rather familiar. "Some kinda sinkhole opened up down the block. Looks like an old mine collapsed."

"The alignments have shifted!" The hound howled in melodrama. "Two trackways have touched!"

The potbellied bunny grumbled, straightened his Crystal Caverns t-shirt, and left her standing in the street. He padded back into his house, past Shane and Sarah, who watched, muzzles agape.

Max and Kylie shared a secret smile and, together, walked back to her fine aquatic automobile.

CHAPTER 19
Renewal

STRANGEVILLE (SAT/4P)

S05E13 "Endgame": Armed with ancient knowledge and a demonic motorcycle, the team has their final confrontation with Tribunal. New dangers and old allies surface as the fate of the world hangs in the balance.

As they arrived home, light had begun to reclaim the town and forest. Bourn Manor still slouched against the hillside, but at least with indifference instead of menace.

The car puttered to a stop. Kylie found herself jubilant, breathless, and numb from the shock of it all. They'd gone up against a predator from another planet and survived.

She mulled that over for a moment, before it bubbled up a squawk of sudden anxiety. "We need to tell people about all this!"

The dog sighed. "I still don't think people will believe us if we say the TV show was real."

"Maybe that's the answer." She double-checked that the safety was on over the can's trigger button.

"Are you signing the 'bring back *Strangeville*' petition?" He cocked an ear. "Because you could just ask your mom."

"This has to all come out sometime, right? Like, it can't be a secret forever. So we warm people to the idea of all this with more *Strangeville*."

He nodded. "A nice idea, but the show's over."

"Not for an aspiring young writer..." She danced around him, chittering. "...who happens to be dating the creator's daughter."

His ears dipped. "You're joking."

The otter grinned. "I'm trying a new way of dealing with my crazy."

Kylie woke late the next morning feeling clearheaded and refreshed, which was nice. She also woke up snuggled next to Max, which was even better. The sound of the front door opening caused her to tense for a moment at the memory of who'd dropped in to visit last night. Then she heard her mother babbling on her phone and setting down luggage. Within a minute or so, the coffee maker puffed, boiled, and sizzled. Eventually, the activity faded to another part of the house.

After drifting in and out of sleep a few more times, Kylie rose and peeked out from Max's room. No sign of Mom. After checking her panties and t-shirt hadn't bunched up in obscene ways overnight, she padded upstairs and grabbed her housecoat, then ambled around the house looking for her mom. It became necessary to raid the coffee pot as she passed through the kitchen. Upon hearing typing inside, she sidled onto the sun parlor. Lush plants lined the glass walls, sunlight streaming in over the well-swept floor. At the south end, near the reflecting pool, her mother sat in a partly-reclined lawn chair, typing at her newest script, a flutter of notes on the floor around her.

The elder otter glanced up. "Hey squirt."

"Hey Mom. Heard you come in." She stretched, muscles still sore from the previous night's battle and chase. "Writing already?"

"Had some ideas on the drive." She tapped out a few more notes. "Wanted to get them down before they get away."

Kylie's paws traced over the leafy greenery. "How was the con?"

"Good." The wilt in her whiskers implied it'd been a long flight back, even with an extra day at the hotel to recover. "It's nice, sometimes, to receive shameless praise from someone who isn't dating my daughter."

"Max's liked your work a lot longer than that."

"True." She crossed her ankles. "At least the kid knows a good thing when he sees it."

The younger otter plopped down at the other side of the pool and cleared her throat. "So, I have this friend…"

Her mother glanced up from the laptop on her stomach. "Ah yes, how is Cliché?"

The slender lutrine deflated backward to the floor. "Fine, it's me, okay?"

The elder otter took a swig from her cup of cold coffee. "Go on."

"Things are good with Max." Kylie held up her paws, studying the light as it played through her webbing. "Maybe even great."

Her whiskers twitched to a smile. "Great."

"Amazing even. He makes me feel…" She grasped for the word.

Laura smirked. "Sane?"

"Yeah." The younger otter's thoughts drifted back to the front entry-way, where she and Max had cleaned up the damage from the fight with Joe. They figured a bunch of scuffed wallpaper and dirty flooring wouldn't go far to proving the existence of aliens.

"That's lovely, dear." A thought struck Laura and she typed it up.

Rolling to her stomach, Kylie angled around and batted at the sun-warmed water. "But…"

Her mother stopped typing. "But?"

"I've been thinking about asking Max to stay a little longer than the summer."

"How much longer?"

The tip of her tail dipped in the reflecting pool. "Not that long, on a cosmic timescale."

"So, forever, as far as the grocery shopping is concerned." She pushed up her reading glasses. "Kiddo, of all the things to come out of *Strangeville*, you two hooking up is one of the coolest. I'm not about to split you up." Her hand rose in a shrug. "Besides, with you two sneaking into each other's rooms the last few weeks, I'm guessing it's a little late to be protective of your innocence."

"Mom!" Heat flushed under her cheek ruffs.

"Oh sweetie, did you really think I had that many real reasons to leave town for a few days at a time?" Her thick tail swished along the foot rest of the chair in amusement. "Maybe you are still a bit innocent after all."

"Anyway!" The younger otter waved the topic off. "I'm worried he might go home." Kylie sat up, dipping her feet in the pool. "He comes from a close family. Can I really ask him to stay?"

"Sure you can."

Tension squeezed her shoulders together as she glanced up at her mother. "I'm afraid to."

"That's normal, dear, but being afraid won't get you an answer." Her fingers drummed along the side of her laptop. "And do you think he's going to drop you like an old tennis ball at this point? By the way, does he like tennis balls? I keep wondering if I should pick some up."

"Worth a shot; I know he liked them as a pup. And I guess you have a point..." Kylie poked one of the water lilies with her toe.

"Are you thinking it's too good to be true?"

"Maybe I'm cynical."

"I haven't seen Max this happy since he joined the show." She wiped a coffee ring from the hand-rest of her laptop. "I think it's safe to say he likes you. And you either trust in that or you don't."

"What if he's unsure about all this, but playing the strong and silent type?" She shrugged. "I mean, I don't think he is, but..."

Her mother rolled her eyes. "Barring telepathy, you'll have to take his word."

"What if Max and I just aren't right for each other?" Her gaze met her mother's. "Over the long term, I mean."

"Well, that at least I can help with..." A few clicks and Laura turned the computer around for her to see a video titled "I Told You So" springing open on the screen. She hit play.

The video feed started in the kitchen of their apartment, then proceeded into the small living room. A younger but still huge Max lay on his stomach on the sofa reading a script. A scrawnier Kylie lay on her stomach on his back, reading the same copy, legs kicked up in the air. The view zoomed in as a nearby fan blew his long hair in her face, which she batted away with a simper. Neither seemed to notice the camera.

The footage turned jittery as, without cutting away, Mom walked back into her room and turned the camera on herself: She was grinning like a cat in a colorful simile. "I'm calling it right now. You guys are gonna be an item." Pure lutrine mischief lit her face. "Because that was the cutest damn thing I've ever seen and anything else would be a waste."

Kylie squawked and squirmed against the floorboards. "I don't remember this! How do I know this wasn't cooked up in special effects?"

"Are you kidding?" Laura laughed, a sound that washed through the whole room. "Effects cost money. I can make fun of you for free."

The slimmer otter squirmed. "Does this mean we should've done this earlier?"

"Being friends first is far from a waste of time." She turned the laptop back to face her with a distant smile. "As I'm sure your father could verify, if he weren't too busy raising another kid in another state."

"Harsh, Mom." The younger Bevy looked up. Her tail curled like a question mark. "Have you had that video on your computer all these years?"

"And other places." She closed the laptop and took a victorious sip of her coffee. "I've been keeping this copy handy since Max got here."

As the otters watched the sunlight play over the lily pool's ripples, Kylie felt a word bubble up from her heart: "Thanks."

Laura glanced around the side of her glasses, smiling. "Sure thing, kiddo."

Max sat up straight on the sofa, trying to keep his cool. He'd never had many interviews and none since the final publicity push. Beside him, Kylie melted across the cushions with lutrine suppleness.

In the middle of the living room, Karl straightened his webcam a little, watching as the video feed recorded onto his computer. Scooting back into view, he scratched the base of his horn, then steepled his thick fingers. "Welcome, fellow Strangers, to a special video edition of Strange Times. Today, I have the super-amazing honor of having—" He paused to get his breathing under control. "—Max Saber and Kylie Bevy as guests." Biting his lip, he turned to toss them a frantic wave.

Kylie waggled her fingers. "Hey."

Max tried not to look at the camera and just pretend it was a normal conversation with Karl, if those existed. "Umm, hi."

"It's really great to have you guys here." He bounced a little in his borrowed kitchen chair, causing a few uneasy creaks. "The podcast has gotten a lot of new listeners since you moved to town."

"I bet." The otter rolled her eyes.

"So! Umm, let's talk about the series finale." A thin veneer of calm fell back of over the rhino as he settled into his comfort zone. "The takeaway for most fans was that Sandy and the crew were tired of fighting monsters and that Cassie and Serge were stepping up."

"That's a fair assessment." The husky nodded. "Tammy and Sandy pretty much go back to their normal lives."

Kylie sat up to use the sofa as intended. "Egbert's life was never normal to begin with, so it doesn't change at all."

"Right. Reading arcane texts, teaching the occasional class, palling around with his simulacrum." Max swept a paw her way. "And Damon sacrificed himself to destroy the Tribunal once and for all."

The rhino got a little misty-eyed. "That was really bittersweet! Especially when he rode into their board meeting on his motorcycle from that other building's roof with the sidecar full of enchanted dynamite."

She chittered a chuckle. "And then he stayed on the motorcycle, drove off set, and we never saw him again."

"Wow, really?" Karl sat and blinked for a moment.

"Yep." The otter nodded. "To this day."

The rhino blinked. "So he's...method acting?"

"Something like that." Kylie smirked. "But my mom assured us our characters would go on fighting monsters."

Karl's little tail whipped against the chair. "We've heard rumors Laura Bevy turned down offers for *Strangeville* video games, just like the episode novelizations and board game." He squirmed, leaning forward. "Why is that? Does she consider the show over?"

Max shrugged. "She wants to make sure any *Strangeville* material is true to the canon and spirit of the show."

The giddy, armored interviewer nodded. "That's good! I mean, that's great, but it doesn't give fans of the show much to work with. Is there anything she's willing to authorize?"

Seated on the sofa next to Kylie, the dog exchanged a quick glance with her. "Actually, she has authorized one thing…"

"Really?!" The rhino froze mid-bounce and cleared his throat. "I mean, what would that be?"

"A blog. From the point of view of Cassie and Serge." Max smiled, nervous ears drooped. "By me. Approved by Ms. Be—er, Laura, of course. Basically, they're whole new episodes." He glanced to his lover; this would be their version of the journals, really.

"Really?" His thick grey jaw dropped.

Kylie gave an amused nod. "Really."

The rhino's brow furrowed. "This isn't like the Season Three dream thing? Because the forums are still debating that."

Max shrugged. "How do you know the dream thing isn't part of it?"

Karl's brain seemed to churn through that notion for a second. Then he snapped back to reality. "And does Kylie have input on these…episodes?"

The otter slithered to a sassier position. "I'm in charge of the steamier scenes."

Heat rushed to Max's ears. "There aren't going to be steamy scenes."

Kylie patted his paw. "He's just shy. They're actually quite sensual."

The rhino double-checked that his system had recorded that exchange, then turned to face them again. "Can I ask who these scenes involve, if they exist?"

A gaze passed between the pair. In full view of Karl's webcam and the world, she kissed him.

Star-strewn night spread over Kylie and Max in all its inconceivable depth. They lay on a hillside at the edge of town, looking up at the heavens. The husky breathed out a contented sigh.

"I'm really glad you didn't leave." As she scooted closer, her paw closed around his. "For lots of reasons."

He squeezed back. "Why would I leave when you give me adventure and blowjobs?"

"You're terrible!" She elbowed him. "I thought you were the modest one."

"I am." He turned to smile at her, cool grass tickling his whiskers. "You should hear what comes out of your muzzle."

She groaned, then studied the boundless firmament. "It's kinda nice to know there's someone else out there."

"Yeah... Now if we could get them to break into our house and throw us around like beanbags..."

"Hey, we took on an alien and made a blog out of it." She sat up, arms around her knees, eyes on him. "I call that a victory."

He wagged and sat up too.

She kissed his nose, then looked back toward the house. "Wanna go in and watch *Vow of Violence?* I finally found a copy with English subtitles."

"Sure." Max pulled her closer and smiled. He didn't know what the future held. He didn't understand unknowable cosmic horrors. But he understood the girl he loved. Not a bad place to start.

In fact, now that he'd fought a monster, telling his mom he'd be staying for more than the summer didn't seem all that scary.

CHAPTER 20
Epilogue

STRANGEVILLE (DOWNLOADING...)

S06E01 "The Return": Cassie and Serge take up the banner in the fight against supernatural monsters as they confront a reawakened threat from their past.

Max careened a shopping cart of butter down the rocky slope.

Kylie scampered after, collecting what few sticks of butter bounced free. "Hurry! It's starting!"

"I know!" The husky growled as he shoved the cart through a deep patch of gravel. His eyes locked on a plume of smoke rising from the shore ahead and picked up his pace. Frantic shouts echoed up the cliffside.

"Oh no! They're already here!" The otter dumped an armload of butter sticks into the basket and hauled it faster. With a spray of pebbles, their emergency dairy supply burst onto the beach.

The shoreline writhed with frantic activity. Waves surged and retreated, revealing a cavorting army of crabs. A dozen otters waded and waddled, snatching up crustaceans to deposit them in willow baskets and commandeered laundry hampers. On the shore, Laura organized the rollick of lutrine chefs who manned the boiling pots over cook-fires.

"We're here!" Arms waving, Kylie called out to the group. "We made it!"

A general cheer arose from the otters; a few raised flailing crabs in salute.

The canine swung his cart to a stop and panted before the row of fires. A chittering wave of chest-high otters swarmed up and took the butter. Though he tried his best to remember their names, they scampered too fast and too many. He'd have been in danger of misplacing Kylie too, had she not gotten his scent onto herself with great enthusiasm an hour before. At the end of the frenzy, he and the cart stood with a single tub of margarine that had been bought by mistake.

Max felt a buzz in his pocket and pulled out his phone. "Karl just posted a photo of us running down the street with the butter."

"Tell him to come out." Kylie beheld the butter as her relations began unwrapping it into pots. "I'm surprised the grocery store let us clear out their whole butter section."

He sent the reply, smiled, then switched apps and tapped out a quick message.

Howl: {I am a lucky dog.}

Kylie's second uncle padded up with a crate of crabs, set it down on the gravel, then hooked his thumbs in the waist of his Bermuda shorts and grinned around a sprig of seaweed in his teeth. "When otters, especially Bevys, show up and try to buy all your butter, you sell them all your butter."

"I can drink to that, Thomas." Laura tipped a bottle of seaweed beer to her muzzle, then crossed her arms at the couple. "Glad my minions got here in time."

Her daughter squawked: "Minion!"

The dog steadied her shoulder. "You seem to have matters under control." He turned to survey the beachfront.

The crowd wore a mix of waders, galoshes, clamdiggers, and board shorts. From the next beach up, another otter sailed a Schwimmwagen ashore, the honk of its horn chasing a scuttle of crustaceans toward them. A few more washed out the supply of clams. Otters too young to be trusted with crab collection heaped seaweed in a large pit for the accompanying clam bake...and onto each other.

"Thomas Creel." Kylie's uncle offered his paw, seaweed sprig sticking from his greying muzzle. "So you're the handsome dog who swept Kylie off her feet?"

Like the well-trained dog he was, Max shook hands. "More like the other way around."

"Seems like just yesterday she was a little cork float." He laughed, looking very much like the otter on his brewery logo. "You're from Montana, right? Rancher? Where's your rope?" The potbellied otter looked him over. "Didn't Laura tell you we wanted you to lasso Big Betsy this year?"

He tilted his head at the notion of crab-wrangling. "Big Betsy?"

"Body the size of a basketball, she has!" He threw his paws in the air, a small slosh of beer sailing from his bottle. "Five meters from claw to claw!"

Nodding slowly, the husky tried to dig up a reply, but a wave of otters rushed over him on the way to the cooking area. He spun to watch their antics.

A general commotion arose around the cooking of crabs. The various pots filled with crustaceans as the air filled with squabbles about optimal cooking times. Meanwhile, the grand clam-master upended baskets of mollusks into the seaweed pit, then commanded the rolling of glowing-hot cannonballs in after them. These hit with gouts of steam, then sizzled under a layer of seaweed, wet tarps, and sand.

The dog watched in awe as the Bevy clan laughed, shouted, and clacked tongs at each other. His family gatherings, while hardly somber affairs, never got this chaotic.

Their food prepared, each lutrine attendee sprawled out in sunbathing chairs, plates of crab on his or her stomachs. A frenzy of crab-cracking commenced like a dozen tiny thunderstorms. Max watched in wonder and faint alarm as carapaces disintegrated under an onslaught of specialized crackers, cutters, mallets, tiny forks, oyster-shucking knives, and devices resembling lever-action can openers. Shards of shell shot off in all directions. Pups, having only a limited attention span for crab, chased each other with empty pinchers.

Beside him, Kylie cracked, shattered, and munched her way through her second crab. Possibly third. Impossible to tell from the discarded shells, which lay in utter destruction. He kept a safe distance, lest his paw be mistaken for an especially furry crab.

As if feeling his gaze, she glanced up with a churr, crustacean in both paws. A tiny string of crab meat dangled from one whisker. Her wide eyes met his as she offered a shrug. "What?"

"Nothing, rudderbutt." He leaned in and licked the crab off her muzzle.

She giggled and fed him another chunk of buttered meat from her plate.

These actions elicited wolf whistles from the accumulated otters.

Ears ducked shy and flat, he woofed a chuckle and turned back to his girlfriend. "I'm just amused you're so in the zone."

"Eat some crab!" Dumping the shells of her supper on the beach, she grabbed another steaming crustacean from a nearby platter. "We won't be running out." She prodded a claw at the ocean, where another wave of cara-paced reinforcements made landfall, undeterred.

Max dug into the offered crab with all the gusto a non-otter could manage, which spared him enough brainpower to watch the mass ingestion.

As the sun set and her clan set upon the clams, Kylie took her lover for a walk down the beach.

Her husky hopped from one foot to the other to avoid the scuttling crabs. He seemed to think it weird, but what could be more romantic than a beach covered with delicious food? A contented sigh left her chest as she watched them pass; even though she'd puke if she ate another one, it was still nice to just look at them.

Kylie smiled. "Okay, so my family's still crazy."

"No more than most." He cocked his ears at her. "Did I ever tell you about my little cousin who chases her tail?"

Smiling, she shrugged. "And it's a good crazy."

The canine scampered past a rock, tail between his legs to protect it from an especially bold crab there. "I'm never going to think arthropods look weird again, after seeing Joe."

"Yeah..." She sighed. "I just wish we'd gotten better proof."

"Hey, cheer up!" He bumped her shoulder. "We saved the town."

"No, we managed to avoid destroying the town." Arms crossed, the otter glanced up at him and blew a sigh through her whiskers. "Not really the same thing."

"Well, we learned your family isn't actually crazy."

"Not all of us, anyway. And we lost our evidence of what Joe really was."

With a wink and a wag, his powerful arm slipped around her. "You did manage to pick up a roguishly handsome boyfriend..."

Her glance dropped to the shoreline, even as she leaned against his bulk. "Well yeah, I guess there's that."

"...who'd really like to find a nice little secluded spot and take your pants off."

She snickered into his sweatshirt.

Max's phone buzzed again. He flipped it onto his palm, only to see his mother's number flash. With only a moment's pause, he clicked the call to voicemail and dropped it back in his pocket.

The couple shared a look, knowing they'd have to deal with his pack at some point. But not now.

For now, paw in paw, they looked out over the sea.

For now, she had a best friend, a boyfriend, and a companion in shedding light onto the shadowy weirdness of the world.

For now, life ruled.

The sun set, the march of the crustaceans tapered off, and the otters staggered back to Bourn Manor. They draped themselves over various beds and sofas and fell into butter-laced slumber.

Kylie padded out to the front porch to find her boyfriend illuminated by the glow of his phone. Stars shone overhead in a scatter of nuclear pinpricks. Crickets chirped over the wind through the trees. Deep in the woods, something skittered, unseen.

Snuggling up next to him, she curled her tail around the fluffy canine. She glanced up at the ladder still propped against the side of the house. "Joe could've at least finished our roof."

"Sometimes, you've got a place you need to get back to." Max slipped an arm around her waist and wagged under her tail. He flipped through images, then turned his phone to her. On screen, Karl grinned while being attacked by half a dozen crabs.

She winced at the one hanging from his left nostril. "Ouch."

"I'm sure he's fine. He's got thick skin." He scrolled to the photo's description. "Sounds like he enjoyed himself."

"Good, I wouldn't want word getting around that the local celebrities sacrificed him to the crabs."

Behind them, the door creaked. Laura emerged, tired but pleased with herself. She tossed a moldy petri dish into the sacks of garbage they'd brought up from the beach. "The last of our guests are settled in and the spare crabs are packed in ice. I'd call this Krabbenwanderung a success." She leaned against the porch railing, her eyes on the couple seated on the stairs. "You kids enjoy yourselves?"

Kylie patted her full stomach. "Did I ever."

The husky nodded. "And your old house is packed with relations once more."

"It's good for the soul." Her straggly whiskers twitched in amusement. "And they're leaving tomorrow, which is good for my sanity."

The night air breezed past them, ushering the day's heat out to sea.

Laura interlaced her fingers up to the webs. "What'd you want to talk to me about?"

Max cleared his throat with a woof, then looked to Kylie.

The younger otter swallowed. "The last few weeks, we've been looking around town. Learning about the local legends and seeing how that matched up to what you put into *Strangeville*. You heard that kind of stuff growing up, huh? How much of it do you believe?"

Concern crept onto her face. "Am I going to regret giving you those journals?"

"It's nothing like that." Kylie waved a webbed paw. "I know they're paranoid fantasies."

Max rested a palm on her knee in support.

Her mom studied the pair. "But...?"

Her daughter squirmed and forced the words to form. "But something had to inspire them."

The elder otter raised an eyebrow. "Yeah, like a brain chemical imbalance."

The husky tilted his ears toward town. "You don't think it's weird your roofing contractor's house got sucked into the ground?"

"Hoaxes are Windfall's stock-in-trade. I'm sure he had a deal with the Chamber of Commerce or some such." Her mother brushed a lock of hair from her eyes. "You'll get used to it."

"Joe was an alien." The younger otter lashed her arms out for emphasis. "He had a disguise to cover up his true form. We watched his basement-laboratory implode when he left."

Laura's ears lifted with concern. "You were there when it collapsed?"

"Alien, Mom. Alien. From another world." She jabbed a finger skyward. "He had weird living technology and tunnels that connect to the old mines."

"Living technology?" She stirred her whiskers. "I think someone's pulled a prank on you, kiddo."

Kylie pulled a the small bone disk from her pocket. "We got this at the site."

The older lutrine adjusted her glasses and studied the alien artifact. "Pretty sure this is a sand dollar, sweetie."

"She's telling the truth." The husky straightened beside his girlfriend. "I saw it too."

"We tried to go back in, but the tunnels are all collapsed, and the whole area makes our teeth hurt." The younger otter tapped a claw on her pearly whites.

"And we recorded another type of creature getting into our garbage." Holding his phone out, he thumbed through a gallery of blurred photos.

She looked away. A rare crack of bewilderment appeared in her demeanor, only to be welded shut by steely resolve. "Kids, it took me years, but I learned to see the charlatans of this town for what they are. You're going to have to learn that lesson for yourself, I guess." With a burst of urgency, Laura waddled back into the house. "Don't stay up too late!" The screen door clattered shut after her.

Kylie started rise and give chase.

Max's paw pressed her thigh and he shook his muzzle.

His girlfriend grumbled: "She doesn't believe us!" An accusing otter paw poked toward the front door.

"I don't think this is the sort of conversation you have in a day." He patted her shoulder. "Let her process everything."

"Yeah, you're probably right. We don't want to make a scene with the family here either."

He nodded. "It's a lot to take in. I'd have trouble believing it if I hadn't seen and smelled it myself."

She slumped against him, a smile dawning in the dark. "Unbelievable things happen now and then."

His tail thumped with joy against the deck.

As his arm slipped over her shoulders, Kylie stared up at a sky of countless stars and listened to her heartbeat settle. "We'll talk to her later, show her this isn't the first step on the road to Crazytown. After all, you believe it and the only crazy thing you ever did was start dating me."

His chuckle rumbled against her cheek. "That's a pretty good track record."

Held in the warmth of his embrace, Kylie watched the heavens haze before her misty eyes, glad she wouldn't be missing Max anytime soon.

www.ingramcontent.com/pod-product-compliance
Lightning Source LLC
Chambersburg PA
CBHW051636050726
47502CB00011B/554